T0365687

DEATH ALL AROUND

DEATH ALL AROUND:

LUKE & LILITH

S. T. MEIER

authorHOUSE®

AuthorHouse™
1663 Liberty Drive
Bloomington, IN 47403
www.authorhouse.com
Phone: 1 (800) 839-8640

Published by AuthorHouse 08/25/2015

ISBN: 978-1-5049-2940-0 (sc)
ISBN: 978-1-5049-2939-4 (e)

Library of Congress Control Number: 2015913070

Print information available on the last page.

CHAPTER 1

Present Day

Then it came. The dreadfully ominous knock at the heavy door to her room. The knock that Grace had been terrified of, since she had watched and giggled as the staff and the other searchers called it quits. The Minnesota State Patrol must have heard me talking to Jake under the bowl of snow made by pine trees where the tree keeps out the snow and forms three-foot tall walls with the boughs for a roof.

The policeman was very polite and told me that the wind could have shed all of its snow and the walls could have caved in on her. He handed me this frozen pinecone and talked about the lethal four-foot avalanche burial requiem on the way to the main building entry. He made a point of telling me that had I been out any longer in the subzero temperatures, I could have froze to death and resembled that stiff pinecone. Honestly, at this point, I could have cared less if I would have died. After all, my family was gone and now I'm trapped in this mental institution.

From a distance, Grace could see the brightly lit interior of the large brick building. Inside the front door, I was treated to posters from friends and concern from the staff, but I knew what was waiting for me. I appreciated that my friends were happy to see me but all I wanted to do was go straight to my room, get into some warm clothes, and go to bed.

It was just after eight o'clock and it had been dark for hours in the Minnesota winter evening. They were just now bringing Grace her supper, cause up until an hour ago, she had been hiding under a tree in the snow. The grounds looked like the face of a Christmas card only dotted with nurses and the men in the blue suits. They had all been out after me since before the sun set down and outside time was over.

I hid in the little fort, the kind that evergreen trees make under their boughs, after the really big storm we had all day. I loved to lie down on the ground in the forts, away from the other kids, away from the doctors with their endless questions, away from the nurses always giving pills and especially, away from the counselor who just wants to talk about my mother, father and all the rest of the family. I guess I loved the winter snow cause it was the only season when I was truly happy.

"You can come in now. I'm in my pajamas and the radiator is warming me up some," called Grace as she rubbed her hands together trying to warm herself.

A stern, middle-aged nurse entered Grace's room. The nurse placed Grace's supper tray on the side table next to the little girl's bed. Without a word, the nurse went to the bedroom door to exit. Grace knew her counselor was going to be mad when the nurse who puts her to bed came in and didn't give her any medicine with her dinner.

Grace ask the nurse "**Why no shot?**"

"**Miss Reagan is going to see you any minute and I will be back afterwards,**" said the evening shift nurse placing the food tray on the side table next to Grace.

Grace looked over the tray of food the nurse had placed before her and wrinkled her nose. The broccoli looked slightly over cooked and limp. The chicken was rather pale looking in color. The color of the almost cold chicken was similar to the complexion of Miss Reagan, and her dark auburn hair accentuated her pallor.

Miss Reagan reminded Grace of her grandmothers. The elderly woman was strict, disapproved when Grace broke the rules and she felt like the counselor wanted to scold her. But with both Grace's Nana and Grandmother Susan, she would just talk and talk until Grace felt bad about what she had done. Before Grace could think another thought the door opened and in walked Miss Reagan practically shouting.

"**Grace Ann Francis! Good grief child, are you all right? What on earth happened today? You terrified the entire staff. You had the entire state of Minnesota looking for you. We had to lock down all of the other friends and the Minnesota State Patrol was searching around the outside of the campus with their dogs.**"

Normally, Miss Reagan had such a soft voice but now her voice filled the small bedroom. As Miss Reagan entered Grace's room, she kind of, looked like a marionette dancing into her room, finally flopping down into an over stuffed chair.

Grace sat on the edge of her bed and said quietly **"I'm sorry Miss Reagan. I just wanted to be alone so I could think. You know, to remember things so that I don't forget them."**

Not always being able to remember, Grace forced herself to remember the many places, people and how they came together to make the times they linked to make her life. It seemed like hiding and thinking real hard let her keep together the parts in her life. Grace may only be ten but she felt so full of thoughts and stories, like movies playing over and over in her head. So when she hid, the pictures slow down, her brain would get quiet and she and Jake, her oldest friend from childhood would sit and talk with her.

As soon as they were alone, Jake would come and the first thing he'd say was "Grace Ann Francis". Her first name was chosen from and is the same as her mother's grandparent's last name. Grace's mother, Lilith, loved that name because her grandparents were extremely wealthy and her mother's thinking was that by naming her daughter thus, their little family would hold higher favor with the affluent grandparents. Grace's mother never seemed to really care for them though. Lilith was like that. Lilith could be nice to a person then behind their back, call them a name as she walked away.

Jake said Grace's mother was a liar because of Lilith's many tricks. For one, Lilith named her daughter after Grace's great-grandparents, in order to have a larger sum of money for her family to inherit. When Jake told Grace about her mom's plan, Grace started to cry. Then Jake held her hand and told her that it didn't matter though cause "Grace" was the prettiest name that any little girl could ever have, and that happened when Grace was five. Now that Grace was almost ten, she better understood the dynamics of her family. Unlike Lilith, Grace learned not to tell lies or to say things to people in order to get them to do what she want.

A lot of adults say that Grace looks like Lilith but Jake can't see why. Grace has very big, blue eyes while Lilith had brown hazel colored eyes. Grace's hair is very long, and light brown in color similar to her dad's hair color but lighter than her mother's black hair. In the summer, she gets natural blonde highlights just like her dad. While Grace may look similar to her mother, everyone agrees that she has the personality of her dad. Her stay-at-home father is what every body talks about when they talk about Grace's intelligence. She'd been told that he was a genius. Her dad was always reading to her. He discussed books, and history, and art and everything under the Sun and Moon. This is the reason that Grace became such an avid reader.

"Now, Grace, are you finally ready to tell me about your family? I would like you to start from the very beginning. You can continue to eat your dinner while I ask you some questions. First, tell me about your father," said Miss Reagan trying to break Grace out of her deep thoughts. **"Start with his name and his date of birth."**

"My father, Luke Philip Francis was born September 6, 1969," said Grace with a distant look in her eye. She'd never noticed before but his birth numbers would appear 9-6-69 and he was married in 1996. Grace was convinced that all those sixes and nines were not lucky for him in the least she thought to herself.

"Dad was extremely intelligent and was considered a genius at his high school. He had several debate trophies with medals, and was active in student government as its president. He was an avid reader that loved books and knew everything there was to know about the value of his treasures. He had gone to college and majored in Art", said Grace. **"I think he majored in Art because it challenged him. Knowledge and facts have only one answer but art has many right answers that make it more complex. Dad always said that art is only right when you can feel the harmony within."**

"So, Grace, was your father an artist or did he teach art?" asked Miss Reagan.

"Dad was a few credits short of graduating with his bachelor's degree, but he was stubborn. My mother said that he refused to take two physical education courses required for graduation. This is all he needed to finish his bachelor degree but he said that these courses were a waste of time and none of us really have that much time on this earth. Never knowing when his time was up, he was not about to

spend it finishing his degree," explained Grace as she remembered her father telling her.

"If your dad didn't do art, what was his occupation?" questioned Miss Reagan.

"Well, at first, Dad had a huge store with Nana, Papa, and Uncle Tommy. Then Dad started working at home, selling things on the Internet and took care of me," responded Grace with a smile as she remembered enjoying her time with her dad.

"How would you describe your father physically? Was he tall or short?" asked Miss Reagan.

"He was a very small-framed man of 39 years of age. He was only 5'6" and the most he ever weighed was 140 pounds for about a week from some medication he was taking at the time. However, he hated the temporary weight gain and dropped the medication immediately. He usually weighed around 120 pounds or less. At times, Nana and Papa would complain that he was so thin that he looked like a Holocaust prisoner. Dad just ignored them and he was glad he was not the other possible extreme", added Grace concentrating on describing her dad to someone that had never met him.

"Do you think it bothered your mother that your father was so thin?" inquired Miss Reagan.

"Yes, I think so. She thought she looked fat next to him. My mother claimed that Dad refused to eat at all-you-can-eat –buffets because the extremely heavy weight people took his appetite away. Actually, my

mother never liked weight-challenged people either and probably just put the blame on him so others wouldn't think that she was so vain. Dad said there were many times that my mother would project her feelings or weaknesses on others. Dad figured that she was insecure and didn't want others to know her downfalls. This way, he said my mother always had the upper hand," stated Grace honestly.

"Getting back to your father, tell me what you remember about him Grace," encouraged Miss Reagan.

"Dad had a long, thin face and wore large dark framed glasses even though I'm not sure that he really needed the glasses. His eyesight wasn't that bad but glasses seemed to fit his intellectual integrity. He had the usual short brown hair that most guys had. He always complained that he never had a good hair day due to the cowlick on the top right side of his head. On the bright side, at 39 years of age, he still had all his hair. He wasn't balding and he didn't have gray hair like most people his age," described Grace as she stroked her fingers in her hair. **"When my Dad showed me his high school pictures from his yearbook, I noticed one thing and that was he hadn't changed in appearance. He really didn't have any frown marks. Dad didn't even have wrinkles. If I didn't really know how old my Dad was, I would guess that he was in his mid-twenties at the most. There were times that we would run into people that he knew in high school and they always looked a lot older than him. The women from high school would always flirt with Dad and if my mother saw it, she**

would get so mad. My mother's temper was fierce and one that if she were even slightly mad, she would not let the issue easily go," said Grace looking scared as she remembered her mother's temper.

"Sounds like your mother was the jealous-type. What would your mother do when she was jealous or angry?" asked Miss Reagan.

When Miss Reagan looked at Grace, she noticed the child looked a little preoccupied. Grace's head was tilted as if to she was listening to something. Then Grace nodded and began to speak.

"Jake wants me to tell you that it was not unusual for my mother to throw things when she was angry. If she were angry with my Dad, for instance, that would be the direction that objects would fly. If my mother was mad at me, she threw things in my direction. Once she threw my favorite doll at me and cracked my doll's head. Dad told me that my Grandmother Bobble also threw items when she was angry. My mother always complained about my Grandmother Susan's temper and that she didn't like her mother. Dad would joke about how funny that we pick up the bad characteristics from our parents, especially those traits we dislike most," said Grace as if in a trance back to a time when her parents fought.

"Well, Grace, it sounds like your father was very intelligent. Is Jake with us right now?" asked Miss Reagan.

"Yes Miss Reagan. Jake has been with us the entire time," responded the little girl surprised that Miss Reagan couldn't see him sitting next to her.

"What can you tell me about your mother?" asked Miss Reagan a little disturbed that Grace was seeing imaginary people again and making note of Jake's appearance to the child in her file.

My mother's name was Lilith Bobble-Francis. She was the same height, if not taller than my father, but complained that she always weighed more than him. On the plus side, she said that they could share a wardrobe if she was at a lower weight. In our house, money was always scarce so this saved them a few bucks. My mother was always telling others the clever ways that she could save money and sharing clothes with Dad was one of them." said Grace as she remembered back to the fights her parents would have over blue jeans.

"Most women are concerned with their weight. Do you think your mother was concerned with her appearance?" asked Miss Reagan.

"Secretly, my mother was always weighing herself. She didn't know that I knew but I saw her using the digital scale several times a day. Sometimes she would tell us how much her bowel moment weighed. If it was a Loch Ness, as we called it, weight loss was inevitable and that made my mother very happy. Sometimes my mother would take a photo of her poop and post it on the Internet. My mother was sort of quirky that way and she would laugh with

happiness when telling us about it," smiled Grace as she recalled her mother's frivolity attitude.

"It sounds as if your mother was obsessed with her appearance. Is there a particular feature that your mother considered her pride and joy?" asked Miss Reagan.

"A lot of people thought my mother looked like Anne Hathaway with waist length hair. My mother's best feature definitely was her long, thick, dark hair that became curly when the weather was humid. Aunt Char who had super fine, blonde hair always said that "Lilith has enough hair for three-people". Being that my mother knew she had great hair, she would do whatever necessary to have people compliment her best feature. She would adorn it with gemmed hair gadgets or twist it around for a different look. My mother was always playing with her hair. When she wasn't playing with her hair, she was playing with mine. If you got it, flaunt my mother would always say," said Grace imitating her aunt and mother.

Grace stopped and thought for a moment. "In my mother's case, flaunting was an understatement. My mother always made sure that she was the center of attention. I got the feeling that she felt uncomfortable if she wasn't. It was probably because she was an only child. My mother didn't have any brothers or sisters, " continued Grace.

"What would happen if your mother wasn't the center of attention?" asked Miss Reagan.

"Well, all I can say is that she wasn't happy and she let everyone around her know it. At least those who knew my mother well enough to know when she wasn't happy like Dad and me. My mother's eyes would turn black, her lips would close tightly and protrude out, and she would throw anything within her reach at her target of anger. My mother's eyes would remain this midnight black color until she was finished being angry. I remember the room would be thick with this really uncomfortable tension. When this happened, I just ran into my room and escaped into one of my favorite movies," replied Grace a little anxious at the nerve wrecking memory.

"So Grace, you feel like your mother was uncomfortable with not being the focus of a group of people? Why do you think your mother feels this way?" asked Miss Reagan trying to relax Grace.

"My mother liked having people pay attention to her. I don't really know why. Maybe it was because my mother was an only child. Or maybe it was because she was a latchkey kid? My mother was always telling me from the time she was in kindergarten through the time she was a teenager that she came home to an empty house," said Grace when her face froze and she remembered a very important detail. "If the house wasn't empty, my mother told me that grandmother was home drinking alcohol. To my mother that was worse than being home alone. From what I saw, my mother got her super bad temper and drinking habits from Grandmother Bobble. Both my mother and grandmother drank, and the more they drank, the angrier they became."

"Your mother was left alone that young?" asked the counselor.

"Being an only child, my mother was frequently by herself until her parents came home from work. She also said that when her parents came home from work, instead of spending time with her, they had their cocktails together in the library. Perhaps this is the reason she was starved for attention. Anyway, she was not shy about seeking attention and a lot of people found her very charming in an odd sort of way," said Grace disgusted at the fact that her mother's family was extremely self-centered.

"Grace, in what way was your mother odd?" asked Miss Reagan.

"Well, my mother had this strange laugh. I don't know anyone else with the same kind of laugh. Her laugh was loud and my Dad told her that she sounded like a horse if she was laughing at him," described Grace her mother as best as she could remember.

"What else can you say about your mother?" asked Miss Reagan noticing that Grace was beginning to squirm with anxiety as she pictured her mother and father starting to quarrel.

"When my mother wanted something, she could be extremely charming. Dad always told me to watch out for mother if she was overly nice to a person. If she were telling you nice things, Dad would tell me that she was plotting something. My mother had a way of making a person feel that they were the most important person in the world when she needed something from them. On the other hand, she could also make them feel horrible, as if they didn't exist, if they didn't comply to do what my mother wanted," said Grace as she analyzed her mother's behavior.

"That's interesting. Did your mother go to college?" asked Miss Reagan.

"My mother was a theatre student at the local community college. Some people say she acted like a different person everyday. Sometimes her voice was *like this* (in a slow, monotone voice) and she was really sad. Most of the time, she would speak and move really fast. Dad told me that my mother moved really fast because she had too much caffeine. My mother seemed like she was always entertaining the people around her. It was like she was always on stage," said Grace trying to describe her mother as best as she could.

"What was your mother's occupation?" asked Miss Reagan.

"As you know, theatre was my mother's first love and lighting was her second. She always said that lighting is an important part of theatre. This is why my mother worked at the Lighting World store in Mayhem. She started working at the store way before I was born. She told me that her first day of work began on April Fools Day in 1997. My mother thought her job was very important because without light nothing would be seen like the stage along with her performance. As long as I can remember, my

mother told me that she wanted to see her name
up in lights and would do almost anything to see it
happen," described Grace.

"It sounds like your mother had a lot of ambitions
when it came to the stage. Was your mother normally
happy or did she seem more sad?" wondered Miss
Reagan as she examined Grace's family history and
knew that Lilith was bipolar.

"My mother was normally very hyper and her hands
always seemed to be moving really fast. My mother
told me she could hypnotize others when she told
them a story she wanted them to know and believe.
So I could always tell how she was doing that day by
the liveliness or slowness of her voice. Wait, let me
show you," said Grace as she stood up to show Miss
Reagan.

"When she was depressed, she would walk around as
if she was literally dead, dragging around this really
heavy shell of a person. Her head would be down
and she would cry for no reason. Her psychiatrist
diagnosed her as bipolar but she never believed
their medical diagnosis. My mother thought she was
a borderline personality. Unless she was angry, I
preferred the hyperactive version of my mother,"
reasoned Grace as she thought about her mother's
personality.

"How did your mother feel about having a college
degree in Theatre and only holding a job as a store
clerk?" asked Miss Reagan.

"I'm not sure. A lot of people thought that my mother should be more than a clerk at a lighting store. Dad told my mother that a college degree wasn't needed to hold that job. Being that the economy wasn't doing very well and the lighting store hadn't been very busy, my mother had a lot of time to plan other activities. My mother would come home from the store and tell me about her plan about things that she could change in her life by using other people and not have to work very hard to accomplish it," responded Grace acting like it was normal for people to do.

"Really? That's very interesting Grace. Can you tell me what your mother disliked in her life?" asked Miss Reagan.

"One thing that my mother hated was being bored. My mother would do anything to make things more interesting. She once told me a story that she was angry about the rising tuition costs at her community college. In order to feel better, she stole a television from a classroom at the community college that she was attending. She would laugh and laugh about how easy it was to do without being caught. The television was on a tall stand with casters. So my mother just rolled the cart out of the building and the television slid right into her back seat of the car. She left the tall stand on casters in the parking lot and laughed hysterically as she drove away. My mother never wanted to be taken advantage of, and would do basically anything to win in any situation," replied Grace. "My mother always had to win or she wasn't happy."

"Was it normal for your mother to steal items?" asked Miss Reagan.

"My mother stole things all the time. One warm night, we were walking past an older building in downtown Mayhem. My mother saw this large mat outside the vestibule of the structure. The mat said Landmark Hotel in Art Deco print. She picked up the large, heavy mat and started running home. I had a difficult time keeping up with her because of my short legs. She didn't need the large mat. She just wanted it so it was rightfully hers as she saw it," said Grace like the incident was no big deal.

"Where do you think your mother learned to steal?" asked Miss Reagan curiously.

"My mother told me that she learned to steal from her father. Grandfather Bobble had photography as a hobby. She told people that my Grandfather Bobble would buy a camera from a store, take out the piece he needed to fix his own camera and then return the product claiming that it was defective. I don't know if this story true? My mother told me this when she was really mad at Grandfather Bobble. She might have wanted to make him look worse than was really true. I never asked my grandfather if the story was true and I probably never will," concluded Grace wanting to see her grandfather in a positive light.

"What else can you tell me about your mother?" asked Miss Reagan.

"An interesting thing I noticed about my mother is that she would always find the negative in someone and make a joke about it, as she would tell someone else in the family about it," replied Grace.

"Why do you think your mother would speak so badly of someone?" inquired Miss Reagan.

"Dad told me about this technique that my mother used. He said it worked great for my mother for two reasons. First, by pointing out the negative in another person, my mother appeared observant. This made her look very smart to other people. My mother always worried about being the smartest person in the room. Secondly, the person she told would be distracted into thinking about another's actions and would be fooled into noticing the other person's downfall and not be aware of any of my mother's problems. This deception trick was so easy and my mother had mastered it with almost everyone," stated Grace. "Dad said that my mother was a master manipulator. Dad and I could see that she was laughing to herself when she got others thinking negatively about her targets. Dad said that mother saw herself as the great puppet master of others. She even started collecting Pinocchio items. Pinocchio made her laugh because she knew she could tell little lies but others couldn't tell because her nose didn't grow which was lucky for her. Dad said that mother lived to trick others and loved taking advantage of others."

In the corridor, the grandfather clock chimed 10 o'clock. Miss Reagan looked down at her watch and was shocked to see that it was so late.

"I didn't realize that it was so late Grace. The nurse will come in and make sure that you get all your medications. Get a good night's rest and I will be in late tomorrow morning and we can pick up where we left off," said Miss Reagan as she walked to the doorway and closed the door.

CHAPTER 2

The next morning was a bright, sunny day. As Grace looked out the small window in her room, she could see that the area had received a couple more inches of snow. The sun bounced off the newly fallen snow and it was so bright that it hurt Grace's eyes to look out the window as she squinted to check out the cardinals looking for seed in the birdfeeder.

Grace went to her closet and found a sweater and pair of pants that would keep her warm in the at times freezing facility. There were occasional cold spots in the facility and being bundled up helped her not to get too cold. After getting dressed, Grace went down to the dining room for a little breakfast. When Grace returned to her room, Miss Reagan was waiting for her to continue their session from last night.

"Come sit down Grace and get comfortable," suggested Miss Reagan as she pointed to the adjacent armchair in Grace's room.

Grace made her way across the room. There was a glass bottle of orange juice Grace carried with her from the dining room and she placed the bottle down on the small square table. As she sat down, she adjusted the chair closer to the side table. As she grasped the container, she slowly unscrewed the metal top.

"Now, I remember you telling me that your mother was an only child. What can you tell me about your dad and his family? Did your dad have any brothers or sisters?" asked Miss Reagan as Grace made herself comfortable.

"My Dad has two brothers – Uncle Jason and Uncle Tommy. Uncle Jason is the oldest. Uncle Tommy is the middle brother and my Dad is the youngest son in the family," replied Grace deep in thought as she tucked her hair behind her ear. **"My mother always laughed that Uncle Jason was the oldest and sucked away all the height from his brothers being 6' tall. Uncle Tommy was the next tallest at 5'7 feet and my Dad was an inch shorter at 5'6"."**

"That is very funny Grace. What can you tell me about your Dad's oldest brother?" asked Miss Reagan joking more than Grace had ever seen her do before.

"Uncle Jason was Dad's oldest brother who married my Aunt Char a long, long time ago. Uncle Jason was most like my Dad in personality. They laughed about everything and they also loved trivia. My Aunt Char was always nice to me except for one year she pinched me on my birthday and told me to grow an inch. I really didn't like that. My mother thought

it was funny that Aunt Char was shorter than her and Aunt Prudence but she had the tallest husband. Uncle Jason had blonde hair unlike Uncle Tommy or my dad. My Uncle Jason and Aunt Char had my favorite cousin Allison. My cousin Allison was the only blonde and Mathew and I got the dark hair from our parents," said Grace as she described her dad's oldest brother and his family.

"Grace, what can you tell me about your dad's middle brother Tommy?" asked Miss Reagan.

My Uncle Tommy was the middle brother and was only a little taller than my dad. He and Aunt Prudence had my cousin Mathew who was just a few months older than me. Just because Mathew was born in August and I was born in October I was in a grade behind him in school," stated Grace discontented that a few months could make a year difference in school. "That is so unfair! I should be in the same grade as him. I know I am just as smart if not smarter than him. That stupid Mathew, he gets all the breaks."

"Now don't get all upset Grace. You are very intelligent. Can you tell me about your cousin Mathew's mother?" asked Miss Reagan.

"Aunt Prudence is married to my Uncle Tommy. My mother says that Aunt Prudence wants the world to know that she is the best Christian ever. My mother also said that Aunt Prudence made her family go to a Baptist church every Sunday whether they were home in Mayhem or not. If they were traveling out of town, they had to locate a Baptist church for that Sunday. What my family found so puzzling is that Aunt Prudence talked about everybody in the family as being so bad. My dad thought if you are a true Christian shouldn't you be finding the good in everyone? Once Nana asked Aunt Prudence how she could judge the family so coldly. In her cold emotionless response, she would tell you that she "was just being honest". At home, my mother called Aunt Prudence "the Church Lady", and imitated her as being very self-righteous. My mother could be very funny when she acted like Aunt Prudence" said Grace laughing as she pictured her mother imitating Aunt Prudence.

"Why do you say that your mother was funny imitating your aunt?" asked Miss Reagan.

"Aunt Prudence disliked noise or social gatherings, well, at my Nana and Papa's house anyway. When we got together with my dad's family, Aunt Prudence would go to a quiet corner of the room and pull out a book or play games on her cell phone. She did most everything by and tried not to talk to anyone in dad's family. When anyone would ask her a question, Aunt Prudence would answer with only a couple of words. Oh yeah, she was a real fun person to be around," said Grace as she rolled her eyes. "My mother said because of her introverted qualities, when it was only my dad and me around at home, my mother would call Aunt Prudence "the Secret Schizoid". She would burst out laughing because it was NO secret. Aunt Prudence is dull, she doesn't show any emotion and never really talks to anyone".

"It sounds like you don't like Mathew or his parents as much as you liked Allison and her parents," remarked Miss Reagan.

"You are probably right. My mother was always going off about getting rid of Uncle Tommy at the antique store and about how stupid she thought Uncle Tommy was in his people skills," added Grace. **"Sometimes she would grunt and laugh telling me to guess who she was talking about. I would roll my eyes because it was like the millionth time she had asked me that question and everyone in the family knew it was Uncle Tommy."**

Uncle Tommy was an angry, resentful and an aggressive person. Before Luke and Lilith were married, Uncle Tommy helped Nana and Papa run and manage the Francis' family store. Uncle Tommy was a hard worker but he was NOT a people person. Most of the time, Uncle Tommy harassed customers and truly hated children in the shop. He had no problem telling people or parents "you break it, you buy it," followed by his trademark of a grunt.

"Was there a specific reason your mother disliked your Uncle Tommy so much?" asked the counselor.

"My mother thought Uncle Tommy was a threat in the percentage of dad's ownership of the shop with Nana and Papa. She feared that when Nana and Papa would die, the store would be split 50/50 between dad and Uncle Tommy. My mother was so concerned about losing control over the store that she started spreading lies to whoever would listen

about Uncle Tommy embezzling from the family company. My mother convinced my dad, Nana and Papa that Uncle Tommy was stealing from the store so he would be ousted from any part of the partnership. It wasn't really true but my mother could be very convincing. Like dad always said, she made good use of her Theatre major," insisted Grace with one raised eyebrow.

"Do you ever wish that you had siblings Grace?" asked Miss Reagan.

"I'm fine not having any siblings. From what I saw from watching my dad and his brothers, is that all they did with each other was argue. One thing I didn't need to see at home was any more fighting. Don't get me wrong my family and I had good times. But, as time went on, the good times became fewer and fewer and the fighting between my parents and my dad's family increased more and more. There are many reasons why we had problems but I will tell you what I know and let you decide, " answered Grace honestly.

"So your dad and brothers fought a lot. What did your mother and father fight about," asked Miss Reagan.

"My mother loved money and would do almost anything to get it. That is if it didn't require a lot of time or work on her part. My mother always preferred that others did her work. After a night of heavy partying, my mother was in no condition to get out of bed. If there were some place we had to go,

I would have to collect all necessary items and pile them next to the front door. Having to do her work made me feel like I was her parent."

"Did your parents do a lot of drinking?" asked Miss Reagan concerned of Grace's parents' lack of being real parents.

"It was not unusual for my parents to drink the night before any family gathering. Eventually, it became a nightly thing. Most mornings I was the first one up so I would make coffee for my parents. I always found that my parents were not as irritable if they had their coffee. This is one way I could stop the fighting before it started," stated Grace irritated by the immaturity of her parents.

"So getting back to your dad and his family. Would you say that your dad preferred Uncle Jason or Uncle Tommy?" inquired Miss Reagan.

"Dad always said that Uncle Tommy was an anal douche bag. He said that Uncle Tommy would nark on him when he was growing up and still did when he had the chance. Dad's oldest brother, Uncle Jason was more similar to my father than Uncle Tommy. Both were very smart and knew a lot of common trivia. Both Dad and Uncle Jason swore if they were ever on "Who Wants To Be A Millionaire" they would be each other's "life-line". When they got together outside of Nana and Papa's house, alcohol was usually involved and Uncle Tommy was the butt of most of their jokes," stated Grace nonchalantly. **"No doubt about it, Dad definitely preferred Uncle Jason.**

I would also guess that Uncle Jason preferred my Dad to Uncle Tommy.

"So Grace, are you finally ready to tell me the entire story of your family?" questioned the sympathetic counselor.

Grace looked out the window as if she would like to run away again but took a deep breath and said, **"I will tell you the entire story and let you decide what happened to cause the tragic end to my family."**

CHAPTER 3

Mayhem is a small town in southwestern Minnesota. Luke's entire family lived a few miles away from each other and it only took a few minutes to get to any of their houses or businesses. Nana and Papa liked having the entire family close to the businesses they ran in town. Luke, Lilith and Grace lived in downtown Mayhem and close walking distance to both Papa's architectural firm and the antique store.

Up Glenwood Avenue from the two businesses, Nana and Papa's house was at the end of a cul-de-sac and behind their backyard, was a very old cemetery. Inside the grandparent's house was referred to as "Nana's fridge" because Nana didn't allow the temperature above 66 degrees inside the house. Everyone was sure to keep a fleece or sweatshirt there so they could stay warm. Nana put socks by the back door just in case anyone forgot to bring them from home. She got tired about the constant complaint about how cold the house was. Sometimes Grace, Allison, and Mathew would go outside to warm up and play in the backyard or the cemetery.

At least once a month, Nana and Papa would try to have the whole family to their house to discuss business. Sometimes they would get together more than once a month if there were birthdays to celebrate.

"Jim, I need you to go to the store right now! It's almost two o'clock. The kids will be arriving at 4:30 or so, and we haven't started the chicken and rice," stated an irritated Nana.

"Mother, I'm working on the broken picture frame you wanted. Can you just let me finish and then I can go to the store," responded an overworked Papa.

"Go to the store right now Jim or I'm getting a divorce! Dinner is at 5:00 and I'm not going to be the one holding up the show. Now get going!" exclaimed a very angry Nana as she pointed towards the door.

"Okay, I'm going. I'm going," responded a defeated Papa.

Grace's Nana and Papa were getting ready for the rest of the family to come to Sunday dinner. Papa went to the store and was back more than an hour before any of the family members even started to arrive. While Papa worked on the chicken and put it in the oven, Nana read her recent paperback novel. Papa didn't mind doing all the work. At least this way, there was peace in the house.

A few miles away, Luke, Lilith and Grace were getting ready to leave their house to go to Nana and Papa's house. Lilith was just buttoning up her blouse as she talked to Luke.

"Spending time with Tommy and Prudence always makes me want a drink," complained Lilith. **"Prudence always acting like she is holier than thou and your stupid grunting brother drives me crazy. Why can't your family enjoy cocktails like mine? It would make getting together with family so much easier, not to mention, more fun."**

"Lilith, you know my mother has a problem with drinking in the house. Think of not drinking as a favor to Dad. He needs as much help as he can get with Mom," stated Luke.

At Nana and Papa's house, no drinking was ever allowed. Past history had showed that when drinking took place in the Francis' residence, Papa, Uncle Tommy, and Aunt Char ended up babysitting those that couldn't control themselves. Therefore, it was understood that if people in the family wanted to drink at Nana and Papa's that they would have to take it elsewhere.

Meanwhile, at Uncle Tommy and Aunt Prudence's house, they were anticipating the activities at the parent's house. Aunt Prudence hated the thought of spending another Sunday night at Tommy's family house. In times like this, Prudence had planted some smaller sized bottles of alcohol where she thought no one would think to look.

Prudence had a small room off the kitchen area in the back of the house where she made her candles. Everyone in the family knew this was her area and that no one was allowed in the room except her. This is where she hid her bottle of alcohol. If someone were to find the bottles of sin, she could come back with a comment of why were they in her space anyway? There was no way that Prudence would look like the bad guy.

Normally, Prudence would secretly drink in this room but she had some work to finish up in the kitchen so took her forbidden beverage there to indulge. When no one else was in the room, Aunt Prudence poured herself a whiskey seven and placed it in the kitchen cupboard. She would secretly gulp when Tommy and Mathew were out of the room. It was getting close to 5:00 when Prudence called up to Mathew.

"Come on Mathew. It's time to put away the bible and come downstairs. We don't want to be late to Nana and Papa's house," said Prudence as she rolled her eyes. Prudence could care less if they never made it to that destination.

Tommy was working in his small, enclosed office off of the living room in the front of the house. He was busy going through the expenditures for the antique store. He looked at the clock above his desk and jumped up and walked toward his wife.

"Yes, we should get going. I can't wait to see the folks. I'm going to tell Mom and Dad how Luke is spending all the store's money on Indian blankets again," said Tommy to his wife Prudence as he was putting on his jacket. **"Boy is he going to be in trouble with the folks. Ha! Ha! Grunt!"**

Uncle Tommy laughed to himself as he thought about his parents' reaction to his little brother's overspending.

Tommy always prided himself on pinching pennies. His nieces, Grace and Allison truly believed that moths would fly out of Uncle Tommy's wallet if he opened it the way their dads talked about Uncle Tommy being a cheapskate.

While growing up, Jason was Tommy's target for getting into trouble. If the oldest brother, Uncle Jason, did anything Uncle Tommy could use to tell their parents, he was sure to tell them. By the time Uncle Jason left for college. Uncle Tommy was known as the family spy and he changed his target to Luke as the young teenager grew up. If there was dirt to be sniffed out, Uncle Tommy was there to report it to the folks. So as soon as Luke decided to try out cigarettes as a rebellious teen, Uncle Tommy was there, reporting to Nana and Papa about Luke's bad vice.

Sundays were typically the day that the family would all get together at Nana and Papa's for dinner. This day was chosen because it was the only day that no one had to work and basically there was no excuse not to attend the family get-together. Small groups would form in various areas of Nana and Papa's house. In the kitchen, were Nana, Papa, Grace's mother Lilith, Aunt Char, Uncle Tommy and in the corner with a book, Aunt Prudence. Meanwhile, in the breakfast nook, an adjacent room to the kitchen sat Grace's dad, Luke and Uncle Jason.

"You should have seen Tommy at the shop yesterday. Some days he really pisses me off. He practically threw out a woman just because she brought her child into the store," said Luke disgustedly. **"I am**

so sick of him telling customers "you break it, you buy it" with his stupid grunt at the end. What a douche-bag!"

"The worst part is that he doesn't know how obnoxiously loud he is when he talks. Maybe if Tommy would just turn the volume down a little, he might be tolerable," said Uncle Jason trying to give the middle brother the benefit of doubt.

"No, no he wouldn't," said Luke stubbornly with a straight face still angry about Tommy's actions from the prior day. "Tommy is driving away all the customers. Pretty soon no one will shop at the store. Some days I wonder why we even bother to open the doors."

The two brothers would look at each other and Uncle Jason would lift and arch one of his eyebrows. It was as if Uncle Jason was giving his statement a second thought. Uncle Jason knew that he wasn't being totally honest with his youngest brother with Luke shaking his head no. Then Uncle Jason shook his head in thought as if "no, Tommy would not be tolerable under any condition".

"You're right. Once a douche-bag, always a douche-bag," agreed Jason annoyed by the family spy. When they both realized how annoying the middle brother was, they then would break out into a roar of laughter while nodding in agreement.

Meanwhile, on the other side of the room was Grace's mother Lilith having a conversation with Uncle Tommy,

Nana and Papa. Lilith was setting the stage for doubt in Uncle Tommy's judgment.

Grace could tell what Lilith was thinking by just looking at her mother. Right now, her mother's look told others "don't waste my time and I won't waste yours". It's something Lilith would say when people didn't talk fast. Grace's mother had no patience for Uncle Tommy or his slow-talking friend Daryl who had spent the majority of his adult life at the Francis' family store. Daryl had a huge heart but talked extremely slow. Daryl having less than a satisfactory home life became a fourth son in the Francis' home.

Daryl irritated Lilith because she feared that he would try to talk his way into the family will. Being an only child, Lilith didn't like sharing anything with anybody. Lilith would imitate Daryl by saying "Duh Daryl" whenever she was going to mimic him to make him sound less intelligent. In the Francis' residence, intelligence was everything.

"Daryl was down at the store yesterday. He was showing this old tin tobacco advertisement and wondered if we would sell it at the store for him," said Uncle Tommy to the family at the small island in the kitchen.

The conversation between Luke and Uncle Jason stopped when Luke heard mention of the store. Luke turned his head to better hear the conversation in the kitchen. Luke motioned to Jason to go join the conversation in the kitchen. The two brothers both got up from their seats and walked into the kitchen.

"Duh Daryl always wants something. When is everyone going to realize that Daryl is just an idiot and to stop taking him serious? Don't you all see that he is just trying to use us," said Lilith trying to remove the fourth non-existent brother from the family business before he had made any progress becoming a part of it.

"Is the advertisement in good condition?" asked Nana liking the idea of something unique coming into the store.

"It's Duh Daryl, of course it isn't in good condition," responded Lilith degrading Daryl. **"We know that he usually buys crap."**

"Well, it does show some aging but it isn't bad," said Uncle Tommy with a grunt defending his friend. At the same time, Tommy's right hand twitched in an agitated manner.

"Is it the real deal?" asked Luke to his brother Tommy as Luke began to listen to the conversation. **"Daryl doesn't always understand the business and his work is sloppy. Good grief, I'm still trying to fix all the problems he caused trying to help us fix our house."**

"Luke, after dinner, Jason & I can drive over to your house to take a look at your problem," offered Papa who was always the family's problem solver.

Grace's mother wasn't interested in solving their house problem; she was interested in downgrading the status of Daryl and Uncle Tommy. Therefore, it was up to her to change the subject. She had to bring up a subject that everyone knew except the one person to who the subject really mattered.

It had been pointed out to Aunt Char by Lilith that the higher number of children in a family meant a higher status symbol in today's society. In other words, only those with a lot of money could afford to give their children a good life. If you weren't rich, one child would be the limit. Being that Uncle Jason was the oldest and only had one child, none of the brothers felt pressure to have two children.

Although Aunt Prudence had expressed an interest in having more than one child, Uncle Tommy had other plans. Uncle Tommy, being the stay-at-home dad, knew that he would be the one to take care of the child. Without telling Aunt Prudence, Uncle Tommy went to a doctor to get himself fixed so there would be no chance of Aunt Prudence getting pregnant.

"Hey Tommy, are you and Prudence planning on any more kids?" asked Lilith knowing full well that Uncle Tommy had the operation and was not wanting any more children.

"(Grunt). Why the hell would I want any more children? We already have Mathew", stated Uncle Tommy knowing that the operation he just had would make additional children nearly impossible. His whole body was stiff but his right hand began to shake uncontrollably hitting his thigh as he stood next to the kitchen island. Lilith could tell that she was hitting a nerve as she watched Tommy's hand nervously twitch. It was obvious to anyone that could read body language that Tommy didn't enjoy being interrogated by Lilith's questions. Tommy's face began to redden and his temples began to sweat.

"Really Tommy? You never want any more kids?" said Lilith with a huge grin seeing if he would crack and confess to Prudence.

"Mathew is all we need", repeated Uncle Tommy wanting everyone to know where he stood on the subject. **"We don't need anymore kids!"**

"I think two children would be perfect. Especially if the second child was a girl," said Aunt Prudence. **"It would be just like my family. I had an older brother and than there was me – the baby of the family. I think Tommy and I are going to keep trying."**

"Really Prudence? Really? Well, good luck with that," said Lilith laughing to her self and looking at Tommy like she had a secret she could share if he did anything to make her mad. That's how Lilith operated. She enjoyed having power to make people sweat.

Uncle Tommy never told Aunt Prudence about the operation. However, I'm sure that when Lilith found out, she was very tempted to tell Aunt Prudence. Lilith found pleasure in seeing other people squirm. If she started a fight, that was worth extra points. Lilith figured that she would keep Tommy's secret for a better time to start an argument. For now, Lilith would use the information as leverage to make Tommy do what she wanted.

Both Uncle Jason and Aunt Char knew about Tommy's operation too but disliked any type of fighting or arguing and chose to sit by and watch quietly for now. In fact, everyone in the family knew about Tommy's operation, except Aunt Prudence and Mathew.

CHAPTER 4

A block away from Nana and Papa's house lived Luke's oldest brother Uncle Jason, his wife Aunt Char and had their only child Allison. Jason and Char had chosen this area for two reasons. First, it was near Jason's aging parents and also, this area had no covenants so Jason could design anything he wanted and build his home. Uncle Jason and Papa were both architects and each had designed their own homes. Uncle Jason had a really, really long driveway with two architecturally designed pilasters. On the other end of the driveway was a new modern home that had been built a few years before Mathew and Grace were born.

Allison was several years older and was Grace's favorite cousin. Uncle Jason and Aunt Char let Allison do to her room whatever she wanted. Allison had millions of pictures of her family and friends taped to her walls. If you weren't in at least one picture in her room, you didn't exist in Allison's world.

Allison had older friends that had written on her walls, her ceiling, and even on her white bookshelves. Allison let Grace write on her wall and bookshelf "Grace was here". This was fun and made Grace feel so grown-up. Many years later, Grace's writing is still there on Allison's wall next to the closet in Grace's handwriting.

Allison would refer to Grace's parents as the "fun aunt and uncle". Allison said that if anything happened to her parents she wanted to live with Grace and her family. As Grace looked at Allison's alternative choices of Uncle Tommy and Aunt Prudence or her parents, Grace wasn't a bit surprised.

Uncle Tommy and Aunt Prudence were not fun people at all. Neither of them ever joked about life or gave any real kindness to other people, but every Sunday, Uncle Tommy, Aunt Prudence and Mathew sat in the front pew at their Baptist church. Aunt Prudence was extremely self-righteous and once told Nana that she had a "black heart" because Nana didn't go to church. Nana and Papa never forgave her for this unkind statement.

Why in the world would a person say such a nasty thing to their in-law in the first place? The truth is that Lilith dared Aunt Prudence to say it and Prudence would do almost anything to get Lilith's approval. Lilith loved drama in her life and could really stir the pot when she had the ammunition.

Everyone in the family wondered what Aunt Prudence would do if she doesn't get into heaven. So far as the family saw it, Aunt Prudence was planning on her every Sunday Baptist church attendance getting her into the desirable pearly gates. Whatever happened to being a good Christian and spreading thoughts of pleasant wellbeing to others? It was because of people like Aunt Prudence that Grace's parents didn't think it was necessary to attend church. Grace's parents wouldn't want to end up being with people like Aunt Prudence and wherever they go.

On the other side of the Minnesota River, in lower North Mayhem, lived Uncle Tommy, Aunt Prudence and Grace's only male cousin Mathew. Their house was big but dull. There wasn't anything about Mathew's home that was remarkable or interesting in viewing or playing. Aunt Prudence didn't allow Mathew to have any toys and only allowed books in the house. Because Mathew and Grace were the same age, there was always a competition on who was the smartest, most talented or whatever.

As Grace saw it, Allison was the first and oldest grandchild. Mathew was the first grandson and then there was Grace, not really known for anything. She was the second granddaughter or the second child born child in 2003 and "first place loser" as Grace's mother referred to those not coming in as the first place winner. Grace guessed that her mother, Lilith felt like a loser for not having a child before Uncle Tommy and Aunt Prudence. After all, Luke and Lilith had been married for five years prior to Mathew's parents.

Luke and Lilith were married seven years before they had Grace. On October 4, 1996, Grace's parents were married at a party room in Lilith's parent's condo in St. Louis Park. Of course, there was an open bar. Lilith's parents never went anywhere that didn't serve alcohol.

Baby Allison was at Luke and Lilith's wedding but she wasn't even a month old at the time of the ceremony. During the wedding vows of Luke and Lilith's ceremony, Uncle Jason was holding the small baby Allison and she fluffed. A loud, booming sound echoed throughout the hard-surfaced room and everyone thought it was Uncle Jason. With all eyes on Uncle Jason, he quickly pointed at Allison, shook his head no and lipped with his mouth "it wasn't me". There were a few giggles at the interruption. Grace's parents always laughed about it and said it was Allison's way of giving her blessing to the wedding.

Lilith must have shared this story with Aunt Prudence. A few years later, in September of 2000, Allison told Grace that when Uncle Tommy and Aunt Prudence got married, Prudence told Allison's parents that 4-year-old Allison better not ruin her wedding. I guess Prudence didn't find the humor of flatulence appropriate during wedding vows. In Prudence's defense, she was so crabby and ugly that deep down she knew that she would never get another chance to get married. This was her one and only chance to get it near perfect. Like Lilith always says "ugly inside, ugly outside" as she rolls her eyes. When Lilith said that, Grace always knew that her mother was describing Aunt Prudence.

As far as honeymoon stories, or any other kind of story, there were never any funny stories told by Uncle Tommy or Aunt Prudence. However, Grace's parents were another case when they honeymooned in Stillwater. Lilith always tells the story that Luke had a little too much to drink. The only way to get him back in their hotel room was to order room service.

"Luke ran out of the room buck naked. So he is running around the hotel lobby and he refused to come back to the room. I was so mad that I grabbed his hands and started dragging him back to the room. The next day Luke had the worst carpet burns I ever saw on his behind. Anyway, after Luke finally agreed to come back to the room I ordered room service. He was so drunk that he started eating the butter pads like it was sliced cheese," laughed Lilith as she told Luke's family the story.

Luke told Grace stories about Uncle Tommy and Aunt Prudence when they were first married. Three years into the marriage, Aunt Prudence became pregnant with Mathew. Lilith was so mad that Tommy and Prudence was pregnant with Mathew before she became pregnant with Grace. After all, Grace's parents had been married four years longer than Tommy and Prudence. Maybe worse than anything, Lilith had to share the limelight with another pregnant sister-in-law.

This never did sit well with Lilith. Mathew was born in early August and Grace was born in October of the same year. Papa loved the idea that he finally had a grandson in the family. Sometimes Grace wondered if her mother would've been happier if she had the only grandson in the family? Lilith always wanted to standout in any family setting and having the only grandson would provide the attention she desired. At the same time, Lilith knew Papa was the key to money in the Francis family. So all a family member had to do in the Francis family was to please Nana and Papa, and the world was yours...

CHAPTER 5

Meanwhile, in the Twin Cities area, Lilith's parents Hank and Susan Bobble along with her grandparents Harman and Judy Grace lived 200 miles away from Mayhem. These were the wealthy grandparents that Lilith had named Grace. Because of the long distance, Grace hardly ever saw them but at the same time, Grace knew that neither of her parents really liked them. That was probably the other reason Grace rarely saw Lilith's parents and grandparents.

Grandmother Susan Bobble was never very friendly or warm. She normally had a haughty, angry disposition with hostile, ice cold, blue eyes. She would rarely give Grace a hug or kiss. Recently, Grandmother Bobble had developed scleroderma and this just made her angrier. Scleroderma is the hardening of the skin and organs. Every time Grace saw Grandmother Bobble, she looked more and more like an angry statue. Grandmother Bobble was just bitter about everything in life and nothing was going to change her mind.

On the other hand, Lilith's father, Hank hugged Grace a little too long – probably to compensate for the grandmother's aloof, detached personality. Grandfather Hank Bobble was a short, thin man just like Grace's dad. He had jet-black hair and a really thick mustache that curled up at the ends. Grandfather Bobble was well liked by most people. For some reason, Lilith did not like her relatives but neither did Grace's dad.

When they did visit the relatives in the Twin Cities, there always seemed to be some sort of drama to follow. Grace's great-grandparents were major stockholders of a large Minneapolis bank. Even though Lilith's grandparents were multi-millionaires, they would not help the young couple or anyone else in the family with their money problems. Aunt Char would always say, "There's a reason the rich stay rich. They don't give away their money and just keep it for themselves. Otherwise, how could they stay rich?"

Now, every family has skeletons in their closet and Lilith's parents considered Aunt Liza their big secret. Lilith's mother and father, Susan and Hank were high school sweethearts. When they were sixteen they had a daughter while still in high school and gave her up for adoption. Grace would later call her grandparent's mistake Aunt Liza.

A couple of years later, at age of almost eighteen, Susan and Hank had a second child coming. The grandparents were not happy about the situation and were against abortions. Judy and Harman said that Susan had to give birth to Lilith even though Susan wanted to have an abortion. Susan still didn't feel ready for a child and did

45

not want to keep Lilith. However, Susan was pressured by her parents to rethink that thought. Lilith's family always used money to get what they wanted. Grace's great grandparents told their daughter Susan to either have the child or they would cut her out of the will.

Lilith didn't know about her older biological sister Liza until she was 14 years old. Had Lilith not been eavesdropping on her parent's conversation, she may have never learned that she had an older sister. Susan and Hank tried to keep it a secret from Lilith but she heard her parents discussing the situation over cocktails one afternoon. After Aunt Liza had been given up for adoption, Susan became pregnant a second time with Lilith. Susan didn't want the baby but her parent's money always pressured Susan to do what she disliked doing.

Harman and Judy Grace made Susan and Hank have the baby and named the child Lilith Marie Bobble. The young couple was only eighteen years old and Susan's parents were only in their late thirties. This is the reason why Lilith still had her great-grandparents and no one else Lilith's age had their grandparents. Needless to say, neither grandparent was happy about the situation. I'm not sure anyone was really happy. Ever…

Growing up, it appears that Lilith had a very difficult time. In her early teens, Lilith had told Grace that a group of boys tried to rape her. Lilith told her daughter that she did the one thing that would cause a bunch of boys to run the other way. She told Grace that she defecated in her pants. You have to admit that if someone pooped in her pants, you wouldn't stick around. Lilith said it smelled really bad and the boys just ran away scared. Imaging all those guys taking off like Lilith was crazy made her laugh hysterically. Lilith loved fooling others. Grace always wandered if the story was true but wouldn't let her mother know she didn't believe her.

Lilith was fifteen years old when she finally met her older, biological sister. Liza didn't meet Lilith's expectations that were pictured in her mind. Whenever Lilith described Aunt Liza she would always point out the fact that her biological sister was extremely overweight.

"My biological sister is a BIG gal," said Lilith with wide eyes and chuckling at Aunt Liza's mass with disgust. **"I'm not kidding you. Her one thigh is as big as my waist. Liza is just huge. Really! I'm serious."**

This is always how Lilith described her biological sister Aunt Liza. Perhaps this is the reason that Lilith tried committing suicide the first time as a young teen. Someone told Grace's mother "Lilith, the teenage years will be remembered as the best years of your life." To that statement Lilith's response was that if this was the best it ever got in life that she didn't want to live and tried to commit suicide.

Even after all theses years, the wealthy great-grandparents were so mad at Susan for the two pre-marital births that they excluded her from their will. Instead, they made Grace, the great-granddaughter, as the future owner of half of their estate. The other half would go to Susan's sister and her family.

S. T. Meier

Of course, Grace still loved her great-grandparents Harman and Judy Grace and grandparents Hank and Susan Bobble. Being that Grace was the only grandchild, they always showered her with attention and presents. However, even through all the gifts, Grace could tell that money was the only thing that mattered to her mother's family. A person was worth the amount of money that came into a household by the individual and Lilith stood by this belief.

In their eyes, Luke wasn't worth much because the antiques in his store didn't bring his family very much money. Needless to say, Luke wasn't really welcome in Lilith's family. Grace once overheard her grandparents talking about Luke and referred to him as being odd and nothing but a hoarder. They blamed Luke for the boxes of antiques in their house even though Lilith was just as bad of a hoarder. Grace's grandparents always blamed people outside the family as being the problem but NEVER their own family. Liza and Lilith were Hank's fault not their daughter Susan's fault. They never made Lilith responsible for any of the family's problems. It was always someone else's fault. In this case, Luke was the culprit.

One afternoon when Lilith, Luke and Grace were visiting Lilith's family and were out at a Twin Cities restaurant. After ordering cocktails, Lilith broke the ice and was buttering up her grandparents in order to get more money.

"Grandma and Grandpa, do you remember Luke's brother Tommy? He and Prudence have a son named Mathew. Remember me telling you about

him? It's Grace's cousin that is just a few months older than her. Well, the other day I asked Mathew what he wanted for Christmas. He said WEGOS. I said Wegos? What is that? Oh my God, he got so mad," laughed Lilith having a problem talking because she was laughing so hard. "It was so funny. He kept saying the word over and over again and I still didn't know what he was talking about. Mathew just got more and more angry. So I turned to his mother Prudence and I asked what are Wegos? She said that he was saying Legos. Good God, I thought. Don't you realize that all your baby talk to Mathew has produced a son that can't talk!" exclaimed Lilith as she laughed, shook her head and rolled her eyes as she thought about the kid that couldn't talk right. "What a couple of losers!"

"It is so important to talk to a child as an adult," stated Lilith's Grandfather Harman as if he was an authority on the subject of raising children, "otherwise the child will never develop properly."

"That is so true Grandpa," agreed Lilith as she shook her head and swigged down her gin and tonic and signaled to the waiter to bring her another, "I have to tell you that Mathew sounds like a complete idiot. No one can understand a word that kid says."

"Well, no one is as bright as our little Grace," added Lilith's grandmother showing she was listening to the conversation and loved her great-granddaughter.

"So true Grandma," responded Lilith "That's why Luke and I want to send Grace to dance and

gymnastic lessons. We were wondering if we could have some money to send her and some extra cash to get through the month. Grace is so talented and that would really help us out."

"Well, I suppose we could find a little extra money to give you," stated Lilith's grandfather concerned if he was doing the right thing. **"So Luke, is the antique store doing any better? We can't just keep giving you money month after month. Maybe it's time for you to find a more lucrative job."**

"The economy isn't doing very well right now. Lilith and I have been talking and we are thinking of closing the shop and are just planning to sell on the Internet. This way the whole world can see our store. In time, we should be raking in money," stated Luke hoping that his financial position would no longer be questioned.

"Judy and I have been talking about your situation. You have nine months, the same amount of time to have a baby, and if the Internet doesn't prove an increase in your income, we want you to find a better job," stated Lilith's grandfather firmly, **"You and Lilith have been married for over ten years. We all have been very patient waiting for you two to get on your feet. If you can't support yourself by than, that's your problem. We aren't giving you anymore money after that and you are going to have to figure things out for yourself."**

After dinner, they returned to the Bobble residence. Grandfather Bobble wanted to talk to Lilith in private without her husband. Luke, Harman and Judy were sitting out in the living room while Lilith's parents wanted to speak to Lilith in the kitchen.

"Say Lilith, can you come into the kitchen for a minute? We need to talk to you about something," said Grandfather Bobble serious about the topic.

Seated at the kitchen table were Lilith's parents with very stern faces. Grace followed Lilith into the kitchen for something to do. There were some crayons and coloring books in the kitchen drawer so Grace decided to grab the box of colors and go sit down and hear what was so important to the adults.

"Lilith, come here and sit down, " said Grandmother Bobble as she pulled out a seat at the kitchen table.

"Your mother and I have been talking and we want to discuss a few things with you. In a couple of years, you will be 40 years old. At your age, your mother and I had $100,000 in the bank. Luke is 39 and you and he have no savings whatsoever in the bank. When are you both going to grow up and start supporting yourself?" asked Grandfather Bobble concerned about his daughter's financial situation.

"Well, we may not have $100,000 in the bank but we do have hundreds of thousands of value in our inventory. Luke and I have been stockpiling inventory as our 401-K plan. If we sold everything, we would have more money. It's just a different way of doing the same thing," defended Lilith.

"No, it's not Lilith! The cash is a sure thing and the antiques are dependent on what people will pay. If the economy is as bad as you say, how can you expect to find that money now when you need it?" asked Grandfather Bobble.

"Why must we always have this conversation? Grandpa and Grandma Grace have the money. Why can't we get some gift money from them?" shouted Lilith wanting others to solve her problem. **"If they really loved me, they would help me with some money."**

"It's their money and they want to keep a reserve in case there are medical issues later on down the road. That is prudent planning Lilith," stated Grandmother Bobble defending the lack of generosity of Lilith's grandparents.

The discussion continued but Grace lost interest and went on to watch some television in another room. Somehow cartoons seemed more interesting then the shouting in the next room. Visits to the Twin Cities never seemed pleasant except to celebrate Grace's birthday but that only happened once a year. Otherwise, it seemed like repeats of the same discussion of money.

Lilith's relatives always had to have drinks when they went out for lunch or dinner. Their favorite places were bars that made the drinks extra strong for cheap. Luke always had to drive home because Lilith was usually intoxicated and this time was no exception. After every visit, there seemed to be the same discussions in the car on the way back home.

On the way home from Grace's grandparent's house, Lilith was slumped in her seat with the seat belt loosely attached. On every return trip to Mayhem, Lilith would start one of her tirades of verbal abuse that was even worse after she had been drinking. There was practically steam coming out of her ears.

"God! My fucking grandparents are such cheap fucking turds! I hate them!" screamed Lilith angrily. **"It wouldn't kill them to give us a million dollars! I've even told them that they could gift us tax-free $12,000 a year each but they still didn't help. God, I hate them! I wish someone would just kill them. All they are a couple of fucking drunken-asses!"**

"I suppose it doesn't help that they hate me so much. Well, at least they bought us the washer and dryer that we really needed," reasoned Luke trying to calm Lilith.

"Well, those fucking assholes can afford to give us more than appliances. Did you know that today they offered me $100,000 to leave you?" replied Lilith knowing that this was a lie but also knew Luke would never ask her parents if this was true.

"Why? Because I don't make more money?" complained Luke. **"I swear that the only thing your parents care about is money. They are such shallow people."**

"Well, those shallow people can put food on the table for their family. For over the past 10 years

you haven't brought home any money you stupid, worthless jerk," insulted Lilith.

There were a lot of things that Lilith wasn't happy about. For one thing, she had a full-time job at a local lighting company. Meanwhile, Luke stayed home with Grace and sold antiques in the store and on the computer. The money Luke did make went straight back into inventory for future profit. Night after night, there were arguments that Lilith told Luke that she was the only one that brought any money into the house and that she was sick of it.

CHAPTER 6

Grace and her family had always lived in the same house in Mayhem, Minnesota. The Cape Cod type house is in an older part of town called the Lincoln Park area. The Lincoln Park neighborhood is one of the oldest areas of the city with many styles of Victorian and Arts & Crafts period houses. The majority of the homes in this neighborhood have shutters on the windows and the peaked roofs had ornamentation that set it apart from the newer neighborhoods in town. A few of the larger homes had a circular tower or turret like Papa's architectural firm office on South Second Street. There was a detailed richness to the homes of the area that gave it a certain charm but this hometown was different.

There is so much history in this part of town. There are two things that Mayhem's history is known for. On the positive side, Martha Hart-Love was the author of Betsy Terry stories. The well-known author of the area, Martha Hart-Love actually lived a few blocks away from Grace's home. The author's childhood home is located on Center Street and it can be toured. The Love's home isn't anything fancy but very interesting to learn about. It was here Hart-Love wrote the Betsy Terry books during the 1940's. Being an avid book collector, Luke had several 1ˢᵗ edition books written by this author. Hart-Love is buried in the Glenwood cemetery behind Nana and Papa's house.

Luke and Grace took many walks through the Lincoln Park and surrounding neighborhoods. Luke would discuss the interesting history behind Mayhem. One day Luke and Grace walked down to the public library on Main Street. As they stood on the corner of Main Street and River Drive, they faced the Minnesota River and Luke started to tell her the darker side of Mayhem's history based on the Dakota-Sioux Hanging. Luke held in his hand a local newspaper clipping citing the events of the horrific event.

"Grace, we are standing in the vicinity where 300 Dakota Sioux were hung in 1861," stated Luke going into one of his intellectual speeches as he put down the yellow backpack, he was carrying onto the ground. **"You would think that the federal government would step in before that many people were hung. However, the local white people, at the time, were so angry they let their emotions take over. See that large carved buffalo across the street? Uncle Jason was part of the committee to have the buffalo placed there. That's where gallows were constructed and thousands of local people watched the hanging right where we are standing. Even now, in 2008, Mayhem still holds the record of the highest mass execution in U.S. history."**

The story begins that in 1855, a Treaty of Traverse des Sioux sold the southwestern portions Minnesota Territory for $1.7 million in cash and annuities. The Dakota Sioux moved into reservations on the Minnesota River.

Problems between the Dakota Sioux and the white settlers escalated in August 1861, when annuity payments to the Dakota were late. In preceding years, the government had made the payment directly to the traders so that most of the Dakota did not receive any of the money themselves. Most of the Dakota were already in debt to the traders. Thus, the traders refused to sell more supplies or provisions to them on credit. In frustration, the Dakota began to kill white settlers.

In the surrounding Mayhem area, over 500 white settlers and militia died in attacks along with 60 Dakota. On December 26, 1861, 300 Native Americans were hung in the city of Mayhem.

"At 10:00 a.m., on the day after Christmas in 1861, the 300 Dakota Sioux were led to a scaffold constructed for the execution. The scaffold was constructed near the area where the downtown Mayhem Public Library is now constructed. Approximately 6,000 spectators crammed the Mayhem streets for the event. It was reported that the Dakota Sioux prisoners sang a song and grasped each other's hands as white sheets covered their faces. The bodies dangled from the scaffold for over an hour before being cut down. Then the bodies were taken to a shallow mass grave on a sandbar between Mayhem's now River Drive and the Minnesota River. It was reported that some

of the Sioux bodies were dug up that same night and used as physician's cadavers," said Luke disgusted by the lack of sympathy for humanity.

This Mayhem Sioux hanging remains the largest mass execution in the entire American history. Luke believed that Mayhem was cursed due to the hangings and that the city is haunted due to this happening. Perhaps the chants sung by the group of prisoners placed a bad, bad curse on the city thought Luke. It was at this moment that Luke felt the hairs on the back of his neck stand straight up. Luke felt that he was awaking something evil by discussing it with Grace.

While Luke was telling Grace the history of Mayhem, suddenly, Luke's cell phone went off in his pocket. He looked at the name listed on the phone and smiled. Both Luke and Aunt Char felt that Mayhem was cursed by the Sioux event. They felt that some ghosts in the older part of town were trapped in this locale. Years later, the area surrounding the downtown gave off uneasy energy that only sensitive people could feel.

At that moment, Luke's cell phone buzzed again in his pocket. Luke saw that Char was calling him. A smile came over Luke's face.

"Hey Luke. What's good?" asked Char cheerfully.

"Hey Char, Grace and I are down at the Mayhem library. I was just telling her about the mass execution of the 300 Sioux Indians," said Luke excited to talk about Mayhem's history.

"Oh wow, I learned that story during Mayhem's sesquicentennial. It's great she's learning about it at her age. It is really a shame that ever happened," replied Aunt Char saddened by the events. **"I don't believe in putting anyone to death for any crime. Nothing good can ever come from it."**

From the side of Luke's eye, he saw a large dark mass run from the corner of the library to the corner of a statue that honored the vets. As Luke's head turned in the direction of the statue, the mass disappeared.

"It's horrible. Don't laugh. I'm not crazy, but it's almost like I can still feel the angry, restless spirits around the library," laughed Luke nervously glancing back at the library building Papa had designed early in his career.

"I know what you mean. I've always gotten a strange feeling down on that side of town. It's really sort of creepy," remarked the aunt not being specific in the details.

"I feel trapped just like those spirits. It's like I can never leave. I don't know why but it's just a feeling that I will never ever get out of Mayhem," complained Luke in his hopeless situation.

"Unfortunately, I know exactly what you mean. It's like I can't leave here ever either. Like something stronger than me is keeping me here," agreed Aunt Char not liking the idea of dying in Mayhem. **"We should get out of town and visit Michael in Waltham sometime. He is the only other person I know that**

feels that Mayhem is cursed. I need to call him. Let me see if I can get a hold of him and then we both can get out of town."

"That would be great – give him a call. I have to let you go. Grace is getting antsy to go home. Talk to you soon," replied Luke as he watched Grace tug on his arm to go home.

"Okay, talk to you later. Bye" said Aunt Char as she went back to her laundry.

As Luke grabbed up the yellow backpack he placed onto the ground, he noticed that the backpack appeared heavier than it did before. Had the pack become heavier? Luke laughed to himself that the backpack had magically become more massive. Logic would suggest that he was just more tired.

Grace grabbed Luke's hand when crossing streets. On Luke's back was the yellow backpack with the black cord slightly loosen, the flap began to open up. As Grace and Luke walked away from the Library, the black mist jumped into the bag and had a ride home with its next target. The mere discussion of the dark city secrets awoke the evil spirits and they were now wide-awake.

CHAPTER 7

Not far from where the Dakota Sioux were hung, is where Luke, Lilith and Grace live. The Mayhem Public Library is located on the corner of River Drive and Main Street. The Francis family lives on South Broad Street. As Luke and Grace walked past the old Mayhem Carnegie Art Studio, Luke told Grace that he had a couple of art shows inside the small, brick building with ivy growing up its sides. A few blocks down from the Carnegie building, was the Mayhem Post Office that Luke sends off his Internet sales to customers in other parts of the United States and internationally. By far, the hardest street for them to cross was Warren Street. This is the road that heads up to the community college.

As Grace and Luke approached the corner, she turned to her left and saw a large white house down the block. There is a large rental house at the base of Warren Street before ascending up to the community college. That particular house has an incredible high turnover rate of college-renters that changes every semester or sooner. Aunt Char heard a story from one of her students at the community college where she taught about living in that house. Her student said that items in the house moved, and her roommate and other heavy items would be flung across the room from some unknown source. One tormented student resigned from college when she became demonically possessed. Aunt Char's student moved out of that large house when the semester was over and she never heard from the possessed roommate ever again. Mayhem has a lot of secrets like that.

As Luke and Grace waited for the light to change at Warren Street, they could see the Catholic Church across the street from their house. Cars drove passed them above the 30-mile per hour speed limit. Eventually Luke and Grace got the walk sign and made their way to the other side of the street.

In 2001, Grace's parents bought their house on an auction. Rumor was that the prior owner had died in the house but that didn't seem to bother Grace's parents. How many other people died in that house is anyone's guess. They moved into this house the same year that Uncle Tommy and Aunt Prudence were married. Papa helped Luke come up with enough money for a down payment on a loan. Papa was always there when anyone needed help.

The outside of Grace's house is stucco of a beige white color. The panes of the windows on their house are painted a dark green that is Lilith's favorite color. From the outside, the house looks rather small but inside is a labyrinth of many, many rooms. One of the reasons Luke and Lilith bought this particular house was for the various rooms in order to place their many collections.

From the outside, one would never guess that the house had five bedrooms and two bathrooms.

As a guest would first enter the home, they would see the bright red front door that instantly grabs everyone's attention. Luke decided to paint the front door this color one weekend during the Fourth of July of 2006. He said that this color told people that they were welcome and that this is the front of the house. At the same time, the red color was to bring luck to the household but that isn't always the case.

As Luke and Grace open the bright red front door to their house, there is a small, enclosed porch on the front of the house. On the left hand side of the porch, is a small built-in seating area for weary travelers. On the other side, Lilith placed a small table, a little taller than Grace, with a candy dish containing an assortment of hard candies for guests. Just to make the area more memorable, Luke left a register for friends and relatives to sign in and leave funny comments. Luke and Lilith were just quirky like that. When Grace was a lot younger, Luke and Lilith would joke around with each other. To anyone passing by the house, they appeared very happy but that was years ago.

When Luke and Grace opened the door into the main house from the porch, this is when the unwanted guest from Luke's backpack decided to ditch the enclosed area of Luke's backpack. The black mist decided to leave its hiding place and wait in the ceiling corner for its next victim. The spirit somehow knew that very soon someone would be coming through the door. The evil mist also knew that it could make an angry individual a living hell for the entire family.

Lilith worked until 6:00 at the store and Luke would try to put something together for the small family to eat. As Luke looked through the cupboards, he noticed there were several cans of ravioli that Lilith had purchased on sale. To Luke this was a logical choice for dinner that evening.

Grace's family wasn't the typical sit down to dinner at 5:00 family. The only time that happened was at Nana and Papa's house. In the summer, Papa would grill hamburgers and it would be like an indoor picnic with all the aunts, uncles and cousins. Those were really good times. Looking back on the fun they had then, Grace now realize that she took these good times for granted.

At approximately 6:15 p.m., Lilith walked through the front door. Grace had noticed that her mother had walked in with very dark, angry, black eyes. The scowl on Lilith's face was an obvious sign to Grace that her mother wasn't happy. Grace concluded that her mother must have had a bad day at the store.

That night when Lilith came home from work, there was a large package on the front steps. At least once a week, there was some package left under the front stoop. As usual, the box was addressed to Luke Francis. That evening, Lilith quickly grabbed up the large box from the top doorstep and stomped into the house. When Lilith saw Luke, she exploded.

"Good freaking god Luke, are you buying another blanket? Really? Aren't the other three dozen we have at the shop enough for you?" yelled Lilith as she threw the large box at Luke's head.

"I'm buying for the future. That's how this business works. You know that Lilith" explained Luke.

"Whatever. I'm hungry. What's for dinner?" demanded Lilith with dark eyes and no expression on her face.

"Well, after searching the cupboards, the obvious choice was canned ravioli stuffed with meat and tomato sauce," replied Luke in a happy tone.

"Again? You are totally worthless as a cook. You would think by now that you could master more than opening a can of food and nuking it. You are such a worthless piece of crap! Why don't you get a job? You are such a lazy husband," yelled an angry and irritable Lilith.

"I have a job. I take care of Grace and I sell items on the Internet. You know that we can't afford daycare for Grace and it makes sense for me to stay home," said Luke in a firm tone. **"We've discussed it several times Lilith."**

"Luke, I am so sick of all your excuses! We need more money and we need it now! Why don't you sell some of these worthless toys of yours?" yelled Lilith as she reached for Luke's Batman figurine and threw it at Luke.

"Are you crazy Lilith? Why don't we sell some these stupid Chinese children that you like to collect?" screamed Luke wanting to break the ceramic figurine but stopped before he did.

"You know Luke, it's all your fault that we are so poor. I'm the only one that brings ANY money into this house. You don't do anything but buy those stupid blankets. Why can't you make more money?" demanded Lilith.

"I make money. I sell things all the time" replied Luke in defense.

"You may sell things but the money never makes it into the house. You stick it right back into blankets or some other crap! For once, couldn't you just STOP buying?" yelled Lilith and she started crying at the same time.

"Don't cry Lilith. I can fix this. I promise that I will fix this Lilith. Please stop crying," begged Luke.

"Don't tell me what to do. You're just a turd and that's all you will ever be. You are so worthless! You don't clean. You don't cook. YOU don't do anything!!! I hate you. I really hate you!" screamed Lilith as she hit Luke in the face over and over again. Lilith had given Luke a bloody nose.

"Stop it! Stop it!" yelled Luke until Lilith was exhausted and stopped the beating the crap out of him. **"Quit it Lilith! Quit it!"**

Luke had gotten the worst of it. His eye was darkened from a punch forming a bruise as tears fell from the corner of his eye. His face was flushed in color as blood dripped down from his nose and bottom lip.

On the other hand, Lilith's hair was messed but she had no bruising or blood. Her face was blotchy from her rise in blood pressure from anger. Her dark eyes glared with hatred and anger.

"I hate you! I really, really hate you Luke!" screamed Lilith as she wiped the sweat from her forehead with her sleeve. **"You need to get a real job you lazy ass-wipe! How could I have married such a lazy husband? Luke, you better find a better paying job. We need money and we need it now!"**

Luke normally just tried to control Lilith's arms from hitting him. As time went on, Lilith learned some new moves that hurt Luke more. There were fights Grace saw that Lilith would knock Luke down and get his neck between her legs and continue beating on his head. Lilith would pummel Luke's head over and over again. This would continue until either Lilith got tired or Luke could stop her. This time was no different.

It was at this point that Grace had heard and seen enough. At least a few times a week, Luke and Lilith would yell at each other. As voices grew louder and louder, Grace made her way up the stairs and walked into her bedroom.

Grace's bedroom was on the second floor of the home. The walls were painted this silver color with planets and stars on the ceiling. The closet was small but fairly well organized. Grace's clothes were from thrift stores but in very good condition and bright colors. There were also more stuffed animals than any child should have. When a relative found out Grace liked a character or toy they always went overboard with the gifts.

In the bedroom, Grace had her own television with many, many videos. On the opposite side of the room from the closet there was a screened door that went out to the top of the roof on the back of her house. Grace's parents told her not to go out there because there was no railing to prevent her from falling off the roof. For the most part, she obeyed them but from time to time Grace would dangle her feet over the edge, and watch the neighbors in their backyards. In the next yard, lived Martha and Bert who would let Grace stay at their house when things got loud between her parents at the house. It was fun to watch Martha work in her yard without knowing Grace was there.

Martha, and her husband Bert Johnson, was an elderly, retired couple. Martha had spent her earlier years on the Mayhem city council but presently enjoyed her leisure time. Now that Martha had retired, she spent all time in her yard or the city park taking care of the beautiful gardens. Martha never said anything but Luke and Lilith's yard next door probably drove her crazy. It was not manicured like Martha's yard and had many patches where the grass didn't grow at all. Sometimes Grace would catch Martha working on the Francis' side of the property trying to make the eyesore of their yard a little less so from her side of the property line.

Being that Lilith was usually at work, Martha and Bert enjoyed talking with Luke during the retail day hours when his wife was at work. At least a couple times a year, Martha and Bert would invite the Francis family for dinner. It was nice for Grace to have them as neighbors and a safe refuge when things got bad at her house.

CHAPTER 8

Over the years, things began to change in the Francis household and the aggressive buying could no longer be hidden. Boxes quickly accumulated in every room of the house that made the problem obvious to any visitor. To Grace it felt like so much was going on because the walls in her house were piled with boxes of valuables that neither of her parents could bare to let go.

Every room had small, thin paths in which a person could walk but there was no blockage to the windows so light could come into the room and so Grace was still able to look outside. To be honest, Grace never knew the color of most of the walls in her house except if she looked above the top of the boxes. Both Luke and Lilith were hoarders that just couldn't let go of any item in case the item was valuable down the road. That included magazines, newspapers and pretty much everything.

Not only was the house filled with boxes of antiques, being that Grace's dad was a partner with Nana and Papa in owning the largest family antique store in town, the store was also stocked. The store was just a few blocks from Grace's house and had been opened for decades. Grace's grandparents, James and Sandy Francis, or Nana and Papa as Grace called them, had kept the store immaculate unlike any other antique store like it. Nana and Papa had washed the antiques and meticulously placed all the similar items together and all vintage toys in one area so that people shopping could easily find what they were looking for. Nana and Papa always made sure that everything was laid out in an organized and very appealing way.

It's funny but Luke appeared to be the complete opposite of Nana. Luke felt organized by creating piles of stuff that only he understood the organization. He would become easily agitated if anyone touched or tried to organize his stuff. For this reason, months would go by at Grace's house and their floors wouldn't be swept, vacuumed or washed. Lilith once told Aunt Char that it had been years since the kitchen floor had been washed because of all the boxes of future profit. Luke didn't like his items being moved and he didn't get mad about much but was very irritated when his things were relocated.

There was only one time that Luke was ever mad at Aunt Char. Occasionally, Char would work down at the antique store when the other family members went to auctions. Over time Luke had cluttered so much of the antique store's merchandise on the counters that customers could not place their item on the purchasing surface. Aunt Char decided that the time to straighten up the store had come. In order to see the top of the purchasing area, Aunt Char started putting the piles in boxes thinking that she was helping Luke and placed the boxes on the floor behind the counter. Luke was livid and Aunt Char was never allowed to help down at the store ever again.

On the other hand, the majority of the antique store resembled Nana's house that was unbelievably clean. Nana told Grace that as she grew up as a little girl, she had maids to clean for her. There was never anything out of place at Nana and Papa's house. Eating on Nana's floor would probably be cleaner than any of the dishes at Grace's house. During World War II, Nana's father had been a Major in the army. Nana was known for flipping quarters on beds to check the tightness of the sheets. Everything had to be perfect or Nana wasn't happy. When Nana wasn't happy, nobody in a ten-mile radius was happy.

Nana made constant lists for Papa and other family members to do for her. Meanwhile, she claimed she couldn't do the housework or drive the car due to the pain in her shoulders. Lilith was convinced that Nana was making it all up to get out of doing any work. Over the years, Lilith became jealous that Nana had Papa to do what she didn't want to or couldn't do. Lilith would have loved to have her own personal slave but Luke wouldn't lower himself to be one.

Luke told Grace that Nana and Papa had the antique store in two different buildings. The original antique store was located in the back of Papa's architectural firm. The firm was located in downtown Mayhem on South Second Street and was even closer to the Sioux hanging than Grace's house.

The architectural firm was the other business owned by the Francis' family. The building was a large Victorian mansion with a turret and had originally been owned by the physician Doctor Harris as a residence back in the 1860's. It was rumored that this was one of the doctors that used the cadavers from the Sioux hanging. Over the years, the building had also been a bakery and a mortuary prior to being an office. Nana's antique store was in the carriage house that now was connected to the architectural firm. Later on, Papa put his office in the backspace.

Strange things had happened in the architectural firm building. One strange thing was that Aunt Char would occasionally have interior design students intern at the firm to gain experience. One young, petite Asian woman that was interning with Char when the intern decided that she was tired and would take a nap for a lunch break. When Aunt Char returned from lunch the intern was shaking.

"Lin? Are you alright?" asked Aunt Char concerned over the intern's disposition. **"You look a little shook up."**

"I was laying down on the floor in that room over there with the turret. I hadn't even fallen asleep yet and all of a sudden I was floating," exclaimed Lin taken back from the experience. **"This place is haunted. I don't want to be here. I need to go home now."**

"Okay?" remarked Aunt Char not sure what to believe **"You do what you need to do."**

Lin quickly packed up her things. Aunt Char could tell how the young lady looked around nervously that something was wrong. The intern never stepped foot in the office ever again. After Lin's haunting episode, Char surmised that because her office was once the area that all coffins were displayed, back when the building was used as a mortuary, that perhaps it was possible that a few spirits lingered behind. Never having seen any spirits in this area of the office, Aunt Char shrugged off what Lin had said.

However, Aunt Char told the Francis family about the incident. This was nothing new to Allison whom had seen several spirits at the office. One that stood out for Allison was a very young, little girl in a white, turn-of-the-century dress. Allison could tell that she died a long time ago from the way the spirit was dressed. Allison wondered if the little girl was at the office because of the building being a mortuary in the past or did the antique store have a possession of the little girl's in Nana's shop behind the office? Allison appeared more spiritually psychic than anyone else in the family.

After more than a decade behind the architectural firm, Nana's antique business was growing and Nana wanted a larger building. The old bargain center building on Front Street was vacant and being sold by the son of the woman who had recently passed.

Papa had a great imagination and could envision the large space for them and the spaces people who would rent in their building. Papa's vision was a small town-like Mayhem with the aisles being streets and each individual booth would be like their own store and what they specialized in selling.

The antique store in its new space was huge. It was a large 3,000 square-feet brick building that took up a major section of a city block on Front River Street. There were two doors in the building with a front door for the customers and a back door from the parking lot for whoever was working that day to enter. If anyone came in from the back the alarm would sound so if anyone went out those working in the front of the building could hear them coming or going. The alarm was security against possible theft.

During the Christmas holidays, the antique store served coffee or cider and cookies as patrons walked in the front door. There were 2 long counters at the front of the store. One of the long counters had a glass top and displayed unique items. Parallel to this display counter is where the old silver cash register was placed in the middle so that two people could take care of customers before leaving the store. Papa had set up the store to give the impression of the old world charm.

As years went by, the number of dealers decreased and the Francis family took over more and more of the space with their items in the store. At one point, over 250,000 items were inventoried at the store. Even with such a high number of antiques, the store was well organized. Each booth had a unique item owned by the family with a few dealers. One booth would have Depression glass another would have Fiesta dishes. Grace's favorite area was the toy booth in the basement. Throughout the store, the festive holidays were celebrated with focus on

S. T. Meier

the decorated colors and home ideas. People came in for both antiques and decorating ideas.

One November day right before Thanksgiving, the owners were getting ready for the Christmas holidays. Grace was at the antique store with Nana, Papa, Luke and Lilith. In the front window, Grace was playing with some toys that her parents kept there for her. In the back of the store, in the kitchen area, she could hear her family speaking rather loud. Nana, Papa, Luke and Lilith were putting up garland and miniature decorated Christmas trees when her parents brought up the idea of closing the store.

"I think you're making a mistake by wanting to close the store. You should keep the doors open and sell on the Internet" stated Nana as she handed garland to Papa as he stood on the ladder nailing the garland to the beam above. **"You could be down here doing both at the same time and make more money. The more opportunities of selling the antiques the better your chance of selling the item and making more money."**

"It's crazy to keep the doors open when we could be using our time selling on the Internet" yelled Lilith acting like her life depended on winning this issue. **"Besides, if people are in here they can rip us off. You know that we have thousands of dollars stolen from some of the customers who have come through here!"**

"Mom, the store will be open through the winter holidays but come summer I want to close. You know that sales go down and it gets really, really slow in the

summer. We can make more money on-line because there is more money in the world than in this tiny town. The people that come in are only coming in to see how much their stuff at home is worth. They don't come in to buy," argued Luke.

"Why can't you two do both?" asked Papa as he nailed the garland to the overhead beams. "You could have a computer down here while the doors are open. The back room could be used as a photo area and packaging center for the computer merchandise. I think you are missing an opportunity here not wanting to keep the doors open."

"I CAN'T work here. I HAVE a job at Lighting World. WE have to pay someone else to work here with Luke and we don't have any extra money to pay anyone" debated Lilith in a determined voice and her eyes becoming dark as coal. "Besides, Luke's back has given him a lot of problems since lifting that jukebox that needed to be moved. It's difficult for him to do any lifting thanks to this shop!"

Grace tried to look like she wasn't listening by busy playing with the chalkboard and magnets that Nana and Papa put up for her in the antique store. As she looked over at the adults, she noticed the usual telltale signs that her mother was about to blow a gasket. Lilith's eyes were super dark, large and her lips were pressed tightly together and pushed away from her face. Her hands were twitching with anger similar to Uncle Tommy when he got agitated. A black aura seemed to surround Lilith's upper body. Grace could tell that her mother was getting very angry would continue to fight until she won the argument.

"Lilith and I want to close the store and only sell on the Internet. We are sick of people stealing from us. Oh, and by the way, Lilith has noticed that Tommy is cooking the store books. We think that he has been stealing from all of us. Lilith and I want to be the only partners with you two. Please don't make me have to keep working with Tommy," complained Luke. **"He is impossible to work with. Tommy grunts at the customers and scares them away. Tommy is driving down the business here with his lack of social skills."**

"Well, the office manager for the architectural firm is retiring. I could probably have Tommy take his place," said Papa trying to figure out a way to make everyone happy.

The antique store was nostalgically organized until Lilith and Luke convinced Nana and Papa to close the doors and sell the antiques through the Internet. This was the last holiday season the store remained open and closed by the slow summer months. Lilith and Luke had won the battle. Reluctantly, Nana and Papa closed the store to keep the peace in the family.

It was a very, very hard decision for Luke's parents. The antique store had been open for a really long time. The store was started decades before even Allison was born. Nana and Papa were getting old and tired. Once the doors closed, no longer did anyone dust the cabinets, clean the glass or vacuum the floors in this once beautiful antique store. The glass and walls soon became covered with spider webs and a dirt -film lined the windows and the antique items. The memories from happier times displayed in the store areas were soon crammed with boxes of thrift store finds in hopes of making big money in the future. This magnificent store was slowly becoming a large, cluttered, dusty, old warehouse similar to the bargain center store before it.

Lilith, the master manipulator, had won by first, getting rid of Uncle Tommy as a partner and then, by closing the antique store. Lilith wanted to continue feeling that victory. To make sure that the store never reopened, Lilith began hauling some of the boxes that had accumulated at their house down to the antique store. The weekly trips to the Goodwill stores were taken directly to the antique store. This space was quickly becoming a warehouse of old and new collection items. The nicely organized areas in the various meticulously laid out booths were becoming huge messes. After months of continuing this ritual, Lilith's plan had successfully ensured that the store would appear as an eyesore and would never open again.

CHAPTER 9

In order to solve Grace's family's income shortage, Luke went to Papa in private with his family's cash-flow problem. The antique shop wasn't giving Luke the income they needed to live. So Luke went down to the architectural office where Papa and his oldest brother worked. Papa's office door was in the back of the architectural firm in the carriage house where the original antique store was. Luke could enter from the back parking lot without anyone from the firm seeing him come in.

"Hey Dad" said Luke as he walked through the door. **"Do you have a couple of minutes to talk?"**

"Sure. What's up son?" asked Papa working over his drawing board as he smoked the delicious, forbidden pipe that was discouraged at home.

Nana would be extremely upset if she knew Papa was smoking his pipe at work. Little did Nana know that the rest of the family had seen Papa driving around town in his big blue Suburban with his window slightly cracked open and a big pipe hanging from the left side of his mouth. Anytime Nana wasn't riding with him, this would be the vice Papa would enjoy. Papa would then pop some gum to cover up any odor left behind. It was amazing that Nana couldn't smell the smoke on him. When she did smell it, Papa would tell a little white lie and blame it on a client smoking in his office.

"Lilith is giving me a hard time about not bringing in any money with the antiques. Is there any way you could give me a little every month in order to make her happy?" explained Luke not wanting to tell him the whole story.

"How much are you talking," asked Papa?

The old man inhaled forbidden smoke from his favorite brown tobacco-pipe between his teeth in order to hold the pipe firmly. He could tell that the couple had another fight by the bruises on Luke's face. It appeared to the father that the young couple was fighting more and more.

"Lilith would probably be happy with $2,000 a month. That's about how much she brings home before taxes," suggested Luke.

"We could probably manage that," said Papa trying to keep peace in the family.

Papa was amazing in so many ways. It would appear to anyone that knew the man that Papa always put everyone ahead of his own needs. All three sons agreed that Papa was the glue that kept the family together. If anyone had a problem, that person would end up going to see Papa and he would fix it every time.

Papa was an architect that owned his own firm with Uncle Jason. During the week, Papa met with clients and designed buildings. On the weekends, Papa would go to auctions with Nana and Luke to get items for the antique store. When Papa wasn't doing those jobs, the elderly man was doing the "Honey Do" list that Nana provided. Papa even cooked dinner at home and cleaned up afterwards. This probably explains why Papa had a heart attack before he had any grandchildren.

Luke told Grace that in the past 15 years Papa had several heart attacks with the end result of 14 stents in his heart. The doctor warned him that if Papa had one more heart attack that was it. There was no more room for any stents and by-pass surgery was out of the question. It was amazing that he was still alive. That wasn't the only amazing thing about Papa. What everyone thought Papa did that was really amazing was take care of Nana and everyone else in the family.

Nana was never calm about anything. It seemed that things had better be perfect or she would tell you about it. Once Nana got excited, it took a very long, long time before she calmed down. Needless to say, Nana had a major blood pressure problem.

When Nana started yelling about things it took her a very, long time for her to quit talking about the issue. One thing that drove Nana crazy was a mess. She was the reason why the antique store had been nicely decorated and super clean. If she couldn't do it, Papa or another family member had to do it. At home, Papa did the cleaning and the cooking because Nana claimed her shoulders hurt too much. Papa did anything to keep the peace at home. He thought it was better to clean than listen to the nagging.

Without Papa letting Nana know right away, Papa started giving Luke $2,000 a month to help with his family bills. Luke was the youngest of three sons and Nana's favorite. Luke reminded Nana of her father because Luke looked just like him when her father was young. Even so, in Papa's eyes, giving Luke the money might just get her upset and no reason would be worthy of the hell that Papa would be put through when she found out. So the payout remained a secret for a little while.

Papa had once again saved Grace's family financially. It was like Papa had a disease to please. If anyone needed anything, they went to Papa. This is probably the reason that his black hair turned grey early in this life.

Although Luke was receiving this money from Nana and Papa, Lilith kept telling her side of the family that she was the only person that brought money into their household. Lilith knew about the new income that was coming from Papa but she loved to have others feel sorry for her. The sympathy Lilith got from others in being the "lone" breadwinner felt great and she didn't want things to change that way. In theory, by making Luke look worse, in contrast, would make Lilith look better.

To those that listened to Lilith, she would convince them that Luke was the laziest drunk, and worthless husband that ever lived. In reality, Lilith was even a worse drunk having a super bad temper. Luke did drink but became extremely submissive when intoxicated. When Lilith drank she got really, really, mean and would start beating up Luke when he was too drunk to fight back.

Over time, Lilith was becoming more and more violent. Lilith was always giving Luke black eyes, bruises and squeezing his neck with her legs. As time went on, Lilith hid his bruises where most people wouldn't see them unless she wanted to embarrass him. How could Luke tell anyone that a female was beating him up? She knew he wouldn't tell anyone due to his embarrassment. After a while, she bragged to anyone that would listen about how she dislocated his shoulder or gave him a bruise. Sometimes she would order Grace to jump on his chest and if she didn't the little girl would become Lilith's focus of anger.

Lilith soon realized and enjoyed that she was causing people to turn against each other and that resulted in arguments and hatred. Uncle Tommy was removed from the antique store and now had a desk job at the architectural office. She appeared not to care about others and continued to create drama. Lilith wanted what she wanted and nothing else seemed to matter.

CHAPTER 10

December 21, 2008

It was a few days before Christmas and it was a family tradition to shop in the downtown Minneapolis area and then to take in The Holiday Dazzle Parade after the stores closed. The parade didn't take place until after sundown and the lights of the various floats lit the dark, downtown air. For years as a holiday tradition, the Francis family would pile into Papa's Suburban and spend a day at Dayton's and do their Christmas shopping. This year Papa's Suburban was blue due to Aunt Char backing into a cement post and ruining the door to the old red Suburban. The red Suburban door never opened the same again after that.

Uncle Tommy and Aunt Prudence were already up in Twin Cities visiting Aunt Prudence's family and would meet the rest of the family in Minneapolis at Dayton's. Besides, Papa's truck could carry eight people at full capacity.

Being that Uncle Jason, Aunt Char and Allison lived a block away, Nana and Papa would pick up them up first. Then, Papa would pick up Grace's family before heading out of town. Over the bridge then onto Highway 169 North he drove the blue Suburban.

"Jim, watch where you are driving," said Nana as she watched Papa looking at new construction along the highway. **"You're driving all over the road!"**

"I'm driving just fine, mother" replied Papa as he shook his head and rolled his eyes.

Nana went back to reading the Minneapolis Tribune until she felt the car jerk again and the rumble strips make a grinding sound on the wheels as the car drove to the right side of the road. She lowered the section of the paper she was reading immediately. Papa managed to get control of the car again before she could see that he was driving over to see her.

"Jim! Would you pay attention to where you are driving?" demanded Nana.

"I'm fine," said Papa a little irritated. **"You know what I really hate on these four lane highways? Look at that guy ahead of us in the left lane. He's driving slower than those in the right lane. Not only that, he is doing 5 miles less than the speed limit! Don't people realize that the left lane is for passing those in the right lane? I always wonder if that person is too stupid to know better or are they just self-centered? Don't they care how their driving is affecting others?"**

From the seat behind Nana and Papa, sat Uncle Jason and Aunt Char were listening to their conversation. They both arched forward pulling their seat belts with them as they looked at the slow moving car ahead.

"What a jerk. That guy is talking to someone on his cell phone. You can tell that he's holding it up to his left ear," said Uncle Jason shaking his head. **"You could flash your lights at them."**

"I've tried that several times and I got nothing," replied Papa irritated by the situation.

"Give him a break. He looks like a really, really old guy," said Aunt Char sympathetically. **"I always thought that people should drive their age. That guy is like 80 or more. You'd think older people would drive faster. After all, don't they realize that their time is running out."**

By this time, the family had reached the suburbs of Minneapolis and was beginning to merge onto eight lane highways. New buildings were going up everywhere. Nana was looking out her car window and was pointing to the restaurant called "Fudge Rockers".

"Hey everybody it's motherfuckers," said Nana realizing what she had just said and as her face turned bright red.

At first, the car was dead silent. Aunt Char's eyes widen in disbelief and shock. Then everyone couldn't help but burst out in laughter. Nana seldom swore so this was a once in lifetime happening. Even blushing Nana was laughing and blushing at the same time about her faux pas.

It was obvious that they were entering the downtown Minneapolis area. The buildings were tall with interesting architecture. There was an exciting energy known only to large cities. Seemed like forever before they finally parked and unloaded the crowded vehicle.

Dayton's always did a marvelous job of decorating for the holidays. There were large Christmas balls probably the size of Grace's head in bright and metallic colors with garland on the top of the tall structural columns. Due to the high volume demand on the elevators, the family took several different escalators to reach the special Christmas display on the seventh floor.

After seeing the Nutcracker Suite display on the seventh floor, Allison managed to talk Papa into going to the cookie store. Being that Papa had a huge sweet tooth this was an easy feat. Papa bought a special cookie for each member of the family. Grace's cookie of a beautiful doll was almost too pretty to eat. Unable to stop herself, she bit off her doll cookie's head and proceeded downward on her delicious treat. After finishing off their delectable cookie, everyone would pair off in order to buy Christmas gifts for members of the family. Grace decided to tag along with her Dad and Uncle Jason.

Not only was it the Christmas holiday season, but it was also a Saturday. People were packed so tightly that at times, Luke and Grace found themselves being carried by the crowd. This was a deadly combination for a child without patience like Grace. Being only a little over three feet tall, Grace swore that she spent most of the day looking at butts. If it weren't for the Christmas display and holiday decorations to look at high above her head, Grace's day would've been a total drag.

"Hey Luke, why don't you come with me. There's a couple of things I want to talk to you about," said Uncle Jason waiting for Nana, Papa and the other family members to pair up and leave the two brothers alone. **"I need to buy a Christmas present for Char and I could use a second opinion. Hey Grace you could help me too."**

The Francis family clan left in several different directions. Jason waited until all his family members were a safe distance away. Abruptly, Jason stopped Luke from going any further by holding his hand to elbow to Luke's stomach. This stopped Luke in his tracks.

"What's up bro?" questioned Luke to Jason.

"I should be punching you in the stomach. Thanks for sticking the architectural firm with Mr. Happy. You really suck. You know that? The way Tommy calls up clients and tells them to pay the firm, he is starting to dry up our business," informed Jason irritated by the situation. **"At this rate, we'll be out of business in no time."**

"Don't be mad at me. It was Dad's idea – not mine," answered Luke trying not to laugh.

S. T. Meier

Jason squinted at Luke not really sure if Luke's answer was totally honest. It was obvious to everyone in the family that Luke and Lilith were trying to get rid of Tommy for years. Being that it was Christmas, Jason decided to let it go.

Did you need to buy anything for Lilith?" asked Uncle Jason wanting to change the subject that really pissed him off.

"**Oh I forgot to tell you. I scored big last month,**" said Luke in a quiet whisper so that Lilith couldn't hear him. "**Lilith is going to love the Art Deco statue that I bought her.**"

"**Nice**" said Uncle Jason as he nodded in agreement. "**Char would love that but I think that I'm going to buy Char some jewelry for Christmas. I've always wanted to replace her wedding ring with something larger.**"

The department store was crowded with large people, short people and various types in wheelchairs. It was hard to walk around without bumping into someone or something. There were people pushing strollers and shopping carts. Grace tucked her head into her Dad's buttocks and moved only when he did to protect herself from the mass of moving objects.

"**Let's head down to the first floor to the jewelry department,**" suggested Jason as looked around and spotted the bay of elevators and pointed to the silver doors. "**There are the elevators, Luke. Come on Grace, let's go.**"

"What floor did you say you wanted?" asked Luke as entered the elevator and looked at the various floor choices listed on the elevator sign. Luke never bought jewelry for Lilith and never really went to any department stores at least since Grace had been born into the family. Luke and Grace were there only to take in the festive sights the big city had to offer.

Without a word, Luke and Graced followed Uncle Jason into a crowded elevator with more people following behind them. The three family members were dead center of the crowded elevator and unable to push the main level button for the jewelry department.

"Floor one please," stated Uncle Jason loudly hoping that someone closer to the button panel would feel obliged to grant his request.

"Two please," requested an elderly lady in the group of mature women that entered ahead of the Francis family but now stood in the very back of the elevator behind the Francis family.

As the elevator door closed from the seventh floor, there boomed a high-pitched sound that lasted several seconds and so horrendously loud like the thundering of a lighting bolt. Although strangers in this crowded elevator, this raging sound was well known to everyone. It was amazing how the strangers around the elevator all had the same expression on their face. Their eyes wide open and void of any smile except for Luke. Instead, Luke smiled and looked forward not making any eye contact. What followed was the all too familiar smell of rotting intestinal matter. The obnoxious odor grew increasingly stronger in the quiet elevator.

"Who farted?" Grace asked out loud enough for everyone to hear, looking at her dad and plugging her nose without thinking.

The same woman who had originally requested the second floor was now in panic mode. The sulfuric gas smell increased in intensity as seconds passed. Basic instincts told everyone to evacuate the area.

"Floor five please. Five please!" shouted the elderly woman feeling as if the guy next to the button panel wasn't moving fast enough.

The elevator stopped and the entire space cleared out taking most of the atrocious smell with them. Only Grace, Luke and Jason remained in the elevator. People that started onto the elevator backed away after catching a whiff of the horribly polluted area. "We'll catch the next elevator," was repeated over and over again by several customers.

In the almost empty elevator, only Luke, Jason and Grace remained behind in the moving space having four more floors to go down. Luke continued to smile but said nothing. Jason glared at Luke but remained quiet until the elevator bounced to its destination. Finally, the elevator reached the first floor. As the three family members quickly exited the small space, Uncle Jason moved closer to Luke.

"Was that you?" asked Uncle Jason with squinting eyes and a disgusted look on his face.

Luke said nothing but only smiled as he walked away from the scene of the crime...

CHAPTER 11

<u>Christmas 2008</u>

During past Christmases at Nana and Papa's house, the family would open presents for hours and then sit down to a fabulous dinner. Aunt Prudence would be in a corner all by herself. She would be reading while the rest of the family would be laughing about past Christmas gifts. One competition Luke would have with his family is who could get the best gift with the lowest cost. Luke loved this game because he normally won.

That Christmas, Aunt Char and Uncle Jason had given Papa a miniature Red Wing brown jug with maroon and gold ribbons that said "Who Will Win? Minnesota or Michigan?" Papa had gone to the architectural school at the University of Minnesota and collected both jugs and university items. Papa was shocked of finally obtaining the item that he had searched for decades and also, at the value of this small item.

The first thing Papa said to Uncle Jason and Aunt Char was **"You can't afford this!"**

"Yes, we can," remarked Aunt Char proudly with a twinkle in her eye.

Luke, who knew the value of everything, was blown away by the gift for Papa. As an antique dealer, Luke realized that this item was worth over $300. He asked Aunt Char where she found this awesome gift. Aunt Char whispered to Luke **"I went to the Salvation Army and they were having a 50% off sale. There was a $12.00 price tag so I only paid $6.00."**

Aunt Char was smiling and whispering so softly that no one could hear what she was saying to Luke. Grace could tell that Luke was jealous of how Aunt Char acquired the best gift at such a low price.

"You suck," yelled Luke to Aunt Char as he realized he had lost that year's great gift at a low cost contest and everyone sitting in the gift circle laughed. Well, everyone but Uncle Tommy and Aunt Prudence.

What bothered Grace and Allison most about the holidays is that Uncle Tommy and Aunt Prudence were absolute downers for the holiday. The couple gave crappy, second-hand books for Christmas and for birthday gifts. The books were never new and always smelled funny like they were stored with mothballs. If Grace wanted a used book, she would just go to the library and check it out. Buy a clue! Kids want cool toys for Christmas. They were such cheapskates! At home, Lilith would call both of them "cheap turds".

How frugal were they? Uncle Tommy and Aunt Prudence didn't want to spend money on Christmas gifts for adults and petitioned Nana and Papa that only the kids get gifts. Nana & Papa gave into Uncle Tommy and Aunt Prudence's request. Each kid had about 5 gifts to open. Compared to other Christmases at Nana and Papa's house, to a kid this one was by far the worst.

Luke and Uncle Jason were really angry about the direction that Christmas was going because of those two cheapskates. Both Luke and Uncle Jason had come to the conclusion of "screw them" referring to both Uncle Tommy with Aunt Prudence and the other two brothers gave all the adults presents. Although Uncle Tommy and Aunt Prudence looked very frugal, this didn't bother either of the cheapskates. They weren't out any money. Over the past years, Allison noticed that Christmas celebrations became shorter and shorter. What was once an enjoyable holiday became that day everyone started to dread.

Lilith decided she would create her own unique little twist to the holiday. This would be the Christmas she wanted to give everyone news that no one would forget. The $2,000 a month was still coming in regularly from Papa and Lilith couldn't wait to brag to Luke's brothers and their wives. This would prove to the uncles that the parents loved them more than the rest of the family. She figured if all of Luke's siblings knew that their parents cared more about Lilith and Luke this would make them angry. The way Lilith saw it was by creating envy she would break up the family of any sort of close relationship. Divide and conquer was Lilith's goal. She She was all about winning, then flaunting it, and she would let it be known by all.

So while celebrating Christmas at Nana and Papa's house, Lilith decided to start the hurt. As usual, Uncle Jason would help Papa make dinner and Aunt Char was setting the table for the celebration. The normal rule at Nana and Papa's house was if you didn't help cook then you would help clean up. For some reason, Lilith and Luke were always exempt from both duties. Grace couldn't ever remember her parents ever cooking or cleaning. Aunt Prudence must also be exempt because she never helped either. It was always the same three people helping at Nana and Papa's. Uncle Jason helped with the cooking, while Uncle Tommy and Aunt Char were normally on clean up duty.

When both Uncle Jason and Aunt Char were in the dining room and away from Papa and Nana's hearing, is when Lilith began her instigating of trouble. As Aunt Char was placing the good china on the glittering placements, Lilith turned to make sure the grandparents were out of sight.

"Can you believe that Jim and Sandy are paying Luke to do art? Every month Papa gives us $2,000 as if Luke is actually working on the Internet. Luke isn't selling things. Little do the folks know he is buying blankets and other crap," laughed Lilith hoping to see any sign of anger possible in the oldest sister-in-law.

"That's nice," replied Aunt Char not really caring about the information Lilith was trying to share. Instead Aunt Char's focus was on setting the table with the correct placement of items and making it festive and appealing. Being an interior designer, a pleasant Christmas table setting for the family was all my Aunt Char cared about at the moment.

Lilith could tell that Aunt Char wasn't really listening. If she was listening, Lilith wasn't getting the reaction she craved. Although Aunt Char could tell that Lilith was slightly irritated at being ignored but she had a task that needed to be finished. Dinner was close to being done. Uncle Jason came into the dining room with the cold food first. The salad was in a large glass bowl that he placed close to the center of the table. When Aunt Char didn't respond, Lilith turned and then directed her focus to Uncle Jason.

"Hey Jason, did you know that Papa is giving us $2,000 a month to run the shop. But you know Luke, he just does art work all day long" sarcastically replied Lilith hoping to get a rise out of the older brother.

"Good for you," insulted Uncle Jason and then looking directly at Lilith he added. **"Don't really care."**

By the look on Lilith's face, Grace could tell that her mother was angry that this news didn't make Lilith's in-laws mad. Uncle Jason and Aunt Char made a lot more than $24,000 a year, or even Luke and Lilith's combined income of $48,000 and they really didn't care about the antique business. In fact, Uncle Jason HATED antiques. The farther away Uncle Jason was away from the family antique business the happier he was.

Uncle Jason was the president of their family architectural firm and had an adjunct professor position at the local community college. Aunt Char worked at the architectural firm, and also taught at the same college. The combination of the various jobs not only kept the aunt and uncle running but also brought in a nice sum of money for their family. Grace wondered if this is the reason Allison's family never seemed to fight like her parents.

Lilith had already done reputational damage to Uncle Jason and his family with Nana and Papa. Back in 2000, when Grace's cousin Allison was only four years old and living in the Lincoln Park neighborhood, Lilith had heard that Allison was still sleeping with her parents. Allison had told Grace that she had seen ghosts living next door to her house on Pleasant Street in the Lincoln Park area. Having this gift, Allison wanted her parents protection from the apparitions and didn't want to be alone. Lilith used this information to make Uncle Jason out to be a pervert to her in-laws and Jason's own parents seemed to believe it. Nana would nag Jason and Char that Allison was too old to sleep with them. Yes, Lilith was that convincing.

Lilith was the master of deception, and she convinced people into thinking the worst of others. She told Nana and Papa that Uncle Jason and Aunt Char "had more money than God". Therefore, it made sense to equal things out by giving Luke the antique store and the architectural office building to Uncle Tommy in the most current will. Uncle Tommy was all in favor with this arrangement and this made Lilith a close friend in Uncle Tommy's eyes. He still hadn't realized that Lilith was the one responsible for his being ousted from the antique store. At the same time, Lilith made sure that Luke requested the best stuff in Nana and Papa's house.

The rest of their things were to be divided out equally among the boys. As a result, Jason was basically written out of the family will.

This arrangement made Lilith very happy. She was still working on how to let Uncle Jason know he was given the least in the will without him getting mad at her but she hadn't mastered this plan yet so Nana and Papa's will remained a secret. Perhaps she figured it is better to keep it a secret after all, otherwise, Uncle Jason could change his parent's mind thought Lilith.

However, now Uncle Jason and Aunt Char were not at all upset and that wasn't how this was supposed to work. This made Lilith very angry but only Luke and Grace could see it. They both saw the fire stirring in Lilith's eyes but the actress in her wouldn't allow others to see her anger. Lilith wanted people, especially Luke's brothers and their families, to be jealous and see that she was winning with Nana and Papa.

Lilith was jealous of Uncle Jason and Aunt Char because they had a new house, cars and great jobs. Even worse, they both seemed very happy. These were all the things Lilith wanted but didn't have in her life. At home, Lilith would say how those two didn't deserve all the good things in their lives. Lilith was obsessed with other people's success and wondered why it didn't exist in her life.

After the celebration, Lilith, Luke and Grace packed up their gifts and went to their car. Snow was beginning to fall as they drove home on the curvy Glenwood road.

Luke drove home as Lilith vented her feelings about the evening.

"I hate them. They are just stupid turds!" screamed Lilith, as she would describe Uncle Jason and Aunt Char on a weekly basis in the privacy of their car.

The next week, when Luke and Grace were out and about, they were close to Nana and Papa's street so they decided to stop by cousin Allison's house. Uncle Jason and Aunt Char loved Luke. All three of them could talk for hours and sometimes be laughing so hard that their sides would hurt. However, now was the time to be serious for Uncle Jason and Aunt Char.

"Hey Luke, we need to talk to you about Allison. Char and I thought if something happens to us, would you and Lilith be willing to take care of Allison?" asked Uncle Jason.

"Sure, we love Allison," replied Luke with a smile **"besides Grace would finally have a big sister that she has been requesting and you know we are done trying for any more kids."**

"I think we are all done having kids, Luke. But I have to tell you that Allison said that she would rather live with you and Grace more than anyone else," said Aunt Char.

"No problem" said Luke **"you can count on me".**

Some of Grace's best times were spent with her cousin Allison. Aunt Char and Uncle Jason told Luke that if anything happened to them they wanted Luke to take care of Grace's cousin Allison. Grace loved the idea of possibly having an older sister and Allison was cool. Allison was seven years older than Grace and she could learn a lot from her older cousin. Grace told Allison about everything in her life and Allison understood how Grace felt.

At home, Luke and Grace realized things were good when Lilith wasn't around and she was busy at the lighting store. How come no one outside the family noticed the drama Lilith would create? Maybe they noticed but just ignored her and Lilith really hated that. If Lilith wasn't the center of attention and having things go her way, she just wasn't happy. So when Luke told Lilith what had happened at Jason's house that day, Grace didn't understand why Lilith was so happy.

CHAPTER 12

January 2009

Until Mathew and Grace went to kindergarten, both of their dads were stay-at-home dads. This was the one thing both Lilith and Aunt Prudence had in common besides enjoying drinking alcohol on Thursday nights at the local saloon. Both husbands were the same size in height and approximately in weight. Prudence and Lilith both outweighed their husbands.

Mathew's mother, Prudence, was a full-time secretary at the local hospital who loved to drink. Once a week, Lilith and Aunt Prudence would go out for beers. Grace never was allowed to tag along with them when they went out to the bars to have drinks but she did notice one thing. Her mother Lilith always came home from these nights and argued more with Luke. The more Aunt Prudence and Lilith went out and drank, the more angry and unhappy Grace's home became.

It's funny that Lilith would go out with Aunt Prudence. Grace was convinced that Lilith never really liked

Aunt Prudence. At home, Lilith would describe Aunt Prudence as "extremely unattractive, socially awkward, and lacking any sort of personality". However, Aunt Prudence was always up for beer so Lilith could always depend on her as a drinking buddy.

Sometimes Allison and Grace wondered if Aunt Prudence was a little lesbian. In public, they could tell Aunt Prudence preferred women and girls to men and boys. There were many weekends that Aunt Prudence would go on trips with her girlfriend but not with her husband or her son. When the families got together, she would pay more attention to her nieces than her own son. Also, Aunt Prudence was always touching Lilith's back and always playing with her hair. Aunt Prudence was also all over Grace with the hugs and she couldn't get away fast enough from the ugly old lady.

One night, when Luke was out, Lilith and Aunt Prudence decided to have cocktails at Lilith's house instead of going out. Uncle Tommy stayed home with Mathew in North Mayhem and Luke was out with a friend. It was no secret that both wives got together to complain about their husbands or their in-laws. Another common factor they agreed on is that they were the only "independent" ones in the family on their husband's side.

On Luke's side of the family, everyone else worked for the "family" businesses in one-way or another but not the two superior sister-in-laws. Nana, Uncle Tommy and Luke worked on the antique store. However, when Lilith ousted Uncle Tommy from the antique store, Papa found him a business management position at the architectural office. On the other hand, Papa, Uncle

Jason and Aunt Char worked for the architectural firm. Lilith worked for the lighting store and Aunt Prudence worked for the hospital. This independence made them feel superior to the rest of the family. They didn't need the rest of their husband's family. They were self-reliant and they didn't need to cooperate with the rest of the family in any way whatsoever.

The doorbell rang and Lilith rushed over to answer the front door. As Lilith opened the door, Aunt Prudence quickly looks inside and smiles. Aunt Prudence was a few years older than Lilith but looked a lot older. Prudence had short, dark brown hair, small squinty brown eyes and old fashion square-shaped glasses. Aunt Prudence also had a very bumpy face. It was obvious that Aunt Prudence had a strong case of acne as a teenager. Now Prudence had a horrible complexion and her face showed signs of indentations from the acne scars left behind from a difficult puberty stage. Plain and simple, Aunt Prudence was really ugly.

Aunt Prudence never turned down the opportunity to have a beer. Due to her self-righteous attitude, most people would never guess that Aunt Prudence ever drank. A non-drinker was exactly what Prudence wanted others to think about her. Besides, she was a die hard Baptist who felt saved for the lord because she and her family attended church every Sunday.

Before grabbing the doorknob, Lilith practiced putting on her stage smile and opened the door. A bottle of beer was held in her left hand as she used the right hand to open the door. No way would Lilith tell Aunt Prudence that she started drinking hours earlier without her and this was Lilith's fourth beer that evening. Lilith loved drinking and after a few cocktails, she could tolerate anybody including Prudence.

"Come on in girlfriend and let the drinking games begin," said Lilith to make it sound as if she was just beginning to consume the beer and had full control over her drinking habit.

"Beer sounds good to me after the day I had. If one more person needs anything from me I am going to scream," stated Aunt Prudence as she looked around the living room as the two women walked into the kitchen. **"I am glad to see that worthless husband of yours isn't home. Good god, talk about the endless blah, blah, blah. It's good not having the two brothers here tonight. No one can get a word in edgewise with those two."**

"No doubt. "I'm glad you left that grunter home too. Every other word is grunt, grunt, and grunt. Any day that I don't see Mr. Happy is a good day. Boy, our husbands are so lucky to have us. I mean really, what would they do without us? We are the two breadwinners in our family. If not for us bringing in the money, those two would be out on the street sitting on their duffs," said Lilith as she opened up the refrigerator door. **"Okay, I have beer or wine. Which would you like?"**

"Beer still sounds good. I'm surprised that there is any alcohol left in the house with that husband of yours," chirped Aunt Prudence after years of hearing

Lilith complain of Luke's drinking. **"What a drunk you married!"**

"I know right," said Lilith not mentioning that she was going on her fifth beer for that evening. **"If we don't have alcohol in the house, I notice that my baking extract goes down real fast."**

Aunt Prudence rolls her eyes in disgust as she recognized that Lilith was insinuating Luke out to be an alcoholic. **"What's new with you these days?"** asks Aunt Prudence as she grabs the beer from Lilith's hand.

"Well, Char & Jason told Luke that if anything happens to them they want Luke and me to take Allison," stated Lilith watching Aunt Prudence to see her reaction and hoping to see a little envy. **"I can't stand them but I do love Allison and their money. Did you know that they have a couple million in insurance money?"**

"Oh really? I can't stand them either. They act like they're better than us. I could care less if they died tomorrow." stated Aunt Prudence. **"Can you imagine having their insurance money, their big house and their two new cars? Wouldn't that be the life?"**

"Yes, it would. Yes it would," said Lilith as she drank her beer greedily and thought about living in her in-law's place. **"So Prudence, have you ever thought about killing that annoying husband of yours?"**

"Of course, who wouldn't?" replied Aunt Prudence with a laugh. **"Wouldn't it be a shame if Tommy took a tumble down the stairs? I would stand there**

watching him roll over and over again. Of course, I couldn't help my self from laughing. Who knows, I might help Tommy down them myself."

"Oh, yeah, that would be a real shame. No more Mr. Happy," answered Lilith with a grin on her face **"It almost brings a tear to my eye – NOT!!!"**

Grace was never sure if they both thought about killing Uncle Tommy together but it wouldn't surprise her if they did. They both disliked him but Aunt Prudence probably thought Uncle Tommy didn't have enough insurance money to make it worth her while. Besides, since Lilith got Uncle Tommy out of the antique store, he was no longer considered an important player in the game Lilith was playing. Therefore, Lilith could care less if Tommy lived or died.

This new, exciting situation of being Allison's guardian really got Lilith thinking. The wheels were turning in Lilith's mind that Uncle Jason and Aunt Char had an overabundance of insurance money between them. They probably had some money tucked away along with their 401-k money, not to mention their brand new home, furniture and other possessions. If something happened to the couple, Allison would be in their custody and everything they owned would become Luke and Lilith's property.

On top of that, with Uncle Jason out of the picture, it would be one less brother to have to split Luke's family fortune. With the oldest brother gone, that would leave only Tommy and he was easy to bully thought Lilith. However, Uncle Jason and Aunt Char would not be as easy to dispose of. The question is how do you get rid of both of them without attracting attention and make a small fortune? This would take some careful planning...

CHAPTER 13

February 2009

Lilith decided that she had to work quickly. After all, a few months earlier, Lilith's grandparents had warned her that she had only six months before money on her family side would dry up. Since that dinner, she had been planning some scheme in order to make a jackpot of money. Nothing was more important to Lilith than striking it rich as soon as possible. It was apparent to Grace and anybody that really knew Lilith, that money was more important to Lilith than anything else and that included people.

Being that Lilith was an only child, Liza, her biological adopted sister, wasn't really in line to inherit from Lilith's grandparents. If this changed, however, Liza could also be disposed of easily thought Lilith. Luke, on the other hand, had two other brothers that would someday have to divide up any inheritance. As Lilith saw it, Uncle Jason was the biggest obstacle on her getting everything. Once Uncle Jason was out of the way, Uncle Tommy would be easy to get rid of. After all, Aunt Prudence wouldn't mind getting rid of Uncle Tommy and getting his insurance money. Who knows, if there was enough money in it for Lilith, she might offer to help Aunt Prudence.

Before Uncle Jason and Aunt Char wanted to make Luke a guardian to cousin Allison, Lilith had considered killing her extremely wealthy grandparents. However, Lilith didn't know their schedule as well as she should to make this happen. Besides, it was too much work to get to the Twin Cities and back again to Mayhem and still look innocent. Lilith has never been about working too hard.

Lilith always thought that working hard was for suckers. Also, Lilith wasn't sure what she would inherit if her grandparents did die. Would there be enough money in Lilith's grandparent's will to make it worth her doing it? Was she still even in the will? These were the questions going through Lilith's head.

As Lilith continues to investigate her grandparent's will, she learned that Grace is the major beneficiary for her great-grandparents. When Grace reaches the age of twenty-one, she will receive ten million dollars plus five million every year for the rest of her life. Lilith is angry that she has been skipped over but she will get a portion of Grace's inheritance in order to take care of her daughter. Therefore, it is very important that she never loses Grace. If Lilith loses Grace, she also loses the money. It was this point of her life that Grace felt that Lilith was trying to keep her happy which was fine with Grace.

Grace overheard Lilith telling Luke that Uncle Jason and Aunt Char had a huge insurance policy on each other. Lilith's eyes sparkled at the thought of owning all their things as she told Luke of their value.

If something happened to Uncle Jason and Aunt Char, Grace's cousin Allison and everything they own would go Grace's parents as being guardians to her cousin consumed Lilith's thoughts. A few months earlier, Uncle Jason had just been arrested for a DUI and Lilith thought he would be very vulnerable to having an "accident". If Aunt Char agreed to "kill" Uncle Jason, Grace's aunt would go to jail or maybe they could kill her too. On the other hand, Lilith could make Char so miserable that she would commit suicide. One way or another, Lilith had to get rid of both of them to make her plan work. With both Uncle Jason and Aunt Char out of the way, Allison and ALL the possessions would be theirs. Grace had never seen Lilith more excited or happier….

CHAPTER 14

March 31, 2009

In late January of 2009, Luke had been helping Aunt Char drive Uncle Jason down to Rochester Mayo for doctor appointments. Luke rarely left Mayhem and he welcomed any opportunity to see a different place. Luke was more than happy to go somewhere and Uncle Jason enjoyed Luke's company.

Uncle Jason had a week of cancer and other testing done due to the removal of Kidney cancer a couple of years earlier. As payment for Luke helping Char take Uncle Jason to the doctor appointments, Aunt Char invited Grace's family to their house for dinner and drinks to say "thank you" for Luke's help.

At 5:00 p.m., on a Friday night, Grace's family rang the doorbell and stood on cousin Allison's doorstep. Grace looked inside the glass door to see if anyone was coming to answer the door. She could see Aunt Char coming from the kitchen. Her head peeked around the counter corner and her pace picked up as she saw that Grace's family had arrived. Aunt Char answered the door wearing a black v-neck cotton long sleeve shirt with a skinny pair of black pants. As Char invited them in, Grace noticed that Lilith was giving Char compliments. Lilith never said anything nice to anyone, unless, she wanted something from that person.

"Wow, Char, have you lost weight? You look great," said Lilith overly enthusiastic to the hostess.

"I don't think so, but I never weigh myself. So, maybe – thanks. Anyway, come on in," said Aunt Char without knowing how to take the compliment from Lilith who never gave them.

Luke and Grace looked at each other as if to say why is Lilith being so nice? What does she want from Aunt Char? As Grace looked around the entry, she wondered where Allison was.

"Where's Allison?" Grace asked bored with the adult conversation and wanting to get away and go be with someone closer to her own age.

"Just a minute Grace," said her aunt as she turned and walked to the foot of the stairs, she cupped her hands and called **"Allison, your cousin Grace is here. Please come on down. Grace wants to see you!"**

Allison yelled Grace's name as she ran downstairs. She picked Grace up like she weighed nothing and carried her into the living room where they could still see what was going on with the adults in the kitchen.

In the kitchen, Aunt Char, Luke and Lilith were having hard alcohol drinks. Allison's mom prepared a pitcher of lemonade for the kids. She brought both Grace and Allison a small glass of lemonade and set the glasses on the cocktail table next to the sofa. Uncle Jason wasn't participating in the drink fest. Uncle Jason had just been in jail a few months earlier for a DUI so the smell of alcohol made him nauseous and the last thing he wanted to do was drink.

Although it was March, it was Minnesota, and there were still large traces of snow on the ground. Uncle Jason avoided the alcohol that everyone else was drinking by grilling out on the back deck. By staying active outside he could avoid the putrid smell of alcohol which now made him rather ill. It was not uncommon for Uncle Jason to wear shorts and grill in the dead of winter. Every once in a while, he would pop into the kitchen from the back deck and join the group but he spent the majority of time keeping busy and stayed on the deck grilling the steaks.

Cousin Allison and Grace were in the living room that faced the kitchen. Grace was playing with Allison's old Bratz dolls. Grace took one brunette doll with long hair and called her "crazy wife". Allison also had boy Bratz dolls so Grace took one that had short brown hair and called him "lazy husband". As Grace grabbed the "crazy wife" doll she said to Allison **"I'm crazy wife doll and you are just a lazy husband".** Then the "lazy husband" husband doll responds, **"I'm not lazy, I sell things on the computer". "You are so lazy! Get a job!"** says crazy wife. This made Allison laugh really hard. Grace wasn't sure if Allison realized that she was re-enacting the same scene Grace saw almost every night in her own home.

When the kids weren't talking about "crazy wife" and "lazy husband" they could hear everything that the adults were saying in the kitchen. Lilith was making some comments about Uncle Jason being a loser for getting caught with a DUI. Grace could tell by her parent's speech they were beginning to have too much to drink. While Uncle Jason was busy with dinner outside, Lilith looked at Aunt Char and began discussing her little scheme.

"So exactly how much do you have in insurance money on Jason?" asked Lilith trying not to look too obvious.

"I guess I have almost a couple of million on him. Why? How much does Luke have for insurance?" asked Aunt Char wondering if the amount she had was too much or not enough.

"I have about $100,000 on Luke - not that much but enough to be comfortable for awhile. Now Char, both Tommy and Prudence have told me that they thought about killing each other in order to collect the insurance money. You can't tell me you haven't thought about killing Jason?" asked Lilith with intense interest and the only thing that mattered was Aunt Char's answer.

As Grace looked over at Aunt Char in the kitchen, she could tell that her aunt was horrified at the question being asked. Aunt Char's eyes were big and her mouth was dropped open. Grace could tell from looking at Aunt Char that she had not had as much to drink as her parents and was shocked by the question.

"No! Jason has made me a little upset from his DUI but I wouldn't kill him over it. Besides, as you can see tonight he isn't drinking and has totally quit drinking. If you couldn't tell, the smell of alcohol makes him sick now and he does what he has to avoid it," stated Aunt Char in defense of her husband's past actions.

"Come on Char. You must have thought about the things you could do with the money from the insurance policies. A couple of million would mean you could live a lavish lifestyle for a while. I even have a $100,000 policy on Luke and thought about paying off the house, buying a new car and getting some new clothes," stated Lilith trying to convince Aunt Char of the benefits of extra cash from an insurance policy.

"No Lilith, I never really have thought about killing Jason. I couldn't do that," said Aunt Char as she tried to end the conversation topic by standing up and began making of the salad that should have been prepared before the guests had arrived. **"Besides, I would imagine that it would be hard for anyone to live with the fact that they took another person's life. A life is precious. I'm sure the guilt would eat you alive if you killed someone."**

Meanwhile, from the sofa in the living room, Grace looked over at her dad who was getting drunk. Luke was having a difficult time sitting on the tall stool even though it had a back and arms. Grace also noticed that Luke was making goofy eyes at Aunt Char as she sat down on her kitchen stool. From looking at Aunt Char's profile, Grace could tell that her aunt was furthered surprised by Luke's flirtatious actions. Aunt Char's eyes opened up and wide in disbelief. Char had always thought of Luke as a little brother and nothing romantic.

By this time, Luke was totally intoxicated and his reactions were not as quick as he needed them to be. At the same time, Grace could see that Lilith noticed the goofy eyes Luke was making at Aunt Char. Lilith got her crazy eye look when she was jealous and was beginning to boil over with madness. Lilith stood up and without saying a word, she started swinging at Luke. Before anyone else noticed, Grace saw her mother take her father down off the stool in the kitchen and drag him into the dining room. Her arms continued to bruise his body. Lilith continued to bash Luke's face with her fists and squeeze his abdomen with her legs. Luke's deep red blood began to stain the ochre colored sisal carpet.

Lilith kept punching him in the face over and over again. Instead of fighting, Luke covered his face to prevent further damage from the slugs he had already endured. Aunt Char froze in place with her eyes widen in shock at the actions happening before her. She covered her mouth with her hands as the violence unfolded in front of her. By this time, Allison had turned around to see what Grace was looking at and her eyes also widen in disbelief and surprise.

This display of violence was not new to Grace. She saw her mother beat up her father all the time at home.

It seemed perfectly normal to her but as Grace looked around the room she realized this must not happen in all families. Suddenly, Uncle Jason came inside from the grill on the back deck with a platter of food. He stared at the scene that was in action before his eyes. Quickly, Jason set down the platter of food on the dining room table.

"What's the matter with you two? Now stop that," said Uncle Jason as he pulled Lilith off the top of Luke.

Aunt Char took her hands off her face and looked at the blood on the yellow colored sisal carpet. Once again, Lilith had given Luke a bloody nose and many, many bruises. Aunt Char ran to Luke with a box of Kleenex pulling out a few as she ran to his side and handed the tissues to him. She then went to her pantry to find the carpet cleaner before the blood set in and couldn't be removed from the carpet.

"I will pack up some food but I think you two should go home. Those sort of actions will not be tolerated here," said Uncle Jason as he went to the kitchen to pack up food in Tupperware to send home with his brother and his family.

As the three ousted family members trudged outside the modern house, Lilith took her position in the driver's seat in their old Jeep, being that Luke was more intoxicated. Although the ride home is less than five minutes, it felt like a lifetime for Luke and Grace. There was little talking done in the car. The message promised by Lilith gave both Luke and Grace the creeps.

"Well Luke, Char isn't up to getting rid of Jason. What are we going to do Luke? We need money and we need it now! Someone has to die so we can get a large insurance policy!" yelled Lilith as she gave Luke a dirty look. **"So how are we going to make some money? How Luke! Come on genius. Tell me how YOU are going to make the family some money?"**

The tension was so thick in the car it could've been cut with a knife. Lilith was the angriest that anyone had ever seen her. She did not win tonight and someone was going to pay for it. If not tonight, very soon...

CHAPTER 15

April 2, 2009

Earlier in the week, Grace's parents had arranged for Grace to go visit Nana and Papa. As luck would have it, that happened to be the night after the disaster at Allison's house. Being that Allison lived a block away from them, Nana and Papa called Aunt Char to bring Allison over so the two cousins could spend the day together. At the same time, Allison would lighten the load for Nana and Papa by playing with Grace.

Grace watched out the large front window in the entry of Nana and Papa's house for Allison's parent's car. When Grace saw Aunt Char's black Volkswagen Beetle, she made sure that Nana and Papa knew they were coming. Aunt Char was driving the Beetle when she brought over Allison. The black car drove up the slightly steep drive way and Allison was the first to jump out of the car. Allison ran to the back door that opened into the grandparent's breakfast nook. Everyone used the side, back door when coming into Nana and Papa's house. Char followed behind Allison. When Grace saw Aunt

Char, she knew something was wrong. Aunt Char looked even more serious than usual.

Grace also knew when adults didn't want little ears to hear things. Aunt Char was no different and she noticed that her aunt waited to talk to Nana and Papa until Grace was out of the kitchen. For this reason, Grace stood outside the kitchen in the entry level and grabbed Alison's hand so she could also listen. This was where Grace was watching for Allison's car and was the best spot where she could listen to the adult's talk in the kitchen.

There were low whispers coming from the kitchen that Grace couldn't quite make out. It reminded her of the Charlie Brown specials where the teacher is talking but it sounds totally muffled. Grace had to sneak in a little closer to the kitchen to hear what the adults were discussing.

"There was blood all over my dining room floor," complained Aunt Char. **"Doesn't that concern you?"**

"That's just how those two work things out," replied Papa **"Nothing that you have to concern yourself with. They'll be fine."**

"That's right Char. It's just how those two have always gotten along," agreed Nana trying to convince Char that the matter wasn't that dire.

"Well, I'm just worried that one of them will end up dead," remarked Aunt Char **"and I'm more worried that it will be Luke."**

As Grace looked into the kitchen, she noticed that her aunt wasn't smiling like normal. Nana and Papa just shook their heads. In our society, no one takes it seriously when a wife beats up a husband. Nana and Papa figured that Luke could hold his own being a male. They overlooked the fact that Luke was thinner and not as aggressive as Lilith. Also, Luke wasn't insane thought Char…

"Well, I have things at home to do. I will pick up Allison at 7:00," said Aunt Char feeling that she wasn't getting through to her in-laws as she turned for the door, **"I will see you then."**

CHAPTER 16

April 19, 2009

One Sunday afternoon, the kids were outside running around Nana & Papa's backyard trying to warm up from "Nana's fridge" house. After a while this game became boring, so the three children all ran into the cemetery for a change of scenery. The children weren't afraid of the cemetery because the family took a lot of walks in the cemetery after big holiday dinner celebrations to feel more comfortable in their tight clothes from eating too much food. They often played in the cemetery but this time the children were more energetic and louder than usual.

"Hey, Grace. Hey Mathew. Come over and look at what I have here," said Allison pulling something out of a paper bag she had in her hand and showing them a creepy Troll doll that Nana had in her doll collection in the basement of her house. The doll had a dark tan complexion with long platinum hair sticking out of the top of its hair. The doll's deranged smile would give anyone goose bump chills. **"This doll really creeps me out."**

"I hate those dolls," said Grace with a wrinkled up nose.

"Me too," agreed Mathew shaking his head up and down.

"I have an idea," said Allison with a huge smile on her face as she looked around them to make sure no one would see her. There wasn't another soul as she looked over the entire wooded area in the old cemetery. **"There's a short tree stump. Let's stuff the doll inside and leave it. It will scare everybody that comes into the cemetery."**

"Can you imagine the look on people's faces when they see that ugly doll in the tree?" laughed Grace.

"They will probably run like this," said Mathew as he started to run in circles with his arms flapping up and down.

"No, Mathew, more like this," replied Grace with her arms straight up in the air as she screamed and ran away from the troll.

The thought of scaring others made the children laugh loudly. All three were laughing so hard that their sides began to hurt so they stopped and bent over. The three children started running around the tombstones. Each child had their own version of how people act when they were scared. There was slugging involved with each other and screaming, **"No! You're it!"**

All of a sudden the three children stopped laughing and looked at what appeared to be bubbles coming from the tree stump where they had placed the troll. As the three children watched the orbs, the small toy troll became larger and larger as it grew taller and taller like a tree. The longhaired, platinum blonde troll grew large enough to break out of the tree stump. The body of the troll turned into a texture similar to the bark of the tree with red vines and his hair turned more of a bright yellow color. The ugly troll had heard what the children had said about it and decided to make them aware that he knew.

The eyes of all three children widen and their tiny mouths dropped as they looked up at the large troll that magically grew in front of them. Quickly the troll grew larger than most adults they knew. The slow moving troll started to step towards them. None of them believed what was happening. It was really creepy as the ugly troll got closer and closer to the children.

They all looked at the troll with a group of orbs behind it and then each other. At first they were shocked in place until Allison yelled, **"RUN!"**

They all had an uneasy feeling and decided to listen to Allison as they ran back to Nana and Papa's without looking back. None of them ever discussed what had happened. Occasionally, the children wondered about Nana's platinum blonde troll but never discussed it. Was it still there or where did it go? Whenever Nana asks about its whereabouts, the grandchildren quickly change the subject. By speaking of the hideous sight in the cemetery, the children feared it would come after them. No one wanted the chance of bringing the troll back to life. Never did the children go back into that cemetery and avoided all cemeteries after that.

CHAPTER 17

June 25, 2009

It was a few months later since the big fight at Allison's house and the weather finally started to really warm up in Minnesota. Everyone needed to forget the prior incident before Uncle Jason invited Grace's family back to his house to grill on their back deck. While Allison was at soccer practice, Grace's family sat at the patio table on Jason's back deck getting ready for dinner. Instead of hard alcohol, Aunt Char gave Grace's parents beer out of green glass bottles that took a little while longer for Grace's parents to become intoxicated.

Allison had three cats and Sammy was the oldest getting close to 20 years of age. Sammy was a long hair orange tabby. While Jason showed Luke his newest hockey jersey upstairs, Lilith was sitting on the deck waiting for dinner. Aunt Char followed by Grace, let Brownie and Mittens out of the house to get some fresh air. Brownie could stay outside for hours but Mittens didn't like being out for very long. For now, the third cat, Sammy chose to stay in the air conditioning.

It had been unbelievably hot and Allison's cat Sammy was shedding profusely. As a kitten, Sammy was ferocious and was personally selected by Uncle Jason at the local humane society shelter. The lady that worked at the shelter told the family that Sammy had come from a home where a little boy use to beat the shit out of him. As a kitten, Sammy was fearless and knocked all the kittens out of his way. Finally, Sammy came upon a huge cat and he hit the big cat. The gigantic cat lifted its paw and swatted Sammy off the table. Uncle Jason knew at that moment that the brave little orange tabby kitten was coming home with him.

The humidity was getting warmer outside on the back deck so Aunt Char had excused herself to go inside to get some ice water. As Char went inside the house, Mittens had also decided that she had enough of the summer heat and ran ahead of Aunt Char. At the same time, Sammy decided to go out on the deck to see where everyone had gone. Sammy was eighteen-years-old at the time and was becoming thin in his old years. The years had mellowed him and he now was extremely passive. Lilith watched the old cat come outside. She walked over to Sammy had seen how matted the cat's hair was in places and shedding at the same time. Lilith picked up Sammy and started pulling out large clumps of Sammy hair.

"Oh, my god Sammy your hair is so fucking matted. Well, I can fix that for you. I will just start by pulling out all your snarls. There we go. That must feel better," said Lilith to Grace and the cat as she grabbed clumps of hair out of the orange tabby's body over and over again.

Grace just sat and stared as Lilith grabbed one handful after another. Lilith started to talk faster and faster while she kept grabbing at Sammy's fur. The balls of fur floated away with the wind. Before Grace knew it, Sammy had little fur left and a stranger would never be able to identify him as an orange tabby or even a cat.

Inside the house, Aunt Char was checking on the Greek chicken in the oven. She finally came out of the door and looked at Lilith's direction. She saw that Lilith was grabbing Sammy's fur and she watched the fur float away as short spurts of wind blew it away.

"Lilith? What are you doing?" questioned Aunt Char freaked out by how much fur Lilith had pulled off the cat.

"Sammy needs a good brushing," said Lilith smiling a huge shit-eating grin **"but there wasn't a brush so I thought I would just do the same using my hand."**

"Well, that looks like enough. Let me take Sammy," responded Aunt Char as she grabbed down to Lilith's lap and snatched up the almost hairless cat.

Aunt Char cuddled Sammy in her arms as she took the cat back indoors. Through the kitchen window directly adjacent off from the deck, Grace could see her aunt showing Uncle Jason the damage that had been done to the old cat. There was little evidence of Sammy being an orange tabby. Uncle Jason turned towards the window and looked outside.

It looked to Grace that both her aunt and uncle were going to keep a closer watch on Grace's mother. Lilith was not acting normal and finally someone beside Luke and Grace knew how strange her mother really was. Grace could tell by the looks on her aunt and uncle's face that they were re-thinking their choice for Allison's guardians.

This was the last time that Allison's family invited Grace's family to their house for dinner. It was the beginning of the end and the writing was on the wall.

CHAPTER 18

June 30, 2009

It was late June and it was really hot in Grace's house. Most houses in the neighborhood had central air but Grace's house did not. When it really was warm, the family would pack up their things and go down to the antique store to sleep in the air conditioning. This summer the family seemed to be staying at the antique store more nights than any other summer that Grace could remember. While Luke and Grace were down at the store, Luke discovers that a book he wanted was forgotten at home.

A funny thing about the Grace's house was that even without air conditioning, there were areas of freezing spots in the old house. There were even drafts that would slam some doors shut. Sometimes there were loud crashes but after an examination of the house, there was no damage done. At other times, objects would fly off the shelves and break all over the floor. Lilith was at work so it wasn't of her doing. Grace often saw dark masses in the corners of her eyes but the black masses quickly disappeared. All these activities became worse as time went on.

When Luke and Grace went back home to get a few more things, the phone was ringing. Luke ran to the living room to grab the phone off the table.

"Oh hey Char, I'm fine. Grace and I were just grabbing some things to take down to the store because this house is so freaking hot. Lilith isn't going to be happy but what else is new? Hey Char, before I forget, there's something I want to tell you. In case something happens to me, seriously, look at Lilith. Remember that night at your house when Lilith beat the shit out of me? Well, now I'm worried that she might try to kill me. I mean it! Lilith is absolutely bonkers! She can be very DECEPTIVE so don't believe a thing she tells you if something happens to me. She is a very good actress," said Luke as if this information was the most important thing in the world he needed to tell someone. **"I can't stress it enough. Lilith is freaking crazy I tell you!"**

Grace could tell from the way her Dad talked, it was Aunt Char on the other end of the phone. Luke was walking around the dining room and noticed the two books that he had been reading on Michael Jackson. He quickly walked over to the dining room table and picked up one of the two books.

This week, it was reported on the television that Michael Jackson had passed away. Luke was obsessed with the circumstances surrounding his death. Reports of a Michael Jackson ghost were even recorded and played on the television over and over again. Right away Luke started to talk about the death of Michael Jackson.

"Oh hey, you have got to read these two books I have on Michael Jackson," said Luke **"Just stop by tomorrow and pick them up."**

"Speaking of Michael Jackson Luke, did you see that recording of the ghost that could be him? CNN has been playing the clip over and over again," asked Aunt Char intrigued by something she had never seen. **"Do you believe in ghosts?"**

"You bet! Yeah, I believe in ghosts," replied Luke and as he realized what he had just said made him look around the room nervously, **"I don't want them to hear me. Wait, give me a minute, I need to step out of the house so we can keep talking."**

"Okay, I can hold," replied Grace's aunt sounding a little uneasy from the response from her brother-in-law. Even Grace was a little spooked by the conversation she was overhearing by the two adults.

Grace followed her dad outside the front door and walked down the front steps behind him. Luke kept talking to Grace's aunt through his motions as he walked outside the house. Luke walked down the last step and sat on the brick pilaster at the bottom.

"I'm finally a safe distance from the house," said Luke as he placed his left hand under his right armpit and used his right hand to hold his phone. **"Hello. Char? Hello?"**

The phone line had been disconnected. That shouldn't have happened thought Luke. He was using his cell phone and there was no reason for it to break off. Luke tried calling Char back but only got a busy signal. Oh well, maybe Char had another call. Luke's brother Jason called Char several times a day. She was probably talking to him. Luke would try and call her later.

"Hey Grace, it's a beautiful day. Let's go for a walk," said Luke as he reached for Grace's hand and they started down the street.

CHAPTER 19

July 1, 2009

The next morning, Aunt Char was in the Lincoln Park neighborhood. Tennis lessons had been cancelled for Allison and Heidi due to the Fourth of July holiday. Aunt Char was just a few blocks away from Luke's house so she decided to stop in and to deliver some banana bread. Aunt Char hated waste, so anytime a bunch of bananas went bad, she felt obligated to make a couple of loaves of bread. So now, after so much work, she definitely didn't want the bread to spoil without someone enjoying it.

It was around 9:30 in the morning when Aunt Char and the girls knocked on Luke's door. Too early for Luke who very slowly opened the front door, Aunt Char felt a chill as she viewed her brother-in-law. Luke looked horrible. Char could see there was a muddy light grey and green aura around Luke. The murky color that surrounded Luke's body and his squinty eyes made Char question the stability of her brother-in-law. Something told Char's instincts that being there wasn't right but she could not put her finger on it. An uneasiness of fear came over Char that told her instincts to get out of there as soon as possible. Char wished that now she would've gone straight home instead of making this one stop.

"Oh, hey Luke, I'm sorry if I woke you. The girl's tennis practice was cancelled and I was in the neighborhood and wanted to give you some banana bread while it was still fresh," said Char quickly. **"The girls also wanted to say hi to Grace and bring her with us if she is around."**

Luke loved her banana bread and smiled widely as she handed him half of a loaf. He brought the loaf up to his nose, smelled and smiled with anticipation of breakfast.

"You make the best banana bread. Thank you so much. No, Grace is over at the Johnson's house so she isn't here right now. Oh yeah, I wanted to give you those two books on Michael Jackson. Let me go get them for you," replied Luke wanting to give Char something in exchange.

"That's okay, Luke. I can pick the books up another time. I just wanted to drop off the bread before it went bad. Enjoy," said Char as she was backing down the steps to his front door feeling like she would like to turn and run. **"The girls want to go back to bed if Grace couldn't come over but we just wanted to stop in real quick. I will talk to you later."**

"Thanks again for the banana bread. You just made my day," said Luke happily as he waved to his sister-in-law and niece.

S. T. Meier

As the black Beetle drove away, Char looked in her rear view mirror and wandered why she felt so uneasy around her brother-in-law. Never had she experienced such anxiety about being at his house or any place, ever.

"Say Allison, did you notice anything weird about Luke?" asked Char hoping that her daughter could answer what she could not.

"Well, he looked and smelled really bad," said Heidi being critical of his appearance.

"That's not what I meant Heidi but thanks for your opinion. I mean I know that I woke him up but I know there's something wrong. Well, it's probably just my imagination," said Char worriedly.

"I'm sure that it's nothing," said Allison trying to make her mom feel better.

"I hope so Allison," said Char. **"I hope so."**

- -

School had been out for over a month and Grace would frequently stay overnight at the Johnson's. However, Grace was also spending more time during the day with her dad. She thought it was great. They would take adventures in the neighborhood and there was a lot to explore. Across the street from their house, was a very active brick church. The Catholic Church always had extra services and the increased number of cars parked on their street throughout the day proved their theory of an extremely busy church.

Not having a proper garage for their car, Luke and Lilith always complained about all the churchgoers taking all the parking places on their side of the street. On that sunny July day, Luke and Grace felt compelled to visit the church across the street so that they could say prayers for their loved, family members. Before Grace would leave the house, she grabbed her small toy Panda and ran to catch up to her dad, grab his hand and to cross the busy street.

Inside the church, there were high cathedral ceilings and hard wood pews. On that sunny Wednesday afternoon, both of Grace's grandmothers were in the hospital so Luke and Grace lit some candles and prayed for them. From the side of Grace's eye, she saw a young boy about her age. As Grace looks at the boy, she was sure that she had seen him around the neighborhood. As Luke accidently knocked over a glass vase, Grace wondered away from her dad and walked toward the other child.

As Grace gets closer to the little boy she recognizes him as the boy who always plays in front of the church. The boy told Grace that his name was Jake and that he liked her Panda stuffed animal. Most of the time, Grace had her special black and white friend with her and would just cry if she ever lost her favorite toy.

Other then seeing the boy play near the church, Grace could tell that there was something familiar and special about this boy but she couldn't really identify what it was. There appeared to be something comforting about her new friend. He told Grace that he lived in the neighborhood and he would visit her every chance he had. Grace told the boy to stay where he was and she ran back to her father to show him her new friend, but when she pointed and turned around, the boy was gone. That's funny thought Grace. His parents must have called him away.

Luke looked at his phone and noticed it was getting late in the day. He felt he had better go home and find something for dinner that Lilith liked or he would have hell to pay from Lilith. Before going home, he wanted to stop at the liquor store for the evening. Lilith liked her vodka so Luke made sure to buy enough for the both of them. He could also use a couple of packages of smokes that he could also buy there. Luke noticed that he had been smoking more now than ever before in his life.

In the few months that had passed since the fight at Allison's house, the atmosphere at Grace's home seemed to go from bad to worse. Both of Grace's parents drank more and more. To make Luke look worse, Lilith started exaggerating the extent of Luke's drinking to whoever would listen. Lilith told people that Luke drank large bottles of vanilla extract when there wasn't alcohol in the house. Lilith wanted everyone to think that Luke had a drinking problem. It was obvious to Grace that Lilith was going out of her way to make a point of Luke's drinking being out of control. Grace knew it wasn't just her father with a problem. Needless to say, Lilith's drinking was just as bad, if not worse.

The physical fighting also seemed to be increasing. Every night when Lilith came home it was the same old thing. Some days Grace swore nothing would make her mother happy. Lilith was hyper, irritable and really unhappy with Luke.

That night as Lilith walked through the front door, after a long, difficult day, it was obvious that Grace's mother wasn't happy. Lilith's eyes were black and her lips were pursed together. She walked in carrying a large brown wrapped package.

"Jesus Christ, Luke! Are you kidding me? Another fucking blanket!! Why do you keep buying so much crap? Haven't I made it clear that we can't afford to buy anymore stuff?" screamed an angry Lilith as she threw the package at Luke. **"What do I have to do to get it through your thick skull that we can't afford to buy for awhile? Can't you go a couple of weeks without buying anything? I work and work and I'm the only person bringing any money into this household!"**

"You know that's NOT true Lilith. My parents give us a couple grand every month so I do bring some money home. So I'm allowed to buy whatever I want," replied Luke. **"So get off my back!"**

"You are home all day and you don't do a damn thing to keep the house clean," complained Lilith. **"Why do you have to be so fucking lazy? I must have the laziest husband on this planet!"**

"You're crazy! I do the laundry and I work on the house while you are at work. You'll notice that I plastered and painted the sunroom. You didn't help me a bit with that. It wouldn't hurt for you to lift a finger around the house. You can help out too you know," yelled Luke at the top of his voice.

Luke's statement sent Lilith over the edge. The nerve of Luke insinuating that she didn't do anything boiled Lilith's blood. Lilith ran at Luke with all her might and knocked Luke onto his back. As Lilith punched Luke over and over again, Luke tried to grab Lilith's hands to stop from being pummeled.

As soon as Grace's parents began physically fighting, the little girl chose to leave the area and go to the sanctuary of her room. Grace trudged up the stairs toward her room and closed the door to leave the fighting on the other side. If her parents' yelling were loud Grace would just turn up the volume on her television to cover up the profanities and other noises. Again tonight, her parents were both drinking and fighting. Grace just made sure that the television was louder than her parents so that her attention would be squarely on the program.

The voices were especially loud this evening. So Grace did as she always did. Grace went to her bedroom, put on the television, turned up the volume when the fighting became loud and became engrossed in her show. Any escape would be better than experiencing the scene downstairs.

After what seemed a very long while, Lilith peeked into Grace's room. Lilith was out of breathe, as if she just ran a marathon. She and the rest of the house seemed eerily calm. Then Grace's mother asked her something that she never asked.

"Hey Gracie, would you like to do something fun? I'm going to show you how to make a black eye with

make-up. Doesn't that sound like fun?" asked Lilith with a crazy look in her eye.

So Lilith and Grace went into the bathroom where she kept her make-up. They sat down in front of the mirror and Lilith showed Grace how they did a black eye in theatre. First you apply a dark color and then apply the darkest blue eye shadow you have. Being an actress, one needed to be able to apply their makeup and Lilith excelled in her technique.

"See, now mommy has a black eye" stated Lilith impressed with the realistic result that she was striving for.

"Let's show Daddy" Grace exclaimed with excitement.

"Yes, let's go show him" said Lilith in a weird, flat tone.

As Grace walked downstairs she noticed her dad at the bottom of the stairs lying on his back. He looked like he was sleeping. But why was her dad sleeping there? It didn't look very comfortable but occasionally her parents fell asleep in weird places. Grace guessed drinking does that to adults. Lilith said that he was probably sleeping and that she should kiss him goodnight. So Grace bent down and kissed him. Funny Grace thought but her dad felt really, really cold. Then, Grace's mother than walked Grace up the stairs and the child went to sleep.

- -

Meanwhile, Jason had worked in Minneapolis on a project and felt absolutely horrible all that day. At about 8:00 p.m., Char drove Jason over to the Mayhem

Hospital Emergency Room. A room was found for the ailing man. The doctor in the emergency room had placed gadgets all over Jason's chest to monitor his heart.

Across the room, Char sat in a chair watching Jason. At around 9:30 p.m., Char looked up and noticed something strange moving around Jason's abdomen area. It was a dark murky, grey-green colored matter that seemed to be dancing on Jason's stomach. That's strange thought Char but she thought it was just Jason's aura showing her that he had some problems in that part of his body. As a child, Char could see auras and even now as an adult if someone was really negative, she could see a dark aura around them.

An hour after Char viewed what she thought was Jason's problem area the phone rang in her pocket. Char could see that it was Allison calling. Allison was having Heidi and her other friend Nicole over to her house for a sleep over. Earlier in the evening Nicole was sharing the fact that she could see tragedies before they happened. For instance, a week before the collapse of the bridge in Minneapolis, Nicole had dreamt about it. Nicole also had the same birthday as Luke, September 6, which Char thought was a funny coincidence. Char answered her cell phone.

"Hi Sweetie, how's everything going with your friends?" asked Char cheerfully to her only daughter.

"We're fine Mom. I have to tell you something. Uncle Tommy stopped by and told me that Uncle Luke is gone," said Allison about to cry.

"What?" asked Char not sure if she heard correctly. **"I don't understand? What do you mean he's gone? Where did he go?"**

"Uncle Luke is dead," reiterated Allison.

"Okay, Dad and I will home soon. Bye Honey," said Char as she hung up the phone and burst into tears. Char had held back the tears until she hung up so that Allison would not hear her cry.

"What? What's wrong?" asked Jason knowing that something important had happened but not knowing what it was.

Jason had never seen Char so upset. Char seldom cried. Fighting back the tears enough so that she could speak, Char told Jason the very important message.

"Luke is dead," said Char as she continued to cry uncontrollably.

Jason quickly sat up on the examination table and started yanking off the heart monitor equipment. The equipment must have told the doctor something was wrong as the doctor rushed into the room and saw Char crying.

"I have to go right now, doc. My brother just died," said Jason as he started to put back on his clothes.

After getting dressed, Jason called Allison and told her to call Heidi and Nicole's parents. He explained to Allison to tell their parents what has happened and have them pick up their daughters. When Jason and Char arrived home they thanked the parents for understanding the situation.

CHAPTER 20

July 2, 2009

A ray of bright sunshine blasted through Grace's window, and instead of waking up rested, she felt totally exhausted. Last night, Grace really didn't sleep very well. It sounded like people were in and out of her house all night long. At one point, Grace thought she heard a police siren but it was probably just a dream - a really, really bad dream.

It was around mid-morning and normally Grace never slept in that late. As she became vertical, there were many muffled sounds coming from behind her closed bedroom door. As she opened the door, she noticed a lot of different voices coming from downstairs. From the corner of her eye, there was a young boy standing outside her room. Grace recognized Jake from the church across the street.

"Good morning Grace. Something terrible happened last night. I'm sorry to tell you but your father is dead," informed Jake to the little girl.

"What? No he's not. My Dad is fine," insisted Grace as she rushed to the top of the stair and looked down to the crowd below. **"He's just sleeping at the bottom of the stairs."**

Jake followed as Grace walked down the stairs. Grace's father wasn't there as she had seen him the night before. However, Grace saw Martha and Bert from next door along with some of the other local neighbors. Grace wondered what were so many people doing sitting in her living room? As Grace walked toward the kitchen, she could see that her mother was surrounded by a group of people and Lilith didn't notice that Grace had woke up. Grace's next-door neighbor Martha verified the news to the little girl that her father was indeed dead. Grace was more stunned than anything. For the rest of the day, Grace's head was in a heavy fog. It was like her father just was asleep and he never woke up. Now her dad was gone...

Grace's mother was still wearing the eye make-up that they had made last night. Grace couldn't understand why her mother would leave on colored eye make-up of what would look like a black eye. This must be a ploy to receive sympathy Jake concluded to Grace.

People came in and out of the house all day. Grace was glad when she saw her cousins Allison and Mathew. Later, Nana and Papa came to comfort her mother.

"How did it happen?" asked Aunt Char.

"I was out jogging and I came back and found Luke at the bottom of the stairs," said Lilith acting like there were a million other things she wanted to do than talk to her sister-in-law. **"I thought he had just passed out but when I touched him he was very cold."**

"Oh, this is just terrible," said Aunt Char with tears in her eyes. **"I am so sorry."**

Grace noticed that her mother was not very nice to Aunt Char. As Aunt Char tried to hug Lilith and console her, Grace's mother just turned away from her. For some reason, today Lilith really didn't like Aunt Char. However, Lilith would cry uncontrollably on Aunt Prudence's shoulder. Grace thought this was really strange even for her mother.

Grace also noticed that Aunt Char was looking at her mother strangely. It was if the aunt wasn't looking directly at Lilith but around her. Lilith was surrounded by a black aura. Aunt Char's eyes widen as if she feared what Lilith may have done to her brother-in-law. As Char looked at Lilith's black eye, she wondered if it was real. She made a note to herself to see if Lilith's black eye turned that awful yellow color in the next couple of days. If not, this could be a complete scam thought Char.

Grace's cousins decided to get away from the adults by going up to Grace's room. There was sadness that Grace didn't really understand with her Dad dying. What is death really? Grace was sad about her Dad being gone, but at the same time, at least her parents wouldn't be fighting anymore. On the plus side, for a while, Grace got to see her cousins more.

S. T. Meier

"Hey Grace, you should stay overnight at my house tonight," suggested Allison. **"Let's go ask your mom."**

Allison and Grace raced over to Lilith to ask the important question. Lilith was surrounded by some local neighbors discussing the horrible event when the kids interrupted her and asked permission.

"Mom! Mom! Can I stay at Allison's tonight?" Grace begged her mother.

"Well, did you ask Allison's mom?" asked Lilith. **"She will probably say yes but you had better ask anyway."**

After asking the adults, permission was granted for a sleepover. Grace felt so lucky to go and stay over night at her cousin Allison's. Grace packed up things for the sleepover. She packed some pajamas, a clean outfit for tomorrow and her toothbrush.

It was normally a five-minute drive to Allison's house, but Aunt Char had to stop at the local drugstore and pick up some medications for Uncle Jason. When the girls got to Allison's house, Grace ask Allison if she wants to play a joke on her mom. Grace says it will be really, really funny. Allison smiles and asks Grace what she was going to do.

"I'm going to go in the bathroom and use your mom's makeup to give me a black eye," laughed Grace as she thought about her make-up lesson from last night and the prank.

"Where did you learn to make a black eye?" asked Allison.

"My mother taught me last night," Grace said laughing as she imaged the reaction that she would get from Aunt Char.

"Go in the bathroom, come out crying and say you hit your head on the toilet," suggested Allison.

So Grace quietly walked into their upstairs bathroom and locked the door. Allison had told her younger cousin to go into her mom's gold and brown make-up bag and see what she could find. Grace used what she could find and she thought she did a very good job. As Grace looked into the mirror, she knew that this black eye would really freak out her aunt.

Aunt Char was in her bedroom making the bed. Grace had to get herself ready to look like she was crying. Grace's mother always told her to think of the saddest thing or pinch yourself really hard when you wanted others to think that you are crying. This is when Grace came running into her aunt's room holding her head.

"Aunt Char, Aunt Char! I hit my head on the toilet," exclaimed Grace finding it hard to hold back the laughter.

"Oh my goodness, Grace, are you okay?" screamed her aunt as she ran to Grace and pushed her hair aside to look at the false damage.

"I got you Aunt Char," Grace laughed as she lifted her hand and Allison walked into the bedroom. **"I didn't hurt myself. Ha, ha, I fooled you!"**

"You got me good Grace," said Aunt Char puzzled by the realistic work done by such a young child of five years. **"You have to tell me how did you learn how to make your black eye look so real?"**

"My mother taught me last night," said Grace who couldn't stop laughing as she looked at Aunt Char and how she had pulled off the lie to her. **"Allison, I got your mom good!"**

"Yes, Allison, Grace got me real good" remarked Aunt Char wondering how such a little girl learned how to apply eye make-up. **"Did Grace tell you that her mom taught her?"**

"Grace told me about everything" confessed Allison as she looked at her mom and realized that this was not normal.

The coincidence of Grace's Dad's death and her mother teaching Grace how to make a black eye made Allison and her mom react strangely. It would be some time before Grace would understand that this was no coincidence…

CHAPTER 21

July 3, 2009

The next day when Aunt Char drove Grace home, there were several large garbage bags sitting on the front steps of Grace's house. As the three trudged up the brick steps, their heads looked back wondering what was in the large plastic bags. Aunt Char, Allison and Grace knocked on the door and could hear movement along with talking going on inside. They both looked down on the floor and could see piles of Luke's clothing and his other possessions on the wood flooring.

Grandfather Bobble and Aunt Liza came to Grace's house and helped Lilith clean out Luke's things along with other household junk. Everyone seemed happy and were laughing and smiling. People grieve in different ways and it looked like the Bobbles cleaned when they were sad. Or were they sad? Maybe they were trying to make Lilith feel better. Somehow Grandfather Bobble seemed somewhat relieved from the situation.

As everyone cleaned, Lilith complained how she could never get Luke to throw out any thing. Both of Grace's parents were hoarders, but Lilith blamed Luke for all the boxes. Now that Luke was dead, whom would she blame? Lilith made it sound like the clutter would go away but it never did and years later, the home would still showed signs of hoarders.

Grace could tell by the look on her Aunt Char's face that this was strange behavior. Luke had just died less than two days ago. How could people get memories of someone that just died out of their life so fast? Grace remembered her Aunt Char once saying that if Uncle Jason died that it would be days before she could get out of bed. Grace's mother didn't seem that sad at all. She was smiling and laughing like nothing had happened.

However, Aunt Char was suspicious that Lilith healed so quickly. Magically, after two days, Lilith's black eye had disappeared and left no evidence of ever being. There wasn't any nasty yellowish brown color from healing. Normally, bruises take several days to heal. Is it possible that Lilith healed in less than two days?

As Char drove back home with Allison, there was only one question running through her mind. Did Lilith kill Luke? A chill ran down Char's spine. She shrugged it off as her overactive analytical mind being pessimistic. She couldn't have really done it could she?

Lilith was chipper than ever and later in the day, went on a spending spree with Grace after everyone left. Normally Lilith would go to thrift stores to buy clothes. Now she was going to department stores and paying full price for her things. Lilith also decided that they needed a new car so she asked Papa to go car shopping with her. Being that Grace's mother acted so grief-stricken around Luke's father, Papa paid for the majority of the new car.

Lilith didn't seem unhappy but quite the opposite. At the same time, everyone was helping the helpless widow and she wasn't turning down any offers. All the attention and new possessions made her mother the happiest Grace had ever seen her. Grace could see her scamming others but they couldn't see it. Yes, indeed, Lilith was a very good actress pointed out Jake to Grace.

When Lilith and Grace were alone, Grace's mom would laugh about how she had people wrapped around her finger. People were helping her clean and would volunteer to take care of Grace. Oh yes, the poor widow was the ultimate puppet-master...

CHAPTER 22

July 4, 2009

It was 4th of July weekend and Aunt Liza, Lilith's real biological sister, helped Lilith plan Grace's dad's funeral. More than anything, Liza felt that she should be with Lilith for emotional support. Neither Lilith nor Liza felt like taking Allison to the fireworks in Mayhem.

That night, Aunt Char and Uncle Jason took Allison and Grace to the 4th of July fireworks at the local community college. People could sit on the bleachers or on the field where football players usually performed. They brought lawn chairs and blankets to the fireworks and sat on the football field.

It seemed like Allison knew a lot of people. Several girls and a couple of boys came up either to talk to Allison or give her a hug. A few people even gave Grace hugs; this made Grace feel so grown-up when she hung out with her cousin Allison. Before the fireworks, they listened to bands play a variety of music. Later they watched the fireworks. The activities helped Grace forget about the past couple of days.

Grace felt like her father was with her and he was, along with Jake. Many people were now watching over Grace and they weren't all alive...

CHAPTER 23

July 10, 2009

Aunt Prudence helped Lilith write Luke's obituary. The notice appeared in the local newspaper a few days before the funeral. Luke's obituary was also printed on the backside of his funeral program:

Luke L. Francis, age 39 of Mayhem, passed away on Wednesday, July 1, 2009 at his residence.

Luke was a BIG surprise to Jim & Sandy Francis on September 6, 1969. Raised on discussing news and politics, gifted in words and expression, Luke was a natural debater, Governor at Boys State, played youth hockey and was active in Scouts. He was a college musician, an artist and a life-long scholar whose interests included: rare books, Native American blankets, forensics (both debating and death), and hockey.

Luke was married on October 11, 1996 to Lilith Bobble who was willing to take on the challenge.

His next greatest love was his daughter, Grace, who wrapped him around her little finger upon her arrival in October 2003 and who enjoyed having her daddy as a stay-at-home dad during her early years. After attending college, Luke was a long time co-owner of Olivia Lane Antiques. He was in demand as an expert and co-hosted "Vintage Connections" in 2007. Luke collected friends, their stories, and was always willing to talk, & talk, & talk.

Luke is survived by his wife, Lilith and their daughter, Grace of Mayhem; parents, James and Sandra of Mayhem; brothers Jason & Charlene of Mayhem and Thomas and Prudence of North Mayhem; niece, Allison of Mayhem and nephew Matthew of North Mayhem.

On the table in the front of the chapel, was a larger picture of Luke along with smaller pictures of him with Lilith and Grace. Guests congregated in front of the pictures to discuss happier times.

Grace's dad's funeral was very surreal for Grace. For one thing, her mother, Lilith had used a yellow McCoy Smiley Face Cookie Jar for Luke's ashes. Yes, her Dad collected many things and McCoy pottery was one of his favorite items. Grace realized that her Dad loved McCoy pottery but a cookie jar for his ashes, Mom? Really? Couldn't you give Dad a little more dignity than that? Behind the cookie jar urn, Lilith had placed brightly colored balloons. It looked more like a party than a funeral. Didn't you even respect him even a little mother? Jake pointed out that this appears to be the turning point when Lilith really began going crazy.

Before Luke's funeral, Lilith went from person to person crying obsessively. This was indeed one of Lilith's finest theatrical performances. One by one people gave her their condolences and Lilith was enjoying the sympathy. However, Lilith became very, very angry when she saw Uncle Jason.

At the entrance door of the mortuary, Grace could see her Uncle Jason, Aunt Char and her cousin Allison coming in. All three were dressed in very dark clothing with extreme sadness in their eyes. Lilith raced over to them immediately and she approached Uncle Jason. Lilith's fists started punching Uncle Jason's chest over and over again. It reminded Grace of how her mother used to hit her Dad and those were not good memories.

"You were supposed to be first!!!! You were supposed to be first to die! Not Luke!! Not Luke!!" screamed Lilith hysterically as she pounded her brother-in-law's chest. **"Not Luke! Not Luke! You! You! You should have been first!!"**

Everyone in the room turned toward the screaming widow. As Grace looked around the room, everyone was frozen in shock from the actions of the grieving widow. All eyes were glued on Grace's crazy mother pounding on her uncle's chest. All the relatives looked at Lilith as if she had really gone over the edge.

The crowd stared but they figured that it was just Lilith getting emotional as Grace overheard others say as she passed by them. Lilith was an extremely emotional and an actress after all. Her husband just died and Jason was the oldest son. Naturally, you would assume or think that the oldest child should go before the youngest brother. However, only a handful of attendees felt that wasn't what Lilith meant. However, Grace was probably the only one that knew for sure and realized her mother's meaning to her screaming words.

Grandfather Bobble saw Lilith making a scene, along with everyone else in the lobby, and intervened. He placed his hands on Lilith's shoulders and pulled Grace's mother off of Uncle Jason.

"Calm down, Lilith. Please calm down," responded Grandfather Bobble as he pulled Grace's mother off of Uncle Jason and gripped her hands so she would quit hitting him. Grandfather Bobble did not know what to make of the situation. Grace's mother was heavily sedated with medications to calm her down but it wasn't working for her.

Grandfather Bobble led Lilith into the chapel so that she would calm down. Soon the music started and people began to sit down for the funeral. The front row included Nana, Papa, Grandma and Grandpa Bobble, Lilith, Allison, Mathew and Grace. The second row included Uncle Jason, Aunt Char, Grace's great grandparents, Uncle Tommy and Aunt Prudence. Behind them sat all of Luke's cousins, relatives, friends and acquaintances.

To add to the surrealism of the event, The Rainbow Connection by the Muppets was one song that Lilith had requested be played:

"Why are there so many songs about rainbows and what's on the other side?

Rainbows are visions, but only illusions and rainbows have nothing to hide.

So we've been told and some choose to believe it..."

The last thing Grace remembered before falling asleep was her cousin Allison reading "The Next Place" by Warren Hanson to the mourners. Grace heard Allison's voice but the only words Grace actually heard "The next place that I go will be as peaceful and familiar as a sleepy summer Sunday and a sweet, untroubled mind"....

Grace was so exhausted from the week of going from cousin to cousin's house that half way through the ceremony she fell asleep. She dreamt about the days when her father was still alive and they would go on one of their "Urban Adventures" as he called it. The day that Luke died he went to the Catholic Church across the street from where they lived. Grace's father had lit the candles and said a prayer for both grandmothers that were in the hospital. Luke accidently broke a small vase and Luke had left a sorry note to the church to let them know what happened. How could this have happened? Now, Grace and Jake were attending her Dad's funeral...

Grace woke up at the end of the service. Some family members hung around after the service. After napping Grace wasn't feeling very social but very sleepy. She hung onto her mother's hand and walked but her eyelids were very heavy.

Uncle Jason and Aunt Char agreed to have people up to their house after the funeral. Their house was big and there was a huge turnout. Everyone was still red-eyed after the funeral ceremony. People shared good stories about knowing Luke.

Grace had a story of her own but she was going to keep it to herself. Ever since her Dad died she felt like he was watching over her to make sure that her mother did not hurt her. Grace's father wasn't around to take her mother's beatings. However, Grace felt Dad was watching over her just in case Lilith started taking her frustrations out on Grace, but Luke wouldn't allow that...

CHAPTER 24

October 2009

A few months later, Uncle Jason had done a memorial for a non-profit organization called A Bright Star. It was a unique, curved, short, orange brick wall located in the Erickson Park next to Victory Drive in Mayhem. Normally, only children under 24 years of age who left this world too soon could be displayed in this memorial. Uncle Jason and Aunt Char wanted to honor Luke for being taken too soon. Being that Uncle Jason had been the architect of the memorial and played a large role in this project, Luke was permitted to have a brick be displayed in his honor at this memorial.

Since the diagnosis of lymphoma, Nana did not feel well enough to go out much and she didn't attend the ceremony. On the other hand, Uncle Tommy and Aunt Prudence had no desire to attend so they did not come. Papa, Lilith, Uncle Jason, Aunt Char and Allison were at the ceremony with the little girl. Grace could tell that her mother didn't want to be at this ceremony. Lilith had been crabby all morning.

"Why do you keep reminding me that Luke is dead? I don't want to keep reliving this," stated Lilith with tears in her eyes and anger she felt towards those that forced her to be at the ceremony.

"We thought you and Grace would like to see that Luke will be forever remembered," remarked Aunt Char. **"At least, Jason and I feel that Luke deserves to be remembered forever."**

Lilith said nothing but glared at Char. Lilith didn't really care if her dead husband was remembered or not. The only reason Lilith was there was because Papa picked her up. Papa was doing everything for Lilith and she knew that she couldn't disappoint him.

A service was given to honor in remembrance all the children in the fall of that year. The ceremony began with speakers approaching the podium and talking about loosing a loved son or daughter from years ago. Then the audience was told to go around the memorial to find their love one. A path of bricks listed Grace's father's name and his living years.

The path led to a long table covered with a white paper protector tablecloth. White balloons and permanent markers filled the table. When everyone had completed the walk and they wrote a message on a balloon. Grace wrote a message to her Dad that said "I love you Daddy ~ Grace". People formed a line and everyone let go of their balloons and watched them float away to heaven to their loved one.

Now, don't think Grace was crazy, but she was sure that she saw her dad grabbing his balloon and he faded away...

CHAPTER 25

<u>Mid-October 2009</u>

A few days later, after school, Aunt Char and cousin Allison went over to Grace's school to pick the little cousin up. Aunt Char was driving her black 1998 Volkswagen Beetle that she truly loved. She always told Allison that she would never need or want another car as long as she had her Beetle. Allison told Grace that when she got her license, this car would be hers and she was going to paint it a Barbie pink paint color. Grace imaged if Aunt Char knew about Allison's plan that her mom wouldn't be very happy.

As Grace left the elementary school's front door, she could see her aunt's immaculately clean black car parked in the front lot. The older cousin got out of the front seat and pushed up the passenger seat so Grace could get into the back seat. Allison could've sat in the front seat of the car, but she chose to sit in the back with Grace. Allison had just finished school and had all her notebooks in her backpack that were already in the back seat.

The back of Aunt Char's front seats had a large pocket. Allison put books, markers, and other items that would entertain us in the pockets. Luke use to give Allison soft covered books that he thought she would enjoy reading. There were a couple of books that Grace recognized and when you opened the book to the title page there was the names Luke and Lilith Francis along with address so that the book could be retuned if lost. Nothing was more precious to Grace's dad than books and the stories they told.

After a ten-minute ride, they arrived to Allison's house. The large glass garage door opened and they drove into the double car garage. Allison with her notebook binders in her arms pushed the front seat forward so that she could get out and then Grace followed. It was proper etiquette to take their shoes off on their black slate tile, before going unto the living room carpet. A tall counter top that divided the kitchen and the great room had three stools where they could sit and work on their homework.

First, Allison helped Grace up to the counter. Grace had heard that one time Mathew didn't wait for someone to help him up and he toppled off causing a huge scene. No one wanted to relive that incident again thought Grace as she rolled her eyes.

Allison sat down and opened up her notebook binder. As Grace looked at Allison, she noticed that Allison's eyes widen in disbelief. Grace had never seen that look on her cousin's face ever before.

"What? What's wrong Allison?" Grace asked not understanding her cousin's reaction but knowing that Allison had a freaked out look on her face.

Allison didn't say a word but just pointed down at the notebook that lay open on the black, granite countertop. There on her notebook lay a small, torn yellow piece of paper with the word "Luke" written on it. It was obvious that Allison was confused on how that message got there. Even stranger, it was Grace's dead father's name and it was his handwriting. Grace knew his handwriting and that was it.

When they told Uncle Tommy about this incident, he told the family about his own strange occurrence. The phone rang and Uncle Tommy said it was Luke's voice on the other end. He said that Luke didn't talk very long but he knew it was his voice. Was Grace's dad trying to send us a message from the grave? Luke had only been dead a few months. Perhaps, he wanted to make sure that the family wouldn't forget him. Believe me, no one would forget him or this...

CHAPTER 26

October 25, 2009

It always seemed like Aunt Prudence was always trying to win Lilith's approval and favor. Being that this was Grace's first birthday after her father's passing, Aunt Prudence and Uncle Tommy threw Grace a birthday party at their house. This was one of the few times that they had the family over to their place for dinner. Grace's mother had dressed Grace in a brand new dress for the occasion. The white lace dress was so delicate that Lilith made sure that Grace didn't rub up against anything on the way over to Mathew's house. Lilith needed to make sure that Grace could wear the new dress to the Twin Cities the next day when she celebrated Grace's birthday with Lilith's relatives.

A tension was felt from the moment the family arrived to Mathew's house. It wasn't typical for Uncle Tommy and Aunt Prudence to throw a party. Also, it was a well-known fact that Aunt Prudence did not enjoy her husband's side of the family. Seeing Aunt Prudence being a hostess was very strange. It was like your face hurt from watching her put on her fake hostess smile.

There was a formal dining room off of their kitchen. Grace being the guest of honor sat at the head of the table. Mathew was at the corner on Grace's left side with Uncle Tommy seated next to him. Allison was on the other side of Grace facing the kitchen entrance. Everyone was really squished tightly together around this really small dining room table.

Aunt Prudence and Uncle Tommy had prepared both vegetable and meat lasagna. Grace could tell that her Aunt Prudence was very concerned about everything going just perfect. She was running in and out of the kitchen and dining room. As Aunt Prudence was picking up the empty breadbasket off the table in the dining room, she fell over next to Uncle Tommy's chair. Those who didn't see her fall sure heard the big thump as Aunt Prudence fell onto the floor. Aunt Prudence quickly picked herself off the floor.

"Fuck you! Fuck you Tommy!" yelled Aunt Prudence as she lifted herself off the floor and punched Tommy as she rose from the floor.

"What did I do?" asked Uncle Tommy feeling his shoulder where Prudence had hit him.

"You tripped me! That's what!!" screamed Aunt Prudence.

The entire table fell silent as they tried to surmise the reaction of the crazy hostess. As Grace looked around the table, she could see puzzled faces. Their faces seemed to say, "what the hell just happened?"

Grace looked at Papa who was at the other head of the table. His wide eyes caused his forehead to wrinkle. Then he closed his eyes, and shook his head like now he had seen everything. Papa bowed his head and went back to eating. If Papa could eat, everybody could go back and keep eating.

After a few awkward moments, things calmed down and Uncle Tommy brought in a black and white panda birthday cake he had made for Grace's sixth birthday. After blowing out candles, he cut off the head and put it on Grace's plate. She couldn't help herself. It was so pretty that Grace just had to touch the frosting. As Grace was bringing the frosting up to her mouth to taste, a large portion fell off of her hand and unto her dress.

"Oh fuck," said Grace loudly enough that everyone at the table heard and as she looked at the frosting that covered her new beautiful dress.

"Grace Ann Francis, that is enough," said Lilith angry that Grace's dress was ruined and that her daughter was using inappropriate language.

"What? Aunt Prudence said it first," replied Grace defending her profanity.

As Grace replied to her mother, another big pile of black frosting seemed to fall in slow motion unto her dress. Without thinking, Grace picked up the frosting from her dress that caused more frosting from her hand to fall unto the dress. While this happened, Grace could feel someone watching her as the black frosting covered her new dress. Terror filled her entire body. Grace's mother was a few feet away and was glaring at her.

Her mother's angry eyes seemed to be saying, "That dress won't be in good enough condition to celebrate your birthday with the other side of the family tomorrow. Wait until I get you home ..."

All this was said with Grace's mother's eyes and pursed mouth. It was easy to read her mother but no one else seemed to notice except Grace's cousin Allison. She knew exactly what "that look" meant.

At that moment, a picture from behind Lilith flew off the wall and hit Lilith on the back of the head. It was a picture of Luke, Jason and Tommy fishing on the North Shore. The picture hit the back of Lilith's head so hard that the glass cracked.

"Fuck! What the hell was that?" exclaimed Lilith as she felt the back of her head. **"That hurt."**

Aunt Char got up from the table and picked up the remains of the picture and had a puzzled look on her face. She had recognized the same picture at Nana and Papa's house of the family at a cabin they rented up north.

"It's a picture of the boys fishing up north Lilith," explained Aunt Char. **"That was weird. How could that picture fly off the wall like that? I've never seen anything like that before."**

"Maybe your house is haunted Uncle Tommy," joked Allison not really serious about her comment.

"Maybe it's time for Grace to open presents," suggested Aunt Char as she was spooked by Allison's statement and wanted to change the subject.

In the corner, adjacent to where Grace sat, stood her Dad who winked at Grace and slowly faded away. Both Grace and Allison turned to looked at each other like "did you just see what I saw"? The girls smiled and went back to listening to the adults.

After Grace unwrapped all her presents, the families gave their thank you and goodbyes to Uncle Tommy and Aunt Prudence. The other family members quickly went home. The combination of Prudence falling down and using profanity with Lilith getting hit with a picture was more than any of them wanted to deal with in an evening.

CHAPTER 27

<u>November 2009</u>

Since Uncle Tommy had joined the architectural firm a year ago, business had steadily decreased. Tommy continued hounding clients that were late to pay their bills and word had spread across the small town of his actions. Papa had seen the sign of a decline in clients as his opportunity to retire. Uncle Jason didn't want to continue working in Mayhem as he found the small projects uninspiring. It was then Papa decided to close the office and sell the building.

Meanwhile, Jason communicated with his connections in the Twin Cities area for employment. It wasn't long and Jason started commuting to Minneapolis for his new job. Jason enjoyed working with his father but understood that his father was in his golden years and should enjoy what little time he had left on this earth in retirement.

An announcement was made to Papa's office about closing the doors of the firm that had been open for over

100 years. Papa would have liked Jason to continue the firm but Jason wanted to do bigger and more important projects. Papa was not going to force his son to do something he didn't enjoy.

Being that Uncle Tommy was also out of a job, Papa gave him the one job that didn't require his socially awkward son to talk to the public. Uncle Tommy had to clean out the office and paint the exterior. For this Tommy was richly rewarded.

CHAPTER 28

December 24, 2009

A month later, it was the family's first Christmas without Luke. The family gathered at Uncle Jason and Aunt Char's house. Everyone was there except for Nana who was not feeling well, and of course Luke. Since the funeral in July, Luke's absence left a void felt by the entire family and the Christmas holiday didn't make it any easier to forget.

Nana hadn't been feeling well since her cancer diagnosis had advanced during a doctor visit the previous month. In fact, everyone could tell that Papa had done all the Christmas shopping this year. Usually Allison, Mathew and Grace were all pestered about what they wanted for Christmas and that they each needed a list of least 10 items. That didn't happen this year.

Aunt Char was the only person in the family to decorate for Christmas so naturally it was the best place to open presents. Actually, Allison's parents were the only people to decorate for any of the holidays. Nana and

Papa were getting too old for the energy it required for Nana's perfection. Mathew and Grace's parents never even put up a Christmas tree – ever. Maybe they thought it was too much work. If you asked them, they would say that Christmas was spent at the daughter-in-law's parent's house so there was no reason to put up a tree.

Everything at Allison's house was ultra modern. The tree was huge and layered in lights and ornaments. The treetop was a beautiful silver angel with gold, silver and red bulbs placed throughout the tree. Under the tree, lay presents for Allison, Mathew and Grace. First, however, the family needed to sit down at the dining room table and eat dinner.

Papa sat at the head of the table. On his right side, sat Uncle Tommy and Aunt Prudence with Lilith sitting in between Aunt Prudence and Grace. On the left side of Papa were Aunt Char,, Uncle Jason, Allison and Mathew. Actually, Mathew and Grace sat at the head of the table, facing Papa at the other end. Jake decided to come to the holiday gathering with Grace. None of the grown ups could see Jake but Grace's cousins could. It wasn't like other past holidays. Normally, Luke would've done most of the talking, but his year was really different.

Aunt Char had put a white silk tablecloth on the long, rectangular dining room table. In the center of the table was a golden sleigh with small red clear bulbs and silver garland. Sterling candlestick holders with white candles were lit on each side of the centerpiece. It was very festive.

After saying a dinner prayer, there appeared to be an awkward silence. Uncle Jason was exhausted from the workweek and commuting four hours each day and was practically falling asleep at the table. Jason's head kept bobbing forward and he would wake up and his head would go straight up only to repeat this motion. Aunt Prudence and Uncle Tommy giggled at the tired host. Lilith was not as giddy as usual but smiled politely. She was probably hung over from her drink-fest the night before.

The same thing was on everyone's mind but no one wanted to say it. A piece of tradition was gone, but two people actually seemed happy about it. Aunt Char facing Uncle Tommy and Aunt Prudence picked up on it right away.

"Merry Christmas everyone!" exclaimed Aunt Char as she raised her wine glass to the group as to say cheers. **"Well, you two look pretty happy today. Want to share with the rest of the group some good news?"**

Aunt Char asked the question while looking at Tommy and Prudence. Except for the kids, by far, the couple looked the most excited about life. Aunt Char tried to make the holiday cheerful and was hoping for some good news. Needless to say, she would be sadly disappointed.

"Well, now that Luke is dead, everything will be mine," said Uncle Tommy with a giggle as if he had won the lottery.

"What do you mean by that?" asked Aunt Char puzzled by her brother-in-law's callous remark.

"Look at Jason over there, he can't even stay awake long enough to eat. Jason with all his health issues will probably be the next to die. Then, Tommy will be the only one in the will," replied Aunt Prudence smiling. **"When the rents die, everything will be Tommy's."**

"You don't know who will die next. After all, I don't think anyone here suspected that Luke would've been the first one to go," defended Aunt Char as she looked at her tired husband who sat drooping next to her.

Everyone nodded in agreement but Papa was appalled at the discussion of his wealth distribution after his death. At this point, Papa was sorry that he told Tommy that he would give all the money from the sale of the architectural office to him. Thank goodness Allison changed the subject and started talking about Christmas vacation activities.

"Hey Grace, what do you have planned for Christmas?" asked Allison trying to drown out the adult conversation.

"We are going to Bloomington to have Christmas with Grandpa and Grandma Bobble," Grace said including Jake in the holiday gathering. Jake didn't like most family gatherings except for the holidays. Jake missed holidays with his family and lived vicariously through Grace's. He would come with Grace for special holidays and her birthday.

"We are going to St. Paul with my grandparents too," chimed Mathew.

"We are spending Christmas with Nana and Papa. We always have steak with mushrooms on the brownstone plates," smiled Allison as she thought about eating her favorite meal.

After eating the holiday meal, the kids took turns opening up gifts. Then Uncle Jason and Aunt Char brought out presents for each of the adults. Aunt Char picked up the gift-wrappings, and everyone consolidated their gifts into baskets or boxes that they had brought.

This holiday gathering was the shortest anyone could remember. After wrapping up a plate for Nana and giving hugs everyone quickly left to their homes. It was definitely the quietest and shortest Christmas yet being that Luke usually kept everyone entertained. Luke wasn't around this year and he'd never be back again. Well, not in a human-like existence that most adults could see anyway.

CHAPTER 29

February 2010

"Grace, I love being a widow. I can be as crazy as I want and nobody will call me on it. Yesterday, I told Aunt Prudence that I really didn't like her. Being that I'm the "Crazy Widow" she just lets me continue to insult her. Prudence thinks she is so smart but boy, she is so stupid!" laughed Lilith knowing that she could say whatever she pleased and get away with it.

After Luke's death, Lilith continued working at the lighting store. Retail was no stranger to working on the weekends and Lilith needed someone to watch Grace on Saturday mornings. She played the poor, sad widow card often and she knew whom she could play. So every Saturday morning Grace was dropped off at Nana & Papa's house. Nana was tired from the cancer and liked to sleep-in but Papa and Grace would make breakfast together.

Week after week, Grace continued having breakfasts with Papa on Saturday. Some Saturdays he and Grace would go to the store and get groceries. Other times, Papa would take her down to the antique store to see what could be sold to help Lilith make some extra income to help pay for the store's mortgage. It seemed that Lilith never had enough money.

Why is it that people that are miserable want to bring you into their unhappy world? Yes, we all want some temporary relief but a lot of us just take care of our problems alone and would prefer not to include others. Perhaps we try to take on more than we should but don't normal, well-adjusted people avoid dragging others into their sad world. If that statement is true, is it only the weak, unstable people that need to rely on others? In Lilith's case, this statement is entirely true.

After being married to Luke for thirteen years, Lilith learned that Papa could always be counted on. Anytime Lilith needed a favor she went to her partners of the antique store. Ever since Luke had passed away, Papa kept giving Lilith the original $2,000 a month for the antique store expenses. Papa was in denial and it was as if Luke had never died.

Originally, the antique store property had been paid off with the selling of the first original comic book that the owners of the store sold off before Allison was born. The selling of this particular comic book was big news in Mayhem. Both Luke and Uncle Tommy had their picture in the local paper. The almost mint comic was eventually sold to the owner of a sports team in New York. The sale of the comic book paid for the entire cost of the antique store. However, a loan was taken out by Luke and Lilith to help them with their money situation. No matter what, there was never enough money in their household. The cost of alcohol and drugs takes a big chunk out of anyone's budget.

When Lilith needed money, she never hesitated to go to Papa. He was a sweet, generous man that could never turn anyone away, especially family. Papa had never had a daughter and he was extra soft with women. Being a master manipulator, Lilith knew she could always get what she wanted from him.

"Jim, I was wondering if you could give me a little more help with the store's mortgage. The economy is still really bad and I don't seem to be selling enough to cover expenses. I'm going to need more than the $2,000 you usually give me," stated Lilith trying to be as charming yet pathetic as she could.

Papa stared off into space for a moment before replying. He was getting old and it seemed that he was becoming more and more worn out and tired. Yet, it seemed that Papa was still sort of a control freak and didn't think others could do anything without him. However, Papa was losing steam and he couldn't do it all himself.

"Well, Lilith I think we need to get both Tommy and his friend Daryl to help sell things in the store. We can have both those guys sell and mail items. They can make 50% and we can make 50% for the store. It will be a win/win situation for everyone," suggested Papa.

Grace could tell that her mother wasn't very happy with that idea. Lilith wanted everyone to work for her for free. Papa's idea meant that future money making items would be shared with others. Papa couldn't afford to keep paying for all the bills that Lilith needed to be paid.

Papa was now retired and already had been the victim of a Ponzi scheme from his first accountant in town. Had Papa's accountant not taken his entire 401-K, Papa would've been a multi-millionaire. However, at this point of time, Papa was far from being rich but always considered others before himself.

"Sure, we could do that," reluctantly agreed Lilith not really wanting to share the antique fortune with others.

Month after month, Lilith continued to keep Papa informed of her financial problems. Being the kind-hearted soul that Papa truly was, he felt bad for the widow of his dead son. Papa decided to get Uncle Tommy involved to help Lilith pay the store's bills. Uncle Tommy and his friend Daryl took over where Luke had left off on the Internet selling antiques. In return, Papa gave all the proceeds from the architectural office building and 50% of the sale of an item to Tommy. All this was done without Nana's knowledge and continued until Papa got really, really sick.

CHAPTER 30

April 29. 2010

It was late April in 2010 and the day before Uncle Jason's birthday. This meant that it was lawn day at Nana and Papa's house. The end of April was marked at the Francis residence as the time to rake the wet leaves left behind and plant new seedlings. Lilith never helped Nana and Papa with any of their work and used the lighting store as a reason for not helping out this time. Uncle Tommy and Aunt Prudence had the excuse of being out of town visiting Prudence's family two hours away.

So those left to help out Nana and Papa was Uncle Jason, Aunt Char, Allison and Grace. The task was to rake up the leaves placed on plants last fall. The leaves served as warmth and protection to the plants over the winter. Each person had a rake in their hands as they accumulated the leaves from the rather large yard. Once the wheel barrel was full, they then threw the piles of leaves over the ravine in the backyard next to the cemetery.

Normally, Papa would've had a rake and been working with all of them. The weather wasn't that cold but Papa wore several layers of clothes. Nana had told us that Papa wasn't feeling that well. Papa sat on a green plastic chair and supervised as they did the work. Occasionally Papa tried to get up and do a little raking. Suddenly Papa stopped and grabbed his chest.

"I'm not feeling so well. I think I need to go to the hospital," decided Papa not looking forward to his destination.

"Take it easy Dad. I'll drive you there and Char can bring everybody else later," said Uncle Jason to Papa as calm as he possibly be at that moment.

Meanwhile, Nana used a cell phone to call Uncle Tommy and Lilith to let them know what had happened to Papa. It wasn't long before Papa was given a bed in the Intensive Care Unit. Everyone congregated in the waiting room down the hall from the ICU. Eventually, a nurse came down to let the family know that they could go to Papa's room. So Nana, Uncle Jason, Aunt Char Allison and Grace followed the nurse through some swing doors.

There was sliding glass doors with small desk areas for nurses to sit and monitor each patient outside every room. Papa's room was located at the very end of the corridor on the right hand side. Papa was there lying in his bed as if he was sleeping. He had a breathing tube projecting out of his lips and he wasn't speaking. A group of doctors were meeting outside the room and after some time, came in to discuss his prognosis.

As the doctors entered the sliding glass door, Lilith, Uncle Tommy, Aunt Prudence and Mathew followed behind. Aunt Prudence pushed her way through the group of people to get near where Nana and the head doctor were talking. Aunt Prudence placed her body strategically in front of Nana's and began talking to the doctor as if none of the other family members were there. Aunt Prudence hated the Francis family so much that she kept her crappy maiden name that no one could ever spell right. Now, she was showing the Francis family that she knew better than any of them the medical science of Papa's condition.

"My name is Prudence Choleiwsky and I am the daughter in-law to James Francis. I work at the hospital here and I can tell you anything you need to know about this man," informed Aunt Prudence thinking that Nana wasn't as capable as she to communicate to the medical field.

Nana's mouth dropped open. At home, Nana was known as "Doctor Mom" due to her medical background when she was a lab tech in her earlier years. Why was Aunt Prudence acting this way? Was she showing off to her colleagues or did she think she was more medically knowledgeable than the rest of the family because she worked at the hospital as a secretary?

"Presently, this man is in a coma and frankly, we do not know if he has the strength to come out of it. He has 14 stents in his heart and he is having problems breathing. If he does pull through he may need a breathing apparatus to keep him breathing. We will continue monitoring his progress. In the

meantime, you may want to consider making funeral arrangements. On the other hand, he may have the strength to come through this but his chances are not very good," stated the head doctor.

The doctor and his staff left the room and Aunt Prudence with Uncle Tommy and Mathew followed out behind them. They left the area without saying goodbye to any of the family. Those left behind were asking if Tommy and his family were coming back? No one knew for sure why Matthew and his parents had just left without a word.

Nana grabbed Papa's hand and bent down to give him a hug. Being that Papa was in a coma they weren't sure if he was aware of his surroundings. Just in case, they all said bye to Papa and went back down to the waiting room area they had previously had been in. As the family sat watching the news, a minister came in to see if there was anything the family needed. They shook their heads and he promptly left. It was quiet in the waiting room area for the longest time.

"This really isn't looking good," said Aunt Char summarizing things as she saw it. **"Does Papa want to be buried or cremated?"**

"Jim always told me that he wanted to be cremated and to have a simple funeral," replied Nana. **"He always said it shouldn't be too extravagant."**

All of a sudden, a nurse hurried into the waiting room. She was happy to see that the family hadn't headed home yet.

"Jim has woke up from his coma and would like everyone to come see him," said the nurse amazed at his recovery.

Nana, Aunt Char, Uncle Jason and Allison quickly followed the nurse back down the hallway to Papa's area. Papa was sitting up with a pained look on his face. The breathing tube that was once placed in his mouth was no longer there.

"If they ever need to place another breathing tube down my throat, don't let them do it. Just let me die! That was the most painful thing I've ever experienced," stated Papa in a difficult to breath manner.

"I'm so glad that you are alright. We didn't think that you were going to make it," said Nana as she hugged him.

"I need to tell you about all the investments in case something happens to me again. In the den at home is a silver binder that is labeled investments that show everything that we have," reported Papa as if this was the most important information he needed to give to Nana and the family.

Eventually, Papa was removed from the ICU and placed in a single room. Neither Aunt Prudence nor Uncle Tommy visited Papa's room after that first day in the ICU. Apparently, Tommy still had a large amount of money left from the sale of the office building. Therefore, there was no reason for Tommy had to visit his father. Currently, he was financially well off so his father's status made no difference to him.

It would've been understandable if Aunt Prudence didn't work at the hospital but a visit from her would've meant going a few floors up to visit Papa in his hospital room. She heard that the doctors thought that Papa had MRSA and there may not be an antibiotic to cure it.

Aunt Prudence was a hypochondriac. During the Minnesota flu season, she was extra paranoid. She would tell people that were getting over an illness not to come near her. Even when there were flu shot shortages and only the extremely elderly or very young were suppose to be the first to receive their shots, Aunt Prudence made sure she had a shot with the group. In times of shortages, she didn't care if others couldn't get a shot as long as she was able to get hers. Therefore, it didn't surprise anyone when she didn't visit Papa at the hospital. That and also, Aunt Prudence was not fond of Uncle Tommy's family, not even of the man that always thought of others before himself.

When the nurses or other staff came into Papa's room, they had to suit up. When they left the room, they all would take off the suit. The staff told the family that the suit was so they would not give the MRSA infection to other patients. Aunt Prudence, Uncle Tommy and Mathew were afraid they might get sick from Papa and never visited him in the hospital again.

CHAPTER 31

<u>May 11, 2015</u>

Papa was in the hospital for three weeks. One cold rainy night in May, Lilith and Grace were going up the elevator at the hospital to visit Papa. At the other end of the corridor, Grace saw Nana and Aunt Char leaving Papa's room. Aunt Char was wearing a bright yellow rain jacket with a fleece underneath and old blue jeans.

As Lilith laughed she said to Grace **"Good God Grace, your Aunt Char looks like a hobo. You'd think that with all their money she would dress up a little. She looks just hideous."**

Lilith and Grace met Nana and Aunt Char about half way down the corridor. As they stop to chat, Grace just couldn't help herself. Grace just had to tell Nana and Aunt Char what her mother just said.

"Aunt Char, you look like a hobo," Grace said with a grin mimicking what her mother had just said to her as she ran up to greet them.

"I look like a hobo Grace?" Aunt Char asked perplexed that someone her age would know that word.

"Yes" Grace said as she turned to her mother laughing. Lilith gave Grace a look like she had better not say anything more.

"Grace!" yelled her mother with the look of don't say another word on her face.

"Well, we will let you get on with your shift," joked Aunt Char not wanting to further discuss Grace's hobo statement. **"See you tomorrow at the same time."**

As Nana and Aunt Char continued onto the elevators, Lilith and Grace proceeded down to Papa's room. Before they were to Papa's doorway, Lilith wanted to have a quick word with her daughter, grabbed Grace and abruptly stopped her.

"Grace, never and I mean NEVER, repeat what I say again. You have got to learn that everything I say is our secret. Never tell people anything about us. Do you understand me?" her mother said as she grabbed and shook Grace's shoulder and arm.

Over her mother's right shoulder, Grace could see her Dad's image. He smiled at Grace as if to insure that he was always watching out for her. Luke put his index finger to his lips as if to say, "don't let your mother know that you I'm here".

"I understand," as Grace glared back at the monster that was hurting her arm.

As Grace and Lilith continued to walk down the hospital corridor toward Papa's room, Luke ran up behind Lilith and with all the force he could muster he pushed her with a mighty shove. Lilith suddenly tripped and fell to the floor. Quickly, Lilith pulled her face off the floor. She lifted herself from the carpeted corridor with her muscular arms supporting her average sized body. Grace's mother looked behind her and all around the corridor. It was as if someone had shoved her from behind.

There was no one there that Lilith could see but she was sure that someone had pushed her. On the other hand, Grace, a small child could see more and knew what had happened. It was the ghost of Grace's dad. Luke smiled at Grace and winked as he faded away.

CHAPTER 32

<u>May 16, 2010</u>

Ironically, Papa came home from the hospital on Aunt Char's birthday. Papa was in the hospital on Uncle Jason's birthday and now he was out on his wife's birthday. Normally there was a birthday cake for both of them to share on a day in between the two birthdays at Nana and Papa's house but no one felt like celebrating this year. The only thing that Char wanted to do was to stay home in her pajamas all day and not get out of the house or bed. She was tired of having to go out of the house to run errands all the time.

There were several discussions where Papa should go to get rehabilitation. Papa was adamant on going home and he didn't want anyone to change his decision. There was a long breathing tube and a machine that Papa always had to have with him as he traveled from room to room on the first floor of his house.

There were many restrictions put on Papa that everyone could tell did not make him happy. Perhaps the biggest restriction that Papa hated was that he would never drive again. Driving was Papa's greatest freedom. He loved Nana but sometimes a person has just got to be alone. At the same time, Papa also couldn't walk downstairs and watch television on the large screen with Nana. Luckily, there was a small screen television in the living room. He was restricted to the main level of the house and this did not sit well with him either. Most of all, Nana had to help him with almost everything and neither of them liked that.

Every day, Aunt Char went over to Nana and Papa's house to help them with errands and to get food. It helped that Aunt Char and Uncle Jason only lived a block away from their house. Papa's appetite was small and he usually just wanted soup from the local Chinese restaurant. He became more and more tired and spent most of the day sleeping. A last memory of him is sleeping with in his bed with his eyes closed late in the afternoon. He looked very tired and didn't talk. The whole family knew that Papa was never one to take naps.

Four days later, after coming home from the hospital, on Thursday, May 20, 2012, Papa had a 10:45 a.m. appointment with his doctor. Nana would have liked Uncle Jason to go with her and Papa to the doctor, but he was commuting to the Twin Cities for his job so Nana asked Uncle Tommy to come over and go to the appointment with them.

Nana was having a hard time getting Papa ready for his doctor visit. Papa kept asking Nana when was Tommy getting there. Papa was still in his bathrobe and in front of the fireplace sitting in the Saarinen Womb chair in the living room when Tommy got there at around 10:00 a.m. As soon as Papa realized that Tommy was there with Nana, Papa was gone.

Needless to say, Papa didn't make it to his doctor appointment. In less than a year, another Francis member had died. The Francis family numbers were quickly dwindling and the group would never, ever be the same...

CHAPTER 33

<u>**May 21, 2010**</u>

After Papa's death, Luke was not alive but was closely watching his family. Luke knew that Lilith would be especially susceptible to any stress. He also knew that his ex-wife Lilith was milking the money situation due to being a widow for all she could. Luke knew his family members well and knew that Nana would never give Lilith everything that Papa had. Meanwhile, over the months, Luke was growing stronger in his afterlife talents, Luke promised Lilith he would show her the strength he didn't when he was alive.

On the evening of Papa's death, Lilith decided to go to bed early and cry herself to sleep. She curled herself up in a fetal position and was rather catatonic. Lilith didn't move except to shiver from the chills.

Over the months since his death, Luke had been closely watching over Grace to protect her. At the same time, he was doing little things that would bother his former wife Lilith. Those actions would be nothing compared to what was coming up in his current plan. Luke knew fully well that Lilith had hit rock bottom due to the death of her cash cow father-in-law and Luke was going to have some fun scaring the hell out of her. Luke knew he had to start slow and build up to some spectacular fright that would rattle her nerves.

To get Lilith further down the road to being freaked out of her mind, the ghostly translucent Luke decided that he would grab the foot of the bed and start to shake it up and down. At one point, the pull was so strong that it whipped Lilith out of bed. Lilith landed on her face down, slowly picked her self off the bedroom floor and cried hysterically.

A large knock came from the bedroom's closet door. As Lilith turned to look at the source of the knock, a large black mist with red glowing eyes stared back at her. Never in Lilith's life had she seen anything so frightening. She bared her head into her long nightgown.

For several minutes, Lilith refused to look up. Then a crash was heard in the corner where the Art Deco statue that Luke had given her at their last Christmas together had fallen and broken in millions of pieces. As Lilith responded and looked at the direction of the crash, a devil's head floated towards her and said, "You must die!"

Lilith wasn't going to sleep in that bedroom! She ran out of the room, down the stairs, and decided to watch television to get her mind off of her problems. This can't be happening she thought. For the first time in her life, Lilith was questioning her own sanity.

CHAPTER 34

May 26, 2010

The Francis family thought Lilith seemed fine when Luke died. However, with the passing of Papa, they noticed that Lilith seemed very depressed and really losing her mind. Her voice was slowing down and at times almost dragging. The man she could always count on and did count on had gone to greener pastures. No longer was there a superman that Lilith could depend on to solve all of her problems. Lilith cried more now than she ever did before. It was very difficult for her to get dress and to go to Papa's funeral.

The day of Papa's funeral was like a distant dream. Allison with her parents Uncle Jason and Aunt Char brought Nana to the mortuary before anyone else arrived. Shortly afterwards, Lilith and Grace walked in. They stood in a circle and talked about memories of Papa. Everyone was saying all the great things Papa did and how they missed him. It was getting too serious for Grace so she decided to make a joke.

"My Mom is going crazy," said Grace as she twirled her finger around her head insinuating that mother was getting crazier by the minute.

Grace wasn't lying. She was just telling it like it was and everyone knew it. Lilith just stopped, in position and threw an ice, cold glare in Grace's direction. Had Grace gone too far? Lilith just stood there and glared at the small girl. Grace felt like everyone in the room was looking at her like she had three-dozen heads. Grace looked around the circle as if to say what did I do? Didn't I just point out the obvious? Aunt Char looked at Grace like she wished she had the guts to talk to the crazy lady like Grace. Please someone say something so this uncomfortable moment can be over thought Grace.

"Oh, you little goofball," laughed Aunt Char as she brushed the top of Grace's head and tried to ease the uncomfortable atmosphere. **"You are so silly Grace."**

Meanwhile, Grace's head throbbed with a fire-burning drill going through her forehead as her mother continued to cast that "wait until I get you home look" with her black eyes. Oh crap, I really crossed the line this time by stating the obvious thought Grace. Finally, the conversation moved to more pleasant subjects. To be honest, anything was more pleasant than the stare of death from Grace's mother.

As Char spoke these words to Grace, both Allison and Jason noticed something odd. In the background, behind Lilith and Grace was a man. This man looked a lot like Luke but that was impossible. Luke was dead. As Jason walked away from the group to catch up to the familiar man, Jason's Uncle John stopped him to chat. Luke had gotten away…

Papa wanted to be cremated just like Luke. In the front of the chapel was a large picture of Papa smiling. It was probably the best picture that Papa ever took. Nana had selected a nice brown crock with a round lid in order to keep him. In a simple, glass triangular vase were some white lily of the valley flowers and dark rocks. The beautiful display showed that Nana truly loved Papa and respected him.

People took turns standing up and sharing stories about Papa. Aunt Char was one of the people that shared a story. Instead of a sad story, the aunt decided to try to lighten the somber atmosphere.

"Hello everyone, my name is Char Francis. I met Jim 26 years ago when Jason and I started dating. Jim has always looked the same to me as he is pictured here (she turns and points to the photo). After months of dating, the idea of a wedding started to come up. Originally, Jason and I were going to live together in Boston and were not going to get married. One day in June before we were to leave for Boston, Jim and Sandy sat both Jason and I down to discuss the serious issue. Jim said that they would prefer that we get married instead of living together. Well, both Jason and I thought that we would probably get married some day and it would probably be easier to have a wedding here than out in Boston. So in two, very short months we put together the wedding and we set the wedding date for August 9, 1986. Because the wedding was put together so quickly, a few guests

asked me if I had to get married. Well, ten years later I had Allison. This was probably the longest pregnancy in history."

The room burst into laughter. Many of these people were at their wedding and probably secretly wondered themselves the reason behind a wedding being put together so quickly.

"If not for Jim, I would not be married to his wonderful son or have this beautiful child Allison. This man would not like us to mourn his death but rather we should celebrate his life. This man earned our respect due to his integrity in family, business and life in general."

CHAPTER 35

<u>Memorial Day 2010</u>

Things were very different at Grace's house after both her Dad and Papa passed away. Her mother moved and spoke slowly. Grace knew that this was not a good sign. After Papa died, Lilith fell to pieces and was extremely unhappy. There were some nights Lilith would wake up screaming from nightmares. After a while, it seemed that Grace's mother stopped sleeping to avoid dreaming.

It was several days since Papa's funeral and Memorial Day dinner was always a tradition at the Francis house. Probably like everyone else in town they grilled hamburgers and had a picnic-like dinner. After Papa died, Aunt Char did all the grilling and cooking for the family gatherings.

Since Uncle Tommy, Mathew and Aunt Prudence had moved three hours away, they never came to Mayhem to celebrate holidays with the family. Lilith heard from friends that Tommy and his family were in Mayhem often but they didn't stop in to see any of the other

Francis family members. Uncle Tommy, Aunt Prudence, and Mathew were at Papa's funeral but none of the family had seen them since Luke's funeral that was nine months earlier. Needless to say, the three of them weren't coming to Memorial Day dinner and declined the invitation from Nana.

This left Lilith, Grace, Nana, Jason, Allison and Char to celebrate Memorial Day together. When Char brought the burgers in from the grill, peopled grabbed plates and started scooping potato salad, coleslaw, fruit salad and placing condiments on their burgers. When everyone had filled their plates, they all walked downstairs and sat in the family room, and were finally able to converse. Grace sat on the floor next to the sofa where Allison and Lilith sat. Uncle Jason sat on the other side of the sofa. Nana sat in her usual spot on the love seat with Aunt Char next to her.

The conversation started out how hungry everybody was and what they all had been doing for the day. Everyone seemed to be having a nice time. However, the status of the antique store and Papa's funeral came up and then things started to become strange.

"The Internet isn't doing very well in selling antiques. I will be needing money for the store loan," stated Lilith thinking that the money train would continue as it had when Papa was a live.

"Well, Lilith, I can help for now but I think that maybe we will have to sell the store and all the merchandise," replied Nana suggesting ways to financially recover their losses.

"I really don't want to sell the store. That's Grace's inheritance. I will see what I can do to get other dealers to come in and buy to cover the payments," explained Lilith not happy about selling any of the merchandise.

"That's fine," stated Nana hoping that Lilith could sell enough to make payments.

"Sandy, I just have to tell you that I really loved Jim. I loved Jim MORE than I loved Luke. Jim was always there for me. I even love Jim more than I love my own father," stated Lilith as a matter of fact.

Grace looked around the room and the best way she could describe everyone's response was that of total shock. Everybody was looking at Lilith as if she had snakes coming out of her head. Wasn't a widow supposed to love her dead husband more than her father-in-law? Everyone in the room looked at the crazy sister-in-law like she was absolutely insane.

"That's interesting that you should say that Lilith. I was wondering if anyone else had seen Luke at Papa's funeral?" asked Aunt Char trying to change the subject and looking around the room to see if anyone was shaking their head yes. **"Both Jason and Allison told me that they had seen Luke at the funeral. To see if they saw the same thing, I asked them separately what Luke was wearing. Jason told me that Luke was wearing a green plaid shirt. Allison told me that Luke was wearing a green-checkered shirt. I couldn't believe my ears. Isn't that amazing?"**

Allison's hazel eyes were wide and she was nodding yes to everyone around the room while not believing her own eyes. Aunt Char wasn't joking. Both her cousin and uncle had seen Grace's father. Grace wasn't the only one. She wasn't crazy like her mother had told her she was.

"I saw Daddy too! I didn't tell anyone because my mother doesn't believe me," said Grace happily that she wasn't the crazy one. **"See Mom! I told you I wasn't crazy!"**

At this news, Lilith looked worried and started to panic. Grace's mother started to comb her hair quickly with her fingers and twirl her hair around her finger then placed the end of her hair into her mouth. Lilith stared in a trance as if she was a million miles away. Her mother's reaction was very strange. Why was her mother scared about seeing the spirit of Grace's father? Grace saw Dad frequently and she liked it. Grace felt like he was protecting her from harm. Why was her mother freaking out?

Shortly after finishing her dinner, Lilith excused herself and took Grace home. Once again her mother got a free meal without having to do any work. The ride home was a quiet one. This was very unusual for her mother. Most of the time, she loved the sound of her own voice and would talk endlessly. Not today. Her mother looked worried about something but she wasn't talking.

CHAPTER 36

July 1, 2010

It was a few months later and July 1, 2010. This day marked the one-year anniversary of Luke's death. As usual, it was sweltering in the house without central air and Lilith and Grace were spending a lot of time down at the antique store enjoying its air conditioning. They had bought some air mattresses to sleep on and used light covers.

Lilith seemed to be sleeping less and less, if at all. She would spend hours moving things around down at the antique store. In plans of re-opening the antique store, Nana and Aunt Char had cleaned out the back room so there was an area to mail items sold on the Internet. One night Lilith got the bright idea to make the back storage room an art gallery dedicated to Luke's artwork. Then, from her home Lilith started to bring down all of Luke's collections and started to replace the items in the glass cabinets with Luke's personal collection and things. Quickly, all of Luke's things began filling up the display cases down at the store and boxes of books filled the walking aisles that now were not easy to walk through. After a while, one couldn't even tell where the aisles use to be.

"Can you believe it Grace? Nana is talking like she wants to reopen the store. I tell you one thing Grace – I'm not going to let that happen," complained Lilith as she was hauling a box of Luke's debate trophies from the car into the antique store.

"I'm going to keep this store just a mess so that they can't open and there can't be any auctions. This is the only way that we can keep this store long enough so that it can be totally ours Grace," continued Grace's mother. **"We own this store with Nana and when she dies it will be all ours."**

"Hey Grace, come over here," said her mother as she caught a large fly on the back door of the antique store. **"You want to see what I use to do to flies to waste time? I would catch a fly and pull off its wings. When I was bored with that, I would pull off its legs. You should try it. We need to get rid of some of the flies in here and its really fun."**

The sun was setting and it was beginning to get dark. There was less than an hour of sunlight left. Lilith was in a hurry to unload her car and continue her plan of destroying the shop's plan of opening while hoping for her mother-in-law's death.

Instead of partaking in the fun of decapitating a poor fly, Grace chose to find a good book to read. The thought of a fly's oozing guts turned Grace's stomach. She would leave the act of torturing to her mother.

- -

Meanwhile at Uncle Jason's house, things continued to be very mystical. By this time, evening had set in. As Uncle Jason was walking down the stairs from his bedroom, he saw an image in his living room but he couldn't quite make out what it was. Next, to the remembrance shrine he and Char had built for Luke and Papa, there was a gray mist wearing a Los Angeles King's jersey. Uncle Jason couldn't believe his eyes. The translucent image looked like Luke. Was this really his younger brother that had passed away a year ago? Jason didn't know what to believe.

"Hey dumb shit" said the image **"I need to talk to you."**

"Is that you Luke?" asked Jason freaked out by the apparition that was before him.

"No shit Sherlock. I don't have much time so just listen to me. I'm worried about Grace. You need to protect her from Lilith. As we both know, Lilith has a bad temper. I am very worried for Grace. Oh, and by the way, Dad says "hi", " said Luke as he quickly faded away.

Uncle Jason wasn't sure if it had really happened or not. The sight of his late brother came and went so quickly. The whole thing was over within a minute. This was the second time that he had seen his younger brother Luke since he had died. Is this normal wondered Uncle Jason?

When Jason went back upstairs, he told Aunt Char what he had seen and heard. Char was a lot more open to the spiritual world than Jason. Although Char had never seen a ghost, she believed that they existed. Char wished she could've seen Luke but that never happened. For Char, this was a sign that somehow they had to help Grace but how?

CHAPTER 37

Being single again, Lilith took a strong approach in always looking good. The $100,000 life policy didn't last as long as Lilith had hoped. The money goes fast when a mortgage is paid; a new car purchased even if it was paid for mainly by Papa, and a wardrobe to attract a new husband is bought.

Before Luke had died, Lilith had outweighed him by at least twenty pounds. Now that she was on the prowl for a new husband, Lilith had become somewhat anorexic in appearance at 5'7" and around 118 pounds. She wanted to make sure she looked her best in her new designer jeans.

With a dwindling bank account, Lilith needed money quickly so she started looking at her dating options in the vicinity. As she considered possibilities, she looked around at her potential victims and focused on anyone easy on the eyes with very deep, monetary pockets. One person she focused her attention was Luke's slightly older, first cousin Lenny. What was really strange was that Luke had died on Lenny's birthday the prior year.

Lenny's mother was Nana's sister Ilene. They lived in a small town about 50 miles away from Mayhem. Their family was known as one of the wealthiest people in the area owning several businesses and half the town. Although Lenny had another brother and sister, he would still be a multi-millionaire when his parents passed away.

Luke's cousin was seven years older than Lilith, at least 6'-0" tall, handsome and known for always attracting the wrong type of women. Lenny had been married three times and now was once again a bachelor. Being one of the wealthier people of his community, he attracted all of the local gold-diggers, and Lilith was among them.

One company that Lenny's family-owned was a major construction company. This would come in very handy in fixing up Lilith's 100 year-old home. Right now Lilith could hire him to fix the windows on her house and get to know him better. One thing would lead to another and she could be Lenny's next wife. At least, that was Lilith's plan. After all, Lilith had known Lenny for years being his first cousin's wife.

One morning around 6:00 a.m., Lilith was experiencing another night of insomnia. She decided to drive over to Belle Plain and see what Lenny was up to. Lilith arrived around 6:50 a.m. when she rang his doorbell.

A surprised look came over Lenny's face when he saw Lilith on his front doorstep. Normally, Lenny would get a call before guests came over. Lenny was an early bird but a visitor at this time of day was ridiculous. As Lilith walked in the front door, she told Lenny that she would be right back as she went out his back door to the garage.

After all the family get-togethers, Lilith knew that Lenny always had a refrigerator full of beer in his garage, and she knew exactly where to find the key. Lilith went back to the garage, lifted a large rock next to the door, grabbed the key, and brought back a six-pack of beer into the house.

Lenny was standing at the kitchen counter having a cup of coffee when Lilith came through the back door. She dropped the six-pack of beer on the counter in front of Lenny. Quickly Lilith grabbed one of the beers, opened it and took a large gulp without politely asking. Lilith figured that it was better to ask for forgiveness than to ask for permission. She then took another beer and pointed it toward Lenny as if to offer the can of alcohol to him.

"No thanks," said Lenny amazed that anyone could drink so early in the day. **"I usually wait until at least noon to start drinking. Even then, there has to be a football game or something with a group of friends. Otherwise, people might think I had a drinking problem."**

"Suit yourself. I'll just make myself at home," remarked Lilith with a huge grin on her face and ignoring Lenny's insult.

"Say Lilith, why don't you bring Grace up to the house. She doesn't have to sleep in the car. My couch would be much more comfortable for a little girl," suggested Lenny.

"Grace isn't in the car, you silly guy. I left Grace at home in her own bed. She'll be fine. She is very mature for her age and can take care of herself. If necessary, my neighbors will take care of her," informed Lilith that the situation was under control and there was nothing to worry about. **"More than likely, Grace will wake up and wander over to Martha's house next door. No big deal."**

Lenny's eyes widen in disbelief. Was this woman for real? First, she comes over at the crack of dawn, helps herself to his beer in his garage and now she left her six-year old daughter at home by herself. This woman was full of surprises and none of them good.

"Lilith, I think you should leave now. Grace is probably scared to death. You should really go home and take care of her," said Lenny concerned for the small child's safety. **"She could be crying right now wondering where you are."**

"She's fine, Lenny. Really," persuaded Lilith as she picked up her beer and took another large gulp while trying to look seductive in Lenny's direction.

"Lilith, leave now before I call social services," insisted Lenny irritated for many reasons by Lilith's irresponsibility.

"Fine, I will go home," stated Lilith in an upset tone.

Lilith gulped the remainder of her opened can of beer and left the empty beer can on his counter. She then, picked up the remainder of full cans of beer and went to Lenny's front door. She walked out the door, slammed it closed and drove away like a bat out of hell. Lilith wasn't happy being thrown out by the guy she hoped would be her future husband and her radical driving proved it. In Lilith's eyes, Grace was the reason that she wasn't getting along with Lenny. She opened beers as she drove back to Mayhem and threw the empty cans unto the highway.

After several beers, she felt herself loosing control of the road. Halfway home, she drove into the ditch and rolled her barely-used, white car. Now what would she do? She decided that having beer in her system was no way to have the police see her. She drove out of the field and back onto the road. The car was an absolute wreck but still able to be driven so she drove straight to the car dealership. The dealership drove her home. What a hell of a day and it was only 8:30 a.m.

CHAPTER 38

<u>**August 1, 2010**</u>

The incident of Lilith leaving Grace home alone left Lenny a little cool toward Lilith. What kind of mother leaves her six-year-old child at home alone and expects the neighbors to take care of her? Lenny stopped calling Lilith. Not hearing from Lenny was an obvious sign to Lilith that things were over and she didn't take it well. Now it seemed that Lilith had only one kind of mood and she was always crabby thought Grace.

Lenny wasn't the only summer birthday in the family. It was the first of August and it was Grace's cousin Mathew's birthday. Uncle Tommy and Aunt Prudence invited Tommy's side of the family to celebrate Mathew's birthday. Everyone that felt well and healthy made it to the small boy's party.

Aunt Char and Uncle Jason had been taking care of Nana since Papa had passed away. The day of the party, Nana called Aunt Char and told her that she couldn't sleep all night due to restless leg syndrome. At the same time, Uncle Jason was exhausted from his four-hour commute each day to and from his job during the week. Aunt Char told him to rest while she and Allison went to Mathew's party.

Although Tommy's family had already moved, their house in North Mayhem still hadn't sold. So they figured one last birthday party for Mathew would be fun. Lilith and Grace were already at Mathew's house when Aunt Char and Allison arrive. Aunt Char explains why Uncle Jason and Nana aren't with her. In some ways, Uncle Tommy and Aunt Prudence are relieved that they aren't there. Lilith, however, just went nuts!

"What do you mean that Nana and Jason aren't coming? Don't they realize that Prudence and Tommy are three hours away and they won't get to see them very often?" screamed Lilith at Aunt Char. **"What's wrong with those two anyway? They are always too sick to do anything!**

"Lilith, Nana doesn't feel good and Jason is exhausted. You have never commuted to Minneapolis from Mayhem for a job so you don't understand how exhausting it is to travel and put in a regular workday. I want to keep my husband around for a while so I told him to stay home and rest," replied Aunt Char not regretting her decision.

"Well, we won't have many opportunities to celebrate so we should get together as often as we can. Those two are always missing parties because of their health," spit back Lilith. **"Doesn't that bother anyone but me?"**

"Lilith, they don't feel good. Let it go. Let's all try to have a good time without them," suggested Aunt Char wanting to change the subject.

Aunt Char was irritated and everyone could see she didn't want to discuss the health of the other two family members that she felt responsible for. Lilith was low on funds again and no one at this party could help her with her cash-flow problem. Nana should have been at the party so Lilith could try to get money for the store mortgage. What made Lilith so mad was that she had made a showing but the right viewers were no-where to be seen. What a waste of time thought Lilith to herself.

CHAPTER 39

<u>**August 4, 2010**</u>

A few days later, Lilith became absolute desperate for money. So Lilith and Grace showed up on Nana's doorstep at dinnertime. As usual, Lilith drank too much diet cola soda and was talking really, really fast. Lilith was also smoking pot and using bath salts but only a few people knew about this. It was this combination that helped her to put on the extra charm on Nana so that she could get extra money.

Not only did Lilith put the extra charm on Nana but she managed to muster up some for Uncle Jason and Aunt Char too. On the past Sunday, Lilith had really irritated Aunt Char and she didn't look like she was buying Lilith's act. As usual, Lilith was talking at 1,000-words a minute and she was moving extremely odd like she had ants in her pants. All Lilith could think about is that she needed money and she needed it now.

It was Wednesday and Uncle Jason was tired from his commuting. He was so tired that he kept falling asleep during dinner. At the same time, the dinner conversation wasn't that exciting to him as Lilith begged Nana for money. A plate of food was in front of each family member. However, Jason's head kept slowly falling closer and closer to the steak and mashed potatoes. Before his head hit the plate or the food, Jason would wake himself up. He repeated this action several times over the course of the meal.

"Sandy, I really, really need the money for the store loan," said Lilith begging as if her life depended on it. **"Between my job and trying to sell antiques, I'm not making enough for the store's bills."**

"Lilith, I think we need to make a plan to open the store and sell things in the shop. First, the back room should be cleaned out so that we can have an area to wrap up antiques sold on the Internet. Secondly, we need to clean the main area so that we can open up the doors for business again," said Nana thinking that this was the most logical way to proceed with getting rid of items.

"But Sandy, I was really hoping to keep the store and the items for Grace to inherit," said Lilith trying to find sympathy from the grandparent of her child.

The combination of being harassed for money by Lilith and Uncle Jason falling asleep irritated Nana so much that she screamed at Uncle Jason to wake up. To Nana it wouldn't seem right yelling at a widow.

"Jason, would you wake up long enough to eat?" exclaimed Nana **"Wake up now Jason or I'm cutting you out of the will!"**

At the same time as Nana's scolding to Jason, Lilith developed a huge grin on her face. Grace could tell by the look on her mother's face that this gave her an idea. It was new tactic to getting more money from her dead husband's family. If Lilith could pay Allison to get video footage of Uncle Jason's sleep apnea, she might get Jason written out of the will and receive a bigger chunk for herself.

Later that night, Lilith texted Allison about getting a video of her father falling asleep and then she would pay her for the footage. Lucky for Uncle Jason, Allison wasn't interested in making any money. However, Allison did tell her parents about Lilith's proposition. They both rolled their eyes.

"Why the hell would Lilith want a video of Jason falling asleep?" asked Aunt Char not understanding Lilith's motives.

"So Nana cuts me out of the will," stated Uncle Jason disgusted about Nana's threats at the dinner table.

"Is there nothing she won't do to get money from people? Isn't the shop with its inventory enough?" asked Aunt Char appalled at the situation and knowing that no one would answer the obvious.

CHAPTER 40

September 3, 2010

After Luke and Papa's death, staying up all night was becoming a ritual for Lilith. Grace thought it was because her mother was having a lot of nightmares. Every night Lilith screamed herself out of her dream state. Sometimes she would go days without sleeping. To help give her some zip, Lilith would drink diet cherry cola or some other high-energy drink. She became more and more animated and ate less and less food. As Lilith became thinner and thinner, she became more and more irritable. The littlest things set Lilith off screaming at those around her.

In order to let off a little steam, Lilith would jog several miles a day. Lilith became more and more manic obsessed with exercising, and with the antique store that she shared as a partner with Nana. The list of people that would bend over backwards was beginning to dwindle. When people did volunteer to help Lilith, for instance at the store, she would complain to their face that their help was "like herding cats". So it wasn't a surprise that people started to avoid Lilith.

At first, Lilith was taking Luke's valuable collections down to the antique store. When Aunt Char and Nana cleaned out the back room of the shop in order to make a space for Internet purchases, Lilith wanted to make it into an art-gallery with Luke's artwork. Instead of getting the store ready to be opened or auctioned off, Lilith was rearranging Luke's things in the cases or in the back room. Lilith was convinced that Nana would die soon, and the store would be hers. This building would contain all the reminders of her late husband that she didn't want at home. The way the store's aisle quickly filled it was obvious to Lilith's relatives that she didn't want any of her late husband's things at her house. At the same time, Lilith was bringing down anything that would delay opening up the store for business.

Meanwhile, Nana and Aunt Char were beginning to get very frustrated with Lilith. Every time they cleaned out a space at the store, they noticed that Lilith would bring boxes from home and clutter the space again. The boxes contained Luke's old college papers and other stuff that couldn't be sold in a typical antique store or even on an auction. Nana was very angry when she noticed that Lilith was bringing trophies that Luke had won in high school were being used to junk up an area. In Nana's mind, these were personal items and were meant to stay at home.

The back room was meant to be an area where people could package Internet sales and send off. Lilith didn't want to cooperate with her relatives. For some reason,

Lilith told Nana that she thought Nana would like Luke's artwork displayed at the store. The faster Nana and Aunt Char cleaned a space, the faster Lilith was hauling down Luke's things and messing things up.

After a few months of playing this game with Lilith, Nana decided that everything was going up for auction and for everyone to quit selling on the Internet. In desperation, Aunt Char contacted Lilith's father, Hank or Grandpa Bobble as Grace called him. She told Hank how Lilith was using the back room as Luke's art gallery and that she was messing up areas as fast as they cleaned the aisles

In order to check out the situation, Grandpa Bobble offered to come down and help with the antique store. So one afternoon, Grandpa Bobble and Lilith were busy taking off price tags so that items could go on an auction. He was shocked to see that everything that Aunt Char had told him was true about his daughter.

"Lilith, I think that it's best that you get that store behind you. Your mother and I think that it's causing you unnecessary stress," said Grandpa Bobble.

"No Dad! This store and all the things are Grace's inheritance. I'm not going to let the store go that easy," shouted Lilith.

"Don't you see Lilith? It's just not worth it," said Grandpa Bobble.

"Yes it is! Yes it is!" cried Lilith trying to get her father to see she was right.

CHAPTER 41

September 6, 2010

Lilith was in a really bad mood and Grace surmised it was because today would've been Luke's 41st birthday. Another reminder that Luke had existed and another reason for Lilith to be in a super crabby mood, so Grace decided to visit Martha next door. It was nice to have a place next door that she could always count on to help her if she needed it. Besides, Martha always had delicious treats that Grace didn't get at home.

"So Grace, how are things going with your mother?" asked Martha.

"My mother? Well, it changes from minute to minute. Sometimes she is happy and wants go to Valley Fun. Sometimes she just mopes and is very sad," Grace replied about her home life circumstances.

"What makes your mother happy?" questioned Martha.

"Well, she loves diet cherry cola. This gives her energy and she really likes that. But she complains that she can't sleep. When she can't sleep for a long time she gets really, really mean," Grace replied. "Now she is telling everyone that she is going blind. It's really weird."

This information got Martha thinking about Lilith's mental problems. Martha was a friend of Uncle Jason's. She decided to give him a call about Lilith while Grace finished the chocolate chip cookie she gave her.

"Hello Jason. This is Martha, Lilith's next-door-neighbor. Grace is visiting with me here right now. From what Grace tells me and what I've observed, I'm a little concerned about her mother Lilith. I'm really concerned that Lilith's manic/depressive episodes are getting worse. Grace says that Lilith rarely sleeps," explained Martha.

"Well, Lilith really hates me. She won't listen to a word I tell her. I think you need to call her father Hank Bobble. He is the only one that she will listen to," replied Jason. "Just give me a minute to find his cell phone number. If she liked me I would deal with her but I think she needs to hear this from her dad."

Right after Martha was finished talking to Uncle Jason, she dialed the number he gave her to call Grandpa Bobble. In Bloomington, Frank picked up the phone.

"Hello Hank? This is Martha, your daughter Lilith's next-door neighbor," said Martha.

"**Is everything alright? Did something happen to Lilith or Grace?**" he asked in a panic.

"**No, that is what I am trying to prevent. Grace is visiting with me right now. She told me that Lilith says she is going blind. Not only that, Lilith has been acting either extremely hyper and not sleeping or she is extremely sad,**" said Martha. "**I'm just worried that she might do something to hurt herself or Grace.**"

"**You are the second person to contact me about their concern of Lilith. I think that I will contact her boss and arrange some mental help. Thank you for contacting me Martha,**" said Hank. "**Good bye.**"

"**Good bye**" replied Martha.

Shortly after hanging up the phone, Grandpa Bobble pulled out the contact list on his phone. Hank had Lilith's boss' number in case he needed to talk to Lilith during retail hours. Don had owned Lighting World for decades.

"**Hello Don, this Hank Bobble. I am Lilith's father. Have you noticed any strange behavior in Lilith?**" asked Hank. "**I just received a troubling phone call from Martha, Lilith's next-door neighbor. She told me that Lilith is extremely manic and not sleeping. Otherwise, she is very sad. Have you noticed anything strange lately?**"

"**Hi Hank, I really hate to give you the bad news but yes. Last week, Lilith was so tired that she feel asleep at the front counter at the shop and I had to wake her up. There are also little vodka bottles I've been** finding everywhere in the store. At first, I didn't know who was leaving them and then I catch her drinking out of one. But what I find most troubling is that at times she tells me that she can't see anything and she thinks she is going blind," answered Don. "If that is the case, how is she able to drive to work?"

"Oh boy, this sounds very serious," responded Grandpa Bobble. "Lilith works tomorrow. I am stopping by your store and picking her up and having her committed at the hospital. She appears very unstable."

"I think you are doing the right thing Hank. I will see you then," responded Don.

"I'm thinking tomorrow afternoon. I will tell her that I heard that she is occasionally losing her eyesight and that I'm taking her to get her vision checked," said Grandpa Bobble "See you then."

CHAPTER 42

September 7, 2010

The next morning, Grandpa Bobble drove down from Bloomington to Mayhem. He contacted the local hospital in Mayhem and told them of his bringing his daughter to their facility. He warned the hospital staff that Lilith might cause problems if she thinks that she may not go home anytime soon.

As Grandpa Bobble pulled up to the lighting store, he took a couple of deep breaths. He knew that this would not be easy. However, he knew that he was the only one that could make this happen.

"Hi Dad, what are you doing here?" asked Lilith as she saw her father come in through Lighting World's front door.

"Well, you told me and a couple of other people that you were having blind moments so I thought that you should get your eyes checked out," said Grandpa Bobble. **"I've already gotten permission from your**

boss to take you. So get your purse. We are heading to the hospital."

"Really? Okay, I will grab my things," replied Lilith, **"just give me a minute."**

Lilith went in the back room to grab her purse and jacket that she had worn to work. Before going back out front, she went to her desk drawer, grabbed a small bottle, and took a swig of vodka and finished off the bottle. Now she could handle anything.

"We will take my car," said Grandpa Bobble as they walked to the parking lot.

"Okay, but you will have to drop me off after my appointment," responded Lilith.

"Of course," agreed Grandpa Bobble knowing full well that he wouldn't be driving her back to her car any time soon.

Being that the Francis family had spent a lot of time staying at the hospital, Lilith was very familiar with the different areas of the local hospital. What she didn't understand is why was her father was taking her to the Emergency Room entrance for an eye appointment.

When they approached the desk, Grandpa Bobble had a message pre-written on a small piece of paper that he handed to the receptionist. Lilith wasn't dumb. She knew something was up. When Lilith saw her father handing a message not meant for her eyes, her instincts told her to get away and she ran to the nearest exit.

As Lilith ran out of the hospital, a security guard ran after her out the door. A backup security car was soon on the scene and followed closely behind Lilith as she ran through the parking lot. In another direction was another security guard car. A couple of large guys got out of the car and ran toward her. It took three security guards to secure Lilith and make sure that she couldn't run away again.

Lilith began to pummel any one of the three men that was in whacking distance. When the three guards had a tight hold on Lilith is when she began to scream.

"Help me! Help! Help! Get off of me! I'm not going anywhere with you fuckers! Get the fuck off of me! Let go of me now," ranted Lilith. **"I told you fuckers to let me go!"**

This was the beginning of Lilith hating her father. Lilith didn't see life in varying shades of gray. In Lilith's world everything was black or white. Either you were with Lilith and her crazy plans or against her if you disagreed. There was no in-between for Lilith. It didn't matter how much Grandfather Bobble had supported and helped her before this incident. Now, she considered her father the enemy.

It didn't take long before Lilith had figured out that she was in the psychiatric ward in the hospital. She was able to wear her own clothes but two sets of doors prevented her from escaping. Lilith was not happy with her current situation.

It would be a week before Lilith would be allowed to go home. What really made her angry about being there is that she would not be able to drink her vodka, enjoy bath salts or smoke pot. Those were things that she really loved but weren't allowed in this facility.

During her stay, Lilith was once again diagnosed as bipolar. However, Lilith didn't buy that she was bipolar. She didn't see her episodes as extreme. She disliked being depressed but saw nothing wrong with her being in the state of mania. When she was manic, she got a lot of things done. Lilith was convinced that she was misdiagnosed. She thought if she had any problem, she was borderline personality like her biological sister Liza. Regardless, she was kept in the hospital until they decided that she could go home.

CHAPTER 43

<u>**September 19, 2010**</u>

When Lilith came home from the hospital, she looked better than she had in a while. She wasn't tired and she looked as if she actually slept. However, she was moving in slow motion. That told everyone that knew Lilith that she was very depressed. Her voice was lifeless and her tone was flat.

The hospital wanted to ensure that Lilith took the medication she was told to take. Therefore, every night at 6:30 p.m. she had to meet someone at the medical facility to make sure she took the pills for her condition. This went on for several weeks.

Lilith did not like taking these medications. She didn't like how she felt. She wasn't moving as fast as she use to and this did not make her happy.

The fact that she had people to make sure that she was taking her medications made her feel like she was being put under a microscope. One thing Lilith really hated is having people looking over her shoulder. Lilith had many activities that she didn't want other people knowing about.

A lot of people told Lilith that she had changed. Lilith has always been a little hyper and she thought that was the "fun" Lilith. Some people told her that too. The people at her lighting store said that they missed the "old" Lilith.

Everyone liked the fact that Lilith was calmer. However, she was just a little too calm. Grace wished the doctors could find a happy medium to her mother's problem. Now she just seemed sad and depressed.

After a day of being out of the hospital, Lilith started her bad, old habits. She was drinking and doing various drugs again. Anyone that truly knew Lilith understood that her addiction and obsessions owned her.

CHAPTER 44

November 26, 2010

Tomorrow is Lilith's birthday. She doesn't really enjoy her birthdays anymore. Maybe it's an adult thing with getting older. This year Grace's mother will be 37-years-old. Lilith and Grace were expecting to go to Nana's house to celebrate her birthday. However, Uncle Jason had a high fever and Nana wasn't feeling well either.

Last week, Uncle Jason had spent the week in the hospital. The doctors said there was something on his lungs. He would be having a PET scan done to figure out what it was. Uncle Jason was now on the phone explaining to Lilith why they were cancelling Lilith's birthday celebration.

"Hello Lilith? I'm sorry but we are going to cancel your birthday dinner for tonight. Yesterday the doctors found something in my lungs and I have a fever of 102 degrees. The doctors don't know what it is but they will be running more tests soon,"

said Jason with all the energy he could muster in his extremely weak body.

Char, who was sitting next to Jason and listening to the conversation, could hear the faint sound of sobbing. On the other end of the phone, Lilith began to weep at the news. Char knew that Lilith did not like Uncle Jason so why was she crying? Uncle Jason rolled his eyes and handed the phone to Aunt Char. Uncle Jason had no time for crying sister-in-laws and hated seeing tears from pretty much anyone.

"Hi Lilith, this is Char. Please don't cry. We don't know if there are any serious problems or not yet with Jason, " said Aunt Char trying to calm Lilith. **"I have to tell you that with the past few years, I can't help feeling that death is all around us."**

On the sender end of the phone, Aunt Char cringed at her last statement. The minute Aunt Char had said that last comment about death she wished that she could take it all back. The problem with Aunt Char is that she was honest and would tell people exactly what was on her mind. Once in a while, this honesty would turn around and bite her. This was definitely one of those times.

"Well, we just wanted to wish you an early Happy Birthday," said Aunt Char trying to quickly change the subject.

"Thanks," said Lilith **"I need to go. I'll talk to you later. Good-bye"**.

"Okay Lilith, bye," said Aunt Char as she heard the phone disconnect on the other side.

Aunt Char knew that something wasn't right but she just couldn't put her finger on it. Maybe it was how Lilith said good-bye. Something was off but what was it? Aunt Char brushed off the feeling and figured that it was just her over-active imagination again. She went back to taking pictures and putting items to sell on the Internet for Nana.

After a few weeks back home, Lilith was back to never really sleeping. The diet cherry cola that she always drank didn't help – the caffeine really makes her move and talk a lot. How much does she like to talk? Well, later on in the day, she was calling everyone hoping to talk. She didn't get a hold of Jason but this is what Grace heard her leave as a message.

"Oh, hi Jason, this is Lilith. You aren't answering your phone now so I suspect that you just screening your calls so that you don't have to talk to me. Nice. I've been doing a lot of thinking lately and I just have to tell you that you are so lucky. Why are you so lucky? You are so lucky to have dodged the bullet of death. It should have been you and not Luke that died. Yeah, there I said it. YOU! You should have died! You should have died first! Not Luke! Two years ago when my uncle died, it should've been Tommy. You and Tommy should've died before Luke," screamed Lilith as she slammed down her phone.

If this seems weird, Lilith has started doing a lot of strange things. When Lilith is house sitting her neighbor's house, like Martha's house next door, she looks through their things. If Lilith sees a magazine she likes in their mail, she just takes it home. If there were an item in their home that caught her eye, she would take it home with her. Everyone knows that is stealing but Lilith didn't see anything wrong with taking it. Lilith would keep taking things until someone called her on it. Someday she would pay a price for her bad habit but for now she was enjoying the buzz from having what she considered the upper hand and laughing that she was winning.

CHAPTER 45

November 27, 2010

Today is Lilith's 37th birthday. Grace's mother does not enjoy mornings especially after a night of too much fun. According to Jake, she seems to have "too much fun" every night. Grace knows that today is Monday and it's a school day for her but her mother is not getting up to take her to school. Grace loves going to school and Grace is not happy that Lilith cannot get up to take her.

Every time Grace goes into Lilith's bedroom and tries to shake her to get up, she slurs something and Grace cannot understand a word that she is saying. Her mother appears even more tired than usual. Grace was getting more and more irritated by her mother's lack of ambition.

All of a sudden the phone rings and Grace answers the phone. The small child recognized the caller. It's Grandpa Bobble.

"Hi Grace, how are you?" asked Grandfather Bobble.

"I'm fine but I don't think my mother is," Grace said **"I can't get her up to take me to school."**

"Grace, give your mom the phone so I can wish her a Happy Birthday," insisted Grandfather Bobble. **"Thank you Grace."**

"Grandpa wants to talk to you," Grace said to her mother as she handed her mother the phone.

"Hi Lilith. Happy Birthday honey!! How are you?" asked Grandfather Bobble cheerfully.

"Hello Dad," said Lilith but after that nothing she said made any sense.

Lilith would slur and most of the time Grace couldn't understand what she was trying to say. Grace could tell from the sounds coming from the phone that Lilith's dad was worried.

"Lilith? Lilith? Are you okay? Lilith, I am on my way to Mayhem," screamed Lilith's dad on the other end of the cell phone.

Grandpa Bobble could tell there was something not right with his daughter. He immediately jumped in his car in Bloomington and was driving to Mayhem as fast as he possibly could without having an accident.

Hank Bobble had a close call in St. Peter. As he was trying to get to his daughter's home as fast as he could, he barely yielded at yellow lights and almost hit someone turning right in front of him. He said a little prayer to get him to Lilith's home in time.

A little over an hour later, Grandpa Bobble arrived at Lilith's front door. He pushed past Grace and ran upstairs to Lilith's bedside. On the table next to her side of the bed, were a large empty vodka bottle and many, many empty bottles of Luke's old prescription bottles. The medications included a plethora of sleeping pills and painkillers.

It was obvious to Grandfather Bobble that Lilith had attempted to commit suicide. He immediately called 9-1-1 and asked for an ambulance at the front door of the Broad Street residence.

CHAPTER 46

<u>December 2, 2010</u>

The next day, Lilith woke up in the Mayhem hospital. It was a good thing that Grandfather Bobble called early in the morning to wish Lilith a Happy Birthday and followed his instincts. A few hours later and Lilith most likely wouldn't have made it.

Nana and Aunt Char went to visit Lilith in the psychiatric ward of the hospital. Visitation hours were from 4:30 to 7:30 nightly. It was roughly 4:25 when they arrived but they thought a few minutes early would probably be okay with the ward.

Before they could go through the double set of doors, they had to clear their pockets of cell phones, keys, pens and any other potentially dangerous items into a locked cabinet in the hallway. Definitely no shoelaces were allowed behind that double set of doors as the shoelaces could serve as possible hanging mechanisms.

Lilith had the first room on the right side of the hallway. Did Lilith have the closest room to the staff because she was the most extreme in the ward wondered Aunt Char? Lilith's room had a bed and window but no television. If Lilith wanted to watch television, she would have to go to the television room with the other patients. Lilith decided that she was not like them so the newest patient didn't associate with the others.

Lilith sat up in bed as the two women walked into her room. On Lilith's bed were a menu and several pieces of ripped up paper with an item of what to eat for each of the days that she foresaw for the rest of her stay at the hospital; being held captive she figured that she might as well make the best of it. If she was this bored, she might as well plan what she would eat for the duration.

"So, Lilith, how are you?" asked Aunt Char.

"Well, I wish my father wouldn't have come to my RESCUE," said Lilith with the emphasis on the word "rescue".

"Can you tell us what happened?" asked Aunt Char.

"That's easy. I DON'T want to live. I drank a bottle of vodka and took all of Luke's old prescription medicines. I wasn't going to kill Grace; she would've probably gone to Martha's next door eventually," said Lilith justifying leaving Grace alone as she killed herself.

"So when do you get to go home?" asked Nana hoping to calm down Lilith.

"If I had my way, I would leave this instant. I was told the earliest that I would be let out by THEM would be Tuesday," said Lilith angrily.

At that moment, Martha walked into the room to visit Lilith. Noticing that they had been there a while, Nana and Aunt Char excused themselves. They didn't want Lilith to feel overloaded with guests. However, the real truth was that Lilith seemed angry and it made them feel uncomfortable.

As they went through the double doors, they told the nurses at the desk that they needed someone to help them get their things out of the locker. They quickly took their possessions and left the hospital. Intuitively they both knew that this wouldn't be their last visit to see their in-law.

CHAPTER 47

December 15, 2010

Lilith was still at the local hospital in the psychiatric ward. She would soon be released but would then be transferred to another facility in the Twin Cities focusing on her drug dependency. It was at this point that Lilith was committed to the Commissioner of Human Services and was in a chemical dependency program in Edina. The State of Minnesota didn't take committing suicide lightly.

Luckily, Grace was able to go to Grandpa Bobble's sister Cindy's house. Cindy lived in St. Paul and was always full of fun for Grace. She had four daughters and Grace loved living there. Cindy was fun and made everything better.

Grandmother and Grandfather Bobble would try to visit their daughter in the facility as often as possible. Sometimes after going to the facility, they would go over to Cindy's house to visit Grace. They would give Grace an update report on her mother's improvement.

Meanwhile, back in Mayhem, Uncle Jason was having his PET scan. According to his doctor, it isn't cancer on his lung. Now the question is what is it? One idea his doctor had before the PET scan was psoriasis on his lung. Uncle Jason did have psoriatic arthritis. Psoriasis on the lungs is rare but it was possible.

Grandmother Susan called Uncle Jason and informed him that Lilith was completely done with the antique shop. Nana was very upset at this news. Lilith really hadn't done anything constructive at the shop and now she wouldn't be around to help get the store ready to open for business or sold off for an auction. It's really funny how Lilith got out of doing any type of work but caused a lot of work for others.

After receiving the news that Lilith wasn't involved with the shop anymore, the remaining Francis family decided it was time to make a final decision on the store. When Nana walked in the back door, after inspecting both floors of antiques, Nana was really upset that Luke and Lilith had made such a mess of the antique store. If they had at least left items in their original place, re-opening the store could have happened. The work would have resulted in just dusting the items, washing the glass cases, and vacuuming the floors. That would've been manageable. However, in Nana and Char's eyes, this store was a total disaster. Nana made the final decision that everything would go on an auction and there would be no turning back.

CHAPTER 48

December 31, 2010

Grace was not able to see her mother for several weeks. The chemical dependency facility in the Twin Cities watched Lilith during this time. This report is the only clue Grace has regarding her mother at the time. It would be years later before Grace would see this information.

Patient History:

Lilith Marie Francis is a 37-year-old White widowed female, resident of Mayhem, employed at Lighting World. Lilith was hospitalized in September for onset mania with psychosis. Clinical information was obtained from her doctor. Lilith is somewhat vague, distracted historian of her past.

Ms. Francis was hospitalized in September when her father and employer became extremely concerned regarding her behavior. Had also reported suicidal ideation that she denied. Now states she was misinterpreted. Her husband died in July 2009. Had made a statement that she had wished it were she who had died. Denied that it was a suicidal statement.

According to records, patient has been reported as always being a little "hyper." This has increased significantly over the summer months starting in July. Ms. Francis states that July was a very hot month. She doesn't not have air-conditioning, therefore, was not sleeping well. In addition, since the death of her husband, she has been running several miles almost every other day. Had been unable to get her running in, therefore, was unable to discharge her energy. She does not believe there is a problem.

Year ago, she had been prescribed a medication by her doctor due to complaints of fatigue and inability to concentrate. She states it worked very well for her. She also has chronic pain and uses a painkiller at least twice daily for the pain. She denied abusing the painkillers prior to her hospitalization. Hospital records indicate that she was positive for cannabis. She also admits that she drinks on a daily basis.

Ms. Francis does not see a significant difference in her behavior or mood over the summer. Continues to contend the suicide attempt was all a mistake. States that medications that she is now taking are sedating and is making her energy somewhat poor. Contends that she remains medication compliant. Made the statement, "I miss the old me." Feels depressed and like giving up. When asked what she meant by giving up, stated that she meant she would just go to bed, not try to work, and just sleep. Despite feeling fatigued and reporting medications as sedating, she continues to have nights where she does not sleep at all. Generally sleeps two nights and then the third night will go without sleep.

States she is trying to do her job but has a difficult time concentrating on her work. Works full-time at Lighting World and is part owner in an antique store that is owned by her deceased husband's mother. Apparently, there have been significant financial problems. Records indicate that family is concerned that some of the financial problems are related to poor decisions on Lilith's part.

Lilith feels quite pressured by her husband's family. She feels shut out of his family. Her husband's father died in May 2010. She had been quite close to him. Believed that he was the only person that understood her. This was extremely stressful for her and she repeats saying that she loved her father-in-law more than her husband. She also has a 7-year-old daughter she is raising alone. Apparently broke up from a fairly short-term relationship lately.

Psychiatric History:

Lilith Francis was hospitalized at age 14 after an overdose of pills. She stayed at St. Michael Children's Hospital. Did not take any medications at that time. Lilith states that it was the thought of life being the best as it gets as quoted by her own mother in her teens that made her attempt suicide. Has not had therapy since adolescence. Currently, does not see a need for therapy. Had a trial of anti-depressant medication and at some point in did not remain on for any length of time. Denied history of anxiety, panic attacks with agoraphobia. Denied history of eating disorder. No auditory or visual hallucinations, although records from the hospital indicate she did allude to auditory and visual hallucinations and appeared to respond to internal stimuli. No history of OCD, PTSD.

Past History of Chemical Dependency/Substance Abuse:

No history of chemical dependency treatment. Lilith states that she drinks on an almost daily basis. States she drank two beers last night. Records from the hospital indicate quite a significant use of alcohol. Lilith admits that she smokes marijuana on a daily basis for pain control. Does not use tobacco products but does chew nicotine gum. She has significant caffeine use. Drinking at least six cans of cola and energy drinks. Lilith was drinking an energy drink during the assessment. Denies that she has ever abused prescribed or over-the-counter prescriptions drug abuse.

Family History:

Lilith's maternal uncle has diagnosis of manic depression that died in 2006 by committing suicide. Maternal grandparents are alcoholics. There is also a history of drug abuse on paternal side of family.

Social History:

Widowed after marriage of eight years *(Lilith has problem performing simple math - actually 13 years)*. Lilith was married in 1996. Lilith says husband died by falling down in July 2009. She has a 7-year-old daughter. Lilith was born and raised in Bloomington, Minnesota.

Graduated from high school and community college with major in theater. Recently experienced the death of her father-in-law, which was very difficult for her. Denies history of physical or sexual abuse. Denies legal problems.

Mental Status Exam:

Lilith reveals a rather tall, thin White female. She is mildly disheveled. Clothes were clean. No involuntary movement but there was significant psychomotor agitation. Uses her hands frequently when talking. Shifted frequently in her chair. Went in and out of her purse. Speech was quite rapid at times. No receptive or expressive language impairment. Reports mood as depressed. Lilith has rapid and dramatic shifts in emotion. Thought process very disorganized, circumstantial, provides extensive amount of superfluous detail when asked very simple questions. Digresses from topic and never returns and is very distracted. Her concentration and attention impaired, has auditory and visual hallucinations. No delusions during appointment. Did not appear to respond to internal stimuli. No suicidal or homicidal ideation. At times appeared to have flight of ideas. Cognitive ability appears to be at least average. Insight is impaired. Insight is quite poor with high level of denial regarding any on-going psychiatric problems. Judgment and impulse control impaired.

Lilith has severe bipolar disorder with psychotic features. Rule out substance induced psychotic disorder. Rule out substance induced mood disorder. Has Daily chemical use - cannabis and opiate abuse. She has problems of bereavement, financial problems, poor psychosocial support and inadequate coping skills.

Assessment:

This patient is quite vulnerable. I am very concerned as to symptoms as they do not appear to be stable. Highly recommend case management and therapy, which she is quite resistant to. Lilith will need close monitoring.

CHAPTER 49

February 24, 2011

Lilith was finally able to come home at the end of February. Grace, however, stayed with her mother's aunt Cindy for a couple more months. Social workers wanted to make sure that Lilith was able to take care of herself first before Grace returned home. If Lilith couldn't take care of herself, how could she take care of Grace?

Lilith was shocked when she walked through the antique store and a large amount of the items were at the local Best Midwestern hotel ready to be auctioned off. The store had been cleaned out. Lilith felt defeated. For once, everyone else in the Francis family was getting what was wanted, but not Lilith. Between Nana, Aunt Char, Uncle Jason and the auctioneer crew, the once hoarder filled space was now clean, orderly, and ready for auction.

Lilith had seen enough. Being a closet smoker, Lilith decided it was time for a cigarette outside the store's back door. While outside the shop's back door, Lilith sucked down three cigarettes. She had not anticipated things to be this far along.

Uncle Jason was at work in the Twin Cities. Grandpa Bobble had driven Lilith down for the signing for the auction of the antique store and building. After the signing, the auctioneer requested a set of keys. Being that Lilith was done with the store, it made sense that she would relinquish her keys and not Uncle Jason or Aunt Char's set. This made Lilith feel even more defeated.

Several months and many auctions later, the store had finally sold all the items. Grace's grandparents from the Twin Cities made sure that Lilith did not go to the shop unless absolutely necessary. The only necessary circumstance was Lilith's signature to get rid of her past. Both Grandmother and Grandfather Bobble felt it was this store and Luke's family that had put Lilith in her current mental state. By summer, all the antiques had been sold, debts were paid and the remaining proceeds were divided up between the two partners.

CHAPTER 50

July 1, 2011

Today is the two-year anniversary of Luke's death. Fortunately, the Fourth of July is just around the corner and the celebrations of the holiday will take everyone's mind off of most sad topics.

Lilith has spent the summer waiting for the legal process to give her share of the antique store. Being that Nana and Papa had started the business over 30-years ago, Nana naturally received the largest amount from the sale of antique store. A large portion of the money has gone to the auctioneer, the accountant and the lawyer involved in the process. Aunt Char and Uncle Jason will not receive anything other than the payment of the hours put in to get the job done. Although Uncle Tommy wasn't around to help, he had some items in the store and was paid $2,300 for the sale of his goods.

The accountant remembered that the loan taken out on the antique store was to benefit Grace's parents. Therefore, Lilith's cut in the sale of store was greatly reduced. In the end, Lilith received a payment of $52,000.00.

Of course, Lilith feels that her chunk should've been much larger. To Lilith, Luke's life was only worth a total of $152,000.00. To Grace, her Dad's life cannot have an amount near enough of his value.

After Lilith cashed the check from the store's auction, she went to the local liquor store and purchased a bottle of the store's finest champagne. Luckily, Grace wanted to stay the night at the Johnson's and Lilith was happy to give her permission. Lilith left Grace at her friend's residence. The excited woman then went home and poured herself a large glass of champagne. Lilith sat back, put her feet up on the cocktail table and thought about the past couple of years.

Being that Grace wasn't around, Lilith felt she could do and say whatever she wanted. In her pocket was a large Cuban cigar that she had bought from the same dealer that sold her marijuana. Lilith was defeated in the selling of the antique store but celebrated that almost anything that reminded her of her late husband was virtually gone.

Lilith took out the Cuban cigar and unwrapped its forbidden contents. For a few minutes, she examined its look and smelled its delicious tobacco odor. Nothing smelled so good to her. Lilith then took out a lighter she always kept in her pocket. She figured that you never knew when someone would offer you a joint or cigarette and it was good to be prepared.

After lighting the cigar, she inhaled a deep mass of the delightful smoke. Her eyes rolled back into her head, as she hadn't felt more alive than right then. In her home she was smoking the forbidden, illegal Cuban cigar and nobody could tell her that she couldn't.

Lilith figured it wouldn't be much of a celebration without a bottle of champagne. Carefully, Lilith popped open the container of the bubbling alcohol and poured herself a generous glass. As the liquid escaped down the outside the glass, Lilith was careful to lick as much as possible so not to waste the buzz that would soon be hers.

"Well Luke, you son of bitch. I finally got the settlement on that fucking antique shop of yours. The total value of your life was a measly $152,000. That's more than I would've ever thought. I'm glad that you are gone," said Lilith holding up her glass of champagne. **"Here's to you being dead, you lazy son of a bitch!"**

Being the two-year anniversary of his death, Luke decided to give Lilith a present of his own. As Lilith raised her glass, a strong force whipped it out of her hand. The glass flew out of Lilith's hand and broke immediately upon contact with the floor. The strong spirit then grabbed the remaining bottle of alcohol and threw it at Lilith's head. Its force knocked Lilith out for the remainder of the night…

CHAPTER 51

August 29, 2011

Lilith awoke early that morning and was feeling hyper so she decided to run up to Uncle Jason and Aunt Char's house. As Lilith approached the front door, she looked in through the glass to see if she could get anyone's attention without having to ring the doorbell. If anyone walked by, they would probably think Lilith was casing the place.

Lilith was dressed in a faded white athletic bra and very small gray shorts. From a distance, Lilith looked like she was running in her underwear. Lilith ran up to the front step and rang the doorbell.

At the time, Aunt Char was making coffee in the kitchen when she thought she heard someone at the door. When she checked the door, she saw Lilith standing there in what looked like her bra and panties.

"Hey Lilith. Have you been out running today or do you always dress that way?" joked Aunt Char.

"It is such a beautiful day I thought that I go and enjoy it," said Lilith ignoring Char's comment.

"Sounds good to me. It is a beautiful morning. Would you like something to drink?" asked my aunt expecting the answer to be water after what looked like to be a long run.

Aunt Char knew that Lilith had been away at a facility but assumed that it was a mental ward. However, Lilith was actually staying at a chemical dependency ward in Edina. Lilith was careful not to tell Luke's family too much about her life. She only told them what she wanted them to know. So Lilith had told everyone that it was a mental institution.

"Do you have any booze?" asked Lilith hoping for a quick buzz.

"Well, Jason doesn't drink anymore but once in a while I like a little," said Aunt Char surprised at her sister-in-law's request. **"Do you like scotch? It's the only alcohol that I keep in the house."**

"Sure, I'll take a shot," said Lilith with a huge grin and a twinkle in her eye. Lilith was glad that Char didn't know that she had been labeled an alcoholic. Had she known, Char definitely would not have given her a cocktail.

"Well, I guess one shot wouldn't hurt," said Aunt Char wondering if this was the right thing to do after Lilith's trip to the mental facility last year. Reluctantly, Aunt Char went to the bar in the kitchen. After all, her sister-in-law had a mental issue not a chemical issue she thought.

Aunt Char walked to the kitchen counter and bent over. She reached for the bottle of Johnny Walker. In the cabinet was a small shot glass. She poured some scotch for Lilith and passed on having any herself. Aunt Char drank maybe one cocktail every six months and wasn't in the mood for it as she had a lot to accomplish before going to the post office before it closed that day.

Lilith had some questions on the subject of Nana and Papa's will. Being that Aunt Char was the main person taking care of Nana, she must know where the family will is currently.

"So Lilith, are you seeing anybody right now," asked Aunt Char trying to make conversation with the widow.

"Can you believe that I'm dating Stephen Horn again? Stephen was the guy I was dating before Luke and I went out. Stephen was really mad at Luke and didn't talk to him ever again after Luke stole me away from him," said Lilith loving the thought of two guys fighting over her.

"It's too bad that Stephen and Luke weren't friends after that," remarked Aunt Char thinking back over a decade ago. **"They were such a great friends and they had an awesome band in college. I loved listening to their sound when Jason took me to 1st Avenue to listen to them."**

"Stephen is still trying to get a band going. Can you believe it? A guy in his forties trying to get a band

going?" replied Lilith. **"I can't believe that I'm dating him again."**

"I don't see anything wrong with that," said Aunt Char trying not to be judgmental of Lilith's life. **"I'm never surprised when old couples get back together after divorce or in your case, the death of a spouse."**

"But he is such a loser! He has this long, grey stringy hair. Oh well. At least he's someone to date. Right? Hey Char I got a question for you. What do you know about the current Francis will? Now, we are all in the will, right?" asked Lilith hoping for a positive answer.

"Sorry Lilith, but back before Papa died, he told me that his will had a stipulation that the son must be alive or the money goes to the grandchild at the age of 25. I didn't know that little tidbit until Luke passed away. Papa told me that if Jason died I would be in the same boat. I wouldn't get anything and Allison would have to wait until she was 25 for her inheritance," reported Aunt Char noting Lilith's anger. **"Would you excuse me? Coffee always goes right through me. I'm just going to run up to the upstairs bathroom but I will be right back."**

Lilith watched as Char walked up to the 2nd floor bathroom. When Lilith heard the door close, she ran to the counter and grabbed the bottle of Johnny Walker. She continued to pour scotch in the shot glass, drink and repeat, until she heard the upstairs bathroom door open with Char's footsteps. She then quickly and as quietly as she could, put the scotch bottle back where she had found it.

At this point, Lilith had gotten all the answers and booze that she wanted. When Aunt Char came back to the kitchen, Lilith decided to say good-bye and head home. Char walked Lilith to the front door and said good-bye. The widow half-smiled as she left Char's house. Lilith held her alcohol well as her sister-in-law didn't even suspect that she was drunk.

Lilith ran down the long drive way and turned right onto the paved street. As Lilith headed down Glenwood she decided take another right and to run up to Main Street. Her current boyfriend Stephen Horn lived on that street. As Lilith approached Stephen's large brick house, she suddenly collapsed and had a violent seizure.

From across the street, a group of teenagers had watched the woman fall down and began to thrust about up and down. As luck would have it, Allison was at her friend's house that was situated across the street from Lilith's current boyfriend Stephen. Allison recognized her Aunt Lilith and called 9-1-1 for an ambulance to come and pick up her aunt. Lilith was taken to the hospital. The nursing staff smelled alcohol and found that her blood had an alcohol level of .303 upon arrival to the emergency department.

This episode caused the local Human Services to do a family assessment of Lilith and Grace. Luckily, the family assessment did not result in a recommendation for service. However, Lilith's luck would eventually run out.

CHAPTER 52

September 6, 2011

Today is Luke's birthday. If Luke were alive, he would be 42 years-old. At 12:01 a.m., Luke decided to give himself a birthday present. Now what could he do to make himself smile wondered the ghost. In life, Lilith had made his mortal existence a living hell. Now he wanted to repay her kindness.

Luke decided to pay a visit to his college band buddy. Someone needed to talk some sense into his old friend Stephen. Luke appeared at the head of Stephen's bed. As Stephen slept, Luke repeated into his ear "Lilith is evil. Lilith is evil. Get rid of Lilith. Lilith is evil. Lilith is using you. She doesn't give a damn about you and never will. Lilith dropped you once and she will do it again. Stephen, you are better off without her."

By mid-morning Stephen awoke in a total fog. All night he had horrible dreams about Lilith being a large, angry monster with red eyes. Ever since they started dating, he had a bad feeling that it wasn't right and now this dream had convinced him to end it.

Stephen, Lilith and Grace were supposed to go to dinner that night. Unable to face Lilith, Stephen took the easy way out and texted her.

Lilith, I don't think we should go out anymore.

Being that it was Luke's birthday, Lilith had woken up in a bad mood. It was another reminder that she was alone. At Lighting World, Lilith's workday was busier than usual and she didn't see the message from Stephen until she went to pick Grace up from the child's after-school program.

Lilith walked into Grace's classroom. Grace lit up as she saw her mother and knew that they would be going out with Stephen for dinner. The little girl got up from her table, grabbed her coat and then ran to her mother.

Lilith and Grace walked out the front doors. Grace took her mother's hand until they reached the car. The weather was chilly and sprinkling a light rain and the two didn't want to get wet. They quickly ran to the white car in the parking lot and didn't talk until they got into the car.

"Where are we going for dinner?" asked Grace.

"I'm not sure. Let me see where Stephen wants to meet," said Lilith looking forward to a nice dinner out.

Lilith dialed Stephen's number and held the cell phone up to her ear. She dialed again and again. No answer from Stephen. That's funny thought Lilith. Why isn't he answering? He's not working today.

"Mom? Where are we going for dinner?" asked Grace again.

"Just a minute Grace. Stephen isn't answering. I'm going to see if Stephen left me a text," said Lilith as she looked at her smart-phone. **"I have a message from him. Stephen says I don't think we should go out anymore?"**

Lilith could feel her face fall and tears well up in her eyes. A week ago, she was telling her sister-in-law what a loser the guy she was dating was, and now he had dumped her. Not taking rejection lightly, Lilith angrily spoke her message back to him.

I killed Luke. My lungs were stronger. I popped his head off with my thighs. I didn't want to win.

Stephen was more than horrified at this message. The middle-aged man had always thought that Lilith was a little quirky but this was beyond that. What would possess Lilith to send him such a message? Was he going to be her next victim?

Fearing what Lilith might do to him, Stephen shared the text with his parents. His mother, who knew Uncle Jason, decided that Uncle Jason should be informed and immediately called him. Jason was not at the house so a worried mother left a message. Uncle Jason called Karen Horn back as soon as he got the message.

"Hello Karen, this is Jason Francis. You left me a message to call you," said Uncle Jason puzzled as to why she was calling him.

"Hello Jason, I'm so sorry to have to call you. Stephen received a disturbing message from Lilith regarding your brother," said Karen. **"I don't know what to do but to have Stephen forward it to you and have you interpret it. What is your email address and I will have him send it."**

Uncle Jason gave her the information and he received the message. This is the message he received:

Hi Jason,

I'm so sorry to involve you in this, but I really don't know what to make of this text message that Lilith sent me yesterday. I'm really disturbed by this. And I worry about Grace. Could she be crazy enough to try and hurt me too? I get my text messages forwarded to my email via Google Voice, so this is exactly what she sent me.

Take care.
Stephen

---------- Forwarded message ----------

I killed Luke. My lungs were stronger. I popped his head off with my thighs. I didn't want to win.

After over-coming the initial shock of the message, Uncle Jason and Aunt Char confronted Lilith on why she wrote the message.

"I wrote that note to scare Stephen. I didn't expect him to share it with you," laughed Lilith feeling uncomfortable that she had been caught in a confession.

How does one deal with someone that laughs off the whole situation? Between the remaining family members, they reasoned that the coroner said the cause of Luke's death was a broken neck but at the same time, Luke did have a high blood-alcohol reading. What really killed Luke?

Uncle Jason and Aunt Char included Nana into the situation. The three discussed the event in the family room at Nana's house.

"I guess I always figured that Lilith pushed Luke down the stairs," said Aunt Char **"But now it sounds like they were fighting and she broke his neck over her thigh."**

"Well, those two were always wrestling. Lilith would always get his head between her legs but I never thought she would kill him. I'm sure it was an accident," said Nana trying to make sense of the situation.

Uncle Jason contacted the FBI agent from the case involving his father's accountant that took millions from his father and other Mayhem families in a Ponzi scheme. The FBI directed them back to the Mayhem police but nothing ever came from Jason's complaint.

Uncle Jason also contacted Grandpa Bobble and told him of the situation. Hank's reaction was much like Nana's. Grandpa Bobble said that Luke and Lilith's relationship could be like the movie where the couple fights over things until they both die in the end. Aunt Char went to Nana and Papa telling them of the bloody fight between the couple and they said that was just how those two work things out.

Why is it okay for couples to physically fight with each other? Why did people just accept it? Society sometimes worries about men beating women but never the other way around. In a world where more and more husbands are staying home and taking care of children, the women are getting the upper hand as being the breadwinners. Why is it that victims that do not make much money are thought as unimportant?

Lilith was always more aggressive and always came out on top in fights with Luke. As Grace saw it, her Dad never really fought back. When her father drank, he became extremely passive. Luke was brought up to respect women and not to hurt them. What everyone started wondering is did Lilith get away with murder?

CHAPTER 53

February 3, 2012

Over the past few months, Lilith knew people were beginning to piece Luke's murder together. Little by little people were beginning to drop off communications with her and she was losing her touch as the master manipulator that she admired as one of her best qualities.

One night, after a long exhausting day, Lilith sent Grace to a friend's house for the night. After dropping off Grace, Lilith went to her favorite liquor store and than drove home. Slowly, Lilith trudged up her front steps with a brown paper bag. The only thing that kept Lilith going anymore was her alcohol and drugs.

In a long, thin brown paper bag, Lilith hugged her old friend the vodka bottle. Instead of pouring the liquid into a glass, she just drank it straight out of the bottle while it was still in the paper bag. In less than a hour, Lilith had consumed almost a liter of vodka. For once, Lilith was feeling rather tired and slowly walked up the stairs towards her bedroom.

As Lilith got towards the top of the stair, the floor began to go up and down underneath her feet. She stopped as she saw a large black mass at the head of the landing. The hairs on the back of Lilith's head started to lift as fear overtook her body. Lilith felt her arm burning and blood begin to rush out of the scratch marks that appeared out of nowhere. There were a couple of long thin blood scratches that burned her arm. Lilith grabbed her arm where she was bleeding.

All of the sudden, the mass pushed her backwards and Lilith tumbled down the stairs. She rolled over and over again. By the time she made it to the bottom of the stair she had been knocked unconscious. At the bottom of the stair, Lilith lay still for a couple of hours and when she awoke she noticed that her right arm hurt immensely. Although her arm still stung from the scratches, she knew it was more serious.

She pulled herself to the nearest phone and dialed 911. Lilith ordered an ambulance. She was glad that Grace was staying the night at a friend's house and didn't observe her mother in this state.

As Lilith predicted, her right arm was broken and would be in cast for a few weeks. The only good thing in this experience was the pain killer medication that she received. The little pills made her feel so good, better than anything else in her life.

CHAPTER 54

February 8, 2012

It was Wednesday and Grace had a horrible start to her school day. The morning was not Lilith's friend and this morning was worse than usual. Lilith got really drunk the night before because she had Wednesdays off and didn't have to go to work the next day.

Lilith was so drunk that she did not help Grace wash her face or change into her pajamas the night before. This morning Lilith was not much better. So Grace went to school in the same clothes that she wore yesterday and all the kids in her class noticed. Everyone that made eye contact saw that Grace's clothes had not been changed gave her a look of disapproval. Grace felt so ashamed.

To make matters worse, Grace was the last child picked up from the after-school program. At 5:30 p.m., after all the other kids had left, Grace noticed that the head teacher kept looking at her watch. After a while, the after-school caretaker made a phone call. It wasn't

Grace's mother that picked Grace up. It was a social worker. Her name was Ms. Susan Cooper.

If Lilith didn't come to pick Grace up, Ms. Cooper was going to take Grace to her mother. Ms. Cooper didn't take anything lightly. Being that the time was close to 6:00 p.m., she wasn't happy about working after hours and she would make Grace's mother know it.

It was around 6:15 p.m. when Grace and the social worker arrived in front of Grace's house. Lilith answered the door still in her pajamas from the night before and her hair a big, knotted mess. Ms. Cooper could tell that Lilith must have awoken her from a very deep sleep. The social worker also noticed that Lilith also had a broken arm at the time, not to mention that Grace's mother smelled really bad. The social worker surmised a combination of sweat, alcohol and vomit.

As Ms. Cooper looked past Lilith and into the house, the social worker saw a plethora of hoarded boxes against all the interior walls. Lilith still had not cleaned out the boxes that she and Luke had purchased at thrift stores over two years ago. Ms. Cooper could tell that housekeeping was not Grace's mother's favorite pastime as she saw food that was unidentifiable and with hints of mold stuck to the living room floor.

"Ms. Francis, my name is Susan Cooper. I am a social worker. Do you understand that by law you need to pick up Grace from the after-school program by 5:30? It's now after 6:23 p.m.?" asked Ms. Cooper as she looked at her watch.

"Thank you for bringing Grace home. Fuck, I must have been in one deep sleep," responded Lilith whom starting to look more awake and realizing the seriousness of the situation as she tried to make her hair less messed.

"Are you taking pain pills Ms. Francis?" asked Ms. Cooper looking at her broken arm.

"Yes I am. When I broke my arm it hurt like a fucking son of a bitch so my doctor gave me the pain killers," replied Grace's mother still groggy from the combination of alcohol and medications. **"I don't know what I'd do without them little bastards."**

"I see," said Ms. Cooper. **"Well, I will be sending you some paperwork in the mail. Be sure to get the information back to me. I would suggest that you not allow this to happen again. There is a possibility that you may lose custody of Grace if this continues. I'm leaving now but I will be in touch."**

Ms. Cooper turned and walked down the front steps. Luckily, there were no church services going on across the street so Ms. Cooper was able to park directly in front of the house. After a ten-hour workday, the social worker was finally able to go home to her little pooch that would need to be let out the minute she arrived home.

When Lilith closed the door, she was pissed. Her dark, black eyes were wide and her forehead wrinkled as she processed what had just occurred. The thought of losing custody played over and over in Lilith's head.

Loosing Grace would mean losing inheritance from her grandparents. Lilith needed to stop the direction this horrible story was heading.

"Ms. Cooper? I think she means Ms. POOPER!!! Right Grace! I bet if I had a husband, this wouldn't have happened," surmised Grace's mother, **"That's it! I need to find you a dad Grace! If you had a father, no one would give a shit what I did. I tell you Grace that Project Find Grace A Daddy has officially started. I'll show that Ms. Pooper!"**

CHAPTER 55

February 13, 2012

It was appropriate thought Lilith to try and find love during the week of Valentine's Day. The month of February was filled with Grace's mother hunting for a husband for herself and a new father for Grace. After the visit with the social worker, Lilith was convinced that if she had a husband all her problems with the county would go away. If she weren't competent to have a daughter, her husband would be able to care and be responsible for a nine-year old. This marked the beginning of finding a new dad race.

The first guy Lilith brought home Grace wasn't even sure of his name. Grace just referred to him as "my mother's 58-year-old boyfriend". He was rather scruffy with a full beard and a huge, filled out stomach. They both worked at the lighting store. This was a prime example of Lilith not wanting to work too hard thought Grace.

Earlier in the day, Nana invited Lilith and Grace for dinner. Without asking permission, Lilith brought her 58-year-old boyfriend to dinner to meet Nana, Allison, Uncle Jason and Aunt Char. Both Uncle Jason and Aunt Char looked at Lilith like she had really scraped the bottom of a barrel. No one really talked during dinner. Lilith and her 58-year-old boyfriend had smoked pot before coming for dinner. Everyone surmised by the evidence of the bloodshot eyes they both possessed, not to mention, the reeking smell of cannabis.

At this point, Lilith realized how desperate she looked by the reactions of her in-laws. The next day, Lilith began to think about all the possible single men she knew that would make a good father for Grace. Then, she thought about this one guy she had met at the bars who knew Luke in high school. He was a few years younger than Luke but the guy admired Luke for his high school accomplishments.

This guy's name was Scott Frey. He was taller than Lilith and outweighed her. Scott was almost as tall as Uncle Jason. There was no chance that Lilith could beat him into submission like she had tried with Luke.

Lilith had run into Scott at one of the local bars. A day later, Lilith asked Scott out. Lilith felt the biggest motivator to get Scott to want marriage was to dangle money as an incentive. She told Scott that her grandfather was worth big bucks and someday it would all be hers by being Grace's guardian.

So not to look like one big scam, Lilith wanted Scott to tell everyone that their family had been friends for years when Luke was alive. That was a BIG lie. Lilith convinced everyone that their family would go over to Scott's house for barbeques all the time. Lilith would tell everyone that Luke really liked Scott and they went way back before Grace was born. She would make Scott look like a great friend that enjoyed antiques and would help Luke load and unload items purchased at auctions. Indeed, Scott was the friend that everyone could rely on or at least his new wife would tell everyone that little lie.

Lilith also told friends and relatives that Scott was a 39-year-old virgin. That was an even BIGGER lie. Lilith told the story so many times that she started to actually believe it herself.

Over time, Scott and Grace had a lot of fun He would let Grace punch him the stomach just like her Dad used to do. Lilith decided that Scott was exactly what she needed in a husband. In Lilith's eyes, Scott was very similar to Papa and Lilith needed someone that could take care of her and Grace. With Scott around, thought Grace, she would have at least one good parent as she often told others.

After two weeks of dating, Lilith proposed to Scott. Spontaneously, she suggested to Scott that they hop the next plane to Las Vegas and get married. Lilith left Grace with a coworker that Grace considered more of a mother than her real mother. The woman's name was Linda and she never had children but would've liked one. Linda had taken care of Grace on many occasions and was glad that she had a daughter on a temporary basis.

Lilith had already had the formal wedding with Luke. Now she was going to experience the other end of the wedding spectrum. This time she was going to have a "funny" wedding at a Las Vegas Wedding Chapel. More than anything associated with Las Vegas, that included an Elvis impersonator. The small chapel had wood paneling and cheap tile flooring. Scott, dressed as Elvis, waited at the altar as the Elvis impersonator walked Lilith who was also dressed in an Elvis outfit down the aisle serenading her with "Love Me Tender". Lilith was laughing during the entire ceremony, as she knew that she would shock everybody back in Minnesota with this video. Three different Elvis outfits and the King's song would forever make Lilith laugh.

While Lilith and Scott were honeymooning in Las Vegas, Lilith's Grandmother Grace passed away. Lilith was glad she had the excuse that she was out of town so she wouldn't have to attend the funeral. At the same time, she felt happy and excited about all the good things that were finally happening to her. With the death of her wealthy grandmother, Lilith was halfway to the money of her wealthy grandparents. Now, Lilith just needed her grandfather to die and she would be set for life. Even though Lilith was an excellent actress, she knew that it would be hard to act sad at the funeral when she was happy about her grandmother's passing.

When the newly weds returned to Minnesota, Lilith told Luke's side of the family that she had gotten married. Lilith tried to convince Nana that she already knew Scott and that she had met him when Luke was still alive. Lilith told Nana that Scott would to go to the auctions with Luke. But Nana didn't remember him and Nana remembered everything.

"Well, you know Sandy I only married Scott so that I would be able to keep Grace," confessed Lilith. **"Otherwise, the county might take Grace away from me. Scott is my stability and even if others think I'm not a good mother, they will let Grace stay with us because of Scott."**

"I have to say this is very surprising, "said Nana **"what ever happened to the 58-year-old boyfriend?"**

"Oh that. We just weren't compatible," said Lilith as she shrugged her shoulders. **"Besides, he seemed a little too old for me."**

Lilith did all of this so when she told people that she had gotten married, the marriage didn't seem like the scam it really was. Lilith loved it when she got something past people. She thought it was really funny to make people wonder if she was telling the truth. Lilith felt like she won something when she got away with a lie. Scott believed Lilith's stories about her grandfather being wealthy and figured that he could come out of this a very rich man so why not.

CHAPTER 56

April 2012

After the Las Vegas wedding, it was Grace's turn for some fun in her life. The Fun Zone in Mayhem is a true child's paradise. There's bowling or miniature golf for the older people. If you want to do something alone there are arcade games. Grace's personal favorite is laser tag that you can play with a group of friends. That night Grace was meeting her Blue Birds troop for an evening of memories. Little did Grace know that it would be her mother that would be making the memory in Mayhem tonight for everyone and leave Grace scarred for life in this small town.

Scott, Lilith and Grace got to the amusement place a little after 7:00. It was a Thursday night and since Lilith quit her job at Lighting World she could be as crazy as she wanted. As always, Lilith had already been drinking at home and knew Scott would be the driver so she didn't hold back in her alcoholic consumption. Besides, Lilith had more time on her hands not being employed.

Grace's parents let her run wild in the children's paradise. Meanwhile, Scott and Lilith both sat in the bowling alley drinking and becoming intoxicated. At one point, Grace had run out of tickets and had to find her parents to get more money. As Grace walked into the bowling alley bar, she noticed that everyone was looking and pointing at something. Grace should have known instinctively that it was her mother they were pointing at. Again, her mother has gained the center of attention if only it was for something positive. Grace was so embarrassed.

In the far end of the bowling area, was a woman with long dark brown hair sitting and grinding on a man's lap. To Grace's disgust it was her mother sitting on Scott's lap facing him. Music was playing and her mother was flashing Scott her tiny boobs to the rhythm of the music. Most of the time Lilith did not wear a bra so it's safe to say that Scott wasn't the only one getting a show.

Less intoxicated patrons were noticing the activity. There was a small group of people circling the manager on duty at the time. Based on the direction of the fingers pointing, Grace would bet it was her mother and stepdad that they were discussing. The manager went to Grace's mother and stepdad and said that they must leave the establishment and never to return. Lilith started throwing a fit.

"Fuck you! You can't just throw us out of here! We have a right to be here just like everybody else. I don't want to be here anyway! Go fuck yourself," screamed Grace's mother and flipping everyone the bird as she walked toward the exit. **"Fuck you all!!!"**

But like most things in her life, Lilith has turned Grace's paradise into a living hell in which she may never be able to return. This happened a couple of times but the last time at the Fun Zone, Grace and her family were told to never return. Maybe in a few years, the management would turn over and Grace's looks would change enough so that she would not be recognizable.

Grace's mother grabbed her hand and started to pull the small child out of her paradise. On the way out, Grace saw her Blue Birds leader who offered to take Grace home. So Grace was able to stay a little longer but her mother pulled her out of the Blue Birds program after this incident. Lilith was probably embarrassed by the situation but why take it out on her child. Grace missed her Blue Birds troop but her mother refused to let her go back to the group ever again.

From time to time, Grace would run into her Blue Birds leader. She would ask Grace how her mother was doing. Grace's face would scrunch up as she thought of an honest answer.

"Well, as you probably know, my mother has gone crazy since she got married and now she's really mean but that's nothing new," Grace remarked when anyone asks her how her mother was doing.

CHAPTER 57

May 6, 2012

It was May 6, 2012 and Allison was having her Lutheran Confirmation party. As Grace looked inside through the window in the front door of Allison's house, she noticed there were a lot of old people. Not any younger teenagers like her mother had predicted earlier in the day. There wasn't anyone Grace recognized except for Allison, Aunt Char and Uncle Jason. Nana didn't even make it to the party.

"Hey Mom! There aren't any kids in there," Grace said as she put her face onto the glass portion of the door and cupped her eyes in order to block out any sun glare trying to get a better view inside.

"What? I expected there would only be kids," said Lilith not believing Grace's observations, pressing her face against the glass next to Grace and looking into the house with disbelief.

Grace rang the doorbell and waited for someone to let them in. Once Aunt Char saw them at the door she walked over to the door and welcomed them in. Lilith was whispering something to Aunt Char.

"I thought that Allison would have a house full of teenagers. So I wore this t-shirt so they would think that I was cool. Now I have to change my shirt," said Lilith as she led Aunt Char over in the direction of the powder room. However, Lilith stopped short of going into the powder room door and closing the door like a normal person. Lilith was still in the entry hallway standing next to Char. This was not a private area, but an open area and someone could come around the corner and see everything at anytime.

Lilith was wearing a magenta colored t-shirt with a short corduroy jacket. As Lilith took off the jacket, Aunt Char was shocked by the front of Lilith shirt that said "FU". Could Lilith be any more inappropriate thought Char? This was Allison's Lutheran confirmation with all her elderly Lutheran relatives. Aunt Char's mouth dropped open as the thought of all her relatives seeing her crazy sister-in-law's shirt shocked her mind. Aunt Char's friends and family would never accept this sort of behavior.

Instead of Lilith going into the powder room to turn around her t-shirt, she decided to turn the t-shirt inside out in the hallway outside of the powder room. Keep in mind this is not an enclosed hallway but part of an open entry that opened between the living room and the front door. Being that Lilith had basically a flat-chest, she never wore a bra. As she turned her shirt inside out, she flashed Aunt Char her little boobies and there was no bra to hide them. Grace, standing off to the side could tell that Aunt Char was embarrassed, shocked, and see that her aunt couldn't speak or move for a couple of minutes.

Well, that was interesting thought Char as she made her way around a corner and over to the long dining room table. Let's hope no one else had to witness the peep show. It wasn't new for Grace to see her mother flashing her chest in public. Lilith was always shocking people with the view. This really was nothing new to Grace as she remembered back to the Fun Zone last month.

Grace really hadn't eaten before leaving home so she went where the food was being served. She spied the meat and cheese plate and made a dent from the selection. Grace looked at possible places to sit. At the long, light wood dining room table sat her Aunt Char and cousin Allison.

"You don't mind that I brought my friend Jake here? He likes coming to special celebrations. I try to tell my mother about Jake and she acts like she can't hear me. Whenever I try to tell my mother about Jake, she screams that there is no one there! My mother can't see him but he is there. Then my mother tells me that I'm a freaking schizophrenic," Grace said to Allison as she sat down at the table. **"My mother doesn't exactly say freaking but I can't use the word that my mother uses because then I get into trouble. When I use that word at school, I'm sent to the Principal's office."**

Everyone in the vicinity must have heard Grace because the room became quiet and everyone was staring at her. Everyone looked at Grace like she had three heads. Maybe they didn't know what schizophrenia meant thought Grace. Grace wasn't really sure she understood what that term meant. All Grace knew is that after she made that announcement everyone's mouth dropped open and none of the friends or family said anything for a while. Allison had seen this expression from many people when she would try to tell them about ghosts that she had seen. Allison wasn't sure if the guests were shocked about ghosts, schizophrenia or the "f-bomb".

"Ah, Grace, you should try the cake. It's really good," said Allison putting on her happy face and trying to change the subject. **"Come on, let's go get some. Bring your plate."**

Allison stood up and reached for Grace's hand. The two girls walked over to the Confirmation cake and cut a piece for Grace. As Allison looked back at the table full of Lutherans, she noticed all eyes on Grace and some pointing. Allison thought it would be best to bring Grace up to her room until the house cleared out.

CHAPTER 58

<u>June 10, 2012</u>

It was June 10, 2012 and school was over for the year. Lilith thought that she and Grace should do something fun together. Lilith had been up late the night before drinking and Grace was not really sure if her mother even went to sleep. Lilith looked tired but she wasn't working so it didn't matter. Scott, Grace's stepdad, was at work and Grace didn't have school for the rest of summer. Lilith decided that they would go to Valley Fun in Shakopee.

Lilith didn't look very good and she smelled even worse. The smell was a combination of alcohol, marijuana and whatever other drug Lilith could find. As Grace watched her mother drive, it was obvious that Lilith was having problems maneuvering the car. Lilith seemed to be all over the road.

By the time Lilith and Grace had reached the city of Jordan, Grace was praying that they would make it to the fun park in one piece. All of a sudden, there were flashing lights behind their car and a very loud siren. Lilith didn't notice right away and almost hit the car ahead of them.

"Oh shit, this is just great," cursed Lilith as she pulled to the side of the road.

"License and registration, please" said the police officer.

"Of course, officer," slurred Lilith trying to act innocent.

"Please step out of the car," demanded the officer **"You need to take a Breathalyzer test."**

"No problem" answered Lilith, **"I'm sure I'm fine."**

The numbers on the machine went higher and higher. Lilith started to sweat as she blew on the gadget. The officer's face blood pressure began to rise and his face reddened. He did not look happy about the reading.

"You are going to have to come with me. Social Services will be notified about your child. We are going down to the station," informed the police officer of Lilith's situation.

Lilith and Grace were placed in the back seat of the police car. Grace could feel the angry tension of her mother's temper. It made Grace extremely uncomfortable. As they approached the police station in Dakota County, Lilith was glaring at everything around her. When the car stopped, they were led out of the car. This is when Lilith's temper really exploded.

"This is all your fault Grace Francis! Why the hell do I even try to be nice to you? If I didn't try to take you to Valley Fun, I wouldn't be in this mess. Why the fuck did I ever have you? I wish you never were born. Mark my words Grace I am going to get you for this. Someday I am literally going to kill you!"

This event caused Mayhem County to put Grace in their child protection system. From this day forward, Lilith and the small girl would be in their focus.

CHAPTER 59

<u>August 8, 2012</u>

It was now the beginning of August and Nana was finally coming home from the nursing home located next to Sibley Park. Back in May, just before Allison's Confirmation party, Nana had developed neuropathy and was unable to walk. Nana felt bad for missing Olivia's party, but between cancer and neuropathy she had been feeling just awful. During this time, Nana had gone to a nursing home. Nana still wasn't able to walk, however, she was finally strong enough to come back to live in her home. She could only move around the house using a wheelchair. Nana had a small, flat plastic rectangular shape board that she used to move back and forth from wheelchair to lounge chair.

Uncle Jason and Aunt Char lived only a block away and could be there to help Nana in a few moments. Allison told Grace that they went over to Nana's house at least once a day, every day but usually it was more often. The teenage girl also told Grace that they couldn't even go out of town for a day in fear that something might happen to Nana being that she was just released from the nursing home. Twice a week, Nana had a physical therapist and occupational therapist nurses coming to her house.

When Lilith heard that Nana was back home, Lilith insisted that she was going to visit the elderly patient. Lilith had been waiting all summer for this opportunity. Nana had told Lilith over the phone that the nurses were there and Nana didn't have the energy for company. Regardless, Lilith was obsessed with visiting Nana.

At home, the only thing that Lilith could talk about was seeing her mother-in-law. Since Lilith heard from Aunt Char that she wasn't in the will any longer, she figured that she would take what she wanted whenever she visited the old woman. After being married to Luke for 13 years, and not the nine years she had reported to her psychologist, she was going to get what she felt was her fair share.

As Grace, Lilith and Scott pulled up in their white, square shaped car, they could see that Nana's lawn had been newly mowed. Scott, Lilith and Grace jumped out of the car. Lilith didn't bother to ring the doorbell and bolted right into the house.

As the three walked through Nana's backdoor, a woman that none of them knew walked in from the living room. She introduced herself as the physical therapist nurse. She questioned them and asked their relationship to Nana.

"Hi, my name is Alice and I am Sandy's physical therapist," said the lady to Lilith, Scott and Grace. **"Who are you?"**

"I'm Grace," said Grace as she walked past the woman and went to give Nana a hug.

"I'm Lilith and this is Scott," said Lilith agitated that Nana had nurses questioning her and her family. **"I was married to Sandy's youngest son Luke until he passed in 2009 because he was such a fucking, lazy drunk. Scott and I were married in March of this year in Las Vegas. Scott is the best thing that has ever happened to me."**

Nana was in her electronic reclining chair in the living room. Being that Nana was unable to walk, she spent the majority of time in the recliner in front of the television. Nana didn't move unless it was absolutely necessary. It had been several months since she was able to walk. As more time passed for Nana not being able to walk, the lower her chances that she would ever walk again. The physical therapist was working with Nana and was scheduled for only an hour, but the nurse could tell that Lilith was not fine. It was close to the end of the nurse's shift, but she chose to stay because Lilith was not acting normal and reeked of pot smell along with alcohol. Alice felt that Lilith may harm the elderly woman and didn't want to leave Nana alone with Grace's crazy mother.

"Hey Sandy! What the fuck is this pink gadget?" asked Lilith rolling Nana's pink walker from the dining room into the living room.

"Jason bought me that walker. The pink ribbon shows that we contributed to the breast cancer society," said Nana trying to be polite in front of her therapist and was embarrassed that Lilith had dropped the "f-bomb".

"Yeah, that's nice," remarked Lilith sarcastically as she walked downstairs not really caring about any contributions that didn't effect her wealth status.

Lilith was going around the basement while Scott distracted Nana and her therapist with small talk. When Lilith walked back upstairs Grace could see that her mother had something under her shirt.

Lilith went out the back door and stacked the postcards she had taken from downstairs and placed them in the box she brought in the car. She then went to the glove compartment and brought out some marijuana and a pipe. A pinch of marijuana was taken out of the baggie and placed in the pipe. She inhaled the substance and blew it out. Under the front passenger seat, there was another small bottle of vodka. She took a fast look around to make sure that no one would see her. Quickly, she placed the bottle to her lips and moved her head back so that feel the liquor could move quickly down her throat. The middle-aged woman wiped the excess off her lips with the lower part of her arm and wrist.

After taking a couple more hits of marijuana, she brought the paraphernalia into the house. Strategically Lilith opened a drawer in the kitchen island and left the drugs in the kitchen. This allowed for easy accessibility while staying in the house. This was Grace's mother's normal routine in hopes that no one would truly see how much alcohol or marijuana she used daily. Lilith again, walked back into the living room where the elderly woman sat.

"Hey Sandy, I would like to have some items to remember Jim. I'm going to go look in the bedroom," informed Grace's mother as she walked down the hallway towards the bedroom. Lilith wasn't going to waste time waiting for permission.

Lilith knew that Nana kept her jewelry in the top drawer of her bedroom dresser. She also observed that Nana had no rings on her fingers thus Lilith knew where she could find what she was looking for. As soon as she located the prize that she desired most, she looked at other items in the room. Lilith grabbed the closest item and returned to the living room.

So not to look guilty Lilith grabbed an old Boy Scout uniform that was hanging in the closet. Lilith didn't really want this item but she had to cover for the length of time she was in the room.

"Did you find anything of Jim's to remember him by?" asked Nana.

"Well, I found a couple of belts of Jim's," said Lilith **"Do you mind if I take them?"**

"No, that's fine," replied Nana.

"How about this Boy Scout item?" asked Lilith not really caring about the reply.

"I'm sorry Lilith but Tommy collects Boy Scout items. There must be something else that you can remember Jim by," said Nana surprised by Lilith's selection.

"Fuck you! Just fucking forget it," said Lilith as she threw down the Boy Scout shirt unto the floor and stormed out of the room. **"Come on Scot and Grace! We are going home! Fuck this place!"**

The back door slammed behind them. Lilith smiled as she left her mother-in-law's house and got into her automobile. What Lilith really desired to remember Jim by was already in her blue jean pocket. She knew Sandy would never allow her to have what she really wanted. Therefore, she must take what she wants.

Scott drove the car home as Lilith reached into her blue jean pocket and pulled out the two rings. Lilith's eyes sparkled as she viewed her victory trophies

"It will be months before those idiots discovered these rings are gone," laughed Lilith as she pulled out Nana's wedding ring and 50-year anniversary ring with a 1-carat-diamond for each 10 years married and for each member of the original Francis family member.

Lilith placed the rings on her wedding finger. As Lilith put on the rings, Grace could tell by her expression that her mother was thinking of Papa. A symbol of the one person that was always there for her, the one person that Lilith might actually love; Papa, and not that good-for-nothing, drunken, late husband of hers.

Lilith then extended her left arm and examined the rings on her vertically upright hand. A large smile came over Lilith's face. In Lilith's sick mind, she was married to Papa and she had the rings to prove it.

CHAPTER 60

August 9, 2012

Today is Uncle Jason and Aunt Char's 26th anniversary. However, they won't have time to celebrate their anniversary. Once again, Lilith will turn the focus of the day in another direction. After all, Lilith loves nothing more than causing chaos and being the center of attention.

By late morning, Nana was up and had eaten her breakfast. Important events were always listed on her calendar and Nana knew it was Char and Jason's anniversary. She wanted to give happy greetings to the couple and to know that Scott, Lilith and Grace had been over to visit her.

"Hello?" Char said as she answered the phone.

"Happy Anniversary Char!" exclaimed Nana.

"Thank you for remembering," said Char happily.

"Did I tell you that Lilith, Scott and Grace were over to visit me yesterday," said Nana. "Lilith was acting really strange. Every other word that Lilith said was "fuck this" and "fuck that". She would run into other rooms and come back smelling like pot. My physical therapist nurse stayed an extra hour thinking that Lilith could be dangerous. I told the nurse that Lilith was harmless. I couldn't believe that Lilith wanted a Boy Scout uniform to remember Jim by."

"Why in the world would she want a Boy Scout uniform? Lilith knows that Tommy is the one that collects Boy Scout items in the family," remarked Aunt Char perplexed by Lilith's request.

"I thought it was an odd request. Lilith was in my bedroom and wanted some belts and I let her take them," said Nana.

"That's fine, Jason already took from Jim's wardrobe what he wanted. Wait. Lilith was just going in your bedroom and wanted things to remember Jim? That's weird," said Aunt Char. **"Just a minute, isn't that where you keep all your jewelry? I don't want to sound mean but you might want to check to make sure all your jewelry is where it is suppose to be. I will let you go check and we can talk later."**

Nana became concerned about the possibility of jewelry being gone and went directly to the bedroom where she kept her jewelry. There was no one more organized than Nana. She kept great pride in knowing exactly where everything was in an exact location.

In the top drawer of Nana's mirrored chest of drawers, was the place Nana had always kept her jewelry. All of Nana's jewelry had small, plastic totes. Each tote had sections and each ring she owned had its own compartment.

She frantically started going through the top drawer in search of her wedding ring and anniversary ring. The plastic tote that she had always kept those special rings in was empty. Nana was so upset that she was shaking as she dialed Aunt Char to tell her of the missing items.

"Char, my wedding and anniversary rings are missing! I always put them in the same spot and they aren't there," exclaimed Nana panicked that her two most prized possessions were gone.

"I really hate to say it, but I wouldn't be surprised if Lilith took those rings. Remember when she told us that she loved Jim more than Luke? This may be her twisted way of making it true. Maybe she thinks if she wears the rings that she is married to Jim," said Aunt Char trying to analyze the logic of a crazy woman.

"Tell Jason to call Lilith. I want my rings back!" exclaimed Nana with panic in her voice. **"I want those rings back immediately. Tell her that we will call the police if we have to. I want my rings!"**

"I hope we can get them back Sandy," said Aunt Char not sure if Lilith would admit to taking the rings or if Lilith would bring them back.

Aunt Char told Uncle Jason about Lilith and her strange behavior. Now Nana's wedding and 50th Anniversary rings were missing. Uncle Jason was very angry as he dialed Lilith's phone number. He told Lilith that he was going to get the rings back today or he was calling the police. Lilith told Uncle Jason that she wanted to show Nana that his security was lax at the house. Uncle Jason told Lilith to bring the rings to his house immediately and not to go to Nana's house. However, Lilith only does what she wants to do and disrespects any authority.

Later in the day, Allison and her best friend, Heidi had decided to walk over to Nana's house and visit. The two young teenage girls were helping Nana with a few things around her house. As Allison was heating up some meatloaf for Nana, Lilith came busting into Nana's house. At that moment, Allison realized that she had forgotten to lock the door behind her and now, she wish she hadn't forgotten.

Lilith didn't count on anyone pegging the theft to her, at least, not this fast. Quickly, Lilith ran through the kitchen and into the living room where Nana sat. Not sure what Lilith would do next, Allison and Heidi ran into the living room to make sure Nana was not harmed. Putting on her best performance, Lilith started crying and tried to explain to Nana how she didn't take the rings and how Nana gave her the rings. That wasn't what happened insisted Nana. Reluctantly, Lilith gave Nana back her rings. However, Lilith did not go quietly. Lilith turned around and glared at Allison, Heidi and Nana with her dark, black, angry eyes.

"You think you're safe when you turn on your alarms and lock your doors. That's just cute. You

aren't safe," said Lilith in a very creepy tone. **"Ha! You'll never be safe."**

Lilith left the house and slammed the door behind her. The powerful pull to the door made Nana's house slightly shake resulting in a small picture to come off the wall. Allison picked up the small plaque and noticed a crack in the glass.

Never had the three women seen Lilith so threatening. The elderly woman and two teenagers were extremely scared and called Allison's dad. Allison explained the whole story about Lilith to her dad. Uncle Jason told the girls to stay there. He was going to call the police and have them meet them at Nana's house.

About a half an hour later, Officer Glen was at Nana's door. He knew Uncle Jason from when Uncle Jason was the Mayor of Mayhem. Nana, Allison and Heidi all told them their side of the story about Lilith.

Officer Glen laughs and says, **"I probably shouldn't be telling you this but this morning Lilith was at a coffee shop disturbing the peace. The owner called us but Lilith ran out of the shop and we are still trying to find her."**

They all just shook their heads. It's amazing how much drama one person could cause. Uncle Jason told Officer Glen that he just wanted to file a police report in case the crazy woman came back and killed them all.

Later in the day, Uncle Tommy called Nana to report that their friend Rachel had to call the police because

Lilith was out of control in her store. Someone had complained that she was smoking pot in the restrooms.

Some people love to be the center of attention. Some people just make drama follow them and some people are just plain mean. Anyway, that's how Grace described her mother to her friends at school. Lilith was all that...

CHAPTER 61

<u>August 30, 2012</u>

It's almost Labor Day and school will be starting soon. Grace noticed that Lilith is very, very crabby. Grace didn't usually study her mother's face but she couldn't help but stare at her this morning. Lilith is tired of everyone watching her every move. The middle-aged woman thought that in order for people not to recognize her that she needed to change her appearance, Lilith decided to dye her thick, beautiful, dark hair this really ugly, dirty blonde color. This was not one of Lilith's better decisions thought Grace.

She no longer looked like Grace's mother. Not really sure why Grace never noticed before, but her mother's teeth had turned this gross, light, pale green color. Perhaps because her mother was now talking non-stop it was easy to see her teeth and notice their condition. Lilith, as observed by Grace, looked absolutely horrible.

Grace should've known by the way her mother was moving that this would not be a good day for a road trip. When Lilith was trying to stand still she was still slightly swaying back and forth. Her eyes were somewhat droopy and her speech was non-stop but she didn't really make sense.

"Hey Mom, school is going to start soon. Can we go to Renaissance Fun sometime this weekend? We can wait until Scott can go with us but can we go?" asked Grace trying not to sound too demanding.

"Grace, we need to go to Renaissance Fun right now," said Lilith as she swayed on her feet.

"That's okay. We can go another day. Maybe we should wait for a day when Scott can take us," replied Grace knowing that her mother wasn't in the best physical shape that day.

"Scott has to work all weekend. Let's just go," suggested the impulsive mother.

Lilith never seemed to sleep, but still she seemed to be in constant motion. Gaining weight was always a concern for Lilith, but between never sleeping, not really eating and always moving, her mother was thin and she looked old and haggard. Her mother's face and body looked like skin right over the bones.

Being that school will be starting after Labor Day, Grace had just mentioned to her mother that she would like to go to Renaissance Fun outside of Jordan before school starts. Her mother acted like they had to go that very minute. Grace had just mentioned to her mother that she wanted to go in the next few days.

Lilith's speech was slurred as she told Grace to get into the car. Reluctantly, the little girl got into the back seat and buckled her seatbelt. Grace noticed that the car didn't really move in a straight line as Lilith drove down the street. They seemed to be going from side to side as the car crossed over the yellow and white lines. Lilith hit and took out one sign before they even left the Mayhem city limits.

Instead of looking where her mother was driving, Grace decided to get lost in a book. This seemed to work for a while. That was until Grace heard that all too familiar sound of a police car siren behind them.

"Oh shit, this is just fucking great! Just great! What the fuck is it this time?" screamed Lilith angrily as she pulled over to the side of the road.

"You were weaving back and forth in the lane. Some other drivers were concerned when they saw that you had a small child in your car. I would like your license and registration," said the officer firmly.

"Here!" yelled Lilith as she threw the information out the window and at the police officer.

The expired license and the registration flew in two different directions onto the asphalt surface. The officer bent over and picked up the items. A glare from the officer was tossed at Lilith's direction before and after picking the information up off the road.

"Please step out of your car. Have you been drinking today?" asked the officer not expecting an honest answer.

"Why the fuck do you care?" asked Lilith angrily not able to keep her balance.

"That's it. You are coming down to the station with me," said the officer as he led Lilith and Grace into his car.

"Well, Grace, this is all your fault. You know what? I never wanted a child! I wish you never were born," yelled Grace's mother as they rode to the police station in the backseat of the police car. **"I should've taken you to a pond and held you down when you were born! It would've been so easy to have an accidental drowning had I just done that! I should've just drowned you!"**

Lilith continued to yell at Grace, but over time, the little girl had acquired the art of blocking out her mother's continuous yakking. Grace overheard many people say that once Lilith started talking there was no getting a word in edge wise. Besides, anything Lilith said right now was not going to be very nice so why listen thought Grace.

Eventually, Lilith and Grace were allowed to go home. However, Scott had to go to the police station to get them out of jail. But Lilith still hadn't cool down. By the time they got home forty-five minutes later, Lilith was still extremely angry.

Lilith was still scalding angry that she went to the police station because Grace wanted to go to Renaissance Fun. Lilith continued to scream how she wished her daughter had never been born and by this point, Grace was agreeing with her. Lilith was repeating the same thing over and over again. However, by the time they get home, Lilith went really ballistic.

Lilith decides to run into Grace's room and the crazy, out-of-control woman starts throwing all of the child's things out the back door of her room. Lilith threw out all Grace's dolls, her stuffed animals, some of her clothes. When Lilith tired of that, she went downstairs to the McCoy Smiley Face Cookie jar where Luke's ashes were kept. Lilith took Luke's ashes and opened up the front door. Lilith removed the yellow, pointed lid and turned the cookie jar upside down.

"See! There aren't any drugs in here! See, I told you that I didn't have any fucking drugs," screamed Lilith as she dumped Luke's ashes out onto the front steps. **"I hate you fucking pigs! Why the hell don't you mind your own business! Go fuck yourselves!!"**

By this time, Martha had seen the items flying from the 2nd floor door and heard Lilith yelling obscenities. Once again, Martha had heard and then seen her neighbor go absolutely crazy. Martha feeling that things were totally out of control at her neighbor's house, besides fearing about Grace's safety, decided to call the police. A few minutes later, two police cars had pulled up in front of the house and observed child's things thrown all over the yard. There were also Luke's ashes on the front step. Police had visited Lilith's house so many times that they knew Lilith by her first name. Lilith continued to scream in the house so loudly that the police could hear her as they walked up to the door.

"Lilith (knock, knock) Lilith, we know that you are home. Come on Lilith. Please come to the door," said one of the two policemen at the door.

"See! I'm not doing any drugs," screamed Lilith as she opened the door and showed the two officers the empty urn. **"See! See! There aren't any fucking drugs here!"**

"Lilith, we received a couple of complaints from your neighbors. You are disturbing the peace and using profanity isn't helping your case. You are coming down to the police station with us," said the other police officer. **"Grab your identification and pack an over night bag with all your medications. We aren't sure when you will be able to come home."**

Grace stayed back with her stepdad Scott at the house. After Lilith left the house, Martha came over with a broom and dustpan and swept up Luke's ashes as best she could. She then gave Scott the ashes she could retrieve. It was quiet at the house after Lilith left. An eerie calm from a burnt out shell remained from the hell that Lilith had raised. After this, nothing would be the same...

CHAPTER 62

September 19, 2012

It was a couple of weeks before Lilith was allowed to come home. After a week at the Mayhem hospital psychiatric ward, Lilith was staying at the St. Peter Psychiatric Hospital for a couple more weeks.

Lilith finally was released from St. Peter facility on Wednesday, September 19, 2012. Lilith and Scott were able to pick Grace up after school but were escorted by her social worker, Ms. Pooper as Lilith called her. Ms. Pooper had shorter blonde hair and new glasses since the last time that Grace had seen her. As Grace looked at the social worker, she figured Ms. Pooper was never married. She was strict and to the rules in everything that she did. Grace couldn't imagine that Ms. Pooper was ever fun.

"I'm sorry Lilith, but Grace cannot come back home to live with you. You are extremely unstable and you have had too many moving violations and jail time. The last DUI and endangering your child was the

last strike. Grace will be awarded to the state and we shall find her a new, more stable family," said the social worker.

Grace could tell her mother was not happy with this news. Lilith excused herself to go to the bathroom. The defeated woman disappeared upstairs to use the bathroom and to get a glass of water to take her medications. As she reached for the water glass on the basin, the water automatically turned on without Lilith placing her hand on the water knobs. A little shocked that the water had turned on by itself, Lilith placed her glass under the running faucet and filled the glass.

Lilith carried the glass of water into her bedroom. She walked over to the bedroom closet where she hid alcohol, drugs and other unhealthy habits. As Lilith grabbed out her reserve of vodka, she noticed the familiar black mist in the corner of the room's ceiling. Lilith dropped a handful of painkillers into her mouth and washed them down with her vodka.

The dark mist moved closer to Lilith so as to be able to whisper in Lilith's ears. As Lilith moved to get away from the large mass, it continued to follow her movement and wrap around her like a thick, unwanted blanket.

"Lilith, you are losing. You are nothing but a loser bitch! If you lose Grace, you will lose everything," laughed an image of what appeared to be a larger than life Luke wearing a navy blue plaid shirt. **"Hey Lilith, why don't you take all those pills and drink that whole bottle of vodka. When you lose Grace, you lose**

all the inheritance money. Isn't that what you live for Lilith? Money!!! You are such a stupid bitch! You are so going to lose everything!!"

Lilith drank more vodka and swallowed more pills. The image of Luke watched as the defeated woman with badly dishwater-colored hair and green teeth consumed more and more of the deadly combination.

"You are such a failure Lilith. You will probably fail to kill yourself again! Can't you do anything right?" continued the image that Lilith saw as Luke. **"Are you going to fail again or are you going to succeed this time? What is it going to be Lilith? Succeed or fail?"**

Lilith emptied the remaining pill bottles in her hand. She cupped her hand and placed all the drugs into her mouth and swallowed. Slowly, Lilith stood up and used the walls around her to steady her walk. Lilith had to use the handrail to balance herself down the stairs. After a few minutes, Lilith returned to the group downstairs discussing the issues of Grace's future. Lilith smelled funny and her speech became slurred. Lilith was finding it difficult to stay awake. Everyone in the room knew what Lilith had left the room to do. However, no one was sure which drug or how much Lilith used to ease the pain.

The decision to place Grace in a mental facility was final and the local county controlled the situation. The social worker had to get Grace to the institution by 7:00 p.m. so that she could get dinner before bedtime. By the time Grace had to leave, Lilith was fighting to stay awake. Grace's mother never took bad news well but tonight Grace felt Lilith's response was worse than usual. Grace had seen her mother in drug-induced states before but this one was the by far the worst yet but similar to Lilith's birthday a few years prior. Lilith made no sense when she talked and Lilith's eyes kept closing.

When Grace arrived to the institution, the social worker called Lilith's house to tell her parents that Grace had made it to the destination and was fine. Scott answered the phone and informed Grace that her mother had gone to bed after she had left.

Lilith was sad about the decision made by the county. Grace's mother never took defeat very well and this time she was loosing a lot. For one thing, Lilith was not in any wills. Lilith wasn't in Luke's family will and she wasn't in her grandfather's will now that Lilith was loosing custody of Grace. There would not be any grand inheritance coming from anywhere. At this moment, Lilith felt that she had lost everything.

Around midnight, Grace's stepfather Scott checked on Lilith. Scott could tell by the empty bottle on the side table that Lilith had drank a liter of Vodka and taken the pills. He felt her hands to see if she was cold yet. Lilith's body jerked forward and had thrown up something that looked like coffee grounds. Scott watched as the puke hit the side of the bed.

"That was really disgusting Lilith. Man, that shit smells. Aren't you fucking dead yet?" asked Scott as he looked impatiently at his watch. **"How long is this going to take? You have always been such a mess. Can you just get this over with?"**

Scott walked out of the bedroom and went downstairs to watch television. He went into the kitchen and threw a bag of popcorn into the microwave. He munched on the popcorn and laughed at the comedy show he was watching. By 2:00 a.m., Scott figured that Lilith must be gone and returned to the bedroom.

As Scott walked back into the bedroom, Lilith looked at Scott with sad eyes. By this time, Lilith was unable to speak but she realized what was going on around her. In less than an hour later, Lilith had that 1,000-mile stare when Scott tried to ask her questions. Lilith was finally stone cold dead.

"It's about fucking time," said Scott in disgust. **"Now that you are dead, my bitch of a wife, I am going to adopt Grace and get your rich grandparent's money. Best money scheme ever. Thanks bitch!"**

Scott smiled about his future wealth and walked toward his own stash of whiskey in the bottom drawer of his chest of drawers. As he brought out the bottle, he unscrewed the cap and took a large gulp. He than went to the phone and called the authorities about his wife's suicide.

Scott than went to his wife's phone for family contacts and texted all of them that Lilith had died. By that time it was 2:50 a.m. and Scott told everyone that Lilith was at rest. But was Lilith really at rest?

In the corner of the master bedroom, stood an enormously large, and even darker black mist of Lilith watching Scott. Lilith had been in pain and was angry but now only the anger remained. Had her second husband ever loved her or was it all about the money? Lilith just watched with stern resentment. Lilith would not let this rest...

CHAPTER 63

September 20, 2016

Today is Allison's sixteenth birthday. The family didn't tell Grace right away that her mother had died in the early hours of her cousin Allison's birthday. It was strange but her mother died approximately the same time that Allison was born sixteen years earlier at 2:16 a.m. The last time Grace's mother tried to kill herself it was on her own birthday two years ago. Lilith always had a thing about birthdays. Grace wasn't sure if her mother had planned to kill herself on her cousin's birthday or it was just a reaction to the events of the night before. Perhaps it was the combination of the two.

Allison told Grace that her stepdad had called a mutual friend Daryl who was also Tommy's friend. It was Daryl that had text Allison to have her mother Char call him. Daryl told Aunt Char that Lilith had died at approximately 2:30 a.m. on Allison's birthday.

Later that morning, Uncle Jason called Scott to get the details of what had happened to Lilith. It was almost the same story as on her birthday two years ago. Lilith had taken a bottle of alcohol with along with a plethora of painkillers and sleeping pills. These were Lilith's favorite choice of escape in a deadly combination.

Aunt Char contacted Kari who was a mutual friend and a fantastic hair designer. Lilith and Kari were very close until the day Lilith ruined the friendship. Lilith had gone down to Kari's work place and started smoking pot in the salon's bathroom. Aunt Char told Kari about Lilith's death before she broke the news to Nana. Kari suggested that Aunt Char not to tell of Lilith's death to Nana until after Allison's birthday. Kari was right as always.

When Aunt Char and Uncle Jason brought Nana lunch, they told Nana of the bad news. Instantly, Nana burst into tears. As Nana cried it was difficult to understand what she was stating. After repeating herself a few times Nana stated, **"Now Grace won't have either parent."**

The news of Lilith's death overshadowed Allison's birthday. Nana didn't feel like celebrating. She could only weep for her youngest grandchild being without either parent. You don't hear the word often but Grace was now an orphan.

The question on everyone's mind is why Scott didn't take Lilith to the hospital at that point, no one knows. Grace's stepfather wasn't the brightest bulb and maybe he didn't understand how sick Lilith was at the moment. Perhaps, he also realized that the quick money schemes were over and Lilith was very, very sick…

Although there was the bad news of Lilith's passing, Allison told Grace that she had a good birthday. Her parents gave her a fancy new bed that she had been wanting so she was super-happy. Grace was glad that her favorite cousin had a nice birthday.

Allison also told Grace that she went to dinner with her boyfriend and best friend Heidi at the Pasta Garden. Later they stopped at Nana's house. They saw a family of eight wild turkey and 3 deer in the cemetery behind Nana's house. Allison summarized her special day by saying that the whole day seemed surreal to her.

CHAPTER 64

Lilith (Bobble) Frey, age 39, of Mayhem, is at peace on Thursday, September 20, 2012 at her home. A celebration of Lilith's life will be held at Mayhem Mortuary.

Lilith was born on November 27, 1972 in Bloomington, MN to Hank and Susan Bobble. She grew up in Bloomington, MN when it was mainly country and not just the Mall of America. Lilith and her dad spent weekends discovering the beauty of the woods and hills. Lilith and her mom loved to talk for hours about Lilith's day at school. While at Bloomington High School, Lilith became a major player in Theatre and Choir. Her love for theatre took her to Mayhem, where she participated in numerous performances. Lilith married Luke Francis and they both enjoyed the antique business along with his parents and family, until Luke passed away in 2009. In 2003, they were blessed with the birth of their daughter, Grace; who will always be the joy and light of their lives. Lilith fell in love with and Lilith married

Scott Frey. They married in March of 2012. Their greatest joy as a family was their visits to Valley Fun. Lilith enjoyed her 12-year career at Lighting World.

Lilith is survived in life by her loving daughter Grace; her dear husband, Scott; parents, Hank and Susan Bobble; sister, Liza Helen. Lilith was preceded in death by her first husband Luke Francis and Grandmother Judy Grace.

It was obvious to friends and family that knew Luke that this obituary was written by Scott and Lilith's parents. Luke was barely mentioned and Nana was very upset that she hadn't been listed as Grace's grandmother. Nana said that the part of Lilith's obituary visiting with her mother was a blatant lie but waited until after the funeral to vent her anger.

Allison and Grace welcomed people to the funeral. Allison was wearing her mother's black dress. Grace was dressed in a red taffeta dress with a tulle skirt that had millions of sparkles and of course, Grace was wearing Dorothy shoes with a sparkling red headband.

Grandma Susan Bobble didn't attend Lilith's funeral and that disgusted Grace. What kind of mother doesn't attend her own daughter's funeral? After all, Grace's grandmother never wanted a child and now she had her wish. On the other hand, Grandpa Bobble would attempt to keep his composure during the funeral and then all of a sudden break down in tears. Lilith's biological sister Liza had a migraine but showed strength and managed to keep socializing with others when it would have been easier to hide away.

Being in a wheelchair, Nana had to be placed on the outside of an aisle. There was room in the second aisle. Char and Jason sat next to Nana. Allison joined Grace in the front row. Tommy and Prudence sat directly behind Char and Nana. All the social workers and Lilith's co-workers attended the funeral.

Before the ceremony began, there were pictures of Lilith from various parts of her life flashed on the screen in the front of the room. All of a sudden, sitting behind Nana and Char, Prudence lets out this loud, obnoxious wail in the room. Both Nana and Char turn around at Prudence and scowled. What is Prudence's problem they wondered? Nana concluded that it was just a show for the social workers and Lilith's family. After all, Prudence never cried at Luke or Papa's funeral.

When the funeral started, slides of Lilith's life stopped. Aunt Liza stepped up to the podium and did most of the talking. This is what Lilith's biological sister said:

Forever Good Bye To My Sister Lilith

"My heart aches more than words can say. Each day I think about how you were so amazing, and creative. Those of us who really knew you, the Lilith that made us laugh. Thank you for placing Grace in my life. I thank you for her. I thank you for being my little sister. I miss you so very, very much

The moments I have from the last year are when you hugged me so very tight after speaking to me at Grandma Grace's 85th birthday party. It was like you knew that it would be the last time that you would ever see me. Grace ran up to me and hugged me. She let me know that she was able to do home school because she was going too fast in school. You and I had the same issues and struggled in going slow with a normal class...

In March while in Las Vegas, you texted me so excited to be Lilith Frey. You were so excited for Grace to have another parent in her life. You were just so happy. Although I had not met Scott, I knew he loved you and you loved him.

August 8, 2012 was our last conversations when you were home in Mayhem. We talked for over an hour. I just listened. You were talking a million miles a minute. It was as if you needed me to hear everything going on in your life. You sounded so happy.

When you left me a voice mail on August 10, 2012, you talked but I just didn't know how to respond to your message. You were having problems with Luke's family. I was worried about you and kept saying how much I love you and how much the family loved you. The last time I heard you speak, Lilith, you sounded so sad. I kept thinking was, "I miss my sister. Please get healthy Lilith. I miss you."

Then on Thursday, September 20 at 8:55 a.m. I received a phone call from my biological father Hank while I was getting off the bus in front of the library at Ohio State University. I learned that at around 2:30 a.m. earlier that day that you, Lilith, my sister, had passed away. I collapsed on the ground, crying my eyes out. I had lost my sister. I lost you.

Why do I share this story? Perhaps it is to reflect upon my life on knowing my sister Lilith was a gift to me and I miss her so very much..."

As Liza began to sob uncontrollably, Grace ran to join her aunt in the front of the small chapel. While hugging her Aunt Liza, Grace looked around the room to see who was present and ready to listen. When the room quieted down, Grace looked toward the crowd and with a tear in her eye she began to speak.

"I know my mother did a lot of bad things but she also did a lot of good things. So please just try to remember the good for me," Grace said with a tear running down her check. Jake stood next to Grace and clutched her shoulder for comfort.

CHAPTER 65

<u>**September 24, 2012**</u>

After Lilith's funeral, it was a mad dash to the county by all of Grace's family members to become the nine-year-old girl's guardian. Scott Frey, Grace's stepfather, thought he was the very first to apply for the adoption of Grace. Stories of Grace's relative's wealth was all Scott needed to know that he would be willing to fight for the child.

Scott drove into the parking lot of the new county court building. He walked briskly from a nearby parking stall into the limestone building. The 40-year-old man had been in the building for various reasons but this time he was hoping it would make him rich. There was an open counter for information.

"I would like to adopt my stepdaughter. Could you tell me where I need to go?" asked the slightly sweating Scott.

"Up stairs, room 215 on your left," informed the heavy-set man at the information counter.

Without saying thank you, Scott turned looking for the elevators. Scott was much too excited to be polite. Behind him, was a set of two elevators, Scott went into the first elevator to open. He pushed floor two and the elevator lifted him to the next floor. Almost in front of him, was room 215, making Scott feel that this was a sign that Grace should be his.

"Hello, my name is Scott Frey. My wife, Lilith Frey passed a few days ago and I would like to adopt her daughter Grace Francis," said Scott as he had practiced his monologue verbatim on the drive that morning in order to sound convincing.

The woman behind the counter thought for a moment before responding but said, **"Well, here are the forms you will need but I have to tell you, there are other family members that are interested in Grace. A couple days ago, her aunt and uncle from Ely, Minnesota were here stating an interest. It's hard to know which way the court will settle on a permanent home for the small child."**

"Well, I don't know much about the aunt and uncle from Ely, but I do know that Lilith had told me that Jason Francis from here in Mayhem is a pedophile. I would recommend that you not let him become involve in the adoption proceeding," said Scott slyly knowing that Jason and Char would be his stiffest competition by being in the Mayhem area.

Scott figured that the county would want to keep everything as normal as possible for Grace like school and friends. Scott did not like competition and this was his way of squishing it before it even began.

"I will make note of your comment but again, you will need a lawyer to go through court proceedings," suggested the social worker.

The response from the woman did not make Scott happy. Lawyers cost money and Scott wanted money but didn't want to spend it on this adoption. For some reason, Scott thought that adopting Grace would be a slam-dunk for him being her stepfather and Grace had already lived with him even though it had only been 6 months since Scott married Lilith. However, due to the various problems the law had with both him and Lilith, this feat would be anything but easily.

"I will fill out the paperwork and bring it back later," said Scott.

With a grimace on Scott's face, he slid the paperwork off the counter and took the county's pen with him. Again, Scott did not thank the county workers for the information or their time.

A few hours later, meeting with another social worker, was Lilith's father and sister Liza. They had stayed at a local hotel for the night after the funeral.

"What do you mean Grace cannot come immediately home with us?" asked Mr. Hank Bobble. **"Lilith was our daughter and we are her family. Grace is my granddaughter and I think she needs to be with us."**

"I'm sorry sir, but other family members have stepped forward as wanting to be Grace's guardian. Grace's stepfather, aunt and uncle have also expressed an interest in Grace," said the county social worker. "There is going to have to be an agreement between all family members over Grace's final home. In the meantime, Grace will be staying at the local mental health facility until a permanent home is decided."

"Is there anything I can do in order to speed up the process?" asked Hank. "I really don't want Grace to be spending so much time in such a depressing facility."

"Until all eligible family members agree on Grace's future, there is nothing I can do," said the social worker.

"Fine, I will fill out the paperwork," said Hank Bobble disappointed that he would have to go through so much red tape to gain custody of his granddaughter.

"Also, like I told her stepfather earlier today that you need a lawyer for the court proceedings," informed the social worker.

"Okay, I will get a lawyer," said Hank as he turned to Liza with the paperwork and rolled his eyes. "Come on Liza. We can always mail these forms back. Let's go home."

Hank and Liza grabbed their coats and left. It was a long, quiet ride back to Bloomington.

CHAPTER 66

October 1, 2012

Since Lilith's funeral, Scott found that he couldn't stop working on the house. The boxes that lined the walls of Lilith's home were slowly disappearing. He was storing all the boxes in the various rooms in the dirt floor basement of Grace's house. Scott wanted to remove all memories he had of his short marriage and start his own life.

It had only been seven months since Scott and Lilith had married in Las Vegas. Now once again, he was single. His first plan was to make this house into a man cave. His first purchase since the funeral was an electronic dartboard which could easily mount anywhere with at least seven feet in front of it. He had bought the dartboard that morning and kept it in its plastic bag in the sunroom in the front of the house.

Scott walked around the entire house looking for the perfect place to play darts and be close to the refrigerator for a beer. He finally decided that the best place would be the wall at the end of the stair. Scott went downstairs to the basement where he kept his tools. He found a couple of large nails and hammer and ran back up stairs through the kitchen. Scott put down the hammer and nails at the end of the wall at the bottom of the main landing.

After Scott marked the wall to place the nail, he reached down for the hammer and nail that he had placed next to his feet on the living room floor. Trying not to loose his sight on the wall of the nail marking, he felt around the floor for the nails and hammer. After a couple of minutes of not feeling the items, he finally looked down and noticed that the hammer and nails were gone.

Was he losing his mind? He just put down the hammer and nails and now both items were gone. The nails may have been kicked away but the hammer he would have felt hitting that. In confusion, he began looking around the entire room. Did he place the hammer on a ledge or in another room?

Scott began retracing his steps from the basement. He walked in the kitchen and looked on all the counters. No hammer or nails so he continued to the basement stairs. As he was walking down the stairs, he noticed that ahead of him on the workbench was the hammer and nails that he was sure that he had brought upstairs. Scott squinted as he stared at the items and shook his head. He didn't know what was going on.

Briskly, Scott walked over to the tools and grabbed them. He wanted to make sure that the hammer and nail made it upstairs this time. Again, Scott had to relocate the mark for the nail. Had it disappeared? Now he had to find the pencil and measuring tape and remark the wall. Now where had the measuring tape go?

This five-minute job was turning into an all day event. He normally kept a measuring tape in a junk drawer in the kitchen. For some reason, there was no tape to be found in the drawer. So he had to go back to the basement and find another to take its place.

Once he had marked the wall and pound in the nail, Scott had the issue of finding the dartboard. He could swear that he had left it in the sunroom but now it was nowhere to be found. Scott decided to look in all the closets. No dartboard was found in any closet.

Scott looked down at his watch and noticed that he had to be to work in an hour. The dartboard would have to wait. Scott had to get dressed and drive to work. The only thing Scott had accomplished was a nail in the wall.

Scott walked upstairs and got into the shower. As he was washing his hair, he noticed scratching coming from the wall. Scott turned off the water to better hear the scratching. When he turned off the water, there was no noise. Had he imagined it all or was there an animal in the wall? This was an old house and it would be easy for a squirrel or some other creature to find its way into a small hole in the façade of the century old house.

As soon as Scott turned back on the water, the scratching sound continued. He decided to try to ignore the noise and continue getting ready for work. As he was rinsing off in the shower, there appeared a large, black shadow that swallowed all the light from where he stood. Scott quickly shut off the water. As he turned around to get out of the shower, coming at him was a dark mass in the corner of the tub with large sharp claws. The claw came at him and took a quick swipe leaving behind three deep scratches on his chest. The frightening sight caused Scott to fall back towards the wall causing him to hit his head and knocked him out. A few drops of water continued to drip out of the shower as the blood washed down the drain.

When Scott woke from the incident, he looked down to find three long, large slash marks on his abdomen. He also felt a large bump on the back of head where he hit the wall. He slowly got off the base of the tub and grabbed a towel to dry off. The towel soaked up a lot of blood from the cuts.

On the vanity was his watch, as he looked down he noticed that he was already late for work. He must have been out for almost an hour. Scott got dressed and headed out the front door. Again, he looked at his watch and he shook his head. Scott noticed how crappy the day was starting out and hoped the worst was behind him.

Luckily, the day at work was better than his morning at home. As he was driving back home, all he could think about was putting up his dartboard and playing darts. Concentrating on a target relaxed Scott and he enjoyed the challenge of getting a hat trick.

Scott walked through the front door of his home; he placed the mail on the side table next to the door with the other bills. He walked directly ahead and turned his head to his left to look at the nail that would be covered with the dartboard. Where was the nail? The wall was perfectly smooth like he had never placed a nail in it. Just great thought Scott. Now he had accomplished absolutely nothing that day...

CHAPTER 67

<u>**November 17, 2012**</u>

A few weeks later, Scott still hadn't been able to locate his dartboard. In disgust he felt that when the karma of the world wanted him to play, he would find the long-lost dartboard. Scott's day improved when the phone rang.

"Hello, Scott? This is Hank Bobble," said the voice on the other end of the phone.

"Well, hi Hank. How are you and Susan?" asked Scott not really caring of the reply but asked out of courtesy.

"We're fine but I wanted to call you and tell you of another death in the family. Grace's great grandfather Harmon passed away yesterday. His funeral is scheduled for this Tuesday, November 20 at 11:00 a.m. If you meet us at our house at 10:00 a.m., pick up Grace first and we can go from there. Let's hope that this is the end of family deaths for a

while," concluded Hank tired of putting on his black funeral suit.

On the other end of the phone, Scott caught himself smiling. Realizing that Hank may be able to sense his happiness Scott quickly wiped the smirk off his face.

"That's a shame that Harmon is gone. Of course, I will pick up Grace and meet you on Tuesday for his funeral," agreed Scott.

"Thank you Scott. Susan and I will see you Tuesday morning. Have a good trip," said Hank as he hung up the phone.

Scott was smiling and squinting as he was looking to his left, he hung up the phone. How ironic that less than a month ago, Lilith had died and she lived only to see her grandfather's fortune. Scott was so close to the family fortune and now, the only thing he had to do for the money was to win the adoption of his stepdaughter.

CHAPTER 68

November 22, 2012

It was bright, sunny autumn morning with a slight breeze in Mayhem, Minnesota. The digital clock on his dresser said it was 5:30 a.m. It would be another two hours before his alarm clock was scheduled to go off. Scott had a difficult time sleeping the night before the funeral. There were dreams of his driving a gold limousine and drinking fluted glasses of champagne surrounded by drop-dead gorgeous woman. Today was the first day in a long time that Scott woke up with a smile on his face.

Scott was in such a great mood that he was early picking up Grace. However, he had to wait 15 minutes for the staff at the mental institution to get Grace ready for her great grandfather's funeral. Grace appeared in a dark green and black plaid dress with white nylons and shiny black patent leather shoes. Her deep blue eyes looked up at her stepfather as she quickly ran to slug Scott in the stomach.

"**Uh, good one Grace. I've missed those powerful punches of yours,**" said Scott as he quickly covered his stomach over a possible repeat from his little gold mine and her robust slugs. "**They are amazingly brutal for your size.**"

"**Ha-ha, good one Scott,**" laughed Grace not believing that a little person as herself could do any harm to a big guy like her stepdad. "**That didn't hurt!'**"

"**Come on Grace. We don't want to be late to your grandparents. They would never forgive me,**" said Scott under his breath and rolling his eyes.

"**Sure!**" said Grace as she ran to the front door of the institution and out to the parking lot. Grace immediately recognized her late mother's white car that still had a few dents from Lilith's accidents. "**Come on Jake, we're going to great grandfather's funeral.**"

Jake, Grace's forever imaginary friend got in the back seat with Grace. Jake enjoyed out of town trips with Grace and her family. Jake enjoyed funerals as he would meet the newly dead as they watched their own funeral. Besides, great-grandfather Harman was always nice to Grace and Jake liked him.

"**Nice punch to your stepdad Grace. You really got him good,**" whispered Jake to Grace and laughing. "**Next time, really make him feel it.**"

Grace laughed a little in the backseat. Scott heard the giggle and looked in the rearview mirror to see what was going on.

"**Is everything alright Grace?**" asked Scott wondering what all the giggling was about.

"**I'm fine,**" said Grace "**Jake just said something funny.**"

Scott knew that Grace saw ghosts or something but he didn't believe in such nonsense. Instead of trying to understand Grace's visions of the afterlife, Scott chose to ignore the situation. In Scott's defense, he had little to no imagination so the thought of something greater than what he perceived as real meant nothing to him.

"**So Grace, how is your stay at the institution going?**" asked Scott trying to change the subject away from the voices that Grace would hear.

"**Well, the other day Jake and I had everyone looking for us. Miss Reagan was so worried. She said that even the police were looking for me,**" said Grace as if it were funny.

"**Why did you hide from everybody?**" questioned Scott.

"**I'm tired of everyone asking me questions and giving me medicine. I just want to be left alone,**" confessed Grace.

Realizing that Scott was questioning the child who was tired of being asked questions stopped all conversation. He turned up the radio until they approached the Twin Cities area.

Meanwhile in the back seat, Grace played hangman in the back seat with Jake. Higher vehicles like a SUV or pick-up truck that passed by Scott's car could see Grace with a pad of paper on her lap and a pencil moving on its own. Once in a while, Grace would look up and see a terrified driver or passenger person in the car next to them. Seeing the scared faces made Grace laugh...

CHAPTER 69

November 30, 2012

Ever since Harmon Grace's funeral, Scott was thinking of possible ways to have a better opportunity of adopting Grace. The one thing he had going for him was that Grace liked him and he was young enough to easily care for Grace. Now Scott was thinking that getting married would further help him.

Prior to marrying Lilith, Scott had dated a woman named Vicki. The woman was a few years younger than Scott but the two had dated off and on for years. They went to high school together in Mayhem. Scott had convinced himself in that moment that it was destiny that they should tie the knot and now he had over a million reasons.

Vicki looked similar to Lilith with her long, brown hair. However, Vicki didn't have as large or crazy of eyes as Lilith. As far as body weight, Vicki was also a little heavier.

"Hello Vicki, this is Scott Frey. I was wondering if you were busy tonight. We could go out for cocktails if you are free?" said Scott hoping for a positive response.

"Scott Frey? Are you kidding me? It's been over a year since I last heard from you. Why are you calling?" responded Vicki sick of Scott's past excuses.

"I know it's been a while but we had so many good times. I thought you should know that I just got in a large amount of dope that you will really enjoy. Besides, I've really missed you Vicki. I thought maybe you should just move in with me and we can pick up from where we left off," suggested Scott.

"You want me to move in with you?" asked Vicki questioning their situation and laughing. "You're married."

"Yes, I was married but I'm sad to say that I'm now a widow. Lilith died last month. I'm in this big house and it's so lonely. I would really love you to move in," said Scott. "Lilith left behind a ten year old girl who I know you will love. After I adopt Lilith's daughter Grace, we will have an instant family. Not only that, we will have enough money to take oversea vacations whenever we want."

"Well, I suppose we could try it. I'll have to call one of my siblings to take care of my mother if I move in with you," thought Vicki.

"Great. I'll be over tomorrow to help move your stuff to my place. You better get packing," said Scott as he hung up the phone.

Scott's smile couldn't get any bigger as he hung up the phone. Everything seemed to be falling into place and he couldn't be any happier. After Lilith's death, bills for all the hospitals and fines had left him in the red. Now, he would not only be in the black, but also have a surplus. It was about time that his marriage to Lilith finally was paying off.

CHAPTER 70

December 1, 2012

Because of the negative information that Scott gave Grace's social worker, Jason and Char were not initially included in the process of Grace's adoption. Besides, Char had her hands full taking care of Nana. The only knowledge Jason and Char had about Grace's adoption was the info that Scott wanted the couple to know. Then, Jason and Char would inform Nana.

"Hey Jason, this is Scott. I thought I'd give you a call to let you know the progress of Grace's guardian," said Scott. **"Right now, besides myself, Lilith's parents and your brother and sister-in-law are competing for Grace. I've been told that the county would prefer a two-parent home to a single parent situation."**

"Well, we know that Grace really likes you. Char and I are hoping that you get Grace and that she remains at the same school. We think the best thing for Grace is keeping in her routine," said Jason thinking that he was doing the right thing.

"I wish I could give you better news about Grace staying in town but it's not looking good for me," said Scott hoping to get emotional support from Lilith's brother and sister-in-law. **"If you want to keep Grace in Mayhem, I think that you and Char might want to get into the process."**

Scott didn't really want them to get into the guardianship battle to win. He was using Jason and Char as a shield for a plan he may have to use if he began to lose in the process. Besides, Scott could use the rumor of Jason being a pedophile to deflect all negative information the county may have on him.

Jason gave Nana an update on Grace's situation. Tommy was slowly working his way onto Nana's unfavorable shit list. Nana was appalled that Tommy and Prudence had applied for Grace's adoption without telling her. Also, in the two and half years since Papa's death, Nana had only seen Tommy and Mathew twice and that was at Papa and Lilith's funeral. Otherwise, Tommy never bothered to call or visit Nana. It was at this point, that Nana worried that Tommy and Prudence might get Grace and she would never see her little granddaughter again either.

"Jason, you and Char have got to get Grace. I would even prefer that Hank and Susan get Grace before Tommy and Prudence," fretted Nana. **"At least with Hank and Susan, I'm sure I would see Grace once in awhile. Grace's grandparents only live over an hour away but with Tommy and Prudence they're over 3 hours away. We can't let Grace move so far away that**

I never see her. It's bad enough that I see Mathew only at funerals. I can't let them have Grace too."

"Well, we can see what we can do," said Char not sure if she wanted to take on another responsibility of a young child. "I would think living in the same town and being able to get Grace to the same school would help us to gain custody. All we can do is try."

"I will call Scott and ask him who I should contact regarding Grace," added Jason.

"I don't care what it costs for a lawyer. I want Grace here with her family here in Mayhem," said Nana firmly.

Although both Jason and Char loved Grace, Char was exhausted from taking care of Nana even though she basically lived across the street. Char also noticed that Jason's stamina wasn't what it used to be. She wasn't sure if she could take on a 10-year-old besides.

Jason and Char were fooled by Scott's manipulative actions, into thinking that Grace thought of him as a father. That was the reason they didn't feel the need to get involved at the beginning. Scott had learned much from Lilith in becoming an amazing actor and played the manipulation card every chance he had.

CHAPTER 71

December 2, 2012

Vicki parked her car outside the address that Scott had given her. Before she opened the trunk, she stopped for a moment and looked at the house that stood before her. There was an uneasy feeling but she brushed it off thinking that it was just nerves. She opened her trunk and began hauling boxes and household items. Scott opened the front door and told her to come on in.

As Vicki moved into her new home, she looked around very happy about her good fortune. There were more antiques and valuables than she had ever imagined. Vicki smiled as she thought that this could all be hers.

Upstairs, in Scott's bedroom, Vicki looked through Lilith's side of the closet. She grabbed a hanger with a little black dress on it and laid it on her chest and let the hem fall to her knees. With a nice set of pearls this would be a great ensemble thought Vicki.

It had been a couple of months since Lilith's death. Now a new woman was moving into Lilith's house and taking her place. Scott wanted to get married quickly so that they would still be considered candidates for Grace's guardians. Another reason for the quickness of everything was so that Vicki wouldn't back out with cold feet.

As Vicki opened the bedroom closet door, Lilith's shoes lined the wall of the closet. Vicki bent over to try on a pair of running shoes that were a little long. Lilith had a slightly larger foot but Vicki figured she could stuff the other shoes like Lilith's stylish pumps so they would fit her foot.

On the dresser, there was a small jewelry case. Inside the box were pearls, diamonds and other gold items. Vicki felt like she had just won the lottery. Vicki opened out the top drawer of Lilith's dresser. Inside the dresser was an antique silver Christmas ornament. All of a sudden Vicki felt a sick feeling in the pit of her stomach. As Vicki watched the ornament spin on its cord, she noticed a creature with fangs on its reflection. As she looked closer, Vicki felt a grip on her throat that squeezed until she couldn't breath. Tighter and tighter was the firm, hold on her neck. The woman clutched her throat as if she had the strength to fight off the grip. Vicki gasped for air and dropped the ornament that smashed into a hundred of pieces onto the floor.

Wow, what happened thought Vicki? She ran over to the floor mirror in the corner of the room. She noticed that she had a light-colored rash like area around her neck.

That was weird. Vicki rubbed her temple and went to sit down on the bed. Maybe she just needed a little nap.

Still in the master bedroom, Vicki lay down in the exact spot where Lilith had lived her last moments of life. Within seconds, she was fast asleep. The dream started out sparkling and beautiful. At first, Vicki danced alone in a spotlight room surrounded by glittering jewels and wealth in a large castle. Then the large, fang creature returned, grabbed her and forced her to dance. Vicki fought to get away from the beast but she was not strong enough to break away from it. Vicki awoke screaming, kicking and struggling to get away. For a few hours, Vicki lay in the fetal position and staring into space.

For the rest of the day, that frightening image with the fangs kept resurfacing in Vicki's mind. It was like a combination of a snake but like a demon at the same time. Vicki hated snakes and she felt that this was the most frightening thing that she had ever seen. It was if someone crawled inside her head and created the most hideous monster ever...

CHAPTER 72

<u>December 5, 2012</u>

As in life, Luke was a homebody in death. Being an avid reader, he would read through books that Lilith had packed away in the far corners of the basement. Sometimes he would invite famous authors to his place to discuss literature. Luke's favorite author was Ken Kesey who wrote "One Flew Over the Cuckoo's Nest." He was over to discuss some of his writings.

In life, Ken Kesey had signed all of Luke's books written by the author. In return, Luke had bought Kesey's designed mailbox with a matching helmet. Luke had told his family and friends that Kesey's son had died with this helmet on his head and it was one of Luke's most prized possessions.

The dark, cold basement was where most of the earthbound souls would hang out. Finally, after over a month of death, Lilith made her way from the master bedroom to the basement. Luke had been in the basement for most of the time since his death three years prior. He had been to various other places like his parent's or his brother Jason's house. Luke could have others see him if he wanted them to take notice.

"Hey Ken, look who's here. It's my wife from another life," said Luke sarcastically. **"It took you long enough to come down to the basement. I was able to travel to the basement in half the time it took you to figure it out."**

"Well, I had to come farther being that I died in the bedroom," spit back Lilith.

"It looks like you two have some unfinished business so I will let you figure it out," said Ken Kesey looking for an easy out. **"Another time Luke."**

"Good seeing you Ken," said Luke as Ken left the area and he turned back his attention to Lilith. **"So Lilith, you finally succeeded doing yourself in. It only took three tries. So it is true. Three is a charm."**

"Very funny Luke," said Lilith not exactly loving her new situation. **"So now that we are both dead, what do you do?"**

"Well, I've tried to make the best of it. Now I have all the time in the world to read. In your case, you've always enjoyed torturing people so you should love being dead," answered Luke.

"Well, I know who I will start with," stated Lilith with determination. **"A month after my death and my second husband has already replaced me. That bitch was upstairs looking through my things and sleeping**

in my bed! I tell you one thing, I'll make her wish she never moved in."

"What? You mean someone has already moved in with the douche bag? I thought you were the only one stupid enough to do that," insulted Luke.

"You are so funny Luke. I have already mastered scaring the piss out of that chick," bragged Lilith. **"You should have seen the dream I put into her head. It was hilarious. She woke up screaming!"**

"That's nothing. The other day, the douche wanted to hang his precious little dartboard. He still hasn't found it back. What a dork," laughed Luke. **"Moving objects is where the action is. It really freaks out the living,"**

Just then, there was the sound of footsteps down the stairs. Vicki was carrying a box of Lilith's personal items down to the dirt floor basement. A tense feeling comes over Vicki, as she gets closer to the bottom of the stair. She feels as if many eyes are watching her.

"Wow! Now there's a babe! Guess who I will be watching in the shower when I get bored," said Luke as he stared at the brunette coming down the stair.

"That's your idea of attractive," said Lilith in a jealous tone. **"Your standards have dropped considerably since we were married."**

"Have you looked at yourself since you died? Your skin is pasty and your eyes are bulging out of their

sockets. And that bad dye job - not a good look," insulted Luke. **"You were never meant to be a blonde."**

"Thanks a lot. I think I'll find another spot to haunt," huffed Lilith as she left the area.

As Lilith left the vicinity, she flew through Vicki. A chill to the bone overcame the middle-aged woman. It was at this moment that Vicki realized that she hated the basement and would limit her time spent in this area.

CHAPTER 73

December 10, 2012

Snow was heavily falling outside as Char glanced out the window. Char loved watching the large snowflakes gently fall from the sky and blanket the yard. She felt she was in a giant snow globe. It was hard to believe that so many beautiful, tiny flakes could cause a disaster in a matter of seconds.

Char was still in bed with the laptop on her lap. Jason sat next to her watching the news on the television. Thanksgiving had just past and most people were placing their family photos on the social network. Being friends with Hank and Tommy, this was how Char stayed connected with them.

It looked as if Grace had been with Tommy and Prudence for Thanksgiving. There were pictures of Prudence's mom and dad at their house. Another photo showed that Mathew and Grace were eating pumpkin pie at Mathew's grandparent's house.

"Jason, look at this photo of Mathew and Grace. Isn't it cute with them eating pie and whip cream all over their face," smiled Char.

"That's funny," said Jason.

"I can't wait to show your mom. She needs a good laugh," replied Char.

A few hours later, Char and Jason dressed to go over to Nana's house. At least a couple of times a day, the couple would check on the wheelchair woman to make sure that she was okay. Nana didn't want to go outside much since Lilith's funeral. Jason and Char worried that the elderly woman was going through depression. Char was hoping to give Nana at least a giggle.

"Hey Sandy, I brought over my laptop. There are some photos of Mathew and Grace that we think you might like," said Char.

Char slowly opened up her laptop and brought up her page. Tommy had an album of that Thanksgiving festivities. There were pictures of Tommy, Prudence, Mathew, Grace and Prudence's parents.

"Here Sandy, this is my favorite picture of Mathew and Grace," said Char as she pointed to the photo of the kids with whip cream all over their face.

Instead of a huge smile on Nana's face, there grew a huge scowl. Char and Jason were confused why Nana wasn't amused by the photo like they were.

"Tommy and Prudence spent Thanksgiving with Grace at Prudence's parent's house? That means that they were in Mayhem to pick up Grace at the institution and never bothered with me to say hello. Well, it's obvious to me that Tommy has chosen Prudence's family over me. The only time I've seen them is at funerals. Tommy never calls me - this is it! Tommy is out of the will!! Jason, I'm going to start writing my reasons for eliminating him in a letter to be read at the will. Call the lawyer and make an appointment for this week," firmly stated Nana. **"I don't care how much I have to spend, I don't want Tommy and Prudence to get Grace. Make an appointment with the lawyer for that too."**

It looked as if Tommy who had proclaimed three years ago at the Christmas table that he was going to inherit everything was now going to receive nothing. It's funny how karma always comes around. Be careful in what you say – the opposite might just happen.

CHAPTER 74

December 13, 2012

It was 6:00 a.m. in the morning and Char was helping her daughter get ready for the day. Jason was taking a vacation break from work. Char let Jason sleep in that morning being that he spent half the night in the bathroom vomiting and now was complaining of a headache. Char gave him some aspirins and told him to go back to sleep.

"Mom, where's my white hooded sweatshirt?" asked Allison.

"I hung it up in your closet. You can't miss it," replied her mother pointing to Allison to go back to her room and look.

"Char? I need to go to the Emergency Room," yelled Jason from his bed.

"Can I take Allison to school first and then drive you over to the hospital?" asked Char to see if it was an emergency or if he could wait to go.

"Call an ambulance. I can't see," said Jason as he got out of bed with his hands stretched out in front of him.

"What?? Allison!! Allison, help me get your dad into the car," said Char in a panic. **"Jason, I will tell you when we get to the stairs. Okay, we are at the stairs. Now, step, step, step, step, step, step, step, step, step, step, step, step, step, step and one last step."**

Between both Char and Allison, they managed to get Jason into the car. Quickly, Char drove Jason to the front door of the emergency area of the hospital. Char ran to the wheelchairs, brought one back to the car and helped Jason into the wheel chair. Char wheeled Jason to the check-in counter. The nurse asked Char questions about Jason's condition. Immediately, the staff checked him into a private area. As soon as Jason was checked into the Emergency Room, Char then excused her self and told the staff she needed to take her daughter to school and she would be back as soon as possible.

As soon as Char had returned to Jason's room, she noticed that his room was filled with hospital staff. Jason was extremely agitated and moaning. Char looked at the monitor attached to Jason and noticed that his blood pressure was 240 over 210.

"Wow Jason, your blood pressure is sky high," said Char never having seen his blood pressure in the 200's.

As soon as Jason heard Char's voice, changes in Jason's demeanor started. Jason started looking up to the ceiling and then he cowered in fear. Char thought that maybe Jason saw something not visible to anyone else.

At that moment, Jason began convulsing. The staff yelled that he was having grand mal seizures one after another. Char's eyes widen in fear and she moved away from Jason scared not knowing what would happen next. Char was hugging the back of the chair, moved so that both feet were on the chair seat and she sat crouch while she watched as several more staff ran into the room to hold Jason down on the examination table. A doctor in a white lab coat walked into the space and turned to Char.

"Is this your husband?" asked the doctor.

"Yes," replied Char in fear as she watched her husband move abruptly.

"We may have to place a tube down his throat. Are you fine with that?" asked the doctor.

"Well, yes, only if it's temporary," said Char.

"I can't promise you that," answered the doctor.

"Please, just do what you can to make him better," replied Char.

Eventually, the staff was able to sedate Jason so he was no longer convulsing. The doctor said that they needed to run some tests. They sent Char home and told her to come back later that afternoon when he was resting in his room.

Later in the day, Char decided that she would visit Jason before picking up Allison from school. She wanted to see what condition her husband was in before bringing in his daughter.

Jason was now placed in the Intensive Care Unit directly across from where Papa had a room a few years earlier before he died. Char opened the sliding glass door and walked into Jason's room. Jason lay in bed with a large tube down his throat also like Papa a few years earlier. Jason was totally sedated and unable to communicate.

Char stood on Jason's bedside and wondered what had happened to the Francis family in the past few years. Before Luke had died, the entire family would sit around a Sunday dinner and joke about their day. Now, Luke, Papa, and Lilith were all gone. It was only time before Nana would be gone. As Char looked down at Jason in the hospital bed, the thought of another death brought a tear to her eye.

From the corner of her eye, Char could see a tall figure standing in the doorway of Jason's room. Char quickly rubbed away the tears and put on her strong, happy face. The evening doctor stopped by and introduced himself as Jason's doctor. The doctor informed Char of Jason's condition. The staff would know more tomorrow morning so he instructed Char to come back tomorrow morning at 9:30 a.m. when the staff had their group meeting. Until then, there was nothing that would change so she may as well go home and get some rest.

CHAPTER 75

December 14, 2012

Char woke up early the next morning. She called Allison's school to let them know that the child would be in later that morning and that Allison's father was in the ICU. The woman on the phone said that it would be fine to have Allison come to school a little later.

Promptly at 9:30, Char and Allison walked down towards Jason's room at the hospital. The doctor from the previous day and his staff walked towards them. The doctor told Char and Allison that Jason had swelling in the brain and that the pressure on the back of his head had caused him to lose his vision. Jason's condition was called PRES or Posterior Reversible Encephalopathy Syndrome. It could take up to five days for his sight to return if it came back at all. The doctor told Char to come back after the tube came out later in the afternoon.

Later on in the day, before picking up Allison from school, Char decided to stop by to see Jason. The throat tube was out and Jason was able to talk. However, Jason was still unable to see. Jason told Char not to bring Allison to visit him; he didn't want her to see him this way. A weary Jason told Char that he was tired. Char stood up and kissed him goodbye.

Char noticed the time and picked up the pace. She didn't like making Allison wait in front of the school. Char opened up the locked SUV. She sat there for a minute in the driver's seat and absorbed everything that she just learned. Char's left arm around the steering wheel and she rested her head on the wheel careful not to hit the car horn.

The thought of a blind husband saddened her and she began to cry. Tears rolled down her cheek as she drove to pick up her daughter. Quickly, she wiped away the tears. There was no way she would allow her daughter to see her weak. Just as soon as Char gained back her composure, the woman drove to the school to pick up her daughter and went home.

CHAPTER 76

<u>**December 15, 2012**</u>

The next morning, things were beginning to change for Jason. He had regained some of his vision but now he was hallucinating. As Char enters Jason's room, she noticed that Jason was picking at his quilt. What was Jason picking at she wondered to herself?

"Hey Sweetie, how are you this morning?" asked Char as cheerfully as she could muster. **"Can you see?"**

"Well, I can see but I'm seeing some really strange things now," replied Jason, **"For instance, this morning I saw this little old, naked man. He's naked but he has no genitals. He's running around my room. He will hide for a little bit but then he comes out a little later."**

"That's interesting," said Char tucking in her lip and trying not to laugh.

"There he goes again," said Jason as he pointed and his finger was following his hallucination as it was running around his room.

"Hey, they gave you a newspaper," said Char as she reached over to look at the local headlines, **"That's cool. I forgot that the hospital delivers a paper everyday to the rooms here."**

"That's another thing," said Jason, **"I can't read the newspaper. The letters look like Russian lettering to me."**

"Wow, that's odd," replied Char not knowing what to say. **"The doctor said that it could be days before your vision came back so maybe all you need is time and you will be fine."**

"Yeah, I'm getting tired. Do you mind if I take a nap?" asked Jason.

"That's fine. I'll come back later with Allison," said Char as she kissed Jason on the cheek.

CHAPTER 77

December 21, 2012

After 8 days of being in the hospital, Jason was becoming antsy to go home. He made a point of being obnoxious so that the staff would be eager to get rid of him; always a sure sign that he was doing better. Char came into the room with the hope of taking him home soon.

"So, how are the hallucinations today?" asked Char hoping for a positive answer of not having any.

"Well, this morning there were doctors and children walking like they were in a parade in and out of my room. There must have been at least twenty of them of various sizes and shapes. Last night, I could swear that I saw some woman swinging outside my window and I'm on the fourth floor," responded Jason.

All of a sudden, Jason's therapist walked into the room. Before Jason could leave, he had to meet with a therapist to gauge his degree of improvement. Jason being an architect was asked some visual and math problems. Char watched Jason as he struggled to do simple subtraction and not always correct.

As far as drawing, Jason was unable to draw the face of a clock without looking at one. Even if Jason looked at the clock, he couldn't draw it. Jason became beyond frustrated as he tried to remember how it looked.

Regardless of his failures, Jason wanted to be released and he wanted to be released now. The therapist told Jason she would report to the doctor and he would decide if Jason was able to go home. A few minutes later, the nurse came in with Jason's discharge papers.

"Mr. Francis, we are letting you go home but you must go to the Cancer Center for an IV fusion every morning at 8:00 a.m. You have an unusual type of bacteria that cannot be treated with normal antibiotics and that IV fusion gives it to you. Also, you are not allowed to drive until the neurologist says that you are okay to do so," ordered the nurse.

"I will do that. Please, please just let me go home," begged Jason.

"Okay, sign here and you are free to go home," replied the nurse and removed his IV.

The neurologist never said that it would be okay for Jason to drive again. After this incident, Jason would never be able to do what he once could do. The PRES changed Jason in a way he would never forget. Jason would never go back to his old job or be an architect again. He was just lucky to be alive…

CHAPTER 78

December 23, 2012

Char and Jason were surprised that Scott was already getting remarried. It was only three months after Lilith's death and Scott had found a new wife. Neither Jason nor Char had met Scott's new bride.

Jason and Char were leaving their home in order to witness this surprise development. This was Jason's first outing since leaving the hospital a couple of weeks earlier. The couple was getting married in a church near the infamous Sioux hanging in Mayhem.

As Char drove to the church, Jason looked out the window. He began to have another one of his hallucinations. As Char drove down Glenwood Avenue, near the hospital, Jason saw people walking in their light blue, hospital garbs. It was if they were walking toward the downtown Buffalo Park and the back openings of the garbs showed their butts. Char laughed as Jason described what he saw.

"Say, Char, I'm really feeling sick. Is it okay if we don't go to Scott and Vicki's wedding today?" asked Jason as he rubbed his temples. **"I'm sorry but I'm not feeling that good."**

"That's fine," said Char worried about her husband's health. **"I wasn't really sure if you were up to going to a wedding or not."**

A block away from the church where the wedding would be held, Char turned the car around and headed back home. Jason started laughing.

"What's so funny," asked Char wondering what Jason found so humorous.

"Well, now that we are driving back home, I'm seeing my hallucination's walking toward us and I see their faces. They are still walking towards downtown Mayhem," said Jason.

"How many are there?" asked Char.

"I'm not sure. Hundreds?" said Jason. **"Some are alone, some in pairs, and some are in groups. There are patients everywhere."**

 "Wow, that is wild," said Char amazed at Jason's hallucinations.

"Tell me about it. I wonder if they are ever going to stop," replied Jason.

"So do I Jason. So do I," said Char sadly.

CHAPTER 79

December 26, 2012

A few weeks after being released from the hospital, Jason still wasn't feeling any better. Jason was sleeping the majority of the day and still having hallucinations when he was awake. The Francis family didn't celebrate Christmas the prior day like their friends and neighbors. The remaining Francis family members were melancholy from the past family deaths, and at the same time, Jason's health wasn't the best.

The family was waiting until Grace came to visit to open Christmas presents on New Year's Eve. Nana thanked Tommy and Prudence several times that day for the delay but not in a nice way. Allison overheard Nana dropping a couple of f-bombs when Tommy and Prudence were ever mentioned and this delayed Christmas celebration was no exception.

It was about a week ago since Char had gotten Jason out of the house when they tried to go to Scott's wedding. Char thought maybe it would lift Jason's spirits if they did go for a little drive. Char needed groceries so she talked Jason into going with her that morning to a local grocery store. If Jason didn't feel strong enough, she could always get him an electronic cart with a basket.

Although it was very cold, the sun was shining brightly on this winter morning. As Char was driving down the Main Street hill, she noticed Jason was looking intensely out his side window. She couldn't help herself from asking him what he was seeing.

"Jason, are you okay? What are you seeing?" asked Char. **"Are you seeing hallucinations again?"**

"It's just like last week, but there's even more people dressed in light blue hospital garbs. There are children wearing some super hero hospital garbs. Some children are wearing neon colored pajama. There are hundreds of spirits, Char, it's amazing," said Jason. **"Again, I can see they are walking toward the downtown. I don't understand why are they all walking in the same direction?"**

"That's a really good question. You're telling me that they are ALL wearing hospital garbs and walking downtown?" asked Char.

"Not exactly. There are also people in normal clothing and some in old fashion clothes. No one is walking in the opposite direction," replied Jason. **"Everyone is walking towards the old, downtown area."**

This was the end of December in Minnesota. There were never many people out walking when the temperature was below freezing. If they were out, it was never for very long. The ones in hospital garbs would definitely catch a death of a cold thought Char.

"Why would they all be walking downtown? What is so important about that area? I'll just keep driving down Main Street and I will turn which ever direction you want me to on Riverfront Drive," said Char very curious about the situation.

"Char, stop! Park here," demanded Jason as he pointed to the curb in front of the library that looked at the Buffalo sculpture across the street.

Char stopped the car in front of the limestone public library. From where she was parked, she could see the old Mayhem Train Depot building. Before automobiles, the people of Mayhem would catch a train to get to another town. Jason could see many spirits getting off the train to watch something across from the library. There was also the Buffalo Park that Jason had helped design a few years prior.

"What? What do you see?" asked Char looking in direction that Jason was facing.

"It's a good thing that I'm not driving. Right now I am seeing one spirit after another chained following in a very long row in the crosswalk in front of us. Their heads are bent downward and they look very, very sad. I swear that prisoners just keep coming. From the Mayhem Depot, there are so many spirits getting off the train. There are literally thousands of spirits in this small block and it's like a party or large gathering of dead people. There are really a

lot of people. The people are young and old. Some are wearing hospital garb, and some are dressed normally. Wow, I think I see Lilith," said Jason as his eyes widen.

"No way. Really?" said Char in disbelief. "What is she doing?"

"She is standing over by the large plaque talking to Jeff from our old office. You know, Jeff Zee. Who died in the plane crash," remarked Jason watching closely to their every move. "Jeff is telling her some crazy story. He is showing his hand going up and then a swift downturn to the ground. Maybe he is telling Lilith about his death. Well, maybe not. Now they are both laughing."

"Are you telling me that these images aren't just hallucinations but that you can see ghosts?" asked Char.

"It sort of looks that way. Oh wow, up there. A large group of really bad spirits, they are sort of causing maelstrom. There's like one ghost flying into others and flying up onto the library roof," said Jason pointing up at the building's roofline.

The ghost flying up and down from the roof caused a huge gust of wind to start blowing around snow. The wind was so powerful that a large amount of snow flew unto the SUV on Jason's side. BAMM! The noise made Jason jump as it hit the passenger window. Char also jumped from the sudden impact.

"Wow! Did the ghosts just cause that to happen?" asked Char not believing what she heard and saw. "The wind isn't blowing at all but that gust of wind just pushed snow up against your window. That's just crazy!"

"Definitely!" said Jason. "A bunch of dead people are watching this one ghost like he is going to do something really crazy. I can tell that this one guy is really bad news. That dude just turned into a really tall, dark shadow with a really sharp nose and a red color is following him. This place seems like a party but also a place where the newer ghosts can maybe learn from the elder ghost," described Jason as he watched the ghosts interact with each other and wondering why they were all congregating in this one place.

As Char looked at the clock in the SUV, she noted that the morning was getting away from her. Char couldn't see what Jason was viewing and tried to be patient as he reported to her his vision. Jason had a therapy appointment at noon and she still hadn't gone grocery shopping.

"Jason, can we go yet? It's 10:00 o'clock, and we should go. We still need to go to the grocery store and your appointment is at noon. Is it okay if I leave now?" asked Char wondering if Jason was done watching his hallucinations.

"Just a minute longer Char, please. You are not going to believe this but I see scaffolding across the street at the Buffalo Park. Oh wow, I see hundreds of men chained and walking really, really slow. They are marching up to the scaffold to be hanged. Char, what day is it today?" asked Jason.

"Well, technically yesterday was Christmas even though we didn't celebrate yet. So today is December 26th. Why do you ask?" wondered Char.

"Don't you remember what happened here in 1861? That is when 300 Dakota Sioux were executed. I'm seeing a re-enactment of that day. All the ghosts are watching that event. I can hear the Sioux singing a song. Now they are being stopped by the executioners and their heads are being covered by some kind of pillow case item," said Jason as he was horrified by the vision he was having at the library area. "Char, we can go now. I really don't want to see anymore."

Char was happy to hear that Jason had seen enough and wanted to leave. Ever since she had parked the car, she had felt very uneasy. Char never really liked being on this side of town. Even though Char couldn't see what was going on at the park didn't make her feel any better. She could easily picture Jason's description in her mind and it freaked her out.

As Char turned left unto River Drive, Jason saw apparitions dressed from a past century walking into the Mayhem Depot. A ghost train took the passengers to another place. Some ghosts noticed Jason watching them. One ominous spirit stared at Jason and mouthed to him "See you soon".

CHAPTER 80

December 30, 2012

Once, in 2007, Jim and Sandy had postponed Christmas to New Year's Eve so Lilith and Prudence could spend Christmas Eve and Christmas day with their parents. Prudence had told the county social worker that the Francis family celebrated Christmas at the end of the year. Thanks to Tommy and Prudence, Grace wasn't at Nana's for Christmas Eve on the normal December 24th date. This intended slight further ignited the fire that burned under Nana's skin.

"I can't believe Prudence and Tommy lied. Those two will do anything to get what they want. Grace is my blood, not Prudence's parents. Prudence just wants her perfect little family with one boy and one girl - just like her family," stated Nana in an extremely sarcastic tone.

"Well, she isn't going to get her perfect family relying on Tommy. Not after his secret operation. I wonder

if Prudence ever found out about Tommy getting fixed?" laughed Char trying to cheer up Nana.

"I'm glad that Tommy had the operation. I don't want to see Prudence get her way. That would make her happy and that shrew doesn't deserve it," seethed Nana.

"Well, at least we'll get Grace for the next couple of days. Let's make the best of it," said Char cheerfully. **"We should get on our way. I don't want to keep Grace waiting."**

Allison, Nana, Jason and Char got into Jason's SUV. The Volkswagen Beetle would be too small for everyone to be seated comfortably. Jason's neurologist still hadn't given Jason permission to drive. Besides, Jason had been having problems with falling asleep during the day, not to mention all his hallucinations, so Char drove.

As the Francis family pulled up to the institution's vestibule, Allison could see Grace sitting with an adult. The minute the SUV pulled up, Grace jumped out of the chair and ran to the door. Allison jumped out of the SUV and grabbed Grace with a huge hug.

"Grace! I've missed you," yelled Allison as she threw the small girl into the air.

Grace giggled as Allison bounced her small cousin in the air. **"I've missed you too,"** agreed Grace.

"Come on you two. Get in the car. We have some celebrating to do," said Char as she stuck her head out of the vehicle to talk to the two girls.

Allison helped Grace into the car. Grace sat in the middle between Uncle Jason and Allison in the back seat.

"Hi Nana," said Grace as she got into the car.

"Hi Grace. How are you?" asked Nana the happiest anyone had seen the elderly woman in a very long time.

"I've been good. Yesterday, I built a birdhouse in art class," said Grace as she showed Nana a picture of her work.

"That's really nice Grace," smiled Nana.

"Wow Grace, that's really cool," said Allison. **"I love the colors."**

"So Grace, is this your friend Jake?" asked Jason having never been able to see him before.

"Yes, Jake wanted to join us today. He loves celebrating holidays," said Grace.

"So Jake. How old are you anyway?" asked Jason.

"I'm ten," answered Jake. **"So you can really see and hear me? How many fingers am I holding up?"**

"Three," said Jason as he continued finding out what he could about Grace's friend.

"Hey Grace, have you eaten lunch yet? We could stop somewhere and get a bit if you are hungry," asked Char.

"I had breakfast but not lunch. I wouldn't mind a little something for lunch," replied Grace.

"Ooh! Let's go to Papa's Kitchen," shouted Allison from the backseat.

"Yeah Papa's Kitchen," agreed Grace.

"Everybody agree?" asked Char.

A unison of "yes" echoed throughout the car. The restaurant wasn't the best in town, but everyone loved and missed Papa so it became a natural choice for the Francis family. Char directed the car to Papa's Kitchen and the family piled out of the SUV when they reached the restaurant. Char opened the trunk and pulled out Nana's wheelchair. Between Jason and Char, Nana was placed into her chair and Jason pushed her while Allison opened doors to the restaurant. Grace smiled as she thought that it was great to be with family again and not that mental institution.

CHAPTER 81

January 15, 2013

Everyone that had requested the guardianship of Grace Francis received a report on Lilith since she had become a focus of the county. A package from the social workers had sent out the following information:

Ms. Francis has child protection history in Mayhem that begun November 27, 2010, with the report received by human service concerns that Ms. Francis had attempted to overdose on alcohol, and various medications. Earlier in the day, Lilith was incoherent upon arrival at the emergency department. Per police reports, Ms. Francis' daughter, Grace Ann Francis, was home alone with Ms. Francis all day, when she had ingested the above substances. The emergency department social worker spoke with Grace, age 7, who said she had not gone to school that day and stayed home with her mom. As a result, Grace went to stay with Lilith's aunt, Cindy Bobble, who resided in the Twin Cities area. A report was filed requesting protective supervision as Ms. Francis had no support here in Mayhem and that parent had expressed a desire to move to the metro area near her family.

The Mayhem County's Human Services opened child protection case management and worked with Ms. Francis and her daughter from February 2011 to June 2011. It was decided that as long as Ms. Francis cooperated with the plan of completing treatment that the county would not pursue court involvement.

Ms. Francis was cooperative with the program but had difficulties with her medications. Ms. Francis made progress, went back to work, and her mental health continued to improve. The case was closed after Ms. Francis completed her case plan.

However, on August 29, 2011, the Mayhem Human Services received another report with concerns. Ms. Francis was brought into the local hospital by ambulance. According to witnesses, Ms. Francis had a seizure while she was running. She smelled of alcohol and had a level of .303 upon arrival at the emergency department. The emergency department social worker met with Ms. Francis in order to find out where her daughter was. Ms. Francis reported that her daughter was with a neighbor. The county completed a family assessment and met with Ms. Francis and her daughter Grace. The family assessment did not result in recommendation for services.

Since February 2012, the agency has received monthly reports from Grace's elementary school with concerns for Grace. In February 2012, the agency made a report with concerns for Grace when she was not picked up from her day-care program. When Ms. Francis was called, she did not answer. The county received a report with concerns for Grace Francis reporting that her mother came to conferences wearing pajamas. Lilith's demeanor was erratic, loud and she described injuries, such as a broken arm that it is in a cast. She has told a variety of stories on how it resulted in becoming broken. For example, she was laughing and ended up breaking her arm. Another report states that Ms. Francis is manic and was up all night due to being intoxicated and fell and broke her wrist. Miss Cooper picked up Grace and drove her home. The next day when Ms. Francis picked up Grace from the day-care program, Lilith smelled of a strong smell, like marijuana. The following day, Grace came to the day-care program wearing the same thing she had worn the previous day and appeared not to have bathed or combed her hair. The report states that this happens often.

A second report came in February 2012, stating that when Ms. Francis came to pick Grace up, Lilith stood next to staff that noted that she smelled of marijuana and that it was stronger than the previous day. 911 was called and an officer stopped at Ms. Francis' home, and she said that she had not smoked marijuana recently but reportedly, she had been around someone else who had been smoking.

In late March 2012, Lilith reported a recent marriage and that she had quit her job. She also reported she had a broken rib from coughing too hard much and pneumonia. They surmised that Ms. Francis was under the influence based on their observations. In addition, there was a report that Ms. Francis had smelled of alcohol at 8:00 that morning.

In early April 2012, the agency received a report with concerns for Lilith. The report states that Lilith had recently married Scott Frey, whom works eight-hour shifts, and does well with Grace. Since Lilith married, she quit her job at Lighting World. The report expressed concern that Ms. Francis appeared to have become very manic lately and appeared to be drinking more. Ms. Francis stated that the medication makes her feel funny and she doesn't like taking it. The main concern is her manic state and that she had been found entering a neighbor's home when the neighbor wasn't there. The reporter indicated that she had taken magazines from the neighbor's home.

In late April 2012, the agency received a report with concerns for Grace Francis and her mother Lilith Francis and her new husband Scott Frey. At the Fun Zone, Lilith was drunk and Scott was drinking and Lilith was giving him a lap dance in the bar. Lilith was exposing her chest to her husband Scott Frey without wearing coverage. The manager asked the couple to leave the establishment. The report states that Ms. Francis has mental health issues and alcohol issues and is drinking quite a bit lately. The report states that Ms. Francis quit her job and has not had much to occupy her time and appears to be drinking more. The report states that Ms. Francis is at the local bar drinking all the time, and she is often there at night. The report had expressed concerns that it was possible that when Grace isn't being cared for by other friends or neighbors, that she may be home alone.

In June 2012, received a report of Lilith Francis' DUI with a child in the car. The incident involves a car accident and being stopped in another city 45 miles away. Grace said that her mom was taking her to Valley Fun. Before leaving Mayhem, Lilith had gotten into an accident near the Mayhem Library. Grace said that her mother was swerving all over the road and driving on the wake-up strips. Grace went to the police station until her stepdad Scott could come and get her. The police charged Lilith Francis with Fifth-Degree Possession of a Controlled Substance, Third-Degree DWI including Child Endangerment, Failure to Stop For an Emergency Vehicle, and Failure to Provide Proof of Insurance. The County Attorney's office called Mayhem Human Services and reported that while in the detoxify center. Ms. Francis made comments about hurting herself and her daughter. A welfare check was then requested.

A follow-up visit from Miss Cooper resulted a week later. She met with Lilith, Scott and Grace at their home. Lilith doesn't remember drinking and reports that she has a condition where she cannot sleep at night. Lilith Francis Frey stated that she had been up three straight nights before the incident. Lilith believes that she was asleep at the wheel and doesn't remember anything until she was pulled over by the police.

In early August 2012, several reports of Lilith disturbing the peace and smoking marijuana in the restrooms had been filed. On August 9, 2012 police report also states that Lilith attempted to steal her late husband's mother's wedding and anniversary rings. It is unknown if these items were returned to the mother-in-law.

S. T. Meier

In late August 2012, they received another report of Lilith Francis' DUI with a child in the car. When Lilith Frey returned home, there were reports of Lilith screaming and throwing items out of the windows at her residence. Police were called on a Disturbing the Peace from a near-by neighbor.

It is questionable if keeping Grace in the same routine with her stepfather, Scott Phillip Frey would be advisable. Mr. Frey was unable to control home life while Mrs. Frey was alive and being a single parent doesn't guarantee that the situation would improve.

Mayhem Human Services believes that it would in Grace Ann Francis' best interest to find a new normal in her daily routine. Therefore, it is their recommendation that the child be placed in the care of Mr. and Mrs. Hank Bobble.

CHAPTER 82

January 20, 2013

Scott went to his mailbox on the outside of his front porch. Inside the regular size rectangular black mailbox, Scott found the packet sent from the county regarding their investigation of Lilith's past. He was not pleased to see the negative writing of his actions. In his mind, he had to do something drastic and he had to do it now.

Scott decided that his chances for Grace appeared more and more unlikely due to the Fun Zone incident. This news made Scott decide that it was time to contact Lilith's lawyer. When they first were married, Scott wanted to take every precaution not to lose out on the money. He talked Lilith into going to the lawyer and telling Harvey Johnston about how Hank Bobbles had molested Lilith as a child. Now was the time to bring out this ammunition.

Lilith had never gotten over her anger with her father, Hank Bobble, for putting her into the psychiatric ward a few years back. After marrying Scott Frey,

Lilith went to her lawyer, Harvey Johnston to make statements regarding her father. Scott decided to use the information to discredit his biggest competitor in the guardianship of Grace Francis. There is nothing that would stop Scott in achieving what he believed was millions of dollars.

Scott put down the large envelope and went to his phone. In his wallet was Harvey Johnston's business card. As he pulled out the card, a large smile came over Scott's face. He dialed the digits listed on the card.

"Hello, I'd like to make an appointment with Mr. Johnston. My name is Scott Frey and the date has to be sometime soon," stated Scott impatient and irritated with the news he had received in the mail. **"Friday at 2:00 would be fine. Good bye."**

Once again, Scott did not thank those that aided him in a legal matter. Scott found that those people were there to serve him, and if they couldn't bring him any money then they didn't deserve any politeness. He only was polite if he needed something from that person.

Scott did not like or respect authority. For years, he had been breaking the law by selling illegal drugs but was lucky enough to avoid the four, small walls of prison. He believed it was due to his keen street-smart ways.

Ever since high school, Scott had been known among his peers as the go-to guy for their drug of choice. Over the years, he had maintained his connections and as his connections' children grew up, he had hooked them on a drug in high school too. This was one of Lilith's attractions to Scott - she didn't have to worry about her marijuana supply.

Scott didn't like feeling that he was being put under a microscope and now wanted to divert the attention to Mr. Bobble. Again, Scott smiled as he thought about his appointment on Friday. Soon all eyes would be on Lilith's father.

CHAPTER 83

February 15, 2013

The courthouse had no carpeting on the main level of the building. The floors were a terrazzo and the walls made of the local yellow limestone. Due to the hard surfaces, Tommy's goofy laugh echoed down below the second floor balcony where the courtroom existed. Up stairs, Char and Jason were seated with their backs to on-coming walk traffic on the second floor and could hear the conversation perfectly. Tommy and Prudence, along with their lawyer, walk behind their relatives and talk louder as if acting like it was one big party.

"So did you enjoy the Super Bowl game last night?" asked Bob, the lawyer for Tommy and Prudence.

"Very much so," chimed in the frumpy secretary known as Aunt Prudence.

"So where's Mathew today?" asked their lawyer

"Mathew stayed at the principal's house last night," bragged Tommy trying to appear important.

"We had the hotel room in town all to ourselves," informed Aunt Prudence loudly enough for everyone to hear her.

The three went into a public room and closed the door. Seated twenty feet away, Char rolled her eyes watching. **"Can you believe those two?"** remarked Char.

Jason just shook his head. Then Jason noticed, coming up from the stairwell was Katherine their lawyer. Katherine's children went to school with Grace and she really liked Grace. It was her hope to keep Grace in Mayhem with Jason and Char Francis.

Just then, Hank Bobble, Liza, Hank's sister Cindy and her daughters came through the vestibule downstairs. It was a déjà vu of Lilith's funeral thought Char as she watched the Bobble family pile into the courthouse. It was as if Lilith's entire family was there with the exception of her mother, Susan who didn't show for her daughter's funeral either. Lilith's mother was probably home getting drunk thought Jason and Char, along with anyone who knew Lilith's mother and family history.

Hank had received a letter from Lilith's lawyer that had complained that he had molested his daughter. Grandfather Hank Bobble requested that information regarding the allegations of him sexually molesting his daughter Lilith and that Lilith wanted to kill Grace are sealed so that Grace may never know the truth. He says that the letter that Harvey Johnston wrote was very graphic. Lilith had reported to Harvey that her father started molesting her at a very early age and continued until she married her first husband. This information was received by those in the courtroom but wasn't discussed in detail.

To begin the process, the judge struck his gavel against a small circular base. Then Judge Anderson takes roll call of all participants. He can't help but make fun of Prudence's ridiculous long, hard to pronounce last name as he almost rolls his eyes but catches himself at the last moment. The county's attorney states that the county continues to recommend the Bobbles, being Grace Francis' maternal grandparents as the choice as guardians.

"I object your honor," stated Harvey Johnston as he stood up from his chair. **"There is evidence of inappropriate behavior of Lilith Francis' father Hank Bobble that she confessed to me. It would seem to me that placing Grace Francis in the care of the Bobbles would be a mistake."**

"Your honor, Mr. Johnston is speaking of allegations that have not been proved. There is no one to prove that these allegations are true," stated the county attorney on behalf of the Bobble family. **"Looking into Lilith's psychological records, there is no discussion of these allegations."**

"Your honor, Lilith told me very graphic details of her childhood," remarked Harvey Johnston.

"Being that the victim is deceased, there is no possible way to verify the information that you are sharing with us Mr. Johnston," stated the judge. **"Therefore, I'm going to throw out this evidence. Hank Bobble has requested that the Harvey Johnston letter be sealed so that Grace Francis would never have knowledge of her mother Lilith Francis' statements of the allegations of Lilith's father molesting her as a child. The judge states that if in future years if Grace wants to see the court documents, there is nothing he can do. Next order of business?"**

Harvey Johnston and Scott Frey, who had sat together, abruptly stood up and left the courtroom. Mr. Johnston said what he wanted to say but was not happy with the result. Scott was especially angry but waited until he was out of the courtroom to voice his feelings.

"That was total bullshit! I can't believe that they won't listen to Lilith's statements," said Scott to his lawyer. **"What can we do?"**

"I'm sorry Scott but I believe that the county has already decided that they want the Bobbles to have Grace. It's typical for the law to go with the maternal parents in these types of cases. We did what we could, " summarized Harvey.

Back in the courtroom, Katherine DuPont represented Jason and Char. It was the first time that Grace's uncle and aunt had been invited to participate in the hearings. Katherine informed the court that the social worker was unable to give her clients a time in which to visit Grace. At the same time, the lawyer pointed out to the court that her clients were the only ones that had filed for adoption of Grace. According to the lawyer, the required adoption filing of Grace Francis had not been done by opposing family members to her knowledge and should be begun if they are serious about guardianship.

At the end of the meeting, the judge stated that he hoped the family could come together and decide a good solution for Grace. The next trial date is scheduled for June 22, 2013 at 8:30 a.m.

Jason and Char walked out of the courtroom to a nearby locker to get their coats. Hank quickly ran up to the couple to talk to them. Hank catches up to Jason and grabs him on the shoulder.

"How dare you!" exclaimed Hank Bobble to Jason Francis.

Both Char and Jason turned around and looked at Hank. They squinted as if to say what are you talking about?

"If you are referring to being the source of saying that you molested Lilith, you are very mistaken," stated Jason. **"If you want to know who started that little tidbit of allegations, look at the money."**

By that time, Liza had caught up to her biological father and she wasn't happy.

"Leave him alone," screamed Liza at Jason as if he was torturing her biological father.

"Harvey Johnston sent the letter but he isn't my lawyer. Follow the money. I know Harvey but again,

he isn't my lawyer. Harvey isn't on my payroll. He's Scott's lawyer and that is where you should be looking," informed Jason to the confused Mr. Bobble.

With sad eyes, Char looked and nodded at Hank Bobble that indeed that this was the truth. A baffled Hank stood there speechless. An emotional Liza, confused by what she was hearing and seeing, walked away from the group. She wailed over the balcony that echoed throughout the entire building. Char grabbed her coat out of the locker and Jason helped her put it on.

"Follow the money," repeated Jason to Hank Bobble as he put on his coat. **"Have a good day."**

Hank was stunned to the point of not being able to move. Liza continued to wail as Char and Jason left the building through the vestibule. Hank went up behind his biological daughter and rubbed her back as if to say that everything will be fine, and please don't cry.

CHAPTER 84

March 24, 2013

Today is Char's sister's birthday. Secretly, Char hates this day because of all the bad luck she has had in the last several years takes place on this day. It isn't that bad things directly happen to Char, to ruin her day, but problems happen to her family and friends on this day every year.

"Hey Nana, it's Char," called Char as she entered through the back door.

"Hi Char, I'm in my usual spot," yelled Nana from the leather lounge chair in the living room. **"How are you today?"**

"I have to tell you Sandy, I'm always really leery on March 24 of every year. It's my sister's birthday and you know how I feel about her," said Char as she rolls her eyes. **"Anyway, remember a few years back when Jason broke his arm on this day. Last year, Allison broke up with her boyfriend on this date. A year ago,**

my friend Janet lost her job at the hospital. Well, you get the idea. So I'm going to keep a low profile this year and not do much or talk to many people."

"You are telling me that you are superstitious against March 24?" asked Nana a little surprised at her daughter-in-law's fear.

"Yeah, you might say that," said Char. "So how are you today?"

"To be honest, I'm a little sad. Tomorrow is Tommy's birthday and he hasn't contacted me once since Lilith died. He didn't even wish me a happy birthday in January," said a disappointed Nana with a somber expression on her face.

"Isn't it funny how our two favorite people have their birthday's consecutively on March 24 and 25?" stated Char sarcastically. "Well, Sandy, I say tomorrow you take the high road and call him. Wish him a happy birthday. What can it hurt?"

"Maybe. By the way, I think my electric blanket is done. I'm getting no heat whatsoever," complained Nana.

"I have to go to the store later today anyway. I'll stop and get you a new one," said Char as she lightly tapped her hands on the elderly woman's lap. "I'll bring it over when I bring your dinner. So, what would you like for dinner?"

"I haven't been that hungry. Just some soup from the Chinese restaurant would be fine," replied Nana.

"**Well, I should get going to the store,**" said Char. "**I'll see you tonight when I bring dinner and a new electric blanket. See you later. Bye!**"

"**Bye Char!**" called out Nana.

A few hours later, Char was back with Nana's soup and the electric blanket she requested. As Char took out the electric blanket from its package, she rubbed the fabric against her face. She couldn't get enough of the blanket's softness.

"**Oh, Sandy, you have got to feel this blanket. It is just so soft. Oh my goodness, this blanket is orgasmic,**" laughed Char as she brought the blanket towards her mother-in-law.

"**That's nice,**" said Nana not near as enthusiastic about the blanket as Char had been.

Usually Nana was much more into conversation but there was something different about her tonight. Char went into the kitchen to heat up Nana's soup. Nana had a favorite brown ceramic mug that Char poured her soup into. Char walked back into the living room and placed the mug with crackers on Nana's food tray.

"**So has anything bad happened today?**" asked Nana.

"**Well, nothing yet but I have six more hours to go and I don't want to jinx myself,**" said a cautious Char. "**How's the soup?**"

"**It's still a little warm but I'm not that hungry,**" replied Nana somberly.

Char noticed that Nana wasn't as hungry or talkative as she normally was. Instead of watching the television, Nana kept looking over her left shoulder as if she was expecting someone. Nana appeared a little distant but Char brushed it off as Nana considering whether or not to talk to her estranged son on his birthday.

"Char, I need to tell you something. I think that it's my time to go," said Nana as if there was nothing more important to say at that moment.

'What do you mean that you think it's your time to go," asked a perplexed Char. **"No, it's not. You are doing so much better Sandy."**

"Char, trust me when I say that it's my time," said Nana firmly.

"Oh, Sandy, you are probably just tired. You are fine. I don't think that it's your time to go," said Char as she patted Nana on her shoulder and she took Nana's dinner into the kitchen.

"I'm serious. I need to go," reiterated the elderly woman.

Char smiled a sad smile at Nana. She didn't know if she should hug the woman or what she should do. It was times like this that Char felt socially awkward.

"Don't talk like that Sandy. You are doing great. You aren't even close to death," said Char. **"You are perfectly fine. I think you are doing better and I will see you tomorrow. You have sweet dreams."**

Nana said nothing as Char went out the back door. Instead she looked ahead and watched the television in front of her. The house was silent except for the low volume of the television.

CHAPTER 85

March 25, 2013

"I wonder how Nana is doing today? She seemed different last night," said Char to Jason when he woke up.

"What do you mean? Yesterday she was just crabby with me. She said that she didn't want to even see me and to just stay home last night," said Jason frustrated with Nana's moodiness lately.

"Well, she kept saying how she should go and that it was her time to go. I didn't know whether I should hug her or what? You know I've never been a hugger but for some reason, I felt maybe I should have hugged her. Instead, I just patted her on the shoulder and told her that she would be okay. Wouldn't it be awful if she did die last night and I didn't take her seriously? Or can you imagine your brother Tommy? Today's his birthday and every birthday you had to remember that your estranged mother passed from a broken heart," said Char in an emotional tone.

"You over analyze everything Char. I'm sure none of that is going to happen," reassured Jason.

"Well, let's be extra nice to her today. Being that it's Tommy's birthday, she might be very sad today," suggested Char.

"In a couple hours, I'll give her a call and see what she would like for lunch," replied Jason.

Char and Jason read the world news on the Internet and drank their coffee with French Vanilla creamer with whip cream. Outside their bedroom door, they had hung a feeder and enjoyed the variety of birds that came to visit. The male and female Cardinal was Char's favorite pair.

"I'm going to call Nana and see what she would like for lunch," said Jason. **"What do you feel like having?"**

"I don't really care. Let's see what Sandy wants and we can go from there," decided Char. **"Remember, be nice to her. She is probably having a really hard day."**

Jason went over to his cell phone and called his mother. That's funny thought Jason. She should really be up by now. But Nana had been sleeping more and more and it was possible that she was just exhausted. After an hour of no response, Jason decided to go and see if she was okay.

"Char, my Mom still isn't answering. I'm going over to check on her," said Jason as he grabbed the keys to his moped for a quick drive to his mother's house. The house was only a block away but it was more fun to drive his mini-bike than to walk.

"Okay, let me know what she wants so I can put it together," replied Char as she went over to kiss him good-bye.

Nana had given Char a large list of things to put on eBay. After Jason went out the garage door, she returned to taking pictures of the merchandise. As Char was ready to start taking pictures of the old dolls that Sandy had given her last week. Just then, her cell phone began to ring.

"Hi Jason, what does your mom want for lunch?" asked Char cheerfully.

"Char, my mother is dead," gloomily replied Jason as he closed her eyelids.

"Oh my God, she can't be! She was perfectly fine last night. A little distant but she was fine," insisted Char not believing the news. **"Are you sure?"**

"Yes, I'm sure. I've called the police department and they are on their way over," said Jason. **"I would really like you to come over and help me answer any questions they have."**

"Of course, I'll be right over," replied Char. **"Did you find her sleeping in her bed?"**

"No, I found her in her lounge chair in the living room," replied Jason.

"Wow, I'm leaving right now," said Char not believing that her mother-in-law was gone.

Char quickly picked up her car keys and drove a block away to Nana's house. The police had not yet arrived. Inside paced a nervous Jason.

"Are you okay?" asked Char.

"Not really. I had a strong feeling that this would happen today," replied Jason not wanting to believe his instincts.

"Jason, do you want to hear something really weird? Both of your parents died in the exact same spot but just in different chairs. Both were in their chairs in front of the television. Nana's chair was the exact same place of your dad's Saarinen chair when he died three years ago," said Char with wide eyes.

"You are absolutely right," said Jason in further shock of the events of the day.

"I wonder if she died last night, because of my sister's birthday or this morning because of Tommy's birthday?" asked Char thinking that it was the bad thing that happened on her sister's birthday this year.

"I think she died this morning because I found her in her leather arm chair and her medications were spilled all over the place," remarked Jason. **"It looks as if she was taking her morning pills."**

Just then the front door bell rang. It was the Mayhem police with the mortuary people. The police asked a few questions while the mortuary people carted Nana out the door. After everyone had left, Char and Jason sat on the sofa that faced the leather lounge chair that Nana had spent her last hours.

On the back of the leather lounge chair, was the soft, brand new electric blanket. Char wondered if the blanket she had bought Nana was too hot and somehow killed her mother-in-law. She still had the box, bag and receipt. Char decided to take back the blanket to the store. There was no way she could put that blanket up to her face again...

CHAPTER 86

<u>March 26, 2013</u>

Yesterday was Uncle Tommy's birthday and cousin Allison was the one to call Grace to tell her that Nana had passed away. Allison told Grace that Uncle Jason found Nana wearing her light colored summer pajama dress in her recliner with eyes and jaw wide open. Uncle Jason closed Nana's eyes but Allison told Grace that her father has been having nightmares of that vision. Jason had awoken the house with his screaming that morning.

Being that it was Tommy's birthday yesterday, Char and Jason decided that they would wait until the following day to tell Tommy that his mother had died. In their eyes, Nana died because she had a broken heart but they figured that Tommy was too dumb to see that he had anything to do with it.

In the three years since Papa had died, Tommy had been in Mayhem dozens of times but had visited Nana only twice at funerals – when he had to see her. Nana had left

Tommy a special birthday greeting with the following note with her will:

"Tommy,

I am broken hearted today having to write this letter to you. Dad & I did everything we could to raise all 3 of you in a loving home and made our priority in life our sons. I will always love you and Mathew and wonder until the day I die what I did wrong that you care so little.

When you told us you were marrying Prudence – we were both happy for you. We had 2 daughters-in-law that we loved and looked forward to a third. Prudence's mother said to me at your wedding when she said something to the effect that "well I guess you're stuck with the crazy one now". Boy was she right but we had no idea how bad Prudence was messed up. Prudence let us quickly knows she did not have room in her heart for another family. I tried my best to draw her into the family by purchasing her homemade candles. I wanted to help her in her new business and hoped we would be able to talk and get to know each other. Since buying her candles, she remained silent. She told me she would never forgive me for not coming to your first anniversary party. If you had told the truth about that instead of calling me a C**t in a temper tantrum all it would have taken was a simple I'm sorry!

Dad felt the same coldness from Prudence and I don't know anyone that didn't like him. He was particularly hurt badly when he and I weren't invited to your house for Mathew's first birthday when even Prudence's friend Rachel and her family were invited. He was excited to give Mathew a remote control car on another birthday but Prudence without even thanking him grabbed it from him saying it was too old for him. Dad took it home where he played with Mathew when he came to our house.

I'll never understand when Lilith died your motives and lies. Then there was your buttering up Grace's parents. Lilith behind your back told everyone – even Kari – that while she went out with Prudence to drink that she hated Prudence after the way she treated Dad when he was in the hospital for the last time. Lilith really loved Dad and said it was because of him that she made it through the first year after Luke died. Everyone came up to sit together while Dad was close to death; that is everyone except you and your family.

Lilith came early every morning before work and after work. Prudence never came to see him or us even though she worked there at the hospital every day. She did come once; the FIRST DAY when she swept into his intensive care room while he was in a coma and on a breathing tube, exactly when the doctors made their rounds. She pushed me aside, and promptly talked over me, as if she was really concerned, and the family spokesman. When the doctors left and her "act" was over – she left and never spoke to me again even when Dad died or at his funeral. You, Tommy, did sit with us and were with me when Dad died and I will always appreciate that.

If you were really concerned about Grace's well being – you would have seen how much it meant to her to have 2 stable families and normality instead of breaking up ours in order for Prudence to have a family just liker hers – a son AND a daughter. Grace wanted to stay in Mayhem and that was why we got involved besides doing what Lilith and Luke would have wanted. Neither of them wanted Grace to go with Prudence. They felt that you were too tough on Mathew with your discipline and your constant – GO TO YOUR ROOM and Prudence was cold unless there was someone around that she could "pretend" in front of at what a great Mother she was. AGAIN more lies! Everything that you told the county including that we had always celebrated Christmas on New Years when you knew that we had spent every year together on Christmas Eve day into the evening for over 50 years!!

BOTH of you were trying to hurt me, instead of really caring for Grace's needs and what she was used to. We had a great time with her for 2 days at New Years and I'm sure Susan and Hank can work out things in the future if they adopt Grace.

It's funny that neither of you could cry at your father's or Luke's funerals. At Lilith's funeral, Prudence was so loud that everyone there heard her. Who was that "act" for? Lilith and I were close and I could just see her laughing with her great laugh at Prudence when she said she couldn't stand her except to go out to drink with. Where were you "the do-gooders" when Lilith was so sick this last year?

According to court testimony – you came down every other weekend until your house was sold and made sure that you only visited Lilith. After she died you were in Mayhem often to gain custody of Grace. More SNEAKING – LIES! Since you have never even called me in the 9 months that I've been sick, confined to a wheelchair and going through chemo, I finally know, as hard as it is, that you never loved me and do not want to be part of the family. I had been told by my 3 doctors not to ever get stressed out as they feel that is what is making me get worse. When I talked to you on the phone that last time and you kept berating me with Prudence talking in the background. I was in tears yet an hour later.

I can forgive, but not forget! I am starting to clean out the house with help and plan to sell the antiques and things I don't want. The rest of everything in my estate when I die will go to Jason and Char. Jason wanted to leave you half as he misses having a brother, but I will never be able to repay them for all they have done for me. I know that Dad would agree with me and say – if they don't bother with you while you are alive why leave our belongings to them when you die. Jason & Char insist if I am not able to live by myself they want me in their house instead of a nursing home but you could've cared less what happened to me.

My sister Ilene & I have grown close these last few years and they check up on me often too. Ilene & I find it nice to talk things over that we couldn't discuss with anyone else. I wish you could have had that relationship with Jason and I know that Jason is very hurt by the way you've treated me too. I have not included Grace as she will be well taken care of and she is picking the things she wants from the house. I would have included Mathew, but he will never know Dad or I, except for the lies he's told.

The biggest lie of all is Prudence's and your version of perverse Christianity. Sitting in church or teaching Sunday school for show and personal gain is about the same as having the moneychangers in the temple. Also telling other people that they have a black heart because they don't go to church does not make you a Christian. I did go to church for 60 years. Christ taught it is what you do with your religion every day and how you treat people that lead you to him! It is a personal relationship with the Lord that matters. I hope one day that you will truly find him because it is only through him that is the way to the Father."

Nana had gone to her lawyer on January 7, 2013 to be signed and stamped. This was a few weeks before her birthday. Nana hoped Tommy would change his way but he never did. If Tommy would just apologized, he would've been back in the will but now there was no turning back for him.

CHAPTER 87

<u>**April 16, 2013**</u>

Jason and Char arrived a few minutes early to Nana's will reading. They weren't surprised that Tommy hadn't arrived being that he had to drive almost three hours to get to Mayhem from his house. The receptionist told the couple to have a seat and that Katherine would be right with them.

"Hello Katherine," said Char as she saw the middle-aged woman exit from her office and walk into the reception area.

"Good morning, how are both of you?" asked Katherine.

"We're great and ready to get this over with," responded Jason anticipating a less than desirable reaction from his younger brother.

"How about you two wait in the conference room while I prepare a couple of items. Thomas should be

here soon and then we can get going," said Katherine. **"Can I get either of you two something to drink?"**

"I think we are all coffee out but we will go make ourselves at home in the conference room," responded Jason while Char nodded in agreement.

The couple closed the magazines that they had been reading and gathered their things. The conference room was adjacent to the receptionist and just a few feet away from where they sat. In the conference room, they selected seats so that they could easily see others coming into the room.

A couple minutes later, Tommy was told by the receptionist to meet in the conference room. As he entered the room, Tommy chose a seat directly opposite from his brother and sister-in-law. Katherine was on Tommy's heels and she carried a pile of papers into the meeting room.

"It looks like everyone is here so we can begin things," stated Katherine as she passed out packets to each individual.

Katherine handed each of the brothers the will and the letter that Nana had typed for Tommy. The pile of information was upside down from where Tommy sat. As Tommy's hand turned the packet so he could read it, he glanced at the top page.

"Before we begin, I would like to say a few things," started Tommy in a firm voice as he looked at Jason. **"Why the hell did you make Mom pay for everything when Dad left you that huge insurance policy in**

order to pay for her? When she went to the nursing home, it cost us $7,000 a month. Why didn't you just take care of her and save the money? Why did she pay for it? It should have come out of Dad's insurance policy."

"We never said that the policy money was going for Mom's bills," replied Jason.

"Katherine, the money that was the insurance policy I signed over should be considered against the estate in my favor," said Tommy smugly.

"The money was used to help take care of her. So Tommy, you want to play it that way? If we are talking about inheritance money, where's the money for the office? You know the money that came from selling the architectural office? You know that it was me that worked with Dad all those years and you got the money for the building. So don't talk to me about being fair about our parents' estate," scolded Jason.

"Before we continue, Thomas, I have something I must tell you," interrupted Katherine. "Your mother told me many things about your relationship and she left you a letter. It is in the packet I just gave you. At the same time, she made your brother Jason the sole beneficiary of her estate."

"You know you could've told me that over the phone and saved me a trip!" stated an extremely irritated Tommy with shaky fingers. "Did she leave anything for Mathew?

"No," replied Katherine calmly.

"**How about Grace?**" asked Tommy agitated by the situation.

"**No, Sandy felt that whoever adopted Grace would take care of her. If Jason and Char get Grace, they will take care of her,**" responded Katherine as Tommy rolled his eyes.

"**Just great!**" grunted Tommy. "**I'm leaving!!**"

"**Tommy, why don't you stay and come back with us to Nana's house?**" said Char saddened by the events taking place. "**There are things there that you will want.**"

"**No!**" said an angry Tommy as he stood up, exposing his shaking left hand to the group. Tommy's hand shook uncontrollably as he gathered up his things, "**I'm going home! You all can go fuck yourselves!!!**"

Swiftly, Tommy left the lawyer's office. The remaining group looked at each other knowing that the meeting was not going to be pleasant but not this unpleasant. Char looked out the window and saw Tommy walking angrily towards his car.

The three remaining people in the conference room heard a loud car in the parking lot. Char looked out the window to see if it was Tommy driving away. As an irate Tommy sped out of the lawyer office parking lot, Char noticed something odd. In the backseat, sat a figure with brown hair. Was that Prudence? The head in the backseat turns toward Char, as Tommy drove away. Char put her hand over her mouth as she identifies the person as Nana...

CHAPTER 88

April 20, 2013

Ever since the will meeting in Mayhem, Tommy noticed that things in his life had gone from bad to worse. No matter what he did, it wouldn't come out right. He just couldn't shake the anger he felt leaving that meeting.

"Tommy, I think we need a new refrigerator. The ice cream is melting no matter how high I put up the cool temperature," said the irritated Prudence as she put back the carton of ice cream. **" All the food I bought yesterday feels warm."**

"Well, the refrigerator did come with the house. Who knows how old that damn thing is? I swear, we replace one appliance and another goes. I am so sick of this!" remarked Tommy annoyed with the fridge and slamming the door shut.

"Well, don't get mad at the fridge. Go get us a new one," ordered Prudence as she rolled her eyes at her husband's immaturity.

"Okay, okay! I'm going," grunted Tommy putting on his coat.

Tommy walked out to the garage. At the moment, he wished that he lived back in Mayhem where he could have several appliance stores in a few minutes. Living in a small town in northern Minnesota was an entirely different story. He would have to drive to the nearest large city to buy a refrigerator. A half hour later, Tommy pulled up to an appliance store. He would have to pay whatever the owner asked. Tommy's only other option would to go home and drive in the opposite direction for 45 minutes, then pay whatever they asked.

Everyone in the family knew that Tommy never liked to spend money. George Washington rubbed his eyes every time Tommy would open his wallet. This was no secret. Tommy was proud of his frugality.

Slowly, Tommy walked into the appliance store grabbing his pocket to make sure his wallet was still in his back pocket. He went directly to the refrigerator section of the store. Being in an area of small towns, the selection was also small.

"Is this all you got?" grunted Tommy not happy about making the purchase or the small selection of refrigerator models.

"Yep," replied the store clerk noting that Tommy wasn't the friendliest person he had been in contact with. **"What are you looking for?"**

"Well, these are a little small. I was hoping for something a little bigger," said Tommy snidely.

"I could special order you a larger appliance but it will take a week to get the order and then to install," replied the clerk.

"A week? I can't wait a week," whined Tommy. "What if I choose something here? Can I get it sooner?"

"Yes, we have most of the floor models in stock. We could have it delivered late tomorrow," replied the clerk.

"Okay," said Tommy as he looked around his choices. "I'll take this one."

"The total for that refrigerator will include $50 to remove your old fridge, and a delivery charge of $75," said the clerk. "The total comes to $2100.

"Sounds like robbery but I guess I'll pay it," grunted Tommy. "Call me when you are going to deliver. My address is on the check."

Tommy quickly tore out the check before he could change his mind. Some of the check tore as he pulled to release it from the clutches of his checkbook. Tommy slammed it down onto the counter and walked out of the store.

On the way home, Tommy listened to a country western station. As he tapped to the sound of the music, a deluge of rain suddenly poured down onto his car. The windshield wipers couldn't keep up with the amount of rain on its surface. Tommy was unable to see the road in front of him. All of a sudden, Tommy misses a sharp turn and rolls into the ditch. The vehicle rolled several times before finally stopping.

Fortunately, a car on the road sees Tommy's vehicle roll and calls authorities. The police arrive before the ambulance and take a statement from the witness. Shortly afterwards, an ambulance comes and takes Tommy away.

Standing and watching on the road above, is a woman in a pale, white nightgown. The woman is standing with her back to the road. With little emotion, Nana waves as the ambulance drives away...

CHAPTER 89

June 10, 2013

A month and a half later, Tommy had come home from the hospital but he was not in good condition. He now was like his mother before she died. Tommy would spend the remainder of his life in a wheelchair. Prudence was not happy taking care of Tommy. In the past, it was always Tommy that had taken care of Prudence. Being the youngest child and a girl in her family, Prudence was her Daddy's little princess. She would never be ready to reciprocate and take care of Tommy.

Back in Mayhem, one of the reasons that Jason and Char had requested Grace was to pacify Nana. The grandmother worried that she would never see her youngest grandchild. The other reason for the request was to keep Grace in Mayhem so she could remain at her school and keep her friends. Jason and Char felt that although her parents were gone, that Grace needed some continuity in her life.

The county, on the other hand, felt that Grace needed a new normal. The county was continuing their stance that Grace would be best off with her maternal grandparents in the Twin Cities. Jason and Char then decided that it would be best to bow out of the competition. The couple decided that it would be in Grace's best interest to get her into her new normal. Jason and Char decided to agree with the county placing Grace in Mr. & Mrs. Bobble's guardianship.

Upon notification of Jason and Char's withdrawal and their own unfortunate events, Tommy and Prudence decided to follow suit and withdraw their request of Grace. Being that Tommy was normally the parent that cared for children and cleaned the house, his being paralyzed caused some issues in the adoption of Grace.

Upon news of the withdrawal of the Francis' families, the court awards Grace to Grandma and Grandpa Bobble.

CHAPTER 90

June 20, 2013

As soon as Scott awoke this bright sunny morning, in his gut he knew that something bad was going to happen. The sunlight that shined through his window didn't make things any better. Inevitable loss was the feeling deep in his stomach.

Scott felt over to the side that his wife normally slept. Vicki had already made coffee and had gone to work. As Scott got out of bed, he slid on a pair of sweats that he had thrown on the hardwood floor the night before. He hit his head on the hard surface before he could catch himself. In the corner of the bedroom, Luke stood laughing to himself. What a klutz thought Luke.

"Did you do that to Scott?" demanded Lilith.

"No! The fool did it to himself. I may have been a slob in real life but I never slipped on anything I left on the floor," laughed Luke. **"That guy is just an idiot."**

"Well, at least he made enough money so I didn't have to work," slammed Lilith.

"Good for you, a money-making idiot," replied Luke sarcastically. **"Too bad you couldn't buy him a brain with all that dough. A few more falls like that and he will have killed all his brain cells."**

Scott started to slowly get up from the floor. That fall knocked him out for a few minutes. As he pulled himself off the floor, he felt his temple. That is definitely going to leave a mark thought Scott to himself.

Scott slowly walked from the bedroom to the upstairs bathroom and slouched near the wall for support as he made his way. He turned on the cold water and grabbed the nearest washcloth. As he looked in the mirror, he swore he could see Luke glaring back. Scott quickly turned around with fear but no one was there. That was it, Scott needed coffee and he needed it now.

Still not able to keep his balance, Scott used the rail for support down to the kitchen. As Scott reached half way down the stairs, Luke gave him a little shove. Scott tumbled over and over again down the stair. This time Scott landed on his side.

"Wow, watching that guy fall just doesn't get old," laughed Luke to Lilith who stood next to him.

"Don't you have anything better to do than to torture Scott?" asked Lilith.

"No, not really," said Luke. **"Who knows, maybe I will just have to kill this guy for grins."**

"Well, I have my eye on his new wife," remarked Lilith. **"I hate how she has taken over all my stuff. She looks absolutely hideous in most of it. Besides, it took me a lifetime to accumulate those riches."**

The thought of these two people taking over their old lives gave Luke an idea. Lilith could tell that Luke had an evil thought by the way his one eyebrow arched over his left eye. At the same time, his left hand cupped his right elbow with his right index finger tapping his right cheek.

"I bet that I can kill Scott before you can kill Vicki," suggested Luke.

"Oh, you think so? You are on mister," replied Lilith. **"It will be my pleasure."**

By this time it was mid-morning and the mail had arrived in Scott's mailbox. Scott saw the mail person walk in front of his window to Martha's house next door. Quickly he walked to his front porch and opened up the mailbox. He noticed one return address listed as from the county. Opening it so quickly, he almost split the letter in two.

Scott moved his lips as he read the letter, he was not pleased that both Francis families had dropped out of the request of Grace and were now supporting Lilith's parents. They had won the child. That wasn't how he had planned on this working out. Scott thought that everyone would be beating each other up for the same reasons why he wanted Grace – the inheritance money.

The angry loser walked swiftly towards his phone and called his newest wife. He pressed the buttons so hard he almost broke his phone.

"Vicki, we got the letter. I can't believe that both Jason and Tommy dropped out and are backing the Bobbles for adoption of Grace. What are we going to do?" asked Scott wanting answers.

"What can we do Scott? We are out numbered," said Vicki trying to calm her husband.

"But we need the money. Lilith's hospital bills left me in so much debt. This wasn't the plan!" exclaimed Scott as he could feel his blood pressure rising.

"It's not worth getting stressed over," said Vicki. **"We'll get through this somehow."**

"I got to go," said Scott too angry to talk at the moment.

Scott slammed down the phone unto the kitchen counter and then punched a hole in the wall. Then he threw close the basement door. This action woke up a few evil spirits in the basement. Out of the walls and floors arose spirits that hadn't been disturbed in a very, very long time.

In one of the storage rooms in the dirt floor basement, an irritated spirit in the wall awoke from the noise coming from the upstairs kitchen. A dusty profile of a face pulled away from the crumbling wall.

"What the hell is all that noise?" asked the original owner of the house. **"It's like he's trying to raise the dead."**

"Don't concern yourself with that guy. Let us younger ones handle this," said Luke wondering how best to finish the job.

"He sure is a loud one. We don't need any more noise around here. Whatever you do - do it quick!" recommended the original owner's wife. **"Get those humans out of here!"**

"We have something in mind. I can't wait to get started," replied Luke with a huge grin on his face. **"Just to let you know, we are open to any suggestions that you may have for us. It's always best to learn from your elders."**

Luke extended out his arms, interlocked his fingers and stretched as he half expected to hear a crack that never came. This would take some careful planning thought Luke. How could he beat Lilith? The challenge of winning over Lilith was all he could think about at the moment. No way would Lilith win this time.

CHAPTER 91

June 30, 2013

It was six o'clock at night and Vicki had a horrible day at work. Vicki wasn't sure if it was because of the insomnia she had the night before or if it was the events of being at a job that she absolutely hated. Ever since the arrival of the final county letter, life was unbearable at the Frey residence.

Six months earlier, this was not how Vicki had thought married life would be like. Scott had told her how she would have an instant family and an incredible amount of money. He told her how they would be taking vacations frequently with her every wish coming true. Thinking back to all these lies, Vicki begins to cry.

Vicki was sitting on the sofa with the television on but she wasn't really watching the program. Above Vicki, Lilith is watching over her in the corner of the room and rolling her eyes. As Vicki sat there crying, she begins to speak aloud.

"Why? Why?" she muttered in-between tears. **"I try to be a good person and nothing good ever happens to me. Everything is the same or worse."**

"Oh boohoo, you little baby. Quit being such a whiner and do something about your situation or I will do it for you," said Lilith sarcastically. **"Why don't you just drink yourself to death? The world would be a better place without you!"**

With Lilith's attention focused on the crying wife, she doesn't notice Luke nearby. He is rolling his eyes at Lilith's comments. Lilith never wanted to work very hard are Luke's thoughts of her.

"Isn't that just like you Lilith taking the easy way out? You are so lazy trying to have her commit suicide. You'll never win the competition that way. After all, it took you three tries before you got it right," responded Luke condescendingly. **"Lord, you are stupid!"**

"Believe me Luke, I will win this competition. I don't see you getting any closer with Scott. How are you going to do him in?" asked Lilith.

"I'm still working on a plan but I tell you one thing; it will be spectacular. More creative than anything you could dream up," spit back Luke.

At that moment, Scott walks in and sees Vicki crying. He is unemotional of her feelings. Scott feels nothing but anger and rage about life. The room feels with tension as he walks through the door. Scott stands in the doorway and stares at his wife crying on the sofa.

"What the hell is your problem?" said Scott as he slammed the door behind him.

"You! You are my problem Scott! Nothing is turning out the way you said it would. That's my problem!" yelled Vicki.

"Well, I'm sorry that I can't give you more than a roof over your head. If it wasn't for me, you would be living in the street," roared Scott unfulfilled in his role as a provider.

"You know what Scott? Maybe we should just get a divorce. We didn't get married out of love. Neither of us are happy," suggested Vicki.

"That would make you happy? Fine, leave. Go see where you can afford to live," remarked Scott.

Scott's harsh words just made Vicki cry louder. The sound of her crying voice irritated and made him so mad that he picked up an Asian planter and threw it at the floor. It broke in hundreds of pieces.

"You knew I liked that vase Scott," said Vicki as she picked up his glass antique inkwell and she threw it against the nearest wall. The inkwell didn't break into as many pieces but did gain a few chips that infuriated Scott.

At this point, the couple was so angry that they begin to throw the closest item to them in the direction of the other person whom they absolutely hated. Vicki threw a plate at Scott that hit him in the face. Scott grabbed a book and flung it at her chest. Then Vicki picked up a lamp and threw it at his legs that came close to hitting Scott in the groin.

"Oh, so you want to get nasty? You picked the wrong person to fight with Vicki," said Scott in a loud voice picking up the nearest item and throwing it at his new wife.

"Bring it on Scott. Show me that you actually have some balls because I haven't seen them lately," insulted Vicki.

The angry woman grabbed Lilith's urn and threw it at Scott. The yellow urn hit Scott in the right arm and broke as it hit the floor. On the wood floor, in large pieces of ceramic were Lilith's ashes. Vicki looked at the pile, at Scott, and then she knew she had gone too far.

In a dark corner, stood Lilith not at all happy with the situation. Lilith was very insulted that Vicki had broken her urn, her final resting area, and was going to make her regret her action. Lilith picked up Vicki, turned her sideways, and slammed her to the floor. Scott, on the other side of the room, could not believe his eyes. What had just happened? One minute, Vicki was standing there and the next minute she looked as if something grabbed her and threw her.

Scott didn't even try to help his wife but like a coward, he slithered out of the front door and left for the night. Lilith followed Scott as he left the house by appearing on the roof of the house. The angry man walked down the front steps and got into his deceased wife's car.

The square white car pulled away from the curve and drove to the downtown Mayhem bars. On the top of his car, was Lilith riding with her head arched over the front window and her hands at each corner of the glass where it met the roof. Lilith had the lead in the death of the couple and she wasn't going to lose now. She was going to make sure Luke didn't get to Scott for a couple of hours.

Scott walked into the Some Place Else bar and ran into some of his best clients. Young and old came up to the dealer and were able to get the drug of their choice. In no time, Scott forgot his problems back home and started consuming several beers in a bottle.

Meanwhile, back at the Frey residence, Vicki lay on the floor for the rest of the night curled up in the fetal position. That was as far as she could move...

CHAPTER 92

July 1, 2013

It was after midnight before Scott came home that night. Scott reeked of beer and marijuana. As Scott entered the front door, he noticed that Vicki lay in the same place as she was several hours earlier. He walked over and placed his hand an inch away from her mouth. He was somewhat relieved that she was asleep but still breathing. How would he be able to explain two deaths of his wives in less than a year?

After enjoying eight beers at the bar and a couple bowls of weed, Scott was famished. As Scott well knew after years of indulging, the munchies were inevitable. He went to the kitchen to find something good to eat. Yesterday, before the fight with Vicki, she was busying baking banana bread. In Scott's mind, the old hag could do one thing right. No one made banana bread better than Vicki.

Scott went to the kitchen drawer and brought out a small knife to cut the bread. As he cut the bread, a small corner broke off. He quickly put the wedge into his mouth. Somehow it tasted a little different but he couldn't put his finger on the difference. Maybe it was the pot he had just smoked. He didn't care. He was hungry. Scott sliced the bread and gobbled it down. A little milk would easily wash it down. Without getting a glass to pour the milk, Scott grabbed out the carton and drank it directly out of the container. Scott felt a milk mustache and wiped it away with the bottom of his sweatshirt and tongued out the bread hiding in his gums.

Scott looked back out in the living room at his wife that lay on the floor. What was he going to do about her? Did he want to stay married? Vicki brought in a little money working retail at a boutique.

Did he want to divorce her? If he divorced Vicki, he would most likely lose half of his property. After six months of marriage, was it worth giving up so much? These were the questions running through his head as he stood there staring at her lifeless body.

Then there was the question of what would the authorities believe happened. Lilith had committed suicide. What were the chances of his second wife doing the same after six months of marriage? He decided that he had to make it look like an accident. But the question was how? What would be believable?

Lilith watched Scott from the corner of the kitchen. The angry ghost couldn't wait any longer. Lilith moved in closer to Scott. She was telling Scott to finish Vicki off. You need the money was whispered into Scott's ear. There's a life insurance policy listing you as the beneficiary Lilith told him. The money Scott – take the money. Lilith reiterated the phrase several times until she knew that he was taking the bait.

Slowly, Scott walked out towards Vicki in the other room. He looked around the room to see what he could use as an excuse. On the wall next to Vicki was a large cabinet filled with knickknacks. How could he explain that entire cabinet falling on top of her? That didn't seem natural so that wouldn't work.

Scott started to notice that he wasn't feeling that well. He needed to do something quick and get out of the house. He decided to go back into the kitchen and turn on the gas burner without lighting the fixture on the stove. The gas will kill her in no time thought Scott. He smiled to himself to what he thought was being very clever. He turned on the front burner without the flame. Scott than went around the house gathering up things that he would need for the next couple of hours and headed towards the front door.

"Good-bye darling," he said sarcastically as he walked pass Vicki who still lay on the floor.

Vicki's eyes opened quickly and wide towards Scott's voice. She grabbed his leg and refused to let go. Scott tried to kick her off but was unsuccessful. His body felt heavy as he fell to the floor next to Vicki. Scott's body hit the floor with a thud.

"Hope you enjoyed the rat poison banana bread darling," said Vicki not expecting a response back. **"I knew you couldn't resist."**

The man lay there motionless. It was hard to say what killed Scott first. Was it the gas or the banana bread? Eventually both bodies lay totally lifeless in the middle of the living room approximately in the same spot and on the same date that Luke had died four years earlier.

Luke, Lilith and the other ghosts stood over the two bodies. Nothing in the house made any noise. Only the gas stove top made a clicking sound while the rest of the house calmed down.

"Glad that's over. Finally, some peace and quiet," said the original house owner. **"Let's hope that word spreads that this is a haunted house and no one wants to live here."**

Both Luke and Lilith's heads tilted in curiously as to whom had won the bet. Now, after only four years after Luke's death, once again, there were no live occupants in the household.

"Vicki had the last word. I'm pretty sure that she was the last to die," said Luke.

"No, Vicki just knocked him out temporarily," argued Lilith not wanting to lose the contest.

"Lilith, just accept it. You lost! I beat you! Yes, I beat you! I knew that idiot husband of yours couldn't resist banana bread and I told Vicki to poison him.

I knew it would work! He was dead when he hit the floor," said Luke. "You may have beat me in life but I'm going to beat you in death. And I would do it again..."